MIDNIGHT WORLD

VOLUME THREE

MIDNIGHT WORLD VOLUME THREE

POSSESSED BY DARKNESS

DALIVIA PLAUT

DARK PLOT
PUBLISHING

● ● ●

First Edition, August 2019
Story by Dalivia Plaut
Written by Dalivia Plaut
Edited by Ireland Lelisio

ISBN: 978-0-9976453-9-2
Plaut, Dalivia, 1983—
Possessed By Darkness
I. Title. Fiction. Dark Fantasy/Horror

ISBN: 978-0-9976453-9-2 pbk.

Cover Design by Low Key
Book Design by Dalivia Plaut
Cover Photograph by peeterv/xijian
(istockphoto.com)

This is a work of fiction.
Names, characters, places, and incidents
are the products of the author's imagination.
Any resemblance to actual persons, living
or dead, is entirely coincidental.

Printed in the United States of America

● ● ●

Author's Note

The world presented beyond this page is a fictitious one, as are its characters. Any resemblance to actual persons, living or dead, is entirely coincidental.

MIDNIGHT WORLD VOLUME THREE:
POSSESSED BY DARKNESS

IT all went down at the start of spring when the blood was scorching through my veins.

To say it was a strange time in my life would be an understatement. It was fair to say I've seen more than most people my age have seen throughout my brief existence, like, for instance, that one time Uncle Jojo took me to the Grand Canyon or another time when we went to the "Talking Caves" underneath the town of Maven or another time when we spent a magical week in Dark Mountain, burning away the mornings by trekking the steep hills along the mountain and then laughing through the soggy afternoons by sifting for speckles of gold through these ancient sieves by the river below: strange places I never imagined existed right here on earth yet resided on another planet, or, suffice to say, only behind the screen of my phone.

On the contrary, I've also seen the worst life had to offer, like, for instance, that one time I witnessed a Street Solider getting capped by a rival gang member right before my eyes—they always say the moment you watch a person die is the moment you become an adult, but I don't know about that.

I guess, if I had to sum it up the best I could without ruining any of the surprises, I'd say it was a time of great confusion. I'd be comfortable using a word like *evil*, but I know such a word is considered to hold religious significance.

And there was nothing "religious" about what was going down in Dover.

It went deeper, beyond religion, faith, politics, science.

Or darkness.

What better place to start?

Of all the moments to begin my story, I felt as if this was the right one: at the change of a season, a birth without all that sweaty labor, pink balloons, congratulatory cards, and all that baby crap—no pun intended—more or less, a rebirth.

Like most stories, mine starts out at a pivotal time in my life.

Forget about the moment when I graduated early from high school—which was cool and all but not deemed pivotal for pivotal's sake—or that one time when I first learned how to ride a bike or threw a first punch in my first fight or locked lips with my very first crush.

I suppose the moment I first heard about Damianos's disappearance is when everything *changed* for me.

What them writers call a "character's arch."

The flowers were out and blooming with all sorts of bright colors. We didn't have much of a winter, only a few weeks where the temperature occasionally dropped below freezing. The heat was back before I even had a chance to miss it, and I could feel a lonely summer around the corner.

I was about to leave the Stop N' Shop when I heard the name of the boy whom I've had a crush on for the past year on the television behind the checkout counter. In the report, a teary-eyed news anchor was powering through words on a teleprompter. News anchors—at least not the few stoic ones Uncle Jojo grew up watching—weren't supposed to act emotional, but this one was.

An eighteen-year-old from Dover was reported missing, said the anchor.

The first thing that ran through my mind was doom and then every word associated with *doom*.

According to how I initially perceived the news report, Damianos was already dead, plucked from the earth.

His world, done.

Mine, shrinking.

The second thing that ran through my mind was guilt— I'm talking about the kind that remains lodged in the back of your mouth, nestled between your gums and that crooked wisdom tooth that rubs against the wall of your mouth every time you bite down, and you'd do about anything to tongue it free.

Somewhere, in that tangled web of thoughts spinning through my head, I felt as if I was to blame for Damianos's disappearance.

Which meant I was the one who was supposed to find him.

And that was when it all started, the strangeness.

But first, let me introduce myself.

CALL me Squints.

On good days—which seem few and far between—I suppose I welcome the name. In a way, the name has become not a label but, more or less, the title of a chapter, *my chapter*, as if it's mine and mine only to keep.

I have to thank the friendly neighborhood hustler, Kushman, or "Kush" for short, and his spazzy pee stain of a friend, Too Smooth, for branding me with the name after I tripped over my shoelaces in front of a group of his gabby butt buddies while I was walking home from the School of the Spoiled and Talentless Losers my freshman year, or what I like to call Dante's Seventh Ring of Hell.

The next few agonizing moments were spent with me squinting for my specs that I had flown off during my stumble—hence the name, "Squints!" which was immediately shrieked out at the first sight of narrow eyes, first while I was crawling my way to my glasses—or what was left of my glasses—scattered all over the sidewalk and then, later, while I was doing the walk of shame with my tail stuck between my legs, looking like an old fool with one cracked lens guiding me back to my withered nest.

On most days, they often referred to me as "Shy Girl." They called me other names, too, which weren't even names at all but more so concealed insults, programmed comebacks, or the need to use the word *black* behind another adjective, like "Shy Black Girl," as if these were all unflattering details or broad labels to not only fit me inside a category in order to make me more identifiable, but also to describe my personality precisely the way *they* saw it: "Introvert," a category which was usually placed at the bottom rung, the unspoken, closed-mouthed kid chilling in the darkest corner of the room with a sign written in bold lettering, *Do Not Disturb*, wrapped around her neck like an unfashionable noose. At times, they treated me as if I was a rabid dog foaming at the mouth, my *Do Not Disturb* sign often mistakened for *Beware Dog!* Not just any dog but one that really sinks its teeth into flesh, a Maneater. If they were in a destructive mode, they called me "Useless," as if, by me being so damn introverted, I was of no use to their world or even worse, the world, as if I contributed nothing to it or for it, as if I was no different than an undigested corn kernel buried in a landfill or a raunchy vessel of waste drifting off to sea—a useless thing, really. No nutritional value. All filler. Filling up the void. Stinking up the air they only breathed. Something that was easily passed through time and space—or what "little" space—then flushed down a toilet and exiled to a Place Where Introverts Do Not Return. They called me lots of names, labels, slams, adjectives, anything to pigeonhole me into their perfect bubble that never ever crossed the other bubbles. Yet, I was supposed to stay inside my designated space, shelled up, unchanging, a fixated image which bares no meaning, and most importantly, with or without any color.

EVEN though I, in similar fashion, place Damianos in the same category as "them" or "they" or simply the "Others," such as my uncle and his ever-changing wives, which I had grown accustomed to, indirectly calling them as one body, a collective unit, my aunt "Lazy Susan," a witch that had a new name and new face every time my uncle felt the itch or the *other* kids who disapproved of me at Brainwash High or the *other* teachers leftover from the hippie generation who peddled obedience, Marxist ideology, and a holy trinity of ideas which would inevitably lead to economic collapse, instead of broadening my mind—or in other words, speaking "to" me, not "down" to me—or the *other* neighbors who shot glares at me whenever I was filling up their taxed spaces or the *other* others who were dead, despite being tragically alive and well, he is nothing like "them" or "they."

Damianos Pipes is both a sheep and a shepherd, his last name, from what I've overheard, pronounced *Peeps*.

The others at Move-Over Dover call him "Domino" because nobody can ever speak his first name correctly. Again, at the School of Twittertards, finger warriors and their backup, the language police, pick and say who you are or what name you go by as if the very mortar which contributes to the foundations of a civil society have been replaced with napalm and the only leaders to turn to come in the single body of a strategically placed oversight committee working underneath the oppressive thumb of an elusive, shapeshifting revisionist whose power moves like the wind. It's Damianos, geniuses—that's Da-mia-nos. How hard it that, really?

Every time Damianos passed me in the hallway after Third Period, I'd mistakenly drawl the name with my jaw primitively slack. "Damn" was me as soon as I laid my bubbly Manga eyes on Damianos because "damn" was the only word that came to mind. Whenever I found myself in his presence either at school last semester or while galloping around town, I could hear the hot blood moving inside me. "Damn. . ." is me gawking at Damianos's utilitarian body as I give my E for Effort attempt at trying to imagine what he looks like underneath that cardigan. "Or, hot damn?" The things I'd willingly let Damianos do to my body. "Or, goddamn!" What in the hell was Picky Nicky smoking when she let Damianos slip right through her fingers after she "allegedly" caught Damianos making out with Shanelle over the winter break. I mean, so what if he was? Damianos and Nicole used to be the hottest "it" couple around campus, like Ken and Barbie, only imagine Ken being a multi-talented athlete who was blessed by the gods with a leg that would make Thor's hammer look like a leaden-ridden toy at the bottom of a Happy Meal. "Or, damn me to a jail cell!" I'd unapologetically murder the stingy bitch who lays so much as a single fingernail on him and gladly spend the next twenty-five years of my life in a jail cell no bigger than the size of my closet thinking about how I prevented what could've been one of the worst tragedies of the twenty-first century.

Despite only having talked to Damianos only one or two times, I practically know everything about him. His little sister, Phaedra—which I swear was named after the *Tangerine Dream* album—attends Corner Heights where all of my "former" friends ended up going after South Winston and rumor has it she's all Lady Gaga over a Goth boy named Derrick. I read that he prefers handheld foods, particularly Mexican food, al pastor tacos being his favorite of the Mexican cuisine. I basically know everywhere he goes whenever he's not saving the world from natural disasters and spreading world peace or playing Theseus in the play *A Midsummer Night's Dream* or putting together short films with the drama team for the morning announcements or scoring an amazing "golden" hat trick during a match against the East High Lions.

🚗

AS I sketch every detail of Damianos's perfect head to go along with his perfectly shaped body, the only two obstacles preventing me from putting down my pencil and talking to him is an unexpected impression of a parallel universe where I envision myself trying to live up to my much-cuter, much-smarter, much-popular, much-blonder and less-nappier doppelgänger, who's rounding first base with Hot "Dam" Damianos behind the bleachers, and the impenetrable cancerous wall of black smoke spewing from the industrial pipe-sized exhaust on the back of some glaring asshole's wannabe monster truck with a ram guard and a license plate that says "BIG SEAN," which is one of the dozens of indicators that he's screaming to the world that he has a BIG dick when, in reality, it's itty-bitty, a turtle head, and the only way to make up for his *lack* of manhood is by proving to the entire world that he is, in fact, a man with BIG impressions because he's been brainwashed by the dispatches on TV that a man's masculinity is only measured by how loud, obnoxious, or unruly he can be. *Loud*—hence the constant revving of his truck accompanied by revolving head turns around the park. *Obnoxious*—hence the yelling at competitive soccer players, who, for the most part, appear to be giving in to Big Sean's notorious anthem and foul emissions. *Unruly*—hence a greasy bag of fast food Big Sean tosses at the nearby trashcan, only to hit the side of the rim in what you'd call a "brick."

Only a year since Dover built a new athletic park, the place is starting to reek like a subbed-out port-a-potty. Smoke-free environment, my ass. The park gives off a particular odor, somewhere between an ashtray, burnt trash, rotten food, and household waste: sort of like the same waste that would power up the Mr. Fusion Home Energy Reactor mounted to the DeLorean in the movie *Back to the Future*. Edwin-Backer Park, also known as the "New Park," has brought in a lot of locals the first couple of months after it was opened to the public, both man and his furry friends frolicking around as if they were both living in a utopia, but after that, it's attracted a certain type of creature that would usually be considered "nocturnal." I see more and more hobos, prostitutes and perverts, shady drug dealers who, unlike Kush, would kill at the first sign of heat, all frequenting the New Park rather than actual athletes or health-conscious individuals.

The trash spills over onto the parking lot, ketchup-covered French fries scatter along the curb like a crime scene, pickles, a half-eaten cheeseburger. Which I can only imagine Big Sean using something like he's, you know, "giving back to nature" or just "gettin' 'er done" as an excuse not to get his lazy ass out of his ridiculous-looking, air-polluting truck.

Big Sean doesn't bother to pick up his trash nor do I even expect him to do such a un-"unruly" thing.

Kids like Big Sean are either too proud or too privileged to pick up something as low as trash. They feel as if their kind has been persecuted for their beliefs, for their tribal rituals, for their politics, for their way of life.

Big Sean is one of many jerkoffs who attends Shithole High; however, it's the kids who are the counter opposite of Big Sean who now run that shithole, kids who'd make Big Sean look like a miniature action figure driving a Hotwheel.

Before Big Sean roars away, he chugs the rest of a beer in three gulps, tosses the crushed can out the window, then cracks open yet another one. Right then and there, I realize he's been drinking and he's possibly tipsy, if not intoxicated.

My blood boils with rage from the sight of Big Sean drinking alcohol behind the wheel of what I can only now refer to as a destroyer of fathers. All I can think about is the pain he may possible cause another individual or how this may be the day another father is taken away from his daughter.

All I can think about is a story that Uncle Jojo once told me a long time ago.

🚗

ONCE all the fumes clear and Big Sean has gone away, Damianos and his crew are wrapping up a friendly.

I finish my sketch of Damianos and it's, by far, worthy of showing off to interested parties—which is extremely rare because most of the time "showing off" my work is followed by heat flashes and a sudden inability to make eye contact. I waste the next five minutes building up my confidence by mapping out what I'm going to say to him as soon as he steps off the field and makes his way to his car.

I see my window. I take it.

As I gather my art supplies from the table, I'm driven back by a sudden gust of wind. One of my loose sketches is blown from my drawing pad.

I glance over my shoulder to the fields and Damianos is nowhere around; in fact, he's already driven off.

Another opportunity missed.

Depression sets over my shoulders and leaves me contemplating my future.

How many more opportunities are going to slip through my fingers?

What if I never get to talk to Damianos before the end of the school year? Or even worse, the end of summer?

Then, all of a sudden, my mind starts racing and I start thinking about worst-case scenarios: Damianos going off to college while poor ole me gets left behind and spends her adult years hanging out at bars, occasionally picking up misogynistic jerks who use me for sex. I have an image of myself sitting at the end of the bar with an empty glass in hand, one eye half-opened, slouched over like a pirate, and slurring at the bartender, "Poor ole me. Poor me." All of a sudden, I brighten up like a two-dimension cartoon drawing with a two-dimensional idea. "Pour me another drink!" As if the thought of hard booze and the numbness it brings about would be the highlight of the rest of my miserable life.

My mind involuntary ventures to darker places as if my conscious, my eternal being, my spiritual compass is showing me the life that waits me in a vicious series of 80's montages: We SMASH CUT to the moment after I hammer down my fifth shot of house whiskey, not even the bottom shelf stuff. I'm talking about the leftover stuff they dump into a spit bucket.

My downfall starts with a guy named "Brad," even though the next morning when I wake up in his contemporary bed that he bought from a Akea magazine all naked and sticky and feeling like I spent a week camping out in the woods, I have a tendency to refer him as "Barf." Maybe it's the Shaggy from *Scooby Doo* look. Maybe it's the harsh fact that I found a bite mark on the inner part of my thigh when I went home and washed the sex from my body.

I lower my standards the next weekend with a guy named Rico. He's more handsome than Brad. If Eldris Ilba and Halle Berry had a child, he'd look exactly like Rico Freako; however, Rico has what I like to call an "anger issue"—in fact, it should be the title of a movie, "Anger Issue," starring a man who treats young women no different than his Teddy during the rough transitions of boyhood. The first time Rico tossed me around, I admit I liked it. Then, Round Deuce, when his knuckles met my chin, I became mortally terrified, so much that, in a strange way, I needed the feeling of terror, as if it had become a new high from an old drug that has been on the market ever since the dawn of mankind.

After two heavy weeks with Rico and wearing bruises that he gave me as if they were my own initiation into another dark world that I only thought existed in scummy night clubs run by Russian mobs, I get so used to hooking up with assholes, like Brad or Rico or any other toxic men who use my once sacred body for sex, that I resort to using my useless talents for money and before I even know it, I turn into one of those girls you'd see hanging out on street corners in the middle of the night with her frail, saggy arm held outward as cars creep by.

I get knocked up by one of my regulars, a lowlife, and soon-to-be cliché of a deadbeat dad who winds up in prison a month later for first-degree murder after he shoots his poisonous load inside me.

For eight long months, I lug around some serpent of a child inside my womb. During full moons, particularly the Flower Moon, I can not only hear but also feel it slithering around inside me, as if it's slowly consuming my soul. I want it out because that's all I can think about, that it's an "it," not a child but an "it," the son of a cold-blooded murderer.

After I give birth to my demon child whom I name after a cereal box, I eventually run out of money from child support and resort to working the streets. By then, my pimp named Cuts has no use for me. He wants to do to me exactly what his name suggests, but he says I'm old. I am old. And diseased. In the heart and soul. I go on welfare since I'm unable to find a decent job since I hurt my back from all the abuse to my body.

Later, after the hopelessness sets in, I find a spot on an off ramp and end up panhandling. Signs vary from day to day. Some days I'm a shrink: "Will listen to your problems for food." Others, I'm putting old talents to good use: "Will draw your picture for food." The signs change as it grows closer to dark, so too does my desperation to return to any state of normal. "Will f**k for food." I deliberately use the two asterisks to leave it up to the customer's imagination. I get creative during the night. The basic "rub and tug" will earn me a milkshake from the dollar menu. If I give you head, I can earn myself a full course meal—and if I'm lucky, maybe even dessert. On nights of desperation, I allow myself to turn into a human dumpster. Above me, a showy billboard reads: "Open To The Public."

After years of destroying and wasting away my body on the streets, I end up becoming a part of the streets as if, somehow, I've evolved into the grim and grit like a chameleon. My black skin as hard and coarse as asphalt, my once beautiful nappy hair as thick and wiry as the power lines running throughout the city, my glowing cat-like eyes like streetlights, even the blood that races through my own network of veins is like never-ending traffic zooming along super highways. I am the city—

I hear a nasally voice call out from behind and I haven't felt so much comfort in the voice yet, at the same time, so much frustration.

Again, the voice: *Hey!*

I turn my shoulder, only to find one of Damianos's friends—Ryan, I think, or maybe Bryan—holding a piece of paper in front of him. I immediately recognize his face from the Instagram photo Damianos had posted over Spring Break. He, along with Peedy and Damianos, are posing on the beach with their shirts off.

I panic for a moment, thinking that Damianos is still hanging around somewhere even though his car is nowhere to be found.

"You dropped something," he says to me.

He's holding the piece of paper with the farthest tips of his index finger and thumb as if the paper itself is laced with some highly contagious disease. Without turning his head, his eyes move toward the sketch. He makes an obvious face in front of me; however, I'm not sure whether he wants to laugh or cry or both.

"I believe this belongs to you," he says, his lips curled in a hidden disgust.

He extends the piece of paper toward my general direction.

I catch a glimpse of the sketch.

It must've slipped from my notebook.

As I reach for the loose paper, I realize it's one of my many sketches of Damianos. Of all sketches, that one—anyone but *that* one!

In the sketch, Damianos, who's rocking a bronze tunic and a flappy red cape, is riding the back of a phallic-shaped serpent named Oh!Orgasmo—an emphasis on the Oh! In a fierce, jousting-like stab, the great Damianos is striking the heart of a pesky dragon that has terrorized the small coastal whaling town of Dovieur. What stands out in the sketch is the "other" feature that's flapping in the breeze—and I don't mean Damianos's cape.

Once, during P.E. last fall—with an emphasis on *fall*—Damianos was hanging out with a couple of his jock buddies on the basketball court. He happened to be sitting with his legs crossed. I happened to be sitting at the perfect angle where I could see through a tiny window-like opening directly below his thigh. I wasn't looking at first. I admit that I was curious. But the second time, I glanced at Damianos something had changed about him. One minor detail. My eyes fell below and as his legs opened up like a door, two balls were exposed and hanging from his shorts. And they weren't basketballs. I'm not sure if he knew—maybe he did because he was staring directly at me with a little smirk on his face. I admit that I found an opportunity to catch a glimpse at what all of the sluts at Spoiled Bitch High had been whispering about behind my back. Being the curious person I was, I untied my shoe without anybody looking and acted as if I was doing what any normal person would do if his or her shoe was untied and retied my shoe. Without Damianos noticing, I leaned forward for a closer look to see the full magic act as I started to tie my shoe and he must've moved his leg or changed positions or readjusted himself because there *he* was, King of Thrones himself, chilling with his other two round comrades, as if he was taking a break from all the bouncing and swinging he was doing during jump rope. I was amazed that Damianos didn't even wear underwear. I've heard the horror stories of guys getting their balls all twisted up and tangled like cable wires from running or doing whatever physical activities they did.

The sketch certainly isn't one I'd like to "show off," especially not to Ryan or Bryan. In fact, I feel my skin flaming just by standing in his presence.

I snatch the sketch from whatever's name.

"Nice *drawing*," he says in the most arrogant way possible. "Very detailed."

"Mind your goddamn business," I snap.

He holds up his hands in surrender; and for a moment, he appears as if he's about to pull out a white flag and start waving it around his head like a coward.

Eventually, he wanders away.

I feel the sudden urge to call out to him and make a deal with him not to tell anyone about the sketch. The time passes before I even get a chance to muster up the courage.

Eventually, he gets in his car and drives away listening to glitchy EDM.

For the rest of the afternoon, I can't stop thinking about whether or not he's going to tell Damianos about the sketch.

THE Stop N' Shop is a place I frequent whenever I'm feeling heavy.

On the far corner of the store, I run into Kush and his ragtag team of losers. They put on a good front, despite looking like cats who could cut with their eyes, pupils dilated, and for any noble warrior to cross them, it'd take the wickedest spell to defeat them for their souls are black and bottomless and impenetrable by any threats. The kind of cats who don't play nice. Who obliterate you with their spoken tongue for the whim of only a foolish man would show them a thin iced curiosity of acknowledgment, which, in any Hollow Street Soldier's mind, is considered an act of disrespect and the ultimate punishment was death.

Spoiler alert: Kush isn't a Hollow Street Soldier, far from one. He's what I'd like to call a "pocketsize thug" who comes with batteries. He's a couple of grades below me, as you can tell from the pimples of his face and his scuffed-up Jordan's and hand-me-down Fubu. From what I've heard, after being held back twice, he's wrapping up his last year at South Winston like a bad, under-budget movie.

Unlike what the name suggests, Kush isn't your typical cliché of a laidback stoner, rather quite the contrary. You see, Kush figured out how to make dough while he wasn't schooling; in fact, he was way too intelligent for school. He was a wiz kid who created an app to hustle drugs. Instead of reading books, Kush read code. He knew about ones and zeros better than he did the English language. Instead of beating his meat to stepsister porn, playing shooters, sniffing glue, vaping, blacking out, filming each other pull pranks or dares and posting it all over the Internet, or whatever bored young, rebellious males did these days, Kush was setting up a vast network across the entire city. He "knew a guy who knew a guy who lived in Colorado" and every month, his guy's guy would pay a visit to town and hook up Kush with enough flavors to gut the Stop N' Shop once Kush's famous Kush hit the streets, resulting in hordes of stoner zombies to raid the candy aisle. I have to give it to him. The kid's only a couple of awareness months away from fifteen, and he's already a "successful" entrepreneur and probably making more money in a week than most stressed, worn out, callused-hand parents around here brought home in a month. Unfortunately, it's only a matter of time before the System catches up with Kush and sends his ass to the place that turns nonviolent boys into violent criminals. If only Kush could put his entrepreneurship skills to better use.

Kush and his motley crew are eyeing these two kids on the street corner outside Stop N' Shop or from what I gathered, competitors of Kush. From the constant surveillance, they're clearly working the corner, their hands dipped in counterfeit suede, denim, and polyester, pushing whatever he can get his hands on.

"You good, Beauty Queen?" Kush says, as he tosses his head up at me.

I feel that urge again to act. I envision myself from a parallel universe snapping at Kush by wrapping both my hands around his neck and strangling the little pocket-sized wannabe thug. A part of me wants to shake the fool out of him and tell him that he could do such much better.

I take a beat and face Kush.

"Didn't I tell you not to call me by that name?"

"Well, you are beautiful," he says, grinning. "And you could be my queen."

"In your dreams."

"Can't a girl take a compliment anymo? Shit," he waves at me, "girls be trippin' nowadays."

"I'd be trippin' all right. Trippin' all over your face."

Like the kid before, Kush throws his hands in the air as if I'm the police.

"Chill, Squints," he says.

I pause and take another beat.

"I'm chill," I say casually, as I open the door.

"You don't look chill," he says, as I ignore him and walk into the store.

Inside, Bernie is scrambling around the store searching for a mop that apparently RJ misplaced. I haven't seen him so jacked up since the robbery last spring. He's yelling at RJ as to where he put the mop the last time he used it, but RJ is being RJ and not giving Bernie any indicator as to where the mop may be.

I make it to the middle of the store where I find the crime scene in the back of the magazine aisle. Vomit has even splashed onto the magazines on the top shelf. I haven't seen so much vomit in my life, which is nothing short of an understatement—being someone who's not ashamed to admit enjoys a good vomit video on YouTube from time to time. The scene appears as if somebody's body had been literally turned inside him. I'm talking full-blown exorcism.

With his face all red and sweaty, Bernie acknowledges me. I realize I'm the last face he'd want to see right now. But he pushes through all the frustration and strangely, laughs off the accident.

"If it isn't my favorite customer, or better yet, that one customer who never gives me any grief?"

"Bad day, huh?"

"How'd you guess?" he returns, pointing at the mess.

"Hello, Bern."

He sighs.

"Hey there, Squints."

"Looks like someone ate too many Cheetos," I say, noticing the orange hue to the vomit.

"Don't even get me started," Bernie says sharply.

"Sorry." My body coils inward in guilt. "Can I help?"

"No," he says, as he turns his shoulder and yells for RJ, who has turned into a ghost. He turns back around and takes a breath. "You want the usual?"

"Yes, please," I say, "if it's no trouble."

"I tell you what," he says, "just help yourself."

"What do I do?"

"There's a number on the side of cash register. Type in that number and it'll print you out a ticket." He pauses. "You know you could just pay at the machine. You know, right?"

"But I like paying you, Bernie."

He tilts his head to the side.

"Well, aren't you precious?"

I can sense the sarcasm in his voice.

"What about the money?" I ask, holding out the five-dollar bill in my hand.

"It's on the house," Bernie says.

"You sure?"

"Go," Bernie says, waving me away as if he has more important business to attend to.

I walk to the cash register and punch in the number into the keypad on the side of the monitor. The cash register opens, revealing an entire row of cash. For a moment, the thought enters my mind. I can't believe it does, but I'd be lying if I said I wasn't thinking about talking a couple of twenties. I think about Bernie and all he has done for me. The thought of Bernie rids any thought of ripping him off.

Before the thought returns, I grab the receipt from the machine, close the cash register, and say my goodbyes to Bernie.

🚗

EVER since I graduated from Ridings Academy, heading to the Stop N' Shop for the "full-works" car wash has become the highlight of my weeks. I practically come here at least three to four times a week as if it's part of my weekly regimen of pissing away the last remaining years of my adolescence.

I punch in the six-digit code into the outdated keypad, which looks identical to the square cubes of an old payphone—another reason why I have so much connection with Bernie: when asked about the ancient payment system, he told me he likes to keep things simple and sentimental, to hell with technology! He's mushy like that.

The streetlight-like light above the car wash turns green.

As I carefully guide the wheels into the two trenches running along the inside of the tunnel, I creep through until the light turns yellow, then, eventually, red.

I stop the car and put the gear in park.

Let the show begin.

On most occasions while waiting inside the car as it gets misted with water, then hosed down by jets of foamy soap, then clobbered by massive brushes, both spinning and oscillating against the car, my mind wanders into the fantasy world, *my world*, a new yet old place filled with walking dragons and flying lions with wings like Pegasus.

But not today.

Today, my mind goes to a dark place where I'm reimagining a previous daydream where Damianos goes off to college without me and I get left behind here in Fucksville. Instead of hanging at bars and wasting away my life jumping from one man to the next, I become a detective trying to solve my own murder mystery where I was a murderer on the run. I had murdered somebody and that somebody was myself—at least another, much smaller version of myself. I start digging up old photos, asking questions where answers came with hidden dangers.

As the water rains down on the windows of the car, I rewind the clocks and remake my previous nightmarish daydream. However, what makes these moving pictures inside my head so real is *they are real*—at least, at one point they seemed as if they were. I go back, way back, before these several limbo-like months of being school-free, before Damianos, before Uncle Jojo and some woman who got a swipe right.

The final buzz of the car wash followed by a *wha-whoof* sound of the air vent turning on pulls me from a distant image, a graphic still frame of a girl screaming out in horror.

Before I have a chance to make sense of the image, it's gone.

Faded to black.

I drive forward over the hump in the track and as I'm about to drive through the wall of blowing air, I spot a dark smudge of dry blood caked on the side of the opening. On any normal day, I wouldn't think anything of it. But there's no such thing as normal days—not anymore—especially after the two people who brought you into this world only live inside a two-dimensional world.

WHEN I get back home, Uncle Jojo and his Lazy Susan wife, Nailah, are at each other's throats. I've heard Uncle Jojo scream before like a singer in a death metal band but never so long-winded during an argument. He even has to pause during the use of several "fuck(s)" and "Jesus Christ(s)."

Nailah flips on the bitch switch.

The blasphemy really gets her revved up something awful, especially being a former radical/professional protester turned Jesus freak and all. She won't tolerate a certain language in "her presence," which my uncle mistakes as "her house."

The fight suddenly shifts gears and instead of the two arguing about a comment Nailah apparently made to Uncle Jojo at the grocery store that involved another cuter and more "affectionate" couple, the real reason for Uncle Jojo's hostility is finally revealed, as if he's a poker player unveiling his hand. *Money.* Nine out of ten times, their fights revolved—or devolved—around money. In Nailah's defense, she was trying to explain to my uncle about the way she has been treated lately—apparently, not so well, or at least not the way she expected to be treated when she first read her vows.

I return the favor and ignore them as I slip past the foyer and creep upstairs. I can't help but notice the news report on TV about yet another missing person. So far, eight missing person cases have been reported in the past two weeks. Most of the cases involved young people, possible runaways. However, the recent report is about a middle-age man. Father of two who works the night shift as a security guard at Dover Place Mall. I don't know why the news report catches my attention, but it does. It's sticks, actually. Maybe it's the notion of being missing that intrigues me. You throw a word like *missing* into the subject and all of a sudden, people start paying attention.

I'm pulled back to reality by a curse word that I've never heard before: *fuckwit*. I have to give credit to the newcomer. She tends to get rather creative when it comes to exercising her emotions. Perhaps it was a sparkle of her glory days as a radical who'd spend her youth stirring up fights with those who opposed her or marching against injustice or lending her voice to a rally which promoted a good cause that surfaced every now and then. A part of me wishes I could be just like Nailah—a younger Nailah that is—and be more open with my emotions. A part of me may be, dare I say, jealous.

The insult doesn't sit well with Uncle Jojo. He returns fire; however, he's no match for Nailah's firepower. She resorts to using every curse word in the book, as well as new ones, which I have never even heard of before, like *dickbucket*. If I know Nailah like I think I do, I know her words will be retracted during prayer. This isn't new at all, the fighting I mean; in fact, I hate to say this but I've almost become accustomed to walking in on a good fight.

Which means I know exactly what happens afterwards.

THE shouting match disappears as soon as I put on a straight-to-streaming movie on my tablet. I turn up the volume, which helps drown out the battle royal downstairs. Eventually, I forget that they're even down there, fighting or making up or doing whatever it is. About thirty or so minutes into the lame movie where some tired detective is trying to find someone's daughter, I decide to remove my contacts and step into a hot shower. The soothing sensation of the running hot water helps wash away whatever frustration I still have clung to my body. I hardly bath, though, hardly even run shampoo through my hair or liquid soap over my skin. I watch whatever dirt I still have in my hair or ink or the various colors of paint on my hands mix into the brownish water moving in circular pattern around the drain in a hypnotic spiral.

Somehow, the heavy cues of action manage to slip through the sound of water.

As I continue to stare at the water below, my eyes suddenly get all swimmy as if I'm rippling away like one of those passé flashbacks from what Uncle Jojo calls "old timey" movies. Which I assume he refers to the Fifties or whenever the movies were shown in only black and white, where lead roles were played by mostly white people who carried an otherworldly aura about them that made them larger than the life projected on screen, who appeared as if they had traveled from another distant world, one which did not, by any stretch, reflect my own.

I hear the *thud* of a door shutting downstairs. I don't even have to stop showering, throw a towel around my body, and check out the commotion. I can picture what happens next while the warm water runs down my face: Uncle Jojo, madder than hell, storming outside to his car. He's so infuriated with Nailah that he'll slam the car door as well.

What do you know?

I hear yet *another* sound of a door slamming shut. Thin and hollow but clear enough for me to distinguish.

As I stare at the pale and pruned skin on the inside of my palms, I picture my uncle speeding off into the night and being gone for hours, into the night and well past a quiet and awkward dinner accompanied by my new aunt trying to relate in any way she can. When he returns, he'll smell like beer and smoke. However, he doesn't return after dinner, when both our bellies are full and tempers have mellowed and iced over an over-the-counter remedy of warm chamomile tea and silly YouTube videos. In my bed with my glasses inching down the bridge of my nose and each one of my thoughts fading in darkness of book pages, I wait to hear Uncle Jojo walk through the front door downstairs. He doesn't.

Yet, the entire night is filled with silence and my mind drifting off into a scenario where something awful happens to Uncle Jojo.

🚗

SOMEWHERE in my violent haze, I end up falling asleep and then waking up to the glare of the sun spearing through my room.

I check the mirror, check my hair first and clear away crumbles of crust from the corners of my eyes.

When I glide my way downstairs, ready to begin my day, Uncle Jojo is sitting at the kitchen table as if he's been here the entire time. He's dressed and all ready to handle insurance claims. He's even bragging to Nailah about a new drone he's going to start using to survey roof damage to residential buildings, which means "goodbye to climbing ladders." He spends his days writing checks to help people fix their homes when he can't even fix his own home: the irony. He acts as if last night's fight never happened, despite his eyes telling a different story.

The sight alone of Uncle Jojo sitting at the table brings me great comfort, yet, at the same time, stirs an unforgivable anger inside me.

Ever since my dad—my real one, that is—died in a car accident, I've carried around an image of him inside my head, at times incredibly vivid, like an image seared in my memory, while others blur and fragmented; nonetheless, it's one of the few ones I have left of him. He's sitting in the same spot as Uncle Jojo at the end of the table. The table happened to be the exact one because my mom and Uncle Jojo's first wife, Konomi, whom I once called "auntie," who happened to be as tight as a twin with my mom, shopped at the same department stores, practically wore the same outfits and hairdos. Most of the furniture inside Uncle Jojo's house was exactly the same as the furniture I grew up around. The image grabs me and holds me tight, as if that voice inside is trying to keep me in the moment. My dad is waiting on me, as if he's welcoming me into the kitchen. It may seem like nothing, but back then, it was everything. It was Dad's way of showing me what a family looks like, that, despite all of the fights parents have, family, in this case, my dad would be there in the morning, waiting for me to appear before his eyes as if he had already put whatever troubles behind him and was ready and willing to move forward.

I shake the image from my head.

Before I can address Uncle Jojo, Nailah walks past me and opens up the refrigerator door. She pulls out a carton of eggs and proceeds to make breakfast.

I slip around Nailah and grab a carton of orange juice. I pour myself a glass. I only take two sips before the moment is gone and the anger is back.

Uncle Jojo asks me how the "school hunt" is going.

He mentions several universities and art colleges, which he thinks I might like. Which immediately ramps up my anger because, last week, he got all over me about art—particularly the "artist"—and how it's nothing but a pipedream and that "nobody gives a damn" about what I have to offer to the world. Last week, Uncle Jojo, who, unlike me, had grown up in Baltimore where fear was embedded in daily life and through the eyes of a pragmatist, the gun held more power than a book, acted as if he had certain "plans" for me, as if he had the course of my adult life already figured out and I, the able body, was going to assume the role and go along with these plans and if not, I, the able body, was going to be living the rest of my existence rotting away on the very streets which Uncle Jojo often scorned. Just imagine a typical parent finishing their child's sentences whether it be among the company of guests or strangers because that child was still slow about how to deliver his or her words. Now, imagine the same parent doing the same thing with that same child who could make rational decisions on his or her own. That now grown child still had that slow delivery; however, he or she was more careful with words and wanted to make one hundred percent certain each one truly embodied an expression nestled inside that very place where ideas flourished. That was Uncle Jojo, except he wasn't a parent, not even my parent. And I was that child, except I wasn't *his* child, only a template, a experimentation to Uncle Jojo, the trial and errors of what it may one day feel like to raise his own creation.

I ignore Uncle Jojo and walk back up to my room. I pull out a shoebox under my bed and grab an old photo of my parents. In the photo, my dad is loading a netted bag of soccer balls into the back of our red Star Cruz'R while my mom is standing outside the passenger door pointing at a watch on her wrist as if we don't have time to be taking photographs. As for me, dressed in my royal blue oversize soccer jersey, I'm standing next to Dad as if I'm waiting on his next commands.

I remember only fragments of that day. For one, I remember being incredibly nervous—and nauseous. Usually, one came before the other. I do remember the car—mostly because of its unusual name—and how it was unlike any car on the road. According to Wikipedia, there were only a hundred Star Cruz'R's manufactured in the US. Rumor has it the "R" in the name "Cruiser" stood for the name, *Rian*, which happened to be the name of the automobile manufacturer, but nobody really knows because, after only a year of production, the company shut down for "unknown" reasons. Which made the car a collectible and quite a rarity.

As I drift into the photo and try to make more sense of that day, I feel a presence behind me.

Uncle Jojo says from behind, "I took that picture, you know?"

I don't turn around, don't even react; yet, my attention remains on the photo.

"Your mother was in one of her epic moods," Uncle Jojo says, as he takes a seat next to me on the edge of the bed.

"I always wondered who took the photo," I say. "I figured it was you."

"Your father, on the other hand," he says, as if he's about to tell a story, "was being himself. I remember after I took that picture he spent the next ten minutes cleaning out the backseat because somebody—not to name any names—" he says, glancing over at me from the corner of his eyes, "—dropped a bag of french fries between the seats." He pauses and for a moment, his face looks calm. "He was a perfectionist, that's for sure—'*nitpicky*,' was what Nana used to say. Even when we were kids, he was always looking for something to fight about. The more I get older, I realize your father's personality. . . wasn't a bad thing; in fact, it was the very opposite of bad." He turns his attention to a painting on my desk. He picks it up and looks it over. The painting is one of two Lycans guarding their cub from an evil warlock. "Your father had the gift as well. He gave it up, though, when he was about your age."

I ask, "Why?"

"It was around the time your Aunt Kaali passed away." He pauses, turns to me, and says from the corner of his mouth, "You would've really like Kaali. She was a go-getter. When Kaali passed, times were tough for us, especially for your father who was closer to Kaali than I was. He needed money, and he didn't want to be just another 'starving artist.' So, he gave it up."

"Because of money?"

Uncle Jojo pauses once more.

A mixture of emotions stirs inside me after hearing Uncle Jojo's words.

He leans in closer to me.

"I'm trying here," he says.

The comment doesn't draw any reaction from me.

Uncle Jojo leans back from my lack of acknowledgment.

"You're right," he says, his tone more forthright. "I'm not your father and I never will be. *But*," he says and takes a beat, "if you need any help or anyone to talk to, then I'm your guy."

I continue to stare at the photo in my hands and for a moment, I try to imagine my dad using his brother as a vessel to communicate with me.

It doesn't seem to be working.

Uncle Jojo pats me on the shoulder and walks away.

The leftover anger from earlier suddenly slips from my mouth.

"Where did you go last night?" I ask and nearly retract the words as soon as they leave my lips.

The words came out bitter, I realize.

Uncle Jojo stops at the doorway and says, "You heard, huh?"

Without looking at Uncle Jojo, I nod my head.

In the tense silence, I finally turn my shoulder and give him my full attention.

"I had to clear my head," he said. "That's all. When you get to be my age, you'll realize that everything in life isn't handed to you. You have to work hard for it and once you've earned what you've worked for, you have to do everything in your power to hold onto it, keep it from slipping through your fingertips, even if it means letting go of the things that were keeping you from moving forward. Otherwise, the world will walk all over you; and eventually, it will eat your soul."

Uncle Jojo leaves the bedroom; and yet, it feels as if he's still standing at the doorway with his words resonating throughout my head. It's not until late morning after I waste hours staring an unfinished piece of work that I finally reach out to Damianos on MyCircle. I end up sending him a "nod," hoping that he'll let me into his circle. I wait around for hours. I even skip lunch and wait by my phone, checking each *bleep* or notification. Each noise that my phone makes causes my stomach to stir and rumble and each time, I'm thinking *this is the one*. Each time, though, it's not the one. It's either an alert telling me to upgrade my OS for the gazillionth time this month or an email informing that so-and-so made a tweet followed by a tale of facial emojis and pictograms about how she paid her first car bill #adulting or a text from a sketchy number trying to trick me into increasing the size of my breasts for little to no charge.

Before I even realize the time, the light of the day has already faded.

The entire day has been a complete wash filled with flashes of great expectations, only to be squashed by advertisements or shady spambots.

I can feel the thorns inside, twisting and turning.

Over the past couple of weeks, I've developed them in my sides and I believe they'll only get worse the longer I stay here. Instead of thorns projecting outward, as most thorns do like any natural defense mechanism, mine are starting to project inward deep into my body, and with each move, each turn, each breath, I can feel them poking and pinching at me, as if they're telling me to "stay still," to "stay here" in Shitsville, where the air is toxic, the ground covered in barbwire, preventing anyone from leaving. Even the leaden water you drink stunts your growth and keeps your ass forever stuck in this hellhole, where its residents grow ripe and thorny.

AT night, I sneak a pill from Nailah's medicine cabinet to help me sleep. When I return to bed, I perch my phone against the lamp on the nightstand and put on the movie, *Edward Scissorhands*.

Only a few minutes into the movie, I fall into a heavy sleep where I'm living in a world without Damianos. I don't remember as to how I entered the dream or how I came to be wandering a desolate street in the middle of the night where soft breezes blow around the very objects that society has discarded and remind me of the tumbleweeds in old Westerns: a sheet from yesterday's newspaper, an empty soda can, a pink flyer promoting a punk band named *Eel-Baby and The Cuts*, or me, the body I just so happen to be currently occupying, cast aside, left to rot, forgotten. I try to backtrack and retrace my thoughts as to how I came here, but all I can find are random flashes of images bolting past me as if I'm fast-forwarding through the good scenes. I find myself here, at the end of the movie, my climax.

All around me, the city suddenly comes alive!

Streetlights bend forward like fingers and shine their lights on me like spotlights. The windows of abandoned buildings light up and hum with life.

As I reach the intersection, I'm struck by a dizzy spell. I lose my balance for a moment. My eyes fall to the street below and I realize it's not my body that is doing all the moving. It's the street!

I hold out my arms, hoping it will help keep my body balanced; however, like the city around me, the street comes alive as well!

First, the street softens. The soles of my shoes start to sink into the asphalt as if it was made of quicksand. I make an attempt to step onto the sidewalk, but the street suddenly turns liquid, moving like a turbulent ocean.

I stagger from the violent current and a part of me realizes that, if I fall into the asphalt, I will never return.

That part of me spreads and before I know it, my mind is consumed with the street. Falling into it will be the end of me, my movie.

Swaying back and forth from the violent flux of the street, the two opposing lanes opened up into what looks like a mouth—or void.

As the streets start to swallow me whole, I bolt upright from bed.

Uncle Jojo's words are back as if they've never even left me.

BY morning, I've already moved on from Damianos. The sketches of him looking all awesome and fantastical shelved. Paintings, oil and acrylic, as well as ink wash paintings, placed inside cachet portfolios and bound construction paper, then tucked away under my bed with the dust demons. As for the more risqué digital paintings of Damianos and all of his lustful, *Heavy Metal*-inspired quests, I transfer them from my desktop to a USB flash drive where they'll be saved in the digital darkness and stashed away in the bot-

tom of a desk drawer, then original copies will be highlighted and then dragged to the trashcan on my dock followed by me simultaneously pressing three keys, Command, Shift, and Delete, on my keyboard and the trance-
inducing sound of paper crumbling peppering my speakers.
I prefer *not* to be able to easily access these drawings.
Maybe that's the whole point: the urge to move on from
"Goddamn It" Damianos.

After eating a civil breakfast with Uncle Jojo and
Nailah, I head into work at My Workspace where I've been
working part time while I'm "currently between schools," or
what I like to call "currently between career paths." Even
though it's not much to look forward to and holds absolutely no avenues to thrive in the most economically viable
way—except for possibly a shitty managerial position where
the hours are much longer and way shittier and the stress is
next level—I've told myself that I'm going to save money
not to throw away on "college" but invest it in something,
maybe a place of my own or whatever, or maybe even a
new drawing tablet or updated version of Photoshop.

While I'm on the touchy subject of "moving forward," I
end up checking out this new dating app called Goin'
Steady during my lunch break. I don't waste my time with
those other apps such as Woo, Cupid's Arrow, and XOXO,
which have been known to be "hookup" dating apps—
digital booty calls.

From most of the reviews I read about online dating, of
all the apps out there, Goin' Steady was one of the most
successful dating apps for people who are looking for more
than a fling or one-night stand.

I create an account and make sure to be as transparent
as I can when it comes to filling out my profile. I list my
"likes" as well as "dislikes." I mention that I'm an artist. I
post the link of my blog where interested parties are able to
check out my work. I list all the artists who've inspire me
throughout the years: Julie Bell; Ken Kelly; Boris Vallejo;
Chris Achilleos; Bruce Pennington; Jeff Easley; Michael
Whelan; Jeffrey Catherine Jones; Pitre; Beksinski. I feel as
if I should name more artists—dozens more—to make my-

self as transparent as possible, but, sadly, I've run out of characters.

Once my profile is created and I've indicated to Goin' Steady as to what kind of person I'm looking for, it gives me a gallery of potentials.

Immediately, I write off the ones who are posing without a shirt—a clear indicator that they came to Goin' Steady for other reasons.

I come across a guy named Mikel Hanson. His features are similar to Damianos and he could pass as a relative; however, he has blue eyes, *not* green. And he's twenty-five, *not* eighteen. Seven years is plenty of time to put on some age. Which makes me wonder if Mikel eats avocados everyday and has perfect genes or he's using an older photo in his profile. Regardless, Mikel Hanson shares the traits as someone I'm searching for: smart, funny, and not to mention, handsome.

I hold my breath and send him a "wink."

Within the first ten minutes of swiping through potential "steadies," I receive a return "wink" along with a message from Mikel Hanson.

In the message, Mikel writes that he read through my profile and talked about how he has a lot in common with me. He also read my background on my personal blog and was completely blown away by my artwork. Based on the message, he sounds nervous—like he spent several botched attempts at correcting his sentences. Which is a good sign—great. He is a human *being*.

I reply to Mikel's message, thanking him for all his kind words. It takes him a couple of minutes to reply and during those anxious minutes, I can't help but wonder what he's doing on the other side.

When the message finally comes through, it's well thought-out. Mikel remains business-like in his response as he informs me about his "afternoon itinerary," which involves a meeting at three, then he has to pick up his Labrador from the vet at five. After Mikel picks up his dog, "Igor," his schedule is "wide" open; however, he makes sure to ask me first if I'd like to meet at The Fire Bowl at seven o'clock. Which seems a shade too early for a date—if that's what Mikel is implying. Meanwhile, a fellow associate, Rick—or who I mentally call in my head or behind his back whenever he's not around, Rick the Dick—bursts into the break room and starts barking orders at me. He says Sasha has been paging me for the past five minutes and that she needs help at the Print Lab.

I agree to meet Mikel at The Fire Bowl. I take charge and tell him I can be there at eight. He immediately messages me back: "Sounds great. I look forward to meeting you." He calls me by the legal name on my profile. I don't take it as a turnoff. I don't even message him back to correct him. Instead, I respond by telling him, "Me too." And I leave it at that.

Cla-clunk is the sound of my mic being dropped.

I leave the break room in a good mood. My face is glowing and everybody in the store can see the light radiating from my smile.

One customer, a middle-aged woman who looks as if she's in charge of some secret club where a whole bunch of angry women get together and vent all about their issues, is waiting at the Print Lab with her arms folded across her chest and wearing the kind of face one would wear before going on a murderous rampage. For a moment, I imagine that mascara running down the center of her cheeks like war paint and the purse hanging from her shoulder like a concealed flail and once spun over her head, I imagine sharp spikes to release outward. She's looking for a fight, her next victim; however, she came to the wrong woman. Like hell she's going to steal my glow.

While the customer—as expected—goes on a scripted rant about our service and how "slow" it has been lately, I think about Mikel Hanson and those heavenly blue eyes.

Instead of wasting away my life picking up assholes from bars, I'm living the carefree life with a dark-haired, blue-eyed man named Mikel Hanson. One date at The Fire

Bowl turns into several dates at The Fire Bowl. It's fair to say we enjoy each other's company. Mikel has a dark sense of humor; however, he makes me laugh even when he doesn't intend to make me laugh.

After the third week of going on dates and eating meals together, we spend a weekend camping at the Great Lodge in the White Mountains. It's there, at a soft campfire shared by other campers from other parts of the country, where we share our first real kiss. The heat of the fire warms our skin. The passion burns hot inside us. Two flames. Madly in love.

Weekend getaways become weekly habits.

One weekend we travel past the mountains, to an amusement park where the clocks magically turn backwards and we're like two grownups reliving lost childhoods together.

The next weekend, we find ourselves at the beach, doing every sexual position in the book as if we're experimenting on how deep the flesh can swing. Everything else falls into place, like a jigsaw puzzle.

Mikel and I have our first fight about moving in together; however, the fight makes our relationship stronger than ever before. Each fight brings us closer together by exposing our weaknesses.

With Olympiad grace, we hurdle over the hump where most relationships fail and we both find strength in each other's weaknesses. I am his "yin" and he is my "yang." And for the first time throughout my once miserable existence, I feel as if I have purpose, as if I finally fit into place, like a jigsaw piece that snaps perfectly into another piece. I no longer take walks on desolate streets. On the contrary, I fear nights, the spell they have over me. I am no longer drawn to the lure of the street creature. Instead, I spend nights wrapped in the comfort of Mikel's arms. He is the sole guardian of my body and spirit, my temple. He is me, and I am he.

We decide over a spaghetti dinner at our favorite Italian restaurant to become one unit. We both make it official and decide to have our ceremony at a beach on a remote island in the Keys surrounded by our closest friends. We multiply, bring other mini-me's into the world. We watch them grow up into individuals and pursue their dreams. When our children decide it's time to pursue lives of their own, we set them free into the world. Mikel and I turn back the clocks again and we're together. We grow young together. And then we die together.

AFTER work, I stop by *Au Courant* to pick up a bottle of shampoo.

They're out of my brand on the shelf.

Thinking that they might have more stock in the back, I track down the nearest employee; however, all of them are busy helping customers.

As I exit the aisle, I make a U-turn around an end cap and head down the next aisle. I look over my shoulder for a second; then, when I turn back around, I find a body walking directly at me.

Startled, I bump shoulders with another customer.

"I'm so sorr—"

Before I can even finish my sentence, my words are severed. I'm left without the ability to speak. Both my mind and heart are racing as if they're one singular organ. I'm aware the mind is not an organ, but more so an element of an individual, a faculty built by feeling and experiences. None of these things matter. All I can hear and feel is the throb, the radiating beat of my nerves wringing against my body, extracting the words from my insides and releasing them all slow and tedious as if they were made from the same consistency as honey.

The words dribble from my lips in a stupid drawl.

Da-mia-nos.

"Squints, right?" he says in return.

My senses are heightened. I hone them. The first thing that stands out is the way he looks at me. He's glowing.

"I am?" My voice is drawn out. I realize I sound like I'm stating a question. I backtrack. "I mean, yeah, right,

I'm Squints." I can't believe myself. I sound like an idiot. My mind starts wandering, and I can't help but think as to what he's thinking of me. I stop thinking and look around the store and point out the obvious. "So, ah, what are you doing here?" I ask, trying not to sound too nosy.

Damianos holds up the bottle of conditioner.

"Just buying some conditioner."

"Conditioner?" I repeat.

"Yeah," Damianos says and points at his head. "You put it in your hair."

I can't tell whether he's cracking a joke or treating me like that third cousin who lives in the woods and can't stand to be anywhere near civilization.

"I know, silly."

Silly?

He doesn't respond. The glow starts to fade from his face.

"I mean," I backtrack once more, "I didn't know guys used conditioner."

"Well," he says coolly, "it's nothing for me to be embarrassed about—"

"—I didn't say you should be."

I sound defensive. Already a couple of lines in and I sound bitchy.

"Most guys I know just use some off-brand shampoo that their mom probably bought for them." He holds up the bottle of conditioner as if he's promoting it to me. "However," he says, his eyes narrowing, "the secret to strong and lasting hair is what you put in after the shampoo."

I remain speechless.

Damianos looks as if he's waiting for me to follow up with something that sounds less-bitchy.

Say something, you idiot.

I say the first sentence that comes to mind.

"*Well,*" I say, "I think it's cool."

Damianos doesn't respond.

I clarify, "You know, for a guy to be using conditioner—"

"—So, I heard you're going to Ridings," Damianos nearly cuts me off.

"Yeah," I say and slow my thoughts. "Well, did. I don't go there anymore. I already finished last semester."

"Get out of here!" Damianos says, the glow back in his face. "You already graduated?"

I nod.

"Yeah."

"That's awesome! I'd wish I could graduate early. I actually thought about doing some online classes. I also thought about Ridings, but my parents wouldn't let me."

I realize Damianos Pipes with a little more encouragements from his family and peers could've possibly been in my class last semester.

For a moment, I hate his parents.

I wish them great bodily harm.

"That's a shame," I say but the comment comes off more flirtatious.

Damianos picks up the heat radiating off my body.

I contemplate about whether or not to ask him about the nod I sent him earlier on MyCircle.

"So," Damianos says, clearing his throat, "my friend, Peedy, said he saw you the other day at the park."

Damianos speaking Peedy's name sounds like a similar tone I had mistakenly used with Damianos after explaining that he shouldn't be embarrassed about buying conditioner and for a moment, I wonder whether or not the rumors about he and Peedy are actually true and that little "fling" that happened between the two during Spring Break wasn't a drunk hookup but two friends expressing their deep affection for one another. I figured it was a jealous girl, maybe an ex who wanted Damianos back, like that snippy witch Nicky Picky, who strategically ran a classic smear campaign on Damianos in order to plant doubts in the minds of potential girlfriends—or boyfriends. I mean, if you can't have him, then why not kill him—or better yet, destroy him and his reputation?

What?!?

I shake away the disturbing thought and for a moment, question as to where exactly such debauchery originated.

"Peedy?"

"Yeah," Damianos says. "He's fam."

I start stuttering words again, as if I'm stuck in a glitch. Any thought I had before the comment falls into blackness.

"I was just going for a run," I say, I think, but don't even remember saying it.

As if the words come out automatically.

I think he knows I'm lying too from the change in his voice.

"That's lit," he says, as if he's never used the word *lit* before. "I like to run. You know, if you're not doing anything tonight, maybe we can go out for a run together or even just a walk. Perhaps grab a smoothie afterwards. Your choice?"

"I love smoothies!"

Too much. Keep calm and kill.

"I mean, I like smoothies."

"Who doesn't like smoothies?"

"I know, right."

"So, is that a yes?"

"What?"

"Do you want to hang out tonight?"

"*Yes*," I say, more abruptly. "I mean," I play it cool, like Damianos, "whatever. That's cool with me, if it's cool with me."

"It's cool with me," he says, keeping to his smooth self. "So, do you want to meet me at the park at seven?"

"Seven's very cool."

"Well, then I'll see you at seven."

"Yes," I say and smile goodbye. "See you."

I finally take a breath once Damianos walks away.

"Wait!" I blurt out. "Your number!"

Damianos turns around and acts surprised by the comment.

"Oh," he says. "Right. I almost forgot. We should exchange numbers just in case, you know, something comes up."

"Right," I say. "It's good to keep in contact, right?"

He doesn't respond; in fact, he looks almost put off by giving out his number.

He holds out his hand.

At first, I actually think about shaking or writing on it.

Then, he says, "Your phone?"

I type in my password on my phone and hand it to him. He types in his contact information in my contacts at lightning speed. I'm amazed how fast his fingers move. Before I can catch my breath, he's already done. He hands the phone back to me. His phone rings. He pulls out his phone and shows the screen to me.

"Got your number," he says and walks away.

As Damianos starts typing in his phone, I look down at mine.

I notice there's a text from Damianos.

I open the text and find a "winking" face emoji.

With my knees buckling with excitement, I reply to the text by sending him a "smiling" face emoji.

Did that really just happen?

THE thought doesn't even dawn on me until I leave the store. Another guy pops into my head, my date tonight at The Fire Bowl. My mind is so preoccupied with replaying the previous conversation with Damianos that I even forget his name.

Mikel who?

As I try to think of Mikel's last name, my mind drifts back to the conversation and all the subjects I could've brought up, like films or soccer. I once played soccer when I was old enough to use the potty on my own. I only played for like a year or two, then gave it up and moved onto dance. But I can get back into it. I could've brought up music as well. According to Damianos's MyCircle page, he likes the band *Eel-Baby and The Cuts*; and from what I read on their tour schedule this year, next week they're going to be in Cedar Springs, which is only two hours from Dover. If the date goes well, maybe Damianos can take me to the concert. I keep a list of all the subjects I can talk about tonight—hopefully, if all goes well, I won't have to use them.

Mikel is like a shadow that keeps entering my thoughts.

What if I can have both?

Once I make it back home, I decide to send a text to Damianos. In the text, I tell him that I forgot about this "thing" I had tonight—a "thing," as in my fictional cousin is playing Black Moses in a play about the Ten Commandments and I told him that I'd be there. It's not until moments after I send the text that I've broken at least two commandments ever since I bumped into Damianos. I follow up with a text suggesting that we hangout tomorrow night. He texts me back saying he's hanging out with the guys—whatever that means. I suggest that we hangout this weekend. He follows up with a lengthy text about how he can't because he's visiting his father who lives all the way in Percy.

I send him a text saying that I'll contact my (nonexistent) cousin and ask him if I can take a rain check. I wait a few minutes in the car and act as if I'm contacting my cousin when, in reality, the only cousin that I'm aware of is doing seven years in Windward Correctional for armed robbery. Once enough time passes, I contact Damianos and tell him that the play has been canceled.

He texts me back: I'll see you at seven.

I text back: I look forward to seeing you.

It feels as if we've just gotten past sending each other awkward emojis.

The earth is back in motion and planets are starting to realign.

🚗

MY stomach is twisted in knots for the rest of the afternoon. Most of the time is spent frantically scrambling around my room, trying on every single outfit in my closet, mixing and matching outfits, tossing aside looks that don't work with a sense of bottled-up frustration.

An hour in of dressing and undressing, I bring in Nailah for advice. She tells me that I look like what a nun would look like if she wasn't wearing the habit.

I switch it up, digging and sorting through outfits that were once on my endangered species list—and other words, pending for Goodwill.

I try on flannel, plaid, holey jeans, hats, wondering whether I should go more punk or hipster. If he's genuine about going for a run or jog, then I should go for a sportier look: checker-pattern skirt worn over black leggings with my *CUTS* T-shirt worn under a dress shirt. Two outfits for two very different occasions. If he wants to actually go on a "run" or "jog," then all I have to do is remove the skirt and dress shirt and I'm good to go. It's what I considered a multipurpose outfit. I bring Nailah back into frame and ask her for advice. I tell her about the upcoming date. She thinks the look is "doable" for the occasion, says the outfit makes my dark shine. Not like I need her approval—perhaps the insecure part of me does—but Nailah basically gives me the green light along with a two thumbs up to sell a much needed-effect.

I undress yet again, lay my outfit on the bed so it doesn't wrinkle, then hop in the shower. Five minutes into the shower I hear Uncle Jojo banging against the door, complaining about how I've been running up the water bill, when, in my defense, he's the one who's always outside watering the lawn with the hose when the lawn doesn't need watering. I know Nailah has told Uncle Jojo all about the date and I figure he's trying to put me in a bad mood so the date doesn't go well because the last thing he wants is for some strange guy to be hanging around his niece.

After I spend hours on my hair and makeup, Nailah's already calling out dinner from downstairs. Nailah makes me a plate, but I don't even touch my food. I tell her that I'll eat later and wrap it up, that way I'm not insulting Nailah since I spent most of the afternoon pulling her from the stove for last minute tips.

🚗

SEVEN o'clock looms closer, and I contemplate changing outfits. I try on a couple of other sporty, more interchangeable outfits but end up going with the one I had on before.

Six-thirty.

I tell myself that it'll take ten minutes to get to the park, and I'd like to be out of the house by twenty minutes to seven.

The next ten minutes I spend racing around my room, thinking about any other things I need to take with me as if I'm about to go on a big road trip. I think of the essentials. For one, myself. Check. My clothes, good. Hair, not the flyest, but good and nappy. Car keys. Phone. A slightly chilled bottle of water just in case we actually do go for a run or jog or both. I try to put myself inside the head of Damianos and all of a sudden, I start thinking in wicked stereotypes. What if the so-called "run" is another attempt at "getting some" action? What about that "winking" emoji he sent me? Was it his way of saying he looks forward to hooking up tonight? What if Ryan-Bryan told Peedy all about my sketch he found and then Peedy relayed it to Damianos? And if so, what if Peedy, in his own twisted words, explained to Damianos what was in that sketch, how, instead of Damianos riding on the scaly back of a fearless sea serpent, was actually riding on the back of a winged dildo?

I'll admit. I don't like hooking up on first outings such as the one I'm about to go on with Damianos. But it's not like he's a stranger. I've known him—at least from a distance—ever since my sophomore year at Dover.

Thinking maybe Damianos is the kind of guy who doesn't come prepared and is more of that in-the-mood type of guy, I decide to raid my uncle's drawer while he and Nailah are quietly finishing up dinner downstairs. I locate his secret stash of Lifestyles condoms, as well as odd clothing articles tucked away underneath an empty box of Icy-Hot in the bottom drawer of his nightstand.

I take a handful of condoms and stuff them inside my pocket.

I reconsider my actions. I only take two. Two should be enough, right?

As I place the other condoms back into the drawer, I come across a black dog collar next to the bowl of condoms. I don't remember Uncle Jojo owning a dog.

I ignore the thought and rush downstairs. My mind is so full of scenarios that I almost forget to say goodbye to Uncle Jojo and Nailah on the way out of the house.

WAITING on a bench next to the soccer fields, I watch the time on my phone creep past seven, and Damianos is still a no-show.

I spend the next ten minutes of silence rehearsing pre-memorized lines inside my head. I tweak each line as to what to say to him as soon as he arrives, how to greet him, whether I hug or don't hug, or should my demeanor be up-beat or, like Damianos, cool like Mellow. What kind of hello? A hey? Or, *heeey*? A what up or sup? More friendly or more like he's my soon-to-be boo? The sun starts to set over the horizon. Twenty minutes pass as quickly as the cars driving on the distant highway. Each glimpse of head-lights brings me a glimmer of hope as well as a string of new maybes: Maybe he got held up? Maybe he ran out of gas? Maybe his car broke down? Maybe he got into a car accident? Maybe maybe maybe!

As soon as eight o'clock approaches, I realize Damianos is not coming. Perhaps he never was. All I think about is Little Bee-Ryan and his ugly ass face, that smirk crawling through his cloudy-red cheeks. Was it all some kind of setup for a joke? All of a sudden, I get all paranoid and start wondering if Damianos and his soccer pals are hiding somewhere in the bushes or snickering behind a tree in the woods and they're all secretly filming me hanging around like a bad punch line, the star character in a sick video to be posted on the Internet. Watch the sad bitch get stood up by white dude. I tell myself enough is enough. I decide to write him a text. By the end of the text, my fingers are sore and I realize that I've written a paragraph at least three-scrolls-of-a-thumb long. Which makes for a decent size paragraph.

In the text, I vent my appropriate female rage against Damianos and his sick crew. I talk about how fed up I am with privileged pieces of dog shit like Damianos, who think they can mess with another person's feelings and not suffer any consequences for their cruel actions, who think they run the entire city, who think they're better than other people, who think they're God and get a golden hall pass at mocking other people who look or act different from them or people who don't follow the crowd.

I reread the text several times, my trembling thumb hovering in suspense over the SEND button.

At the very last second, I come to my senses. I delete the text and drive back home in a silence so heavy it hurts.

FOR a second, time travel seems like a legitimate concept once I find myself pulling my car into the driveway. I don't recall the car ride home, don't even recall driving for that matter. One second, I was leaving the park and then the next I'm drifting into the driveway. I turn off the ignition and can't get out of the car quick enough.

I storm from the car to the garage. I punch in the code to the garage and head straight to the door, not even bothering to remove my shoes from my feet. I can't stop thinking about the commendatory joint that Kush gave me the other day as if it was his own way of telling me to keep my lips zipped about his little drug operation, stashed underneath my lava lamp and smoking it till there's nothing left of it but ash.

Midway through twisting the doorknob, I suddenly stop from the sound of a dog barking inside the house.

Immediately, I'm freaking out.

There's a wild dog loose in the house!

Cautiously, I creep into the house. I hear more barking; however, the barking doesn't sound like a dog anymore. It sounds like a man, specifically Uncle Jojo. But why in the hell is he barking? I pinpoint the sound coming from upstairs.

As I inch up the staircase, I get a weird tingly feeling inside me, as if soon my world is about to be turned upside down and I'm soon going to be stuck in a kind of strange Bizarro world where everything is opposite. The barking stops midway up the stairs. I hear *moaning* and *grunting* followed by the sound of someone being slapped.

I reach the upstairs hallway. The door to Uncle Jojo's bedroom is open. The light is turned on inside the bedroom; however, it's dim and reddish in hue. I hear the *squeak* of a bed followed by more bizarre sounds, nothing sexual or anything like that, but just bizarre, like the croak of a frog or the pumping sound an air gun makes. I reach the end of the hallway and lean my head past the doorway of Uncle Jojo's bedroom.

Inside Nailah and Uncle Jojo are both naked on top of the bed; however, it's what they're doing that disturbs me on another level.

My uncle, my own flesh and blood, has been handcuffed to the posts of the headboard. He's wearing a pair of purple panties over his face as if it was a blindfold, as well as a dog collar with a leash around his neck.

Meanwhile, with her back facing the headboard, Nailah is crouched over Uncle Jojo's chest in a still and flexed position. She's making a tight fist with one hand and in the other, she's holding the other end of the leash and forcing my uncle's head between both of her butt cheeks as she repeatedly pushes out *squeaky* farts directly into his face.

Strangely, Uncle Jojo appears aroused by the farts. The thought alone of my uncle, my own flesh and blood, being into fart fetishes as if it's his guilty pleasure causes my body to tighten with utter disgust.

My eyes close so tight that I wish my eyelids were permanently sealed shut; in fact, I squeeze so tightly that the thought actually crosses my mind that they'll forever being stuck, like some sort of reflex or pulled muscle that never heals.

Loosening the strain from my eyelids, I coil up like a rattlesnake, compelled to shout out to the top of my lungs.

As Nailah continues to flex out airy farts, I do what comes natural. I run. In this case, I ease away from the doorway and backpedal into the hallway. But, in my mind, it really feels as though I'm running.

Like I'm caught in an awful nightmare and I'm running as fast as both of my legs will take me, but I'm moving so slowly.

I want to vomit all over the hallway walls, decorate them as if it's my own way of retorting against such licentious acts. I want to stick my fingers down my throat so far down I can touch my last meal and force myself to vomit, even if I don't have the willpower to vomit. I want to dart to the bathroom and vomit the very idea from my head, as if, by doing so, it will never enter my head ever again. Yet, it will spiral down the toilet as soon as I flush it away into the sewage below. My purge. Vomit or not, I feel as if I've been forever scared. I realize that these are the moments that stay with people. Phobias, hesitations, obsessions, or unorthodox rituals: all stem from witnessing something truly scarring.

From now on whenever I hear the sound of a dog barking, I'll think of Nailah and Uncle Jojo.

Whenever I see a neighbor walking a dog, or any dog in general, I'll think of Nailah and Uncle Jojo.

Whenever I hear the sound of someone innocently or accidentally passing gas in another room or quietly within the confines of their personal space, I'll think of Nailah and Uncle Jojo.

Whenever I sniff out something criminally foul in the air that may or may not have come from a silent fart, you guess it, I'll think of Nailah and Uncle Jojo.

In a slow and wayward backpedal toward my room, I hear rustling sounds of bed sheets followed by frantic whispers beyond the thorn-covered darkness of my eyelids.

They know.

They know I know.

Somewhere in the darkness, I hear Uncle Jojo's voice: *I thought you said she was on a date, woman?*

In my angry black world, I realize I can no longer be here anymore. I cannot be here, in this moment, in this house. I manage to force open my eyes to a world that I don't understand anymore.

I grab the squashed joint from my room and rush downstairs while at the same time I hear distant stomps of heels pounding against the floor behind me.

I can't face him. I can't face either one of them.

I dart from the house and hurry to my car.

I start up my car and drive into the night.

I don't know where I'm going.

Anywhere far from here.

AFTER driving around and listening to music for what feels like hours, I pull into Lake Greenwood park and fish out an old lighter underneath a pile of crumbled up and folded receipts, from mostly fast food receipts to pink US letter sized copies of oil change and car inspection receipts.

Using the overhead light, I check the Butane at the bottom of the lighter and from what I can tell, there appears to be a spit of Butane left, hopefully enough to ignite a flame.

I reverse my car into the back of the parking lot, that way I have a good look at the entrance and turn off the headlights of my car. Lake Greenwood is an older park and based on its remoteness, doesn't receive too many visitors, except for the occasional fisher, Mountain biker, or kayaker, but I don't take any chances. Cops have been known to patrol parks, especially at night.

I place the joint to my lips and as I begin to light up the end of the joint, all I get are sparks in return.

For a moment, I actually contemplate venturing out into the woods and starting a fire the old fashioned way since I've run out of options and I'm in absolutely no mood to drive to the nearest convenient store.

On the last try, I get a flame. I figure it's going to be the only flame I can get so I puff real hard and make sure the joint is lit before removing my finger from the trigger.

Instead of chilling with the joint, I smoke it down with steady hits till I can feel the ember burning the ends of my fingertips.

I end up inhaling the entire joint within a couple of minutes.

After I'm done, it doesn't take long at all for the weed to kick in. Since I'm also in no mood to do anything at all productive, I tilt my seat back to a recliner position and switch on the radio and do exactly what the weed wants me to do and that's *chill*.

Once I hear the sound of the DJ's silky voice followed by the opening song of the Monday night program, I realize it's already midnight. DJ Hooray is host of a weekly show called *Monday Marauders*, a six-hour music fest of all the hottest jams from the 90's. Which, for me, a child who was born at that edge of the twenty-first century, is like my own Black History. These men and women, as I looked up to them like gods and goddesses, weren't "martyrs" of *The Movement* nor were they victims of being black or whack in America, not like what the teachers at Dover-Schmover had crammed down our throats *every* February, teachers with faces that didn't share the same color as mine nor re-lation, teachers who reminded us, Students, of all the pain and hardship my ancestors endured during the transi-tional—often bloody and violent—times in the country I lived in through outdated DVDs of "Historical Moments" which somehow dredged up way more heat out of me than clearer understandings of how things were "Back Then," as if, ironically, "Back Then" was still, in subtler ways, "Right Now," with all the unwanted police shootings and brutality against particularly the "young," "black," "male." What I gathered from the three years at Dover High School—and the passive-aggressive years before—was that history was unforgiving, no question, violent, and anyone could best describe it as a dark and starless night without any dream of daylight. Music from the 1990's, however, had done something that history had never done before: it gave us an entire constellation of stars that were as bright and relentless as the sun.

Unlike what my teachers had taught me, these people were alive, and through their music, they still are. Which makes them immortal. As if they created something profoundly original and the generations who came after were trying to replicate what the generation before had brought down to Earth, like a knockoff trying to formulate the same ingredients that made a popular soda so popular.

Funny to say, I wasn't even born when 90's music was being blasted through the eardrums of America, especially the young ears of America, The Youth, trembling throughout streets like aftershocks. Yet, a part of me feels as if I grew up in that time period, had lived and died, was born and reborn, only to be resurrected in a new decade where everything appeared to be a copy of a copy, a lame imitation, a meaningless replication, Wannabe-Cola.

Every Monday night at midnight, the program begins with the opening song "Midnight Marauders Tour Guide" from Tribe's third album *Midnight Marauders*—that's "Tribe," as in the *only* Tribe, A Tribe Called Quest, one of the greatest hip-hop groups of their time.

I find myself falling into the words of the opening song. I'm falling and yet, at the same time, I'm floating into another world. I'm high, really high, drenched in the high. I start spinning. My brain bubbles. At first, I don't fight the high. I ride it, see where it takes me. I keep going up and up. An inherent fear kicks in. I'm afraid of heights, I realize, or at least used to be, afraid of not having anything to hold onto if I should fall. Then, as my body hovers over the car seat, I react. I try to shake away the high. The music isn't helping me in my quest to resist gravity. So, I reach and while doing so, I fall back down to my seat.

I turn down the volume; however, I mistakenly turn the knob the wrong way. That sudden blast of volume causes the blood to punch through my veins!

In a bright flash, the jolt brings a tidal wave of violence. My jacket is caught in the door. The wet, heavy arms of the spinning brushes of a car wash bat me back and forth. I'm screaming to the top of lungs.

I find the right knob and switch off the radio, forcing me back into the natural silence.

I crack down the window and watch the curling smoke being sucked through the opening.

Outside, I hear frogs and crickets singing in night darkness. The sound comforts me and helps tame my high. Then, I tilt my seat to an upright position. The change in position also helps lessen the intensity of the high.

Once the car is clear of smoke and sound, I notice through the rear view mirror that the woods behind me are smoking.

I check the side view mirror along the side of the car.

Not smoking, I realize. Yet, it's the fog creeping through the woods.

I decide to step out of the car and stretch my legs.

Intrigued by the fog, I walk around the car for a closer look. It's thick, really thick, like a creepy scene written in a Koontz novel.

Through the fog, I spot two lights flashing past the trees. One is brighter than the other. The less bright light is longer as well, like a reflection below the bright light. After scouring for a path, I eventually find one next to a torn down fence. I take the path to a dock along Lake Greenwood.

I search for the light but am unable to find it.

Since I'm already here, I might as well enjoy the view. I sit over the edge of the dock and let my feet hang inches above the moonlit water.

Basking in the harmony of nature all around me, I hear the water moving below me. I lift my feet from the water and lean over for a better, safer look.

Tiny waves start to hit the side of the dock. I peer out into the night darkness and use both my eyes and ears to guide me to the source of the disturbance. What makes it even odder is that the air is still, not a single breeze. I search the lake for a boat or any kind of vessel that could contribute to roughening the water. I don't hear or see anything out there, only a beating flame from what I suspect is an oil drum in the middle of a trailer park, as well as tiny lit windows from distant million-dollar homes perched on the sides of rolling hills like fortresses.

A powerful dread comes over me, an impending doom.

Inherently, I find myself backpedaling away from the rising water. A round silhouette swells over the water. It's way too large to be a hippopotamus, and it's way too round to be some kind of undiscovered prehistoric super crocodile.

Cautiously, I take a step forward. Its head is the shape of a hull; however, I know it not to be a boat because the surface of its skin is scaly, reptilian-like. The Pink Moon casts out two beady black eyes, which may or may not be eyes.

The lake creature suddenly opens its mouth.

I find myself taking a step back, way back.

Inside its gaping mouth a skinny, sickly pale man dressed in wet, black rags comes forth. A Ferryman. Who's holding a lantern in one hand and a rusty chain attached to the roof of the creature's mouth in the other hand.

He doesn't say a word to me. He can't. He has no tongue, I realize. He just stands there, staring at me with his glassy white eyes, as if he's waiting for me to board the creature.

Finally, I step forward as the creature drifts closer to the edge of the dock, as if it's luring me into its gnarly cockpit. I carefully step inside the creature's massive mouth, using its sticky tongue as good footing. I cross the point of no return and despite the realization that at any moment its jaws could crush me as if I was a soda can, I make sure not to cut my legs on the intricate layers of teeth outlining the inside of its mouth as if they're street cones marking a barrier.

I use the soft, gummy walls of the creature's mouth to keep myself balanced and upright.

The captain of this vessel, the Pale Man, pulls down on the chain. The sound of the mouth closing sounds no different than the *crank* of a rollercoaster.

A flash of panic sends me into a dizzying state from first glance at the shrinking, as well as darkening of the mouth. Before me, a jagged horizon paints a dark view. The mouth doesn't close all the way, though. Which I find strange yet, at the same time, comforting. I mean absolutely no harm to the lake creature or the frail fellow who appears as if his body is riddled and sunken with cancer.

As both the sickly man and I ride in silence with moments of warm breezes of the foulest, most guttural gas emitting from the dark, circular hole behind me, which I believe to be a gateway to the creature's throat, I realize why the mouth is only partially shut.

We approach a triangular-shaped cave on the side of a cliff. A waterfall acts like a curtain of water in front of the cave. The creature swims directly through the waterfall. The roof of its mouth prevents me from getting completely soaked.

I turn to the sickly man, who, in return, turns to me.

As he has been doing throughout the ride, he doesn't say a word. He can't.

Yet, he stares at me as if he knows a specific detail about me that I don't.

He nods his head toward a flickering light ahead, which is the first and only gesture he's made to me throughout the ride.

Not too far away, a more homey light appears ahead of us and helps bring out both the stalactites along the ceiling, as well as the stalagmites randomly scattered along the pointy floor of the cave like ancient fangs of a subterranean beast that once existed when the giants roamed the earth.

Along the bank of the tributary and surrounded by spire-like stalagmites rests a long medieval-like table. Several stalactites, as well as stalagmites, have joined together and formed what look like columns in front of a plantation house. The source of light is coming from dozens of lit candles on and around the table. The wax of the candles has

has melted, hardened, then remelted into taller waxy mounds. People—strange-looking people—are seated like dolls at the table. From my angle, I can't make out who these people are, whether they're real or not—or even alive for that matter—however, both their stillness and monk-like patience has me intrigued.

As we arrive at the edge of the bank, the sickly man cranks the mouth back open, wide enough for me to step through. I duck my head underneath the creature's sharp teeth and watch my step as I walk out onto dry land. I feel an instant relief from the feel of actual land on my feet and not the tongue of whatever that thing was back there.

I look up the steep undulated path winding its way toward the cavey room where my hosts wait for me. Before I have a chance to ask the sickly man if he's coming with me, the lake creature already swims away. I realize they're waiting for me. Only me.

I make it to the top of the landing where four people are seated at the table. I have to look several times to make sense of them. I can't help but stare. They're me—well, not exactly. They're all dressed the same as me. However, they're wearing their clothes backwards. What separates them from me—the real me—is the silicone mask of my face, as well as wigs of my own hair that they're wearing. The sight alone of the wigs tempts me to yank on them, hard and aggressively too, as if I'm ripping off a week-old band-aid. The circular cutouts along both of the eyes, nostrils, and mouth of the mask, as well as the dark makeup shadowing their visible skin underneath, try to cover up not who but *what* these things really are. They can't fool me. The skin is not human. Similar to the lake creature, the skin is rough and scaly, reptilian-like. Their breathing isn't at all natural either. Yet, it's extremely fast as if they're hyperventilating. The skin around the mouth hole appears different than the skin around both of the eyes and nose. I look closer and realize it's *not* skin. It's duct tape. Lastly, their eyes. Of all the features, it's the one that gives away their disguise. I can't help but wonder if they—or whoever it is behind all of this—ran out of money to buy contacts at

Party City. Their eyes are like a bright tapestry, filled with what looks like every color of the spectrum and depending on what angle you look at them, glowing the same as the eyes of a cat.

As I try to register exactly what I'm actually looking at, I hear footsteps behind me. . .

In the corner of my eye, a small dark figure passes me.

I turn and find a small person dressed in a red cloak escorting me to the chair at the end of the table. He pulls out the chair and tells me in his small voice, "Sit, please. She'll be out in a minute."

She?

"Excuse me," I say, my voice cracking. "*Who* will be out?"

He doesn't answer. Yet, he looks at me with a serious face.

"Who?" I ask again with my patience running thin.

"You sound like an owl," the dwarf says to me and then exits through a dark entranceway along the side of the cave.

Eventually, I end up taking a sit at the table next to the other weirdos. One of them robotically turns its head toward me, as if its entire body is tied down to the seat. Another one makes a noise, which sounds similar to a growl underneath the duct tape. The other one snaps his head away and faces forward, as if they're not supposed to interact with me—or even *look* at me, for that matter.

A minute of awkward silence passes.

The dwarf finally returns with a wheelchair. On the seat is a silver tray holding a wool sack. He pushes the wheelchair to the side of the table and places the tray with the sack at the other end of the table. He pulls on the string, untying the sack.

My only reaction is a gasp, a gasp of losing words, a gasp of not even being able to find the words as if somehow they have all been wrung from my mouth, a gasp of the breath inside me escaping from my lungs. All I know is a gasp, as if it is my only way of incoherently saying, "No-he-didn't."

But the little man did.

And a part of me is bullied to stomp on him for doing so.

The dwarf exits the room as I remain in a state of shock. The only word I can muster from my trembling lips. . .

Mom?

"Hello, dear," she says in return.

She looks just like I last remembered her, except for not having a body.

"You seem uncomfortable," she says over my frozen, fragile state. Her forehead wrinkles and her brow curls in apparent distress. "Can I get you want something to eat? Dear, what's wrong?"

"Your head. . . I mean, your body. Where's the rest of you?"

"I forgot," she says, her tone strangely casual.

She calls out to someone named Dab.

The dwarf, whom I suppose is Dab, returns to the room. "Yes, ma'am," he says to her.

She doesn't respond immediately. Instead, her eyes do most of the talking as they lure him closer. She whispers something into his ear. I try to listen in, but I can't tell what she's saying. Dab goes away, only to return moments later with a few items in his hands: a machete, a stool, and a white nightgown.

He places the stool beside the closest look-alike to Mom and before I have a chance to suspect the next action, he swiftly chops off its head. The head lands with a soft *thump*, then rolls and bounces around on the ground. A strange blood, which is the same ever-changing color as its iridescent-like eyes, squirts out from the severed neck in a similar fashion as water squirting from a perforated hose.

Dab carefully kneels down over the top of the stool, grabs Mom's head, and places it on top of the severed neck, which is still running colors with blood. He gives the head a slight jerk and twist from right to left, as if he's trying to screw in a carriage bolt.

"Righty tighty, lefty loosey," Mom says bluntly.

Starting from left to right, Dab twists the head and does so in two three hundred and sixty degree clockwise rotations until the head is secured to the neck.

After Mom works out the kinks of her new body by working each digit, each muscle, ligament, and tendon of her hand, Dab guides her arms into the sleeves of the nightgown.

Once dressed, Mom turns to me with her eyes wide and maddening.

Despite what the rather masculine reflection in the silver tray—which I suspect is only a distortion from a poor weld job—she's my mom, looks identical to Mom, even sounds like Mom, even uses words that Mom would use and delivers them the same exact way Mom would deliver them, directly and to the point, no filler, no filter; however, there's a feeling inside me, beyond the gut, that is telling me she's *not* my mom—says that strange manly reflection—but someone else, an imposter or foreign entity that has hijacked Mom's conscious.

"Better?"

I nod my head.

I think I say something. *I think.*

Whatever does come out of my mouth doesn't sound like any word I know. Yet, it shares the similar tone as a grunt.

All of a sudden, she makes that facial expression again, forehead wrinkling, her brow bending into the top of her nose and forming into the shape of a lazy w. She tilts her head to the side the same way a dog would when given commands in cartoonish voices. The expression is like a universal gesture indicating confusion. Even though my expressions remain concealed in front of her, a part of me—that beyond-the-gut part—is screaming at me not to give myself away, to remain emotionless in front of this entity who claims to be *my* mom.

With her head tilted in the most exaggerated slant, she says, "You're scared, aren't you?"

I shake my head.

"Baby," she says, "you don't have to lie to me. It's me. It's Mom."

Hoping that talking will help take my mind off the situation, I ask her, "Why are you like that?"

"Why am I like *what*?"

"Like that," I say louder and point at her head. The emotion mistakenly starts to break through my voice. "Your head!"

The confused expression falls from her face. She leans back and drifts into a thought. Then, her face grows long, her lips form into a perfect circle.

"Oh," she drawls. "You're right. My head." She looks at me again with a confused look. Behind the confusion, though, yet another expression appears: the slight crease of the corner of her lip. Not a smirk entirely, but more so a partial, deceptive one. "Don't be so dramatic, Squinty Poo—"

"—You never called me that name before," I say to her. "You died before I was given that name. So, who are you? Really. . ."

"Why would you ask me that?" For a split second darkness spreads over her face. Then, an artificial light. "It's me. Mom."

"My mom is dead—"

"—You're mother is sitting right in front of you," she says in a way more like Mom would say. "Excuse me for the way things look around here, but I didn't bring you here to judge me."

"Then, why did you bring me here?" I ask her.

"You're stuck," she says. "And you need my help to get you where you need to be."

Emotion floods over me. My eyes burn and water. My face starts to break.

"And where do I need to be?" I ask, trying to keep myself together.

"*Unstuck*," she says, leaning closer.

During the brief pause, I'm drawn to the three other bodies seated around the table. The way they're breathing starts to really get to me. I try to block out the sound of their frantic breathing. I find myself taking in deeper breaths.

Mom stands to her feet. She staggers, at first, as if she's not at all used to her new body. Eventually, after a couple of stumbles that force Mom to brace herself against the table, she straightens up her body, smiles off the awkwardness, and lets go of the table. By the third wobbly step toward me, she masters her walk. She kneels down beside me and once more, braces the side of the table to prevent her new body from falling over.

"You see, Squints," she says closely, as she holds my hand with her two cold reptilian hands. Sudden panic washes over me. I move my attention away from the hands and lie to myself that they're her hands, Mom's hands, only cold and scaly from being out in the cold all day. I concentrate on her eyes and to the best of my ability, attempt to decipher the secrets behind them. "Like you," Mom says, "I'm stuck as well. Stuck here." She looks around the cave. "In this awful place. *This* world hidden beneath yours. I need your help. And you need mine. Which puts us both in a particular position where we can both benefit one another."

I still don't know whether or not to believe a word she has to say.

But I want to. A more accessible part of me wants to believe that the person in front of me is the very woman who brought me into that other world she speaks of as if it's a more forgiving place than the one where she currently dwells.

"I know you are alone, Squints," she says, her tone soft as only I can remember from the hazy times when she used to read me bedtime stories. "You're alone because you *want* to be alone, because you feel as if you're not complete, because you're not whole inside. Instead, you're carrying around a weight inside you as if it's your burden. But it's *not* your burden because you had absolutely no control over what happened. Until you accept that, Squints, that the only control you have is the 'now,' the weight will pull you down all the way to the bottom of the ocean where all the 'forgotten ones' dwell." She turns her head toward the others wearing the masks—whom I assume are these forgotten ones. The only questions running through my mind are how these people—if that's who they are—wound up down here: Were they gunned down by the police? Did they lose their past lives from the streets? Drugs?

Mom directs her attention to me. The look of her faces suddenly changes; in fact, she doesn't wear a look at all. The expression alone reminds me of the same exact ones worn on the faces of the black and brown people in those grainy black and white photographs from the 1960's, during sit-ins, pickets, or protests. These expressions never conveyed bitterness or any kind of resentment nor emotion, for that matter. Yet, these looks, these expressions appeared as if they were piercing right through the photograph, through the opposition of those who considered themselves white, hollering out obscene gestures to the same people who wanted equal rights, through the white cop who was clinging to a water hose or that club ready to be soaked with the same color of blood that men bleed, through the country, through the world itself as if it was a look that didn't belong to them, yet, a look that had found them. I didn't know anything about such a black and white world where the only color came in the form of words and posted signs. These men and women reminded me of oracles who knew the fate of the future and how, one day, they, along with their mothers and fathers or brothers and sisters or sons and daughters, would live in a world without ridicule, without being stared at or laughed at, without being followed or chased, without being profiled, without being harmed, into another world where they could be better than the very ones who enslaved them.

With her tone more serious, Mom says to me, "We are here, Squints, and you are there. Down here, we have no more meaning. But there, the world where you come from, one door may lead to another door. Your world is filled with doors still left unopened. Rooms left unexplored. You've been searching for meaning in what you feel has become a meaningless life. I am here to tell you that the answers you seek are right in front of you. Forget about everything you know—or everything you think you know—find the door you're looking for and *open it*."

Her words grip me like a blanket.

"I can't," I tell Mom.

"But you can, Squints," she says, more convincingly.

I can hardly look at Mom. The emotion floods over me but doesn't break me.

As I lower my head, I feel a sudden prick against the bottom of my chin. The sharp end of a claw presses harder against the bone, hurting me.

With the pain poking at my chin, I slowly lift up my head.

"In time," Mom says villainously.

I ask, "What do you want from me?"

"I'm tired of talking," she says. "You know what I like to do whenever I'm feeling down?"

I don't even know how to answer the question. Honestly, I don't even know where to begin. What the hell is there to do down here?

Mom stands upright, more balanced. She stares at me with a strange look on her face as if she's waiting for me to answer.

"No," I finally say. "What?"

"I dance."

"Dance?"

Mom nods at the small person, Dab who, in return, walks to what looks like a radio wedged between the rocks in the wall. The wax from the candles acts like a hardened waterfall between the knobs. Dab switches on the radio.

I hear DJ Hooray's voice from a distance. He's introducing the next song on the program *Monday Marauders*. The song is "The Power" by SNAP!

As the song plays, Dab turns up the volume to the highest setting.

Mom backpedals to an open area to the right of the table.

The other three bodies suddenly wiggle with life as if their bodies have been zapped by an electrical current. They push back their chairs, rise from the chairs, then push the chairs back underneath the table. While remaining in-sync with one another, they moonwalk to the space behind Mom; and before I can make sense as to what's happening in front of me, the three bodies break out into a well synchronized dance routine while Mom bops along to the beat as she lip-synchs the lyrics to the song, "The Power."

A minute into the song, the three dancers place their scaly hands on the sides of their heads and violently rip off their heads and start passing and juggling their heads to one another as if it's all a part of the dance.

Meanwhile, Mom is wearing a creepy little smile on her face and looking as if she's having the time of her life.

I push past the creepiness of the dance, the disturbing violence or gore of it, and I embrace it. I start laughing, not really *at* them, but sort of with them in my own strange kind of way. My throat tightens. I try to clear my throat, but it feels as if something is lodged in my esophagus. Maybe a piece of food that squirmed itself free from a tooth during the burst of laughter. I struggle to clear my throat. I resort to coughing and hope the cough will loosen whatever is stuck in my throat.

The coughing only makes it worse.

I realize I'm choking.

While Mom and her crazy crew continue to dance like it's the start of the millennium, I fall to my knees and grab a hold of my throat.

I motion for them to help—anyone!

Mom continues to dance and rap as if she's the illest MC in her world.

And as for me, I don't even exist anymore.

At least, not here.

In this place.

This world.

I lurch forward, coughing, my hand strangling a door handle.

On the radio, the song, "The Power," is playing. The lyrics, "*It's-getting-it's-getting-kind-of-hectic,*" are still running through my ears and the repetitiveness of the lyrics is causing my head to spin.

I'm no longer inside a cave.

I'm back in my car.

I frantically search for a bottle of water. I find one underneath the passenger seat. I take a couple of sips, which helps clear my dry throat. My breathing eventually calms.

As DJ Hooray's voice returns over the radio, I find myself returning as well.

Returning from where exactly? A dream? Bad trip? A spiritual voyage into the Great Unknown?

Forget about all that noise.

I go directly to the source and the only rational thought that comes to mind is the weed I smoked. Maybe Kush rolled the joint from a bad batch that was laced with a hallucinogen. But then again, Kush is Kush. Based on the quality of his product, most of his clients look at him no different than they would a loyal chef whom they would trust to toss out tainted food before serving it.

I shake off the paranoia and check the time on the dashboard. I can't believe it. I check the time on my phone. The time reads the same 2AM time.

Next, I check the text messages on my phone.

I expect a text from Uncle Jojo asking me where I'm at, even Damianos informing me as to why he was a no-show tonight. I get nothing.

I start up the car. A cold feeling of dread washes over me as I switch the car out of Park and into Drive. Somehow, I feel as if I'm still trapped in that strange cave, that other world, and this body I'm in doesn't exist anymore.

🚗

BY the time I make it back home, it's already three o'clock

The drive home had me thinking more about that dream or whatever it may have been. A lot of the deeper-thinking contributed to Monday Marauder and the carefully selected playlist after two o'clock.

First, DJ Hoorah played jams straight out of Oakland, starting heavy with En Vogue and the song "Don't Let Go (Love)" from their *EV3* album.

DJ Hoorah stayed in Oakland and went for a more laid-back tone with Soul of Mischief's "'93 Till Infinity" followed by The Pharcyde's "Runnin'" from 1995 *Lacabincali-fornia*, then Deltron 3030's "Time Keeps on Slipping;" then, he kept it flowing in the same vein with the super-group the Hieroglyphics.

After Oakland, DJ Hoorah ventured north to the City of Angels, starting with Janet Jackson's "If" from her 1993 self-titled album *Janet*, which was produced in Minnesota. Next: Tupac, Mob Deep, Kris Kross's "Jump" from *Totally Krossed Out*, then making detours and pit stops along his Marauder tour with Erykah Badu and Salt-N-Pepa before trekking all the way across the country to the Big Apple. DJ Hoorah slowed it down with "At Your Best (You Are Love)" by Aaliyah, who was born in Brooklyn but raised in Detroit, then picked it back up with Wu Tank Clan, then Salt-N-Pepa, then the opening song from Method Man's *Tical* album, then Busta Rhymes's "Woo Hah!!! Got You All In Check" from the 1996 album, *The Coming*. After DJ Hoorah managed to make it out of New York in one piece, he went straight global with what he described as the "quiet storm" of Sade, first with tracks "No Ordinary Love" and "Feel No Pain" from *Love Deluxe*, then tossing in a joke about the "spike of babies being born" after Sade hit the scene. After DJ Hoorah flew back to the States, he stopped in New Jersey with The Fugees and the trio's "Ready or Not" song from the 1996 album *The Score* before he wound up in the south, particularly Dirty South. It was there, deep in the grind, where he played an icy jam that effortlessly paired with the previous song: "Black Ice (Sky High)" by Goodie Mob featuring OutKast from their 1998 album, *Still Standing*.

The two tracks were perfect in the way it set the stage for a more investigative mind, that sleekness, as well as the silkiness of the tracks. Both the songs had me thinking more about Mom—or even if that was really her and if so, was she right? I think so. . .

I notice the lights are off, except for the porch light. Uncle Jojo and Nailah are expecting me; otherwise, they wouldn't have left the light on.

Before I head inside, I grab the bottle of Visine from the glove compartment and squirt a drop into both of my eyes just in case Uncle Jojo is waiting for me on the recliner in a pitch-black living room like a secret agent about to pull a hit job on a foreign spy.

I creep inside the house. I open and close the door behind me as if it's armed with explosives. I grab a plate of leftovers from the fridge and scarf it down as if I've been stranded on a deserted island for the past month. Since my high is at the point of mellowing with a soon-to-be headache surely on the way, I don't get too creative in the dessert department.

I grab a box of chocolate-chip cookies from the pantry, spend the next couple of minutes roaming back and forth from the fridge to the pantry, debating whether or not I should decorate them with caramel or chocolate syrup or cashew butter or ice cream or even grab Uncle Jojo's fig bars and double-layer different cookies on top of one another like a cookie-on-cookie sandwich. I'm not in the mood to deal with Uncle Jojo, if I should wake him from his slumber by making a racket in the kitchen. Instead, I scarf down a handful of cookies like the cookie monster and wash them down with a glass of milk.

With my belly full, I tiptoe up to my room. I can breathe a little easier once I hear the sounds of Uncle Jojo snoring from his bedroom. I imagine Uncle Jojo's snoring isn't so pleasing to Nailah. As of now, I could care less about that gassy bitch.

I make it to my bed, undetected.

I fall into bed and slip my body beneath the cool bed sheets.

Never has my bed felt so comforting.

🚗

THE next morning, I sleep in and manage to ignore Uncle Jojo.

After he's off to work, I roll out of bed. In the kitchen, Nailah asks me about my date. I give her the universal I-

don't-want-to-talk-about-it answer with a short response:
"Fine."

The subject is off-limits. I say only a couple of words to
Nailah while I make a quick breakfast. She can sense my
frustration; however, I know that she knows that I know
about the licentious acts she and Uncle Jojo do when I'm
not around.

I take my breakfast to my room and plan out ways I can
erase Damianos from my head. I do what any normal person would do. I stay busy.

🚗

EVEN though I'm not scheduled to work today, I give My
Workspace a call to let my supervisor know that I can come
in to help. He's pleased by me taking the initiative and can
gladly use the extra hands at the store.

🚗

AFTER working for five hours straight, Bradley, the manager
on duty—or who we grunts often refer to as simply the
"M.O.D."—insists that I take at least a thirty-minute
lunch break. I don't want to take a break nor do I want to
allow myself a single moment to think. I want to keep
working until the image of Damianos has been eradicated
from my head. Except for a comment that a strung-out
customer made about "losing" her "head" over a looming
"*dead*line" and how she has spent the entire night drafting a
"top secret" pitch to a new employer, I haven't thought
about last night either. And, to be honest, I don't think I
want to either.

During the downtime away from work in a quiet break
room, I try to squeeze out a conversation from one of the
cashiers named Gabriella but soon realize after about ten
seconds into the forced conversation that she's in no mood
to talk to me; in fact, she only takes two bites from her
soggy mayonnaise-based sandwich that she brought with

her, tosses in the trash, and hurries back on the floor as if she's not allowed to talk to me.

Once the quiet sets in, so too does last night.

I turn up the volume on the TV, which has been set to a "friendly" local news channel. I try to keep my mind busy by watching each cherry-picked story on the news, but they're all scandals or blurbs or Twitter-based opinions and polls, mob-created dumpster fires, nothing newsworthy, only deliberately-plotted distractions intending to distract me from not only the real issues, but also the truth.

My truth.

Frustrated, I switch off the TV and pull out my phone.

I check out a new artist's website that I recently discovered on the dA. I skim through her bio, as well as her portfolio. She's all into the "cyberpunk" genre. I make sure to earmark her page. I jot down her contact information in my Notes for a possible future-collaboration. As I'm about to finish looking over her page, an advertisement for *Monday Marauders* pops on the corner of my screen. I can't help but take it as a sign. Or, on the other hand, maybe I'm being watched.

Either way, I can't take it any longer. I google SNAP! as well as the song, "The Power," which is from the 1990 album, *World Power*.

I watch the music video for "The Power" on YouTube. Maybe I've seen the video before because the dance routine, except for the part where the dancers remove their heads, seems similar, if not, identical to the one I witnessed back in the cave.

After the video is over, I watch it again. Then, again.

Then, afterwards, I decide to research the lyrics to the song. The one bar that stands out is one with a number, two numbers: 7:14. I'm not exactly a churchgoing person, never have been, but the numbers must have some meaning to them. Immediately, I think about the Bible, those numbers.

I google chapter 7, verse 14, only to be redirected to the website called Bible Thumper. There, I'm given references from Mathew, Chronicles, and then Isaiah. Each verse is different from one another. Isaiah is the one that grabs me the most, chapter seven describing the preludes and prophecies about a young woman who will bring a "child into the world." However, none of the verses make any sense to me. At this point, I feel as if I'm going beyond stretching. I feel delusional.

🚗

I work for a couple more hours before Bradley thanks me for coming in today and basically, kicks my ass out of the store because I'm pretty sure he's tired of seeing my face.

Out of options, I drive around for a while before I feel a rumble in my stomach as if it's my stomach's way of giving me an excuse to stop by the one and only safe space that has always felt like home: The Stop N' Shop.

Once I step inside the store, I notice that it's pretty dead inside. Another slow day at the Stop N' Shop. I see Bernie's face behind the counter, and he's waiting there as if he's expecting me. The sight of Bernie puts a smile on my face.

"There she is, the Squints-inator."

"Squintsinator?" I roll my eyes. "Lame."

"Queen Squints?"

"Super lame."

Bernie shrugs.

"Well, just say it's a WIP. You know, what the kids call a beta test."

I'm surprised Bernie even knows what "WIP" or "beta" means.

"Hey, Bern."

He reaches his hand over the counter and gives me a low five as if he already knows that I'm in no mood for a high five.

"So, how's your day going so far?" I ask him.

"Ah," he says. "You know. The same ole, same ole. You?"

"Just got off work."

"Look at you, Ms. Workaholic."

"I guess I can say the same about you."

"Hey, well, somebody's gotta run this place and it sure as heck ain't going to be RJ."

I look around for RJ but don't see him anywhere in the store.

"He's out back," Bernie says, as if he can read my mind.

"I see," I say, thinking more about Bernie than RJ. "So, you didn't tell me that you were building another Stop N' Shop just outside Midway."

"I am?"

"Yeah," I say and backtrack. "Well it wasn't exactly a Stop N' Shop. I mean it had the same font and logo and all."

"I'm not aware of it."

"You're not?"

"Nope."

"They're trying to rip you off then."

Bernie smiles off my concern.

"What you doing all the way out in Midway?"

"I went there last month for the weekend."

"Do anything fun?"

"Hung out at the beach, did mostly girl stuff," I say, "you know, nothing that would interest you."

"Is that so?" Bernie lifts up the sleeves on his arms. "Try me, Squints. You may be surprised."

"Yeah," I say, once more changing the subject. "So what, Bern? You gonna sue these scam artists or not?"

"You must've mistaken it for another one of Harold's places."

"Harold Who? I saw the construction site with the sign in front of the highway. Had the same logo and everything."

"Well, even if Stop N' Shop or anything related to Stop N' Shop was, in fact, franchising, I wouldn't know anything about it. I just run this place."

"But how wouldn't you know about it? It's your store, ain't it—"

"—Point exactly. I run *this* place and this place only." He crosses both his arms across his chest. "You thought I owned Stop N' Shop?"

I stutter for a moment.

"Yeah," I say, feeling myself shrinking in embarrassment.

"The man you're thinking about is Harold, Harold Roman."

The last name immediately jumps out at me—*Roman*.

Row-Man.

Roman Noodles.

Roman numeral.

I ask Bernie, "Why does that name sound familiar? Roman?"

"Well, Mr. Roman has businesses all over the country, several of them in the valley. Believe it or not, he actually grew up right here in Mimosa. Now he's got houses all over. From what I've heard, he spends most of his time in Jersey. He's a good man, Mr. Roman. You've probably heard his name in the news. Mr. Roman has done a lot for the community. He's helped out a lot of people, including my niece."

"You never told me you were an uncle."

"I haven't?"

I shake my head no.

"I thought I did."

"I wish my uncle was more like you," I say without thinking.

"What's wrong with your uncle?"

"Nothing," I say. "I mean, you know, he's like this black cloud always hanging over me. Every time I'm around him, I feel like Dark Sidious ready to shoot lightning bolts from my fingertips."

"Dark who?"

"Nothing," I say again. "So, what? Your niece into drugs or something?"

Bernie hangs his head for a moment.

"No," he says. "Not like that. She has—or had—a heart condition."

"How old is she?"

"She's a few years younger than you."

"Sorry to hear."

"Well, she's all better now thanks to Mr. Roman."

"What's he like a doctor or something?"

"He's not a doctor, but let's just say he knows plenty of them. He even paid for Christine's surgery."

"You mean like open heart surgery?"

"About six or seven years ago, we started a fundraiser page to help pay for all the hospital bills because she had been in and out of the hospital for most of her life and all the hospital debt was starting to drown her parents. I tried to pitch out whenever my sister and her husband needed money. But it wasn't enough. They were both drowning. And they both had decent jobs too. After a while, their insurance company cut them off and could no longer do what they were supposed to do. Christine had been on the donor list for years, but she was considered a 'low priority.'"

"That's messed up," I say.

"Tell me about it," Bernie says, as a customer comes into the store and pays for some gas.

I step aside, as the customer pays.

The man leaves.

Then, Bernie continues, "Once Mr. Roman found out that my sister's family was having some financial issues, he stepped in to help. Two days later, a miracle happened. My niece receives word that she has a donor. She immediately goes into surgery. The surgery is successful. Christine doesn't reject her new heart. It's strange to even say this," Bernie pauses, "but if it wasn't for Mr. Roman, Christine would've died. She had an angel looking after her and his name was Harold Roman. Anyway, that's one of the many things Mr. Roman has done for this community."

"Sounds like a great man. I wish there were more men out there like that."

As Bernie is known to do, he reads me like a book, my tone, my expression, whenever the word men is projected from my voice.

He leans over the counter and asks me, "What's bothering you, Squints? You know me. I'm a good listener. Think of me as your shrink."

"Shrink? I don't need no shrink."

"Whether you like or not, everybody needs a shrink. Think of people, especially people in the service industry, as shrinks in disguise. A man goes to a bar. The bartender is his shrink. A sinner goes into a church. The priest is his shrink. The list goes on and on. Indulge me, Squints."

I look around the store and all the merchandise and snacks in the aisles, the people coming and going like ghosts, grabbing what he or she wants, paying for it, then leaving, off to the world outside, beyond a cowbell, which acts like a tone indicating a gateway which takes you in and out of two worlds.

Bernie says over the hum of the air conditioner, "It's a guy, isn't it?"

"How'd you know?"

"It's always about a guy—or girl. I swear, if you could funnel the power they have on our weak souls, you'd be able to solve the world's energy problem. So," he says, leaning in, "what'd he do?"

"He stood me up last night." I wave off the previous and then, surprisingly, find myself explaining myself. "Besides, I'm over him. Plus, he uses hair conditioner in his hair. I mean, what guy uses hair conditioner in his hair? Honestly," I say, the words coming out more freely, "I think he's playing for the other team."

"Other team?"

"You know, the *other* team. . . "

Bernie rolls his eyes.

"What? Because he uses hair conditioner?"

"He's incredibly neat too."

"Neat?"

I shrug and struggle to find a response.

Bernie leans in, as if he's about to drop knowledge.

"The body—male or female—is no different than a car. Every now and then, it needs to be washed or given a tune-up. I mean, you can't polish a car without any wax, am I right?"

"I guess I never really look at it like that," I say, drifting off.

"Well, did this 'guy' have a reason as to why he stood you up?"

"No. He didn't even text or call."

"Maybe something came up."

"If something came up, then he would've contacted me and told me that he wasn't going to meet me."

"How about his friends? Have they talked to him?"

"I don't really know them."

"Well, I'm sure he had a good reason. If not, and he *did* stand you up, then the guy must be out of his mind. Clearly. What kind of fool would stand up such a beautiful woman like yourself?"

I blush from Bernie's kind words. Every now and then, Bernie has a particular way of making my skin warm despite the obvious age gap. I still don't exactly know how old Bernie is—and I don't plan on asking him—but if I had to guess, he'd probably qualify for an AARP membership.

"So," he says seriously, "do you want me to kill him for you?"

"You? You wouldn't even squash a mosquito if it was biting at your neck."

"I know a guy who knows a guy."

"You do not."

"Sure I do."

"Serious?"

"What'd you think?"

Bernie's mouth quivers as if he's holding back a laugh. All of a sudden, he bursts out laughing. I laugh as well. Spending time with Bernie, talking to him, makes being stood up by Damianos last night feel so trivial, if only for a moment.

"I tell you what, Squints," Bernie says and pulls out two tickets from underneath the cash register. He hands the tickets to me. I read the name, "Eel-Baby," on the ticket, then ROW 4, SEAT 37. The other one is ROW 4, SEAT 36.

"What are these?" I ask, even though I already know exactly what they are.

"Two tickets to Eel-Baby and The Cuts."

"Yeah," I say, "but why do you have two tickets to Eel-Baby and The Cuts?"

"Because I'm giving them to you," Bernie says slower, as if he regressed to the mental state of a child.

"I'm confused—"

"—I was gonna give them to my niece, *but*. . ." Bernie sighs, ". . . she hasn't been returning any of my calls."

"Why not?"

Bernie drifts in thought; his eyes turn red and glossy.

"Well, she's growing up on me faster than I can ever imagine. It's crazy how fast they grow up. One day, you're going places, doing stuff together. Then, the next day, they act like you've come down with bubonic plaque."

I try to hand the tickets back to Bernie.

"I can't take these, Bernie," I say. "Try again."

"I want *you* to have them, Squints."

"I can't—"

"—They're yours," he says, holding out his hands. "It's already done."

I look down at the two tickets.

If only I had someone to go with me to the concert. . .

"You know," I say bluntly to Bernie, "this doesn't mean I owe you."

"No," he says. "Just don't forget about me."

"Forget you? Why would I forget about you?"

He shrugs.

I can tell from the look in his eyes that he's still broken up about not being able to go to the concert with his niece.

"I'm not going anywhere anytime soon," I reassure Bernie. "I mean, I wish I could. For now, I guess I'm stuck here."

Bernie waves off my comment.

"The best way to not be stuck is to be 'unstuck,'" he says to me, the word *unstuck* sending this strange, tingly wave of déjà vu through my body. "You just have to find what's keeping you *stuck* here."

I have a vivid image of Mom in front of me, her face basking in the flickers of candlelight. Her eyes wide and fascinated.

As I hear my name being called out in front of me, I snap from my momentary daze.

"I guess. . . " I utter, ". . . I guess I never really thought of it like that. Well, thanks for the tickets."

"My pleasure, Squints." He lets out another sigh, a deeper one as if it's been trapped in his chest for the past couple of weeks. "So, you gonna buy something or what? Or, did you just stop by here to bug the hell out of me?"

"You know I enjoy bugging the *hell* out of you, Bern."

"I know you do," he says, grinning.

"The usual," I finally say and grab a bag of sour cream and onion chips from the rack. "And these."

I hand Bernie a ten-dollar bill.

"Those things will kill you, you know?"

"You watch too much TV, Bern," I say, as Bernie hands me my change.

"That's what Christine be saying to me all the time. Uncle Bernie," he says, doing his best impersonation of his niece, "'you watch too much TV.' Enough already. You have your phone. Let me have my TV. To each his own, right?"

"Whatever, Bern," I say, grabbing the receipt for the car wash and the bag of chips from the checkout counter. "I'll see you later."

"See ya, Squints," he says.

On the way out of Stop N' Shop, another familiar image catches the corner of my eye. Then, the sound of a name, Damianos's name. . .

I come to a sudden halt underneath the doorway and turn to the small TV set next to the wall of cigarette cartons. On the TV a photo of Damianos is blown up on the screen. The photo looks personal, maybe a year old. Damianos is turning his shoulder as he's stepping into his car and he's smiling from ear to ear. It looks like the kind of photo a worried mother would give to the news channels to show their audiences that "her boy" was still a boy and a mighty good boy, a compassionate one who often smiled even when caught off guard or surprised by a proud mother who simply just wanted to take a photo of her handsome son.

A customer suddenly shoulders by me, nearly pushes me out of the way, and my first reaction is to ball my hand into a fist and punch his lights out.

"Excuse me," he says, giving me a cold look.

I ignore the asshole and wander back into the store. I tell Bernie to turn up the volume on the TV. He does so right on command.

According to the report, Damianos was reported missing by his parents earlier this afternoon and they want anybody to know if they have seen their son. All the details of his car have been displayed on the TV screen, a make and model of his car, which is a Prius, as well as the license plate number. As of now, it's been twenty-four hours. I've watched plenty of crime shows to know that, if the report is serious like the news is claiming it to be, then Damianos only has twenty-four hours left before his mother can really start to worry.

I hear Bernie chirping in my ear, but his words seem so distant. I tell Bernie I got to run. Then, I take off as if I'm running away from the TV.

WHEN I arrive back at home, I'm still freaking out about the news report. Nailah asks me about where I've been, but I keep it extremely short with her as I head to my room:

"Went to work."
I wasn't aware that you were scheduled today.
"Yup."
Well, it's nice to know that they're giving you more hours.
"Great."

As soon as I make it to my room without being further grilled, I pull out the ancient TV box buried underneath junk inside my closet. I locate an outlet with a cable connection behind my dresser. Which means I have to rearrange my furniture inside my room. I take a few minutes to move around bulky furniture in order to accommodate the TV. Once everything is out of the way, I plug in the TV. I turn it to the same news channels that Bernie was playing while at the same time I pull out my laptop, as well as my tablet and phone and start checking each website of each news outlet for any updates on Damianos's disappearance. I find the same "missing persons" report from earlier on the same channel's website.

After I've exhausted each news website, including the town's current newspaper, *Mimosa Times*, which is best used to roll joints or wipe your ass with, I decide to go on social media, starting with Facebook and Twitter.

First, I check Damianos's Twitter page. I scroll through a couple of "political based" tweets but none of them pique my interest. He made one tweet about "his new pair of Levi's" being "too tight on his bird legs" at around two o'clock yesterday afternoon, nine hours before his mother apparently reported him missing to the police. He even posted a photo of his new blue jeans next to what looks like a clothing rack.

A couple of Damianos's friends are actively tweeting throughout the day, but none of them mention Damianos's name in their tweets. Which makes me wonder if they even know about Damianos's disappearance or if detectives have contacted them and specifically told them to lay off the "tweeting" until they can find Damianos—or what's left of him.

🚗

FOR the rest of the night and throughout most of the next day, my eyes stay glued to every news outlet.

At around nine o'clock during a refreshed news cycle, I hear a news report about Damianos. No new details have emerged from the case; however, the reporter interviewed Damianos's mother. She tells the news reporter that Damianos never came home last night or the night before, which is unlike him. He's not the   type of kid to just run off without informing his parents. She says that he always lets her know where he's going at "all times." I also can't see any reason as to why he would run away, either. If he got into a bad fight with his parents, I don't think they would've have contacted the news station. At this point, it's all speculation.

🚗

TWENTY-four hours later from when I first heard the news story, Damianos is still missing.

Nailah calls out "dinner" from the kitchen downstairs. I've remained in my room for most of the day, glued to my laptop, not being able to draw or paint, and I'm sure Nailah has informed Uncle Jojo all about my "unusual" behavior. Nailah calls out once more. Not too long after, I hear the sound of footsteps on the staircase. From the deepness of the footsteps, I can tell it's Uncle Jojo, who happens to be a functioning heelwalker. He knows. But he's got no room to start barking orders. I know about him, too, and his perverse reaction to farts. Or, it could've been like some kind of dominatrix-thing. I internally scream away the thought.

Of course, Uncle Jojo answers the door.

"Dinner's ready," he says.

I don't even allow myself to be within a farting distance from Uncle Jojo.

"I'm not hungry," I say from across the room.

"Squints," he says, more stern, "I'm not going to tell you twice. Come on. Come eat with us." He pauses before heading out. "I tell you what. You don't even have to say a word while you eat, if we make you *that* uncomfortable."

"It's not that."

"Then, what is it?" he asks. "Nailah tells me you've been cooped up in your bedroom all day—"

"—Fine," I say before the conversation turns into a thing. "I'll be down in a minute."

Uncle Jojo looks me over, studies me. His narrow eyes tell me that he wants to project his frustration onto me. Let me have it, if you will.

He withdraws from the soon-to-be shouting match and says softly, "Ok."

He doesn't close the door. Yet, he turns away with his head down and walks back downstairs.

I end up dragging myself from bed and force myself downstairs where Uncle Jojo and Nailah have already started eating dinner. Of all the dishes, meatloaf. I think Nailah deliberately cooked the dish to draw a reaction from me, considering the woman knows I can't stand eating anything that once had a name. She even mentions how she done messed up on the meatloaf by overcooking it too long, as if she also deliberately made the meatloaf extra rubbery just for me so, by the time I'm finished force-feeding myself, my jaw will be all sore.

Only a couple of awkward minutes of picking through my vegetables while at the same time struggling to move my eyes away from the plate, Uncle Jojo is first to cut through the silence. He clears his throat and asks me what I've been doing all day. Uncle Jojo chose those particular words to start with because he knows that I know they're good words to begin a fight, like a cloaked version of a captain yelling out "charge" to his troops. I feel cornered in by the words and whatever answer—or lack of answer—I give him will inevitably result in a fight.

"Squints," Nailah says in his defense, "your uncle asked you a question."

I turn my keen eyes up at them and before I unleash on them, I see Damianos's face on TV.

"Squints?"

My eyes are locked on the TV.

"Squints, what's going on?"

I stand up and leave the table.

My uncle is telling me to sit back down, but I ignore him and wander into the living room where the TV is playing.

I grab the remote and unmute the TV.

On the TV, the news reporter is reporting from an open field out in the countryside a couple of counties away.

As she starts talking, Uncle Jojo yells out, "Get back in here and eat your—"

"—Quiet!" I yell back.

I turn up the volume, drowning out Uncle Jojo's yelling.

Back to the reporter: "*Around three o'clock this afternoon two fisherman discovered a wallet with Damianos Pipes's driver's license inside, as well as several articles of bloody clothing that may have belonged to the missing teen. Police are now questioning the two fisherman, hoping that they can shed some more light on an on-going investigation that has become all too familiar around here.*"

Uncle Jojo creeps up behind me.

"What's going on?" he asks me.

The words start to tremble in my mouth.

"You know that missing boy?" he asks.

I turn to Uncle Jojo. I can no longer hold in it. My eyes rain with tears.

Uncle Jojo holds me in his arms.

🚗

AFTER I wring the tears from my eyes, I sit down on the couch and confess everything I know to Uncle Jojo and Nailah. I tell them about Damianos and who he is to me. I tell them about the date and how Damianos and I were supposed to meet at the park at seven o'clock but he never showed up. Uncle Jojo is precise in his questions, which I'm sure he picked up from his job and knew how to spot a phony claim. He wants to know how I know Damianos, where I met him, what's my relationship with him. I leave out all the stalker-stuff and tell him that I knew Damianos from school and that we met at the beauty store—which had caught me off guard, seeing a guy in there buying hair supplies. Then, we arranged to meet up at the new park around seven o'clock. He wants to know what Damianos and I were up to—"*to do what exactly,*" are his precise words—but Nailah cuts in right before the conversation turns more heated. She acts as if she's been through this kind of thing before. Her words are soft and gentle. For the first time in all of the years—or more like months—that I've known her, I've never witnessed a compassionate side in her. But right now, Nailah gets me. It's fair to say that her understanding helps bring us closer together.

UNCLE Jojo and Nailah step out of the room for a moment to talk among themselves in the hallway and when they both return, Uncle Jojo is holding his phone in his hand.

He looms over me and from the look on his face, it appears as if his armor is back on.

"I'm going to call the cops, Squints," Uncle Jojo says, "and I want you to tell them everything you told us."

"Cops? What?"

The word alone—*cops*—unearths a fear inside.

I do what comes natural. I rebel.

Shaking my head, I say, "I'm not talking to the cops. . . "

"And why not? You got something to hide?"

"No," I say, my armor worn proud and comfy.

"If you like this boy, if you care anything about this boy, then you must talk to the police. It's for your own good."

I take his words personal.

"What do you know about my own good?"

"What you told us might help with their investigation." The anger returns in his eyes. "Don't you want to help them anyway possible in finding this boy?"

"Yes, but—"

"—But *what?*"

His words are sharp, like a jab.

"Be honest."

"Honest? You want to talk about honesty?"

I stand up from the couch.

Here comes my right uppercut.

I'm knocked back down with another jab. His words turn squeaky. His lips remain puckered when he speaks, as if he's blowing out nothing but air. Not just any air but the smelly kind.

I can't bring it up. I won't.

The thought only drives me away. I dart from the living room.

Uncle Jojo starts to chase after me, but Nailah holds him back. I race up the stairs to my room, grab my phone and keys, and rush back downstairs.

By the time Uncle Jojo asks me where I'm going, I'm already out the door.

🚗

MAYBE I'm overreacting.

Maybe I'm losing my mind.

Maybe the truth is that I just don't want to deal with Uncle Jojo anymore and his questions and judgments, his constant badgering.

Maybe I felt—if only for a moment—a glimpse of what it truly means to be ready and willing to open up every inch of myself to a person of the opposite sex, to be one hundred percent committed to go *all* the way, to be, dare I say, in love, and now, I'm ready to be done with it. Had my short run. Now, it's time to hang it up and get on with the slow process of decay. But it's still hanging around, that nagging screw intricately turning and twisting inside me, a feeling I get whenever I think of a world without Damianos.

I plug my mp3 player into the auxiliary cable and shuffle to a new playlist of songs that I downloaded earlier that day. The songs are the same ones that I tried to memorize from the other night.

I drive around aimlessly.

After driving around for a bit, I watch the sunset from the same dock on Lake Greenwood. Waiting for something. A light maybe? A sign? Something? Anything!

81

Everything in my body is telling me to do the right thing, go back home, talk with the police, inform them about Damianos and what I know, even pitch in and make myself available, and maybe my information might add more clarity into his disappearance.

Eventually, as night starts to weigh on me, I give in to reality.

🚗

WHEN I arrive back home, I notice a strange car parked on the curb in front of the house. It looks similar to a cruiser, but it doesn't have any markings on the side of the car. I realize it is a cop car—possibly one that belongs to the local detective—as soon as I spot the siren in the back windshield. My palms turn sweaty on command. My breath heavier. I tell myself over and over that there's absolutely no reason to be nervous. It's just a natural body response letting you know that you *still* care, that you want to do good. I *am* doing a good thing. I'm helping out the cops, contributing, playing my part.

Without thinking, I wipe the sweat from my palms and crack open the door in the garage. Muffled murmurs suddenly come to a halt. I can smell a combination of perfume and aftershave in the air. I can feel their presence inside the house and their soon-to-be pounding stares.

Once I stepped into the living room, both Uncle Jojo and Nailah are standing by the kitchen doorway. A middle-aged man and a younger woman, whom I guess are detectives from their stern demeanors and their well-ironed crime show clothing, are sitting on the edge of the couch, ready to stand.

They're waiting on me. They're *all* waiting on me, the star of the hour. All I think about is what Uncle Jojo has told them. Being able not to speak for myself makes me want to talk to these possible detectives even more.

Uncle Jojo introduces the two people for me.

Detectives, as I guessed.

Detective Tice and Detective Núñez. I give them what they may recognize as a wave coming from a wounded animal. I figure Uncle Jojo has filled them in on my relationship—or lack of relationship—with Damianos.

The man, Detective Tice, stands up and shakes my hand. Detective Núñez follows suit and shakes my hand.

"Shall we talk here or in the kitchen?" Detective Tice asks me politely.

I shrug.

"Here's fine."

He sits back down on the couch. Uncle Jojo saves the recliner for me. I take a seat.

"Your father informed us—"

"—Uncle," Uncle Jojo interrupts.

"Right," Detective Tice says. "Apologies. Your uncle has informed us about some information you may have on the missing teen, Damianos Pipes."

"It's pronounced peeps."

"Like the candy?"

"Huh?"

"Like my peeps," I correct, "my people, my peeps."

"I'll keep that in mind."

An awkward silence fills the room.

Uncle Jojo calls out my name, as if he's giving me a cue to cut the shit.

"We were supposed to go on a date the night he disappeared," I tell the detectives.

"You were 'supposed' to?" Detective Núñez repeats. "So, you two actually never went on the date? Correct?"

"That's correct."

"And where was this date arranged? Was Mr. Pipes going to pick you up?"

"No," I say. "We were going to met at the new park at seven o'clock."

"The one off Backer Street?"

"Yes," I say. "That one."

"How long did you stay at the park before leaving?"

"I waited for, I dunno, at least an hour, but he never showed up."

"Did you try contacting Damianos?"

I feel as if the detective has cast a trick question, as if he, along with his nicer partner has already obtained Damianos's phone records and now, they're fishing for holes in my story.

"No," I say, then correct. "I mean, I was going to text him, but considering what was in the text, I felt as if it was best not to."

Detective Tice asks, "What was in the text?"

I look at Nailah, who's nodding her head.

"It's all right," Detective Núñez says over the awkwardness, "you don't have to tell us anything you don't want to. However, whatever you think is important to tell us, then it might steer us in the right direction."

I ask the obvious question, "So, Damianos isn't dead?"

"As of now, we haven't found a body," Detective Tice says bluntly. "No."

Just the sound of the detective being so grim stirs a little bit of emotion inside me, which causes my stomach to twist and turn with gas.

Detective Núñez takes charge of the conversation, "We will find him. That's our job."

Detective Núñez works a Jedi mind trick on me and all of a sudden, I feel as if I can tell her anything. For instance, like showing her the un-sent text. Then, I realize that they might want to confiscate my phone. Which means they'll have an all access to my phone. Then, I realize what exactly is on my phone. My mind starts racing and I can't help but envision a whole bunch of filthy cops standing around the office, scrolling through my selfies and rating them as if I'm a contestant to whatever fucked-up game they're playing.

"I was going to tell him about what an asshole he was for standing me up and leaving me waiting around like an idiot. That's all."

She asks, "How long have you known Damianos?"

"I dunno," I say, as if it's my strange way of letting her know that I'm thinking of a better response. "About a year or two," I say. "We went to Dover High together."

"Are you still at Dover High School?"

"No," I say. "I graduated last semester."

"That's impressive," Detective Núñez says. "Any particular reason why you graduated early?"

"'Cuz I hate school. That's why. Do I really need to give you a better reason than that?"

"So, how did you get a hold of Damianos in order to arrange this date? Social media? Snapchat? Twitter? Facebook?"

"I bumped into him at a beauty store."

"Which one?"

"The AC."

Both the detectives make a long face.

"Au Courant," Nailah says for me. "It's located off 3rd and Helm."

"And you two sort of hit it off?" the detectives doesn't ask but more so suggests.

"I guess you can say that," I say, more bashfully. "I've, ah, I've been waiting to, you know, hang out with him for a while but I haven't really had the nerve to ask him out."

"Who hasn't been in that predicament before?" Detective Núñez says, trying to break the tension in the air. "I remember when I was around your age I used to follow a boy around. I was obsessed with him, but I can't strongly say he felt the same about me. His name was Jonathan. He liked to play hard to get—"

"—Can we get back on subject?" her partner asks, as I witness a clear tension between the two detectives. Detective Tice turns to me. "After Damianos didn't show up for this date, what happened next?"

"I went home," I say, thinking about the moment I "*went home*" and walked in on Uncle Jojo receiving a face full of farts. "I went to bed."

"Is this true?" the detective asks Uncle Jojo and Nailah.

Uncle Jojo immediately follows, "Yes. She came home at around ten o'clock or so," he turns to Nailah, who, in return, confirms Uncle Jojo's statement with a nod of her head, "and then went straight to bed."

I turn to Uncle Jojo, who then looks at me, as if he's staring right through me. His face changes, as if he committed a crime for me, one where neither party was innocent or guilty, a white lie that he wears like an itchy mask, eager to remove it; however, I know that he'll never speak a single word about what I saw Nailah doing to him the night Damianos disappeared. After all, he's a Leo.

AFTER Uncle Jojo lies about my alibi, the two detectives wrap up the conversation by handing both Uncle Jojo and Nailah business cards with names and numbers in order to reach them in case I remember anything else. I add in one more final say, about the blue jeans. I know I shouldn't mention it because, obviously, it'll give the impression I've been cyber stalking Damianos. Personally, I think being curious isn't considered a crime. But I throw it out there anyway.

"The blue jeans," I blurt out, "the ones that were found in that field, are you certain that they belonged to Damianos?"

"I'm afraid we can't talk about that kind of information," Detective Tice says and squares up to me. "The investigation is still on-going."

"But if they were Damianos's jeans, I think I know where he bought them."

"Oh yeah?"

I nod.

"I saw that he posted a photo of the jeans on his Twitter page," I say. "In the photo, I recognized the store." I didn't, but I tell the detectives what they want to hear. "I'm pretty sure the photo was taken at Stitch. The carpet looked familiar. I was thinking that he was buying the jeans for our date. Maybe he just wanted to look nice, that's all."

Detective Tice struggles to make eye contact with me.

His partner, the nicer one, says that they'll be in touch.

Then, the two take off.

I stop the other detective, Detective Núñez, before she walks away.

Merely out of curiosity, I ask the detective, "So, about that boy you used to follow around, whatever ever happened to him?"

She smiles at me in a big sister kind of way.

"He became my husband," Detective Núñez says and fades into the night.

🚗

FROM my bedroom window, I watch the detectives drive away.

I expect to hear a knock on the door behind me and see Uncle Jojo entering the room, ready to finish what he started back in the kitchen.

Round 2.

For the remainder of the night, time draws out like a jammed switchblade. The house remains freakishly quiet. Everybody avoids one another. Uncle Jojo spends most of his time in his own little space in front of the TV set in the living room watching CBN as if he uses political arguments and pea-brained conspiracies as his way of refueling the man rage that keeps his engines going, as if without it—that anger—his armor will be exposed and vulnerable. Nailah goes to her own nook inside her cramped studio where she sews together new outfits for her clothing line.

As for me, I stay in my own quiet, undisruptive space, tirelessly searching for Damianos on the Internet.

The house no longer feels like a home anymore.

Instead, it feels like a building that we're currently occupying.

🚗

THE next day drags on.

Uncle Jojo and I are civil to one another; however, we're still not talking or even addressing the "elephant in the room," which was the lie that Uncle Jojo told the detectives. Instead, we've regressed to the communication of the deaf using hand signals or head nods, like two strangers from two hostile countries acknowledging one another but not really acknowledging one another.

DAMIANOS'S story has officially gone "viral" on the Internet.

I've always hated that word and what it has become. To me, it sounds like a sickness, a necessary sickness, and everybody is down with it. It's a word associated with disease and infection, a virus. A word that rots flesh, corrupts the soul, then spreads to its next host, rotting and corrupting. Yet, somehow, everybody is okay with it.

Ever since the story went national, the vultures in the media world have been relentlessly shoving Damianos's story down viewers' throats like a necessary vaccine. Damianos's face has been marred; he's become a billboard ad with slogans used by power-hungry politicians and self-absorbed opportunists in order to gain support and attention to themselves. It's not about them, these parasites who latch onto Damianos's story, but, in a way, it's *all* about them, their words, their faces, their agenda. These people could care less about Damianos.

SEVENTY- two hours after Damianos was first reported missing, the police pick up their first suspect in Damianos's case. The local news channel displays his ugly mug all over the TV. According to the report, a police cruiser spotted Damianos's Prius parked in the parking lot of an abandoned textile mill off Howard Street. Howard Street is located in a rough part of town, the part where Uncle Jojo warns me not to go near. Most of the violent crimes around here, like shootings or stabbings—at least, according to news reports—comes out of the east side of Attlee County. Immediately after hearing the report, I know something isn't right at all. *Why*—or what—*would Damianos be doing near Howard Street?*

The police officer on scene found a man inside the parked car. According to the report, his name is Calvin Young, but he prefers to go by the name "Zig-Zag." Which I'm not sure is a street name or a new slang word for a drug on the street. I figure a name like "Zig-Zag" is for a person who's either destined to be a football or basketball player— or any other sport that involves a player to zig or zag—or a common thief. From the dated mug shot that was taken ten years ago after he was arrested for possession of narcotics—according to the report, Zig-Zag has priors, mostly drug and alcohol related—he doesn't look like the killing-type. But I guess some people will do about anything out of desperation. The story doesn't add up, though. Zig-Zag is homeless, been homeless for six years according to a former lover. When he was apprehended, he was sleeping inside Damianos's car. If Zig-Zag was the one responsible for Damianos's disappearance—considering the license plate, as well as the make and model number of Damianos's car being plastered all over the news—why would he still be driving around in Damianos's car? Any person with about any kind of sense would've either ditched the car or found another one. It doesn't make any sense. Lately, it seems like nothing has.

TWENTY-four hours later, I receive a notification on my phone while I'm taking a walk with Kush, my temporary miniature-sized bodyguard, through the neighborhood. According to the recent news report, the police have released Zig-Zag from holding. He is no longer considered a suspect in Damianos's case. I have mixed feelings, some strong and coming in like tidal waves. In a way, I feel relieved that Zig-Zag was not responsible for Damianos's disappearance, yet he was looking for shelter and just so happened to find it in a well sought-after vehicle; however, I'm still frustrated that Damianos might be still out there, alive or dead, nonetheless, out there, as in waiting to be discovered like a lost artifact. I'm frustrated detectives still haven't found a legitimate suspect who screams cold-blooded murderer, frustrated with the news, the media that has now callously ruined the image of a now innocent man, frustrated with all of these pretentious celebrities offering support or donations to Damianos's family, "thoughts and prayers" and dirty money, frustrated with the hashtags like #Damianos or #WhereIsDamianos or #HelpFindDamianos, frustrated with people using words like *viral* or *tragedy* when it comes to Damianos's story, frustrated with the campaigns, both smear campaigns by political asswipes, as well as awareness campaigns by people who only see fit to whet their own agenda, as if they're using Damianos and his well-maintained body as a pawn to forward into their chess match—they, whoever they are, have even designated April, of all months, as Abduction Awareness month. Professionals lend their faces as well as their voices but mostly their faces and inform us "dumb-asses" on what to do when approached by strangers. I'm frustrated with the sharks lurking inside this digital sea that has somehow found a way to take over the material world and hijack what we read or how we speak, "trolls" in disguise flooding the Internet like unstoppable tidal waves crashing onto the shore that has become our lives, watering down comments about Damianos—or anything remotely "good" about Damianos and who he was and what he stood for—through their threads of impersonal tweets or opinions. I'm frustrated with Uncle Jojo, who's still having a hard time talking to me, yet, behind my back, he tells Kush to watch over me until the cops catch the person responsible for Damianos's disappearance.

Most importantly, I'm frustrated with myself.

🚗

THE next day after I spend the entire morning bugging the hell out of the two detectives, Detective Núñez informs me about yet another search party that she and her partner,

Detective Tise, are putting together this afternoon, and she says that, if I really want to help, then being a part of the search party will be a good start. I decide to volunteer in the search.

When I arrive at an open lot a couple of miles away from where Damianos's clothes were found, one of the rescue team members named Ronnie hands me a stick, a flag marker, and gives me specific instructions about what to do during a search, what to look for, what to mark, where to go, and who to follow. I partner up with a guy around my age, maybe younger. His name is Chris and when I ask why he came out, he tells me that he's a volunteer himself. He says it's an obligation for him. I don't know if he means well—but why would a stranger from another town spend his time looking for Damianos? Either he means well and has a good heart or the kid's no different than all of those celebrities and "thoughts and prayers" people all over the Internet and to him, this is all an Easter egg hunt, like the first person who can locate the dead body gets his or her name in the newspaper and a fifty-dollar gift card to Red Lobster.

After about two and a half hours of tirelessly combing the fields and using up all my markers on mostly litter, I come across Detective Núñez at the edge of the woods. I bring up Zig-Zag's name, tell her that Damianos wouldn't have been in or even around that side of town, wasn't like him, but Detective Núñez still acts as if talking about the on-going case is breaking protocol and she dances around my concealed inquiry with a diplomatic response: "We're doing everything in our power to find Damianos Pipes and with your help, we'll find him."

Silence swells between us.

She seems convinced that she'll find Damianos still alive in one piece even though she's probably lying and telling me exactly not what I want to hear but what I *need* to hear by offering up a slice of hope when I know her partner, Detective Tice, more "seasoned," as the TV crime shows typically call his type, tends to mostly hang around cadaver dogs because, through his mindset, they'll be the first ones to let everybody know that Damianos has been found—or what's left of him.

Through the corner of my eye, I can see Detective Núñez looking at me.

She finally asks me, "How are you holding up?"

"Fine, I guess," I say, struggling to look at her. "*Frustrated*, to be honest."

"You're not alone, Squints," she says.

Her words are reassuring, his presence alone comforting.

"Are you sure?"

"Yeah," I say. "I think so. How about you? How you doing?"

"I can't complain. Thanks for asking." The detective turns to me and smiles. "You know, your uncle showed me one of your paintings when you were gone."

"He did?" I ask the detective, "When was this?"

"The night we first met," she says to me and pauses in thought. "You're very talented, Squints. You know, when I was your age, I was too busy doing what my parents told me to do as if they were living vicariously through their own daughter. See, mamá played college ball. My pop missed his chance to play in the major leagues. When he was a young boy, being a professional baseball player was what every boy from the Dominican Republic who moved to the States wanted to be when they grew up." She stops for a moment and looks at the ground, as if she's found a piece of evidence. She continues, "It was engrained in him," she says to me. "In a way, it was his escape. He ended up being drafted to fight in Vietnam; he got shot in his throwing arm; and when he came back home after being medically discharged, he just wasn't the same. But it didn't stop him from pushing his 'Dream' onto his daughter. My childhood, as well as adolescence, was consumed with doing what *they* wanted me to do. When I reached college—the 'age of reason'—I finally put my foot down and decided to pursue my own path. I wanted to be a cop because, in a way, it felt as if my parents had robbed me of my childhood, my innocence." Detective Núñez stopped walking. I stop, as well, and face her. "Even though your uncle may not act like it, deep down inside, in a place where men usually have a hard time expressing, he's proud of you and your art."

"How'd you know?"

"I can tell," Detective Núñez says. "I have sort of a good eye for these types of things. Hence why I became a cop."

"Which piece did he show you?" I ask Detective Núñez.

"The one with the elf-like warrior fighting a half-dragon, half-lion creature."

"That's the great *Ahkashi*."

"Ahkashi?"

"He's an ancient nomad who was raised by orcs from the village of Orcadia during the Blackout Period. When Ahkashi was old enough to go into battle, the leader of the orc tribe granted him a hatchet and let Ahkashi loose into the wild in order to achieve his *mak-yana*, which in Orcish stood for 'manhood.' With only a hatchet to protect him, Ahkashi set out on a grueling journey to find his origins. In that particular piece, Ahkashi ran into a cave dwellin' beastie named Sihlo. He crafted a bow from the finest hickory in Elmwood, arrow from cedar, arrowhead from the tooth of a gogomon—"

"—A gogomon?"

"He's just a bottom feeder who dwells in the swamps of Nelic."

"Oh," Detective Núñez says, her face slack. "I see."

"As for the string, Ahkashi acquired it from the lock of a unicorn; however, the unicorn put up quite a fight and nearly trampled Ahkashi to death."

Detective Núñez appears baffled from my response.

"Sounds interested," she hesitates.

Detective Núñez is lying, I can tell.

I have a good nose for these kinds of things.

THE search party goes on well into the night. A couple of volunteers decide to go on food runs. They bring back a spread of platters and a variety of boxes of fried chicken, burgers, sandwiches, and pizza from local restaurants to help the searchers keep up their energy. After combing the woods and getting eaten up by mosquitoes, I end up calling it quits around ten o'clock. Plus, if I stay out any later than eleven, Uncle Jojo is going to start worrying about me. He's given me a curfew and I'm not even trying to fight with him, especially with everything going on.

When I arrive back home, Uncle Jojo is watching a "LIVE" broadcast of the search on the local news channel. He immediately turns the channel as soon as he hears me walk in. He knows I've caught him and as soon as the subject comes up, he flips it back to the news. I never saw any reporters during the search, but apparently after I left, the search turned into an "event."

"Looks like a circus," I say to Uncle Jojo without even realizing that the comment sounds like me trying to start up a conversation.

"You want to talk about it?" Uncle Jojo asks.

He adjusts the recliner to an upright position.

I take a seat on the end of the couch.

"People are losing hope," I say to Uncle Jojo but, really, in a way, it feels as if I'm speaking it to myself. "People are scared. You can see it in their faces, their eyes and the way they look at you."

"They have every right to be, don't they?"

I ask over Uncle Jojo, "You think someone killed him?"

"I don't know, Squints. What I do know is that if you truly care about this boy, which I think you do, then you should never give up on trying to find him." He leans closer. "He's out there somewhere. People just don't disappear off the face of the earth. *But* you must also prepare yourself for the worse. Most of these missing cases never end with happy stories. I truly hope I'm wrong. I hope they find him. I hope he's okay. And all I can do right now is hope."

"I hope he's okay, too."

"Nailah and I are praying for him."

A warm flare of anger comes over me.

"Prayers aren't going to help find him, Uncle Jojo."

"Maybe you should try it something."

"I have."

"And?"

"And obviously, it's pointless."

He leans back in his recliner.

"Only if you think it's pointless. But if you believe in it, don't underestimate the power of prayer. I mean, you believe in magic, don't you?"

"Yeah," I say. "Sure. I believe in magic."

"There you go."

Uncle Jojo points at me. A smile creeps onto the corner of his face, not a full smile, but clear enough to show me that he's fooled me. I don't quite understand the gesture until I think about what I said to him. When I turn back to Uncle Jojo, he's pointing again but not at me.

"Harold Roman," Uncle Jojo says, shaking his head with what looks like disgust. "You didn't see that man there, did you?"

I turn to the TV. On the screen, a man in his early fifties is talking to a news reporter. His face—I know his face. Whenever he's not speaking to the reporter, his lips press into a hard line.

"Yeah," I mutter. "I think I saw him in the search party. That's Harold Roman?"

"Sure is." Uncle Jojo glances my way. "A few years before the accident, he and your old man worked together—briefly."

"They did?"

"That's right," he says. "The two were good friends. I'm surprised he didn't talk to you."

I remember bumping into this Harold Roman guy not too long after I finished chatting with Detective Núñez. He looked at me as if he knew me, but he didn't speak a word to me.

"What do you mean?" I ask Uncle Jojo. "Good friends, how?"

"Like they used to grab a beer and go bowling on the weekends, that's how." He throws in a side-comment from

95

the corner of his mouth, as if he's thinking out loud. "*Never did like the fellow.*"

I leave the living room with Harold Roman's face seared in my memory.

I've seen his face before.

But I don't know where.

☒

AFTER I step out of a warm bath and dry myself off, I still feel a little off.

My body is still exhausted, legs heavy, back sore. Usually a warm bath helps calm me down. But my mind is racing like crazy, even when I slip underneath the cool bed sheets.

Despite my restlessness and the constant images flickering inside my mind like embers, I manage to drift off.

Somehow, I find myself back in the woods. The flashlights burning all around me appear like distant fireflies hovering through the night darkness. The moonlight is bright and creates a pale ambience throughout the woods. Before me I witness a dark silhouette standing between two trees, staring at me. I can't make out the person's shadowy face. But whoever they are, they're like me. We share similar height and weight, same do.

As the stranger walks the other direction, I follow.

I follow the stranger to an opening in the woods where the moonlight is the brightest. In the beam of moonlight, the stranger is revealed to me. It is the same person—or thing—from the cave. The creature wearing a mask of my face. It's here to show me something, I realize, something buried deep inside the woods.

The creature points to a clearing not too far away.

Then, it continues walking.

I follow the creature to the clearing.

Before I exit the woods, I hear a sudden *snap* of a tree branch behind me. . .

I turn around; and in a sudden jolt, I wake from the dream.

With the previous images fresh in my head, I check the time.

It's only been thirty minutes.

I want to go back in, inside the dream, but in the back of my mind I know I'm not going to sleep a wink unless I find what's gnawing at me.

I decide to roll out of bed.

Doing my best not to wake Uncle Jojo or Nailah, I tiptoe downstairs. I make it to a pitch-black living room undetected. I flip on a lamp and pull it close to the bookshelf along the wall. I start pulling out photo albums. All thanks to Nailah, the photos are in order.

Having spent most of her time around the house, from running her own business in the upstairs guest room, which had been converted to a studio, to cleaning up after me, Nailah put in extra time in the photo albums by reorganizing each one a couple months after she moved in with Uncle Jojo. She's what I like to call a "neat monster" who puts a freak to shame. Only weeks after she moved in, she completely flipped Uncle Jojo's house, adding her own touch by sprucing up the living room with foliage and knickknacks you'd only find in the OCD-edition of *Pottery Barn*. Even the inside of Uncle Jojo's fridge pre-Nailah was like digging through piles of garbage in order to find, for instance, the elusive blueberries that always seemed to disappear and then when eventually locating these ever-so elusive blueberries hidden underneath a slimy pack of year-old bologna, realizing the mutative power Uncle Jojo's fridge possessed. The once bluish-purple blueberries somehow found a way to both change color and texture, and after their transformation, looked like fuzzy white balls of mold and nastiness. "Now"-Nailah meant the inside of the fridge was neat and organized, no more clutter or strange science experiments, yet a fridge neatly monstrous. Each container of each color-coded Tupperware labeled with a name, as well as a date. Each tightly sealed cup of yogurt stacked and filed into straight rows according to flavor. Leafy greens, such as spinach or bunches of kale, designated to specific temperature-controlled drawers. Any food that was two to three days past its expiration date was tossed. The neatosaurus, however, contradicts what I discovered her doing to my uncle in bed during their private time away from the ornery nineteen-year-old who's currently occupying the bedroom located three rooms away—the audacity!

The thought alone makes me cringe, like there's a royal rumble going on inside me and my vital organs are laying the smack down.

I focus my attention on the photos.

Apparently, Nailah has touched and spread her "neatness" to the albums.

Unlike the photo albums pre-Nailah, each photo has been arranged into specific timelines, starting from Uncle Jojo's birth to the fart-loving man he is today.

According to the last couple of pages—or months—in the album, the photos were taken on Nailah's smartphone and then printed out through a new app on her phone. If there is one thing that I do like about Nailah—which is rare to say—it's that she still has an appreciation for tangible things, like books, vinyl, clothing—of course—photographs, which all share a common theme that I think everybody can relate to: authenticity.

The last photo, I notice, was taken a few weeks ago during a church barbeque. Nailah took the photo of Uncle Jojo as soon as he was biting down on a pork rib. Uncle Jojo is a carnivore; and clearly, he's not ashamed to admit it.

I pull out the photo from the sleeve and look it over. He looks so, dare I say, happy.

I skim through other photographs until I reach the ones that were taken by actual cameras, not phones.

I flip to the time around my birth, flip through the baby and toddler photos, as well as the few years that followed, and come across a photo, which was taken at a birthday party, particularly my fourth birthday party. In the photo, I'm wearing a crown. My cheeks spotted red with ketchup. I believe the photo was taken at Burger King. Behind me are other four and five-year-olds, who I think were either friends of mine or sons and daughters of my parents' friends and their colleagues. I look closer. A face in the background next to my dad. A familiar face. I hold the photo up to my face and realize the face belongs to the same man who was recently on TV.

Harold Roman.

He hasn't aged much; in fact, except for the graying hair, his face looks the same today as it did fifteen years ago.

I keep flipping. I find one particular photo of Dad and that Harold Roman-fellow at a fundraiser to help raise money for a cure to leukemia, the same disease that killed Aunt Kaali.

They're both smiling for the camera. Harold's arm is wrapped around Dad's neck the same way a "good friend" would—or is the open bromance for the camera only?

🚗

SOMEWHERE between flipping photographs of Uncle Jojo and researching Harold Roman on the Internet, I doze off and wind up back in the woods.

I wander through the moonlit woods until I reach a clearing cut out in a perfect circle in the woods.

In the middle of the clearing stands the look-alike from the cave. She, he—it—is staring at me with its colorful eyes, its reptilian-like hand reaching out.

I walk over and just as I reach the look-alike, the ground suddenly opens like a mouth. After a closer look, I realize the hole is exactly that, a mouth, one of a larger creature. The mouth stretches open in a gaping yawn, the sides circling the mouth and throat lined with layers and layers of jagged teeth, parasite-like.

I inch closer to the edge of the mouth and stand over the opening, which can easily pass as a fissure above a cave. Below me, in the belly of the beast, is me, but not really me, a fake copy of me in the form of a creature with scaly reptilian-like skin wearing a mask of my face, walking up to Mom's head, which is lying on a piece of flat boulder. The look-alike gently picks up Mom's head and holds it up for me to see.

I turn to the other look-alike standing next to me. It grabs me by the arm and tosses me inside the hole.

I wake up from the sudden feeling of falling to warm sunrays pressed against the side of my side.

I'm in bed, but I don't remember getting into bed.

I roll out of bed and shake away the dream from my head.

I wander downstairs to both Uncle Jojo and Nailah, who are both standing at the edge of the kitchen. They're watching a news report on TV.

Immediately, I assume that they found Damianos's body last night, that he's dead, that soon they will have a funeral to finally lay his body to rest. I make my way into the living room for a better angle of the TV and notice another person's face on the screen.

The news anchor is talking about a young man named Justin Devoid. He's a twenty-eight-year-old from Seattle who's currently finishing up a business degree at a community college called Troxler—or the TCC—which is located not too far from where we live. The TCC is similar to Dover but with ashtrays. It's a place where all the losers who didn't get a scholarship into a real college or Ivy League school go to enter the real world. According to classmates, Justin Devoid hasn't shown up for class in a week. He last spoke to his mom the Saturday before last. The news doesn't mention his father, which means he's either dead or no longer in the picture.

Each one of Justin's classmates, who are being interviewed by the reporter on TV, describe Justin as if they're reading from the same script: Justin was a "quiet" person, "shy," "nice," "kept to himself," "loner." These *words*—strategic as they may be—as well as descriptions, sound all too familiar. Also, apparently, Justin, unlike Damianos, is a social leper on the Internet. He's on there a lot, maybe too much than he needs to be. Unlike Damianos, who has thousands of followers—in fact, he has more followers than the entire population of Dover High—Justin only has eighty-nine followers on Twitter and twenty-three on Instagram. From what I gathered from the interviews with the people who know—or knew—him, his current real life status basically mirrors his online life. He rarely uses hashtags in his tweets or posts, even though he comments frequently on headlines or hot garbage. From the often long-winded rants on his Tweeter page, he appears as if he's not trying to impress anybody by any means.

After the report is over, I go back to my room and grab my phone. I start going through the rest of Justin's timeline on his social media pages, his most recent tweets and posts.

I find myself doing exactly what a detective is probably doing right now.

🚗

THE night Justin Devoid's story surfaced on TV, the town is going to hold a vigil for Damianos.

Since Nailah has been bringing casseroles and desserts, like her famous pineapple upside down cake, over to the Pipes household without consulting with me and has apparently created a new bond with Damianos's mom, she decides to join me. I'm not upset about her wanting to participate; in fact, a part of me feels as if things are improving between us.

Nailah and I arrive at the vigil ten minutes before it starts, and there's a pretty decent sized turnout. Most of Damianos's friends from Dover are here, his soccer pals— his crew—as well as his confidantes from the drama tribe. Damianos has tons of friends and would hang out with a variety of kids—and tribes—who you'd think would never hang out with him. Some of the kids who I used to hang around with at Dover are here too. They weren't exactly friends with Damianos—at least not when I was at Dover. Not even sure if their circle of friends crossed paths with Damianos's many circles, perhaps at parties. I have no interest in talking to them; in fact, I do everything in my power to ignore them.

Nailah spots Cybele at the front of the crowd, lighting candles for her son.

She tells me that we should go say hi to Damianos's mom. I spot several of Damianos's friends, including Ryan—or was it Bryan?—standing next to Cybele, consoling her.

I tell Nailah to wait a little while till everything settles down before we talk to her. Nailah doesn't approve—clearly from her expression—but she doesn't want to make a scene. So, we hang back until after Damianos's father speaks.

As I'm standing among other townspeople and waiting for the vigil to begin, I witness a woman in the crowd who can pass as Mom's twin. I even excuse myself from Nailah for a moment and tell her that I'll be right back.

Mom's vacant face drifts farther into the crowd as if it's floating.

I shoulder my way past townspeople, even at one moment getting stopped by a couple of "old" friends whom I was friends with during my sophomore year—old, as in that's all they really mean to me, old and outdated, nothing more than afterthoughts. Kerry, cracks a joke about a junior named Diesha, who's standing within listening distance, and talks about how Diesha is so fat that she shouldn't be allowed to eat, then Janique, Joel, Cynthia, with her jacked-up weave, Bradley, then M.J.—whom I once had a thing with, but now he's grown out his dreads past his shoulders, which make him look like the *Predator*. I briefly chat with them, these people whom I once referred to as friends, keeping my words short, simple, and to the point. M.J. tries to act as if he's still into me by that starry look in his gaze as if he can somehow summon such a look on command, but I don't pay him any mind. I know it's all a front for M.J. He's not aware that I know he just broke up with Anita. Just because I don't attend Dover anymore and have already graduated early doesn't mean I'm out of the loop.

I ignore him. I ignore all of them and proceed through the crowd.

The crowd tightens at the front of the vigil, so much that I end up having to shoulder my way through a sea of bodies.

During my teetering shuffle, I'm rerouted by a sudden bump to my side—purposeful or accidental still remains a mystery.

With my body all coiled up, I rotate around and track down the bumper: first, her face, Nicole's face, then her thin yet curvy Instagram-body. I struggle to find the right words—any words for that matter! Everything about Nicole, every perfect feature of her face, every article of clothing, which compliments one another in the softest yet loudest tones: hella-flawless. The beating of candlelight causes her silky blonde hair to glow like a winter's fire. The white of her eyes like embers, yet the irises, so blue and vivid, look as if the oceans were captured and bottled up by her thoughtful creators. Her skin, like diamonds. Her lips, plump like a black girl's lips, but less busy. All I can muster from my mouth is a "hey." She acknowledges me, my wounded "hey," and returns with a "hey" herself, only her tone smoother and a smile to go sell it. Then, just like that, our moment passes. Nicole vanishes—or more so glides like an angel—back into the riptide. And I'm left standing by myself, searching for answers to deeply-planted riddles.

Eventually, I find Mom standing before the candlelight.

I tap her on the shoulder.

She turns around in surprise.

I nearly speak her name; in fact, the name remains dangled on the tip of my tongue, as if it's half-spoken, a noise that sounds close to a "Mah. . ."

I look at the woman and that's exactly who she is, just a woman who kind of looks like Mom but is not Mom.

The strange woman waits for me to say something, but the words fall short.

🚗

TWO days of more searching and less finding, two days of more worrying and less guessing, I hear a heavy *thud* of a knock on the door followed by the ring of the doorbell. Uncle Jojo answers the door. I creep from my room and wait at the top of the landing. At the door are two FBI agents and they want to talk to me. They want to ask me just a few questions. Uncle Jojo inquires about their presence and why they want to talk to his niece. One of the agents—a rather deep-voiced man who goes by the name Agent Smart—tells him it's in regards to a manager who runs the Stop N' Shop.

Bernie?

🚗

MOMENTS later, I'm back in my room pressing my face against the dusty window for a closer look at the two agents. They're no longer standing on the front porch. Yet, it appears as if Uncle Jojo's already shown the two agents inside the house.

As soon as the door closes downstairs, I hear the sound of one set of footsteps on the staircase.

I remove my face from the window. I can't help but notice the partial imprint of the left side of my face that I have left behind on the window. Before I get myself lost in the thought of the impression, I hear yet another familiar sound.

Uncle Jojo opens the door and pokes his head inside the room.

"Two FBI agents are here to talk to you," he says sternly.

"Me?" I can only imagine how confused I look to Uncle Jojo. "Why me?"

"They want to ask you about a man named Bernie Shore."

"Okay," I say. "So what about him?"

Uncle Jojo's face hardens like clay.

"Just get down here and talk to them," he demands, not asks.

"Okay," I say shortly, as my chest tightens.

I follow Uncle Jojo downstairs where two FBI agents are standing at the edge of the kitchen.

They're both standing by the fridge, one with her hands nestled firmly in her pockets and the other with his hands holstered over his hips, pushing back a beige trench coat, revealing his pistol. They're both waiting for me, only me.

Somehow, the copper-coated canned light above the kitchen table gets a little brighter.

The light feels strange and warm, like sunrays on my skin.

TWENTY-two strenuous minutes later, the two FBI agents are gone, clicked away, and I'm forced back into a common commercial—my commercial—filled with an uncle, whom I think means well, offering to prepare me any of the boxed and packaged choices of foods that contain minimally processed dry ingredients that he has at his immediate disposal; and by the way he holds up each choice, it feels as if he is trying to strike a deal with me. If I eat, then I will speak. A happy tummy is a happy mind. A happy mind is a happy girl.

Uncle Jojo holds up the many options for me, first Aunt Jemima, then Keebler, then Nabisco, Quaker Oats, all of whom I'd considered lifelong companions who have gotten me through troubled times.

As I mentally siphon through the previous encounter with the two FBI agents, I tell Uncle Jojo that I'm going out for a minute—to think mostly. Hoping that he hasn't been keeping tabs on the weekly maintenance of my car, I decide to use the most available excuse at my disposal and tell him that I need to put some gas in my car since my car is on low. I can already feel it happening, the weight pressed against my shoulders. He's starting to smother me, asking me more and more follow-up questions about where

I'm exactly going—Am I going directly to the gas station? Or, am I'm going to be driving around afterwards? And, if so, what am I going to be doing? Ever since Damianos's disappearance, Uncle Jojo, as well as Nailah, have become closer to me. However, at times—actually, more often than not—it feels as if they're getting *too* close by the way they treat me. I want to tell them—in fact, scream at them until my insides expel from my body—that I'm not that little five-year-old girl whom they took in fourteen years ago. Yet, at times, it feels as if they treat me as if I still am. I don't know how much longer things can go on like this, don't know if I can stay here, in this cold house, before I start to freeze. I resort to the only old tactic I know.

I lie.

When I arrive at the Stop N' Shop, Bernie's there to greet me. He immediately notices that there's something on my mind. It's written all over me, I guess.

"The FBI came by to see me today," I say, looking around the store. I draw my attention toward the cameras scattered around the store, including one pointed directly at me. I didn't notice this before, but Bernie has a lot of cameras. Which is strange for a little convenient store. I squash the doubts, remember the robbery last spring, and how Bernie nearly lost his life after a Street Soldier stuck a gun in his face. The gun jammed, I remind myself.

Doubts aside, I can't help but wonder if the FBI is watching over the place, camped in shady cars parked at a distance while peeping through nice binoculars or even disguised as customers.

"About?" Bernie finally says.

"About you. They wanted to know what my relationship was with you."

"What did you tell them?"

"I told them the truth," I say. "I told them you're a friend."

"I see," he says with his head down. "I tell you what. You hungry?"

"Starved, actually."

"Let me buy you a slice from Luigi's."

I think about Bernie's offer.

"Who's gonna watch over the store?"

"RJ can."

I think once more about his proposal.

"Sure."

WHILE RJ covers for Bernie, Bernie and I walk to Luigi's, which is located within walking distance in the strip mall across the street.

Bernie is first to speak.

He says, "They came by here yesterday to talk to me about that missing boy case."

I ask, "Which one?"

"You mean there's been another disappearance?"

"Yeah," I say, nodding. "Two days ago."

"Geez," he says and shakes his head in a typical annoyance that has spread to most of the townspeople. "Sometimes, I think this town is cursed. People going missing all the time. It's like it's become a trend."

"Have you ever thought about, you know, leaving?" I ask Bernie, as we approach the intersection leading to the strip mall.

"I have. Once. So," he says, more clearly. "Anyway, the Feds wanted to ask me about that Damianos Pipes kid. They also wanted to look through my tapes. So, I let them. They told me you knew him. Squints, you should've told me."

"I did," I say to Bernie, "well, I didn't exactly mention his name. But, yes, I did know him."

"I see."

"But why did they want to talk with you?"

"A new witness came forward, said he saw Damianos here the day he disappeared. The Feds came by, collected surveillance footage. Turns out he was here the day he disappeared."

"He was?"

"So many people come and go," he says. "I must've for-gotten his face. According to the footage, he stopped by for a car wash. I reckon he wanted his car to look spotless be-fore he saw your pretty face."

Even though I should feel flattered by the compliment, I feel more depressed than anything from the very notion of Damianos wanting his car to look clean and spotless. I can't help but think that maybe Damianos wanted to drive me around in his car. Maybe Damianos wanted to take me somewhere, to the movies, to an ice cream parlor, maybe to a place where it was just the two of us, maybe to hook up, maybe just to talk, to get to know each other, to solidify what could've been a meaningful relationship.

I keep talking, thinking maybe, by talking, it'll help rid the thoughts of *what-if.*

"So, what else did the FBI want with you?" I ask. Then, throw in a side note. "Be honest with me, Bern."

"You're not wearing a wire, are you?"

I can't tell whether or not Bernie is joking.

He smiles.

I try to smile back but I come off grimacing.

"Yeah," I say back. "Okay."

Bernie sighs, then stops halfway through the parking lot in front of Luigi's.

"The real reason they showed up was because of RJ."

"What about him?"

"He has a past."

"What kind of past?"

"When he was around your age, he got into some trouble with the law. But all that nonsense is behind him. He's moved on. He's a different person."

Bernie starts to walk again.

I follow.

"What kind of trouble?"

Bernie stops again, turns to me.

"He was charged with indecent exposure."

I ask, "What's that?"

"It's where you show the parts of yourself that should remain private."

"Serious?"

"Yeah," Bernie says. "Serious."

We keep walking.

"To who?"

"College girls, I think," Bernie says, more unsure. "He was young and dumb. He did his time, spent a couple of years behind bars. He's move on. Like I said, he's a different person."

"Knowing what he did in the past, you still hired him?"

We make it to Luigi's.

Before entering, Bernie steps aside.

"It wasn't up to me, Squints," he says.

"Who was it?"

"Harold Roman," Bernie says, looking around. "It was his call. He felt as if RJ had moved on from his past and deserved a second chance. Harold was right. RJ did. *But,*" Bernie emphasizes, "let me tell you this, Squints. RJ is only a man who bleeds the same blood you and I bleed. He's not perfect, not by any stretch. *No-body* is. All men— all women—*we* all have a past. We all have our dirty little secrets which we feel are best hidden than exposed. And those who say otherwise haven't really lived."

"Yeah, but—"

"—It's not society's job to exploit or hold people accountable based on their past or wrongdoings, but instead, celebrate the individual who has come out clean on the other side. That's the beauty of time, Squints. *Time* has a way of cleansing a man of his past."

Bernie holds the door open and walks me into Luigi's.

As Luigi himself greets us, Bernie turns to me and asks what I'd like to order.

I'm still trying to wrap my head around Bernie's words, about a man's past, about time.

"Squints?"

I snap from my trance.

"Yeah," I say, skimming over the selection of pies behind the counter. I find the one with the most colors on it. "I'll take a slice of the veggie pizza."

"One veggie coming up," Luigi says robustly.

Bernie goes with a house salad—"no meat," he specifies.
Says he's watching his diet.
Which doesn't exactly earn him more points with me.
But I'd be lying if I said I wasn't impressed.

🚗

TWO weeks pissed away.

Still no new updates on neither Damianos nor Justin.

From the daily reports as well as the brief and, at times, emotional interviews with friends and family members coming in and out of Damianos's parents' house or Justin's mother's house outside Seattle, the investigations have hit a wall.

People are growing more frustrated. Most have given up hope.

The fact is people just want answers.

🚗

TONIGHT is the prom for Dover High, and I stay locked up in my room for most of the night, painting a new piece, but mostly drifting off into moments of deep thought.

Considering the recent disappearances, last week the superintendent met with a special committee to vote on whether or not Dover, as well as the other schools in the district, should hold a senior prom this year. The vote was overwhelmingly in favor for a prom, except for several members of the committee who let their religious views get in the way of their vote. The majority of the vote was driven by resiliency, as well as a cardinal reminder, to the parties involved in the disappearances that the Dover Wildcats—and any other school in their district for that matter—weren't going to succumb to fear.

All I can do is wonder, wonder if that date between Damianos and I had gone perfect, wonder if we'd go on other dates, wonder if he'd ask me out to the prom.

I've never been to the prom.

So, I guess I'll never know.

But I can wonder.
All I can do right now is wonder.
And Dream of what could've been.

🚗

UNCLE Jojo wakes me up from a deep sleep.

I look around, confused and unsure as to where I am. I check the time on my nightstand. It's only six o'clock in the morning.

"Squints," he says, shaking my arm.

I snap back, "*What?*"

"There's been a break in the case," he says to me and pulls me out of bed.

I follow Uncle Jojo downstairs to the living room where the TV is blaring.

On the TV, a reporter is standing by the aftermath of a car fire on the front lawn of Courtney Allen High, which is located in San Pedro, the town over. Firefighters are at the scene putting out the remaining flames with water hoses. The smoky limo, which is charred and wrecked, appears as if it was deliberately driven into the tatted-up school rock of the high school. The front end of the limo is smashed in like an accordion.

The reporter says that firefighters haven't discovered any remains inside the limo, no driver or passengers. So far, they've found a gas can, which they believe was used to start the fire.

As of now, still many unanswered questions.

🚗

AT exactly 9:08 AM FBI, agents discover the limo driver Ezra Kontos with a self-inflicted gunshot wound to his head inside a two-bedroom apartment off Cober-Dhanial Avenue, which happens to be located a couple of blocks from where Damianos's car was discovered.

🚗

AT 1:15 PM, the FBI, as well as the police chief of the Dover Police Department, hold a news conference regarding new information in Damianos's case. The FBI is extremely vague in their statements and mostly dodge around the most important questions, which are mostly due to investigators still processing evidence from Kontos's apartment; however, the FBI agent provides specific information about the driver licenses which were discovered inside the limo driver's apartment. So many licenses that the FBI agent doesn't even give a number. However, he only gives us two numbers. Two licenses which belonged to one, Damianos Pipes, and one, Justin Devoid. According to Ezra Kontos's background, he has had multiple run-ins with the law. The FBI did a background check on Kontos. The FBI agent lists the crimes: attempted murder back in 2002; sexual assault back in 2008; drug possession, DUI. The man definitely has a sketchy past. He also points out that Kontos was, in fact, driving the limousine under a false identity and also that, when his body was first discovered inside the apartment, both his hands "reeked" of gasoline. There was also a significant amount of "dirt" underneath his fingernails, which is obviously still inconclusive, but he threw it out there anyway, as if he's planting a seed in the imagination of the listeners.

I'm still left in a state of wonder, not by the recent discoveries of who may be the person responsible for Damianos's or Justin's disappearance, but by the fact that the FBI or the Dover Police Department can't answer one simple question: *Where is Damianos Pipes?*

🚗

ONCE the news conference is over, my appetite is ruined. I end up throwing away half of a roasted red pepper hummus sandwich and walk back upstairs to my room where I try to piece together the recent news. I try to break down the news, first with the discovery of the driver licenses.

For one, if Ezra Kontos is a murderer, where did he hide the bodies?

And two, how long has he been committing these crimes?

According to the FBI, they discovered a driver license dated back to a missing girl four years ago. It was a Utah license.

Except for Damianos and several others who had been reported missing over the past few years, most of the licenses are out of state, which means each one of the victims was either abducted while driving in a car, possibly pulled over by a person claiming to have a flat tire or in need of help—which seems unlikely. I'd never stop to help out a stranger, unless he or she looked legit. More than likely, I wouldn't stop for a man like Ezra Kontos. I'm still not excluding the cops. They pull people over all the time—and for all I know, they planted all of those driver licenses inside Kontos's apartment. Either way, the victims were captured in public. Maybe even in broad daylight. I can't possibly see why Kontos would break into a victim's house, capture his victim, then steal the driver license unless it was like a trophy for him.

I try to put myself in Damianos's shoes, put myself in the driver's seat of his car, driving through his timeline: first, stopping by Stitch to pick me up a fresh yet tight pair of Levi's for the upcoming date while, at the same time, live-tweeting to help calm my nerves, and then, making a minor detour to the shoe department and giving the new kicks that'd put the *What are those?* haters to shame for a quick spin. Finally, after my new look is all set and paid for, make a pit stop at the Stop N' Shop for a car wash.

I feel the wind get knocked out of me from the thought of that "busted pipe," as Bernie explained to me.

The car wash. . .

A few months back, I was filling up my tires with air at a pump station outside the car wash when all of a sudden I heard a clank followed by a harsh *grating* sound coming from within the car wash. I drew my attention toward the car wash and saw a brown-looking liquid splattering over the steamy window of the tunnel. The mist was thick and making it hard to see inside. When I grabbed Bernie from the store, I remember he specifically told me it was a "busted pipe," but for some reason, I felt as if he wasn't being real with me.

Then, I remember the spot of blood at the edge of the car wash a few weeks ago.

Then, Bernie cleaning up the vomit all over the floor inside the store. In the corner of my eye, I remember seeing the look on RJ's face. I remember not initially thinking much of the look. But now that I remember, RJ was looking at me and not Bernie. He was giving me a look, like he wanted to kill me.

Bernie's words suddenly start ringing through my head: *That's the beauty of time, Squints. Time has a way of cleansing a man of his past.*

I travel backward, farther into not just my past, but *his* past, where our pasts crossed.

The day I first met Bernie.

I didn't like him at first. He was pushy, very intrusive. He asked me a lot of questions about myself, who I was, where I was from, where I grew up, where I'd like to hang out. After a couple of times of bumping into Bernie at the store, he started to strike up more conversations with me. I specifically remember him asking about my parents, asking me if they know where am I, what I'm up to. Then, apparently, he had seen me talking with Kush several times. He asked me about Kush, what my relation was with him. Which I thought was strange coming from a man who was more likely three times my age. A part of me always knew that Bernie knew what Kush was doing outside his store, how he was peddling drugs to out-of-touch kids and desperate junkies. But not once did he ever call the cops. Which made me believe that maybe Bernie was buying drugs himself from Kush. I always thought about these things, but I never suspected Bernie as someone who would be up to no good since I consider him a friend.

Bernie said he didn't know about Justin Devoid or his disappearance. Yet, a part of me knew he wasn't being straight with me because he spent nearly his entire day watching that damn television behind the checkout counter. Even said how, besides his niece Christine, the TV is basically all he has.

Mentally, I travel back some more, to the day I was five years hold, screaming out for Mom's help as my body is batted around like a pinball.

The entire incident is surrounded by blackness, a gap in the timeline.

All I can remember is Mom's face through the passenger window.

The ground suddenly opened up underneath me and swallowed us whole.

Then, blackness.

WITH a concealed pocketknife that I manage to steal from Uncle Jojo's drawer, I sneak out of the house and drive to the Stop N' Shop.

Bernie saw the recent news conference earlier today.

"I've been thinking about you, Squints," Bernie says, as I stand at the checkout counter.

"Thanks," I say, looking around the store for RJ.

I don't see him anywhere.

"Squints, if you need to talk to somebody, anybody, I'm always here for you. You understand that, right?"

"Of course," I say. "But right now, I'm just sick of talking."

I buy the usual from Bernie. I hand him the money. Instead, he hands me the receipt with my number. Says the car wash is on him.

"Well," he says, as I make my way to the door, "whenever you feel like it, just know that I'm here, Squints. I'm here for you."

I stop at the door, open it, and say to Bernie, "I know you are."

As I pull up to the car wash, my insides start to knot up.

My palms are sweaty, other areas in my body damp and swampy.

My breathing becomes shorter, heavier.

I find myself taking in deeper breaths.

I don't know why, but somehow, I feel—I know in my gut that all of the answers to my questions wait for me beyond the wall of mist.

Before punching in my code into the keypad, I look over my shoulder at the camera facing at an angle on the top of a street post. I look around for other cameras but can only find one, just that one facing the back corner of the car wash.

I punch in the code. I'm given the green light to enter the car wash.

The mist intensifies, making it harder to see inside.

I slowly creep through the wall of mist and align my tires in the tracks on the ground. Once my tires fall into the trenches, I pull farther into the car wash tunnel until my front two tires reach the two grooves at the end of the track. Instead of driving the car into the grooves, I put the gear in park and hurry outside.

With the mist spraying all around me, I investigate the inside of the car wash. I don't know exactly what I'm looking for, but I know something is here, maybe a piece to a greater puzzle.

In my frantic search, I don't find anything out of the ordinary inside the car wash. I check the over-under conveyor belt as well as the trenches with the rollers underneath my car. Then, I check the brushes, first the top brushes, the wraparounds, mitter curtains and wheel and tire brushes, rockers and low side washers. I check the pipes above, the bulky machinery and tanks.

I start pulling and tugging on random things, thinking that they may open up some kind of secret chamber, like in those whodunit movies.

I don't find anything suspicious about the car wash.

In fact, I don't find any signs of struggle.

No secret chambers.

No bodies.

No Damianos.

No answers.

A blaring alarm suddenly sounds off, startling me.

The yellow caution light starts to flash.

I hurry back to my car, get inside, and close the door.

As I drive my car into the grooves, my car is forced to a jolting stop. The red light comes on. The alarm cuts off. I switch the gear to park.

As the soap starts to spray my windshield, I find myself getting dizzy. I look around me, then try to set my eyes on a particular dirt smudge on the side of the window. I never take my eyes off that smudge. Yet, I keep them there, glued, as if, by doing so, it'll rid the dizzy spell. Despite my sharp concentration, my head continues to spin out of control. My fingertips start to tingle. My entire body tingles. My mind even tingles.

The brushes switch on, violently thrashing around my car as if they're unfettered beasties trying to get inside, to grab me, to drag me down to the underworld. The spinning brushes make my head much worse.

Once more, my breath becomes heavier and heavier to the point where I can hardly catch my breath.

I'm not only spinning, but also fading.

The world goes gray.

Before I realize what is happening, I'm falling.

I'm taking the car down with me.

The entire world feels as if it's plummeting straight to oblivion.

🚗

I rise from the blackness.

I'm five years old, again.

Trapped inside a memory, again.

Remembering, again.

In the memory, I'm trying to tug away the corner of my jacket that is stuck in the door.

As I yank on the jacket, I'm suddenly batted against the side of the car like a pinball by brushes the size of a giant's arm. The soggy padded arms slap and beat against my body in repetitive strokes, and at times, I'm forced to thin out my body and flatten it against the side of the car to prevent myself from being crushed by another massive brush.

Mom is calling out to me from the driver's seat, yelling at me to hang tight while she struggles to unbuckle her seatbelt. She's acting strange, though, not her self. She fumbles with the belt buckle. She even has a hard time locating the red button, which, if pressed, will free her from the seat. Eventually, she frees herself from the seat-belt; however, she can hardly sit up straight. Her head bobbles back and forth, her face wearing the same one as that old foul-mouthed lush who lives next door, whose breath always smells of liquor and who walks sideways. The air conditioner is running inside the car; but somehow, I can see the air—actually, see it. A visible gas is pumping from the open vents inside the car.

I bang my palm against the passenger side window, screaming at her to open up the door.

But she drifts into sleep.

While continuing to bang on the glass, screaming at Mom to "wake up" and "help me," I hear the sound of metal gears shifting followed by a rattling *cranking*-sound!

As the front of the car tips forward in a sharp angle and starts to descend into the ground, I manage to unzip my jacket and pull myself from the car door.

I fall backward onto my back.

I'm free.

The ground opens up wider, revealing a large ramp at-tached to a set of clunky gears. The ramp lowers the car below into the blackness below.

A new set of tracks extends from the edge of the ramp. The tracks start moving like the tracks below a roller-coaster, guiding the car farther into the dark hole.

Mom still remains inside the car.

I scream out to her, but she will not wake up!

As the car finally reaches the bottom of the hole, it rolls off the track and hits the ground with a *thud*. Even through the blast of water being sprayed all around me, I can still hear the sound below. I lean closer and hanging from the shattered windshield is Mom. Her head crashed through the crushed glass, her forehead cut and bloody. I scream out to Mom once more.

As I lean closer, my foot slips on the slick soapy surface on the ground.

I find myself falling, again.

Into the blackness, again.

🚗

I come to inside the car.

The last thing I remember is a memory once soaked in blackness, then, out of some blinded yet wielded instinct, remembering to close all of the air vents before the sleeping gas filled the inside of the car, then using whatever mobility I had left in my arm to punch the gear from "P" to "D" in a drunken-like haze, then pressing my foot against the gas pedal and gunning the car off the track.

Then, bam!

The blackness.

I push through the haze and touch a knot forming on my forehead.

I pull away my hand and rub my wet fingertips together. I flip on the overhead light and check the rear view mirror. I'm cut bad, might need a few stitches when this is all over, but I tell myself it's nothing too serious. I locate more blood over the steering wheel, as well as the dashboard. The bottom part of the windshield appears cracked with a splotch of my bright red blood. The grill of the car is smashed and smoking a little.

Out of desperation, I try to start up the car but all I get in return is the sound of an engine choking. The battery, however, still has juice.

I switch on the headlights. Only one headlight comes on. It hangs from the front of the car by a couple of wires like an eyeball that's been dislodged from its eye socket. The other bulb is destroyed. It's dark outside, beyond the windows, but I manage to get a somewhat better view of the hole. I appear to be trapped in a secret lair stretching out into the darkness.

From the oval-like design and the almost smooth walls before me, it appears to be manmade, the lair possibly chiseled out many years ago. From a distance, I can see other cars. All sorts of cars. Newer and older models. Even vintage cars.

Above, a soft light slowly starts to fade.

I poke my head from the window and witness the ramp folding back into the floor of the car wash. Eventually, the light goes out, leaving me back in the darkness.

I step out of the car and stumble over rocks on the ground before making my way to the lone headlight. I grab the headlight, hold it carefully in my hands, and shine it around the lair. The back ends of other cars become clearer. I can't help but notice the different states on the license plates. Nevada, Arizona, Texas, Wisconsin, Montana, Colorado, Oregon, Washington, North Carolina, Ohio, New Jersey, Tennessee, *Utah*. Of all the states, that particular state stands out the most—Utah. I find hundreds of these cars, all parked and facing the darkness like cars at a drive-in theatre, waiting for the feature presentation.

I shine the headlight on a bluish rectangular light flickering along the side of the wall.

Of course, the headlight starts flickering as well.

I give it a tap, bringing it back to life.

Before the headlight inevitably burns out like a cue, I catch a glimpse of the strange light and realize it's coming from a door; and behind that door, voices are speaking.

Mindful of the tripping hazards below me, I inch back to the car and fish a dead lighter from the glove compartment. Then, I clear my head for a moment. *The emergency kit*, I remember. I go to the trunk and pull out a special kit that my uncle left me just in case I found myself in these types of situations—you know, if my car was ever eaten by a car wash and stuck in a pit of doom. In the kit, I find bandages. I use the gauzes to wipe away the blood on my forehead and patch up the cut the best I can with a couple of Band-Aids. I also find a small, handy flashlight, as well as a tire iron.

Thank you, Uncle Jojo.

With both my flashlight and my newly found weapon in hand, I walk to the door where the voices become clearer. Two men screaming at one another; however, I can't tell what they're screaming about.

As I approach the door, I feel a crunch below my foot.

I shine the light on waterlogged trash and random junk littered on the ground. One item catches my eye: a ruined corsage.

Immediately, the thought of the missing prom kids comes to mind.

With the recent discovery at the forefront of my mind, I tiptoe to the door and press my ear against the side of it.

Inside, I hear the sound of Bernie's voice; however, his voice is thinner and gravelly distressed.

From inside, I hear a *thump* and then a soft *thud*.

Then, the sound of leaves *rustling*.

I cut the flashlight and with the tire iron gripped tightly in hand, I crack open the door. Before me, I find dozens of Bernie's, laid out in the back aisle of Stop N' Shop with a puddle of blood forming behind his head. Above Bernie towers a slender man, who, not once, looks up to reveal his face to the cameras.

I scan the surveillance room and find other monitors displaying other areas of the store, including the front entrance of the store where several customers come and go. Some knock on the door. Some peek inside. Some try to open the door, but it appears locked. Once the customers realize that the store is "closed," as the sign reads on the door, they get back in their cars and drive off.

I even shout out "HELP!" but none of them hear; in fact, they act as if I don't even exist.

I direct my attention back to Bernie, who's not moving. Scattered all around him are items that looked as if they had fallen off the shelves. Candy, snacks, batteries, school supplies, like pens and pencils and paper. One shelf near the refrigerators is overturned on the ground. From the chaos in the very back of the store, it appears as if there was a struggle.

Bernie's attacker puts down a fire extinguisher on the ground next to Bernie, goes away for a moment and then comes back with a fire blanket. He places the blanket over Bernie's body, grabs Bernie's ankles, and drags his lifeless body to a utility room.

While he's dragging away Bernie's body, he glances up at the camera.

Holy shit.

Just as I thought.

"RJ."

I always knew there was something up with that guy.

I can't find another camera inside the utility room.

I frantically search each monitor until I come across the kitchen monitor. In the background, I can see a clear angle of the utility room. RJ places Bernie aside and pulls back a shelf with cleaning chemicals. The shelf opens up like a door. . .

RJ grabs Bernie's ankles once more and drags his body through the door.

Once through, RJ closes the door.

In a distance, I somehow hear the echo of a door closing!

I leave the surveillance room and listen closely for RJ, my chest pounding.

Over the thrumming sound of my heart beating through my eardrums, I hear the muzzled screams of somebody struggling inside one of the many cars around me. I find a white Toyota crossover with Washington license plates. I recall the news report about Justin's car, this exact make and model displayed on TV.

I shine a light on the driver's seat.

Inside, a person—can't tell whom exactly—is attached to the driver's seat. If it is Justin, he's not moving. However, I can hear the sound of a struggle.

As I carefully approach the driver's side of the crossover, I shine the light on the person's face. Two wide eyes laced with fear immediately snap toward me. I shine the light on the person's face. I can tell whether or not the person is a man or a woman. Except for the opening around their eyes, their entire face and body is wrapped in duct tape and bound to the driver's seat like a cocoon of duct tape. The only way of breathing comes from the two tiny incisions below the nostrils. I search the ground for something sharp. I find a piece of broken glass. I open the door. The potent smell of shit and piss knocks me backward. I power forward.

With the shard of jagged glass, I cut through the duct tape, first along the side of the face. I slowly—and carefully—peel away the duct tape.

The twenty-something male appears to be Justin Devoid; however, his face is gaunter and paler and spotted with red blotches.

I ask the person, "Are you Justin Devoid?"

The guy barely has enough energy to open his mouth to speak; however, he clarifies that he is, in fact, Justin Devoid.

Mindful about cutting Justin with the shard of glass, I cut through duct tape along the side of the seat, as well as his body, and peel it away. While doing so, I rip the hair from his skin. He slightly grimaces during each forceful yank of tape. But I think having hairless arms is the least of his worries. His body is incredibly weak and delicate after being mummified for God knows how long—days, weeks, who knows? However, when asked, Justin says he'll be able to walk on his own, but a part of me believes–in fact, knows—that he's just saying this to me because he doesn't want me to run off to go find help.

Finally, once his body is totally free, I tend to his hair. I end up having to cut off handfuls of hair in order to free his head from the duct tape.

"Careful," he says, hissing with pain.

I set him straight.

"You have two options: you can either rot away down here or shut up and let me free your ass."

Justin goes with the latter option.

After I'm through cutting free his hair from the duct tape, he's left with a do that would only fly in the maybe the punk-rock scene. But even those kids would question the look.

Hairdo aside, I notice Justin's lips are red and raw and his mouth is parched. He tries to swallow, but his saliva is like sand.

I help him out of the car and set him down next to the back left tire. I tell him to wait here and rush back to my car to fetch a bottle of water from the backseat. I bring the water back to Justin and nurse the water into his mouth.

"Thank you," he says, exhausted.

Realizing that at any moment RJ may show up, I skip asking Justin how long he has been down here and help him to his feet. A sudden dizzy spell forces him back to the ground. He rests on what looks like his left butt cheek. From the way he's sitting on the ground I can only imagine what Justin's carrying in his pants—considering that awful smell in the car.

"Wait," he says dizzily. "Give me a minute, will you?"

"We don't have a minute, Justin. Can you walk or not?"

Justin pauses.

"I was no. . . no use to him," he stutters, as his eyes trail toward the ground in a sense of shame. "He said I was '*irrelevant*' to him."

I hear a distant noise that sounded like footsteps in the darkness behind me.

"Irrelevant? What you talking about? Was it RJ who did this to you?"

"I dunno," he says, holding back tears. "There were two of them. I've seen one of their faces on TV before. That piece of shit. Harold Something—"

"—Harold Roman?"

Justin nods. His eyes light up for a moment.

124

"That's the one."

"How you know this?"

"I overheard him talking to some other guy. Whoever they are, they're some twisted fucks." The tears start to flow. The anger makes its way to his face, as if it's surfacing from deep within a tender spot inside him, then strangles his words. "They're doing these. . . these strange experiments on people."

"Experiments?" I ask, "What experiments?"

Justin nods at me to turn around.

"Look for yourself," he says.

I turn and look.

I don't see what Justin's talking about, at first. Then, I step closer to a cherry red sports car with Virginia license plates parked in front of Justin's crossover. I notice something "strange" on the hood of the car. I have a suspicion of what this "strangeness" might be, but I figure it's only a bitter cocktail of stress and anxiety fueling my imagination. It can't be, could it?

I walk past the red sports car.

The hood ornament, I realize, has been replaced with a round object no bigger than a basketball.

My suspicions become true as soon as I witness the dirty blonde hair, as well as the ear. I step in front of the red sports car and on the edge of the hood perches the head of a human. From the detail of each feature of the face, I realize that the head once belonged to somebody. The head is, in fact. . .

I suddenly back away in horror.

"What the fuck? Is that what I think it is—"

"Yes," Justin utters. "It's a head."

I look around at the other cars parked in the angled row. Each and every vehicle, from sedan to truck to crossover to SUV to hatchback to convertible to even motorcycle— which is a stranger sight to see and makes me question exactly how a motorcycle was able to fit inside the car wash—is sporting what looks like human head as a hood or fender ornaments. I spot an older Mustang, like the ones I used to see in the campy crime TV shows Uncle Jojo watched, with a skull on the end of the hood.

"Who'd do such a thing?" I ask Justin, as the horror grips me and causes my body to tremble.

Somewhere in my mad scramble to find reason in a place of no reason, those footsteps are back.

And they're *real*.

Real as the heads on the cars displayed all around like the sick collection of a psychopath.

I rush back to Justin.

As the footsteps make themselves more present, I grab Justin by the arms and try to carry him. He forces my arms away.

"Just go," he whispers. "I'll distract him."

He pushes the tire iron in my general direction.

I pick it up.

Staring at the tire iron in my hand, he says to me, "You know what to do with that. Now, go!" he whispers sharply. "Hide!"

Before RJ makes his presence known, I dart toward the pick-up truck wearing the head of a trucker with a scraggly beard and take cover the back tire.

As soon as RJ steps in front of Justin, I don't waste any-time.

I make my move.

"Where is she?" he asks Justin.

Resting against the tire, Justin looks up at RJ with a stupid expression on his face.

"Don't you act like you don't know what I'm talking about," RJ says, louder. "Where is she?"

Justin throws his head in a nod.

"Right behind you," I say to RJ before Justin can speak for me.

As RJ rotates around, I swing the tire iron as if I'm strik-ing a softball.

At the very last second, he throws up his hands and shouts out.

His arms only make it to his chest. Then, stiffen out-ward like a manikin. His word is completely cut off by the furious blow of the tire iron connecting with the side of his jaw. I hit RJ so hard that his entire jaw cracks and pops and shifts to the far corner of his face and nearly rips clean off.

With his jaw dangling from the side of his face, he comes at me with his arms erected outward like Frankenstein's monster. He tries to speak but cannot utter a word. His eyes are red and maddening, the eyes of a man who wants to kill me.

I do want comes natural. I defend myself.

I swing again, harder than the time before.

The tire iron connects directly with his right temple.

He immediately goes down. His legs start twitching.

Eventually, the twitching stops.

Justin crawls over to RJ.

Having watched many horror movies where the crazy killer or monster pops back up after being shot, stabbed, or even burned alive, I say to Justin, "Don't go near him!"

Justin leans closer.

He looks at me with a vacant expression. Then, leans closer to RJ. He places his ear over RJ's mouth. Then, he turns to me.

"I think you killed him," he says and crawls back to his car.

I scramble to Justin's car and search inside for a key.

Justin asks, "What you doing?"

"Trying to get the hell out of here," I say. "That's what I'm doing." A rage comes over me and for a moment, I want to scream at Justin to help instead of sitting there questioning me.

Justin manages to stand on his own. He wanders to the front of his crossover. Checks the hood.

"No point," he says, as I search for a key inside the car.

"What?"

I poke my head out, ready to scream.

"Battery's gone."

"Shit," I say, looking around. "Well, check other cars."

Justin follows my demands and starts looking through cars. I do the same as well. Some of the cars of push-starts, the newer models have had their GPS systems stripped out for obvious reasons. Some, like the older models, require a key. Which gives me a glimpse of hope.

"*Here,*" Justin calls out from inside a midnight blue Oldsmobile.

I run over to Justin. He's inside, trying to hotwire the car.

"You know what you're doing?" I ask.

"No," Justin says. "But I once saw a video on YouTube showing me how to hotwire a car. Seems pretty simple."

"And why exactly would you be watching videos on how to hotwire a car?"

Justin looks up at me. Then, he directs his attention on the two wires sticking out below the steering wheel.

"Forget I asked," I say.

Justin rubs the ends of the wires together.

The Oldsmobile suddenly starts up!

"You did it!"

"Told you," he says and looks back up at me.

We share eye contact.

"Well," he says, "you wanna get out of here or not?"

For a moment, dread comes over me.

I ask Justin, "What about RJ?"

"Who the hell is RJ?"

I turn to RJ, who's still lying motionless on the ground next to Justin's crossover, and as I turn back to Justin, I notice another car in the corner of my eye.

I start walking toward it.

Justin calls out from behind, "Where you going?"

"Just give me a sec, will you?"

He doesn't respond. Yet, he stands outside the Oldsmobile, waiting just as I asked him.

As I approach the familiar car, I realize it's Mom's same Star Cruz'R from the "Peace" symbol bumper sticker on the back of the car. I make my way to the Star Cruz'R. The windshield is missing. The left side of the car is dented up. As suspected, I find what remains of her on the front hood of the car. I don't want to look, but curiosity wins and forces me to look closer. It's her. Her hair is cov-

ered in dust, skin dark and decayed. The top of her forehead, which was once covered with deep lacerations that
hadn't properly healed, looks like wiry mesh. All the blood
gone from her warped face. Unlike the others, her head
leans slightly to the right on the edge of the hood. I can
hardly recognize her, but I know it's her.

I break down from the sight of Mom. She was down
here, I say to myself, all this time. All the looking, the
wondering, the guessing. All of the casseroles and cakes,
pop-ins by those tall strangers who often pitied me, the
expressionless men dressed in nice suits who showed me
emblems inside their wallets and asked me questions about
Mom, the hints of metal like some undiscovered spice on
their breath, then the constant hugs, the variety of perfume
and cologne that, at times, stung the insides of my nostrils,
the comforting touch of nana's silky hands rubbing mine
with a bar of soap before we sat down to eat together even
though I often pushed my food around the plate as if it was
the origins of an artist, then all of those half-hearted
thoughts and prayers, the blessings, sad faces followed by
involuntary shaking of the head, awkward silences and distant whisperings behind my back or from the farthest corner of the room, the worried faces, long days of watching
the kids play on streets from my window, longer nights of
watching the stars above from my sliver of roof and wondering if she was *still* out there, maybe watching me from the
stars, the light guiding me through darkness.

An entire childhood gone from my five-year-old eyes,
taken away from me, innocence erased like chalk.

I stand up from my kneeled position and open the
driver's side door. Faint smells bring back pieces of what
was lost so many years ago. A part of me knew that the
dust still existed in another realm like my own—that magic
and its holiest of powers—despite what the tall strangers
had told me, their truth, not mine.

I crawl over the center console, then lean over the backseat. I remember being right *here*, tucked in a fetal position
in the trunk, holding my breath and waiting for the mon-

sters to disappear. I step back outside and open up the back door.

As the memories start to come back to me, I open up the back compartment to the wheel well and find a miniature figurine inside. I grab the toy and pull it up to my face. *Ahkashi*. Who wasn't a man at all but a woman. An elf-like warrior who was the noblest of fighters, who wielded the ancient sword of Zenethica, who shot from a legendary arrow past down from her lost tribe, with the tips of her arrowheads so keen that they could cut through steel platted armor like butter. She was mine, I remember, all mine. While other girls my age were prancing around with new and hip Barbie dolls or clinging to Elmo, Ahkashi and I were going on journeys together, exploring the rocky depths of Naromon.

That day I slipped into the hole and safely hid inside the back of Mom's Star Cruz'R, I left Ahkashi behind to look after Mom, to watch over her, to protect her with her life, while I ran through the blackness to escape the monsters.

I remember slipping out of the back of the Star Cruz'R and running while the monsters chased after me. I ran out of instinct, didn't look back—not once—until I reached a massive drainage pipe along the runoff of a creek. I remember crawling out of the metal pipe, my feet sinking into prickly mud along a bank that was littered with trash and debris. I wandered through the woods, found a road, found civilization. By the time I got done wandering, a new day was upon me.

I never hated and at the same time, loved the sight of the sun as I did that day. It was Heaven *and* Hell. Life and Death. A five-year-old girl gone, erased, only to be replaced by a copy of a girl who was just trying to forget what had happened to her Mom in another life.

I break down again from the sight of the Ahkashi toy.

As I pocket the toy, a car pulls up behind me.

I turn around and see the Oldsmobile running good as new. The inside of the car is dark and I can't quite make out who's inside.

A feeling of dread quivers through my body, thinking maybe RJ is still alive and jawless with his tongue dangling like a necktie from the gorge of his face, and he's pissed off something awful by what I done to him and is ready to take me to not my final destination, but *our* final destination.

As I take step back toward the Star Cruz'R, Justin pokes his head out of the window.

"What you waiting on?" Justin chirps. "I'd like to get out of here while I'm still alive, if you know what I mean."

I'm relieved from the sight of Justin's face, as well as his voice.

I close the back door of the Star Cruz'R.

"You okay?"

"Yeah," I say, more confidently.

Before getting into the Oldsmobile, I fish through the glove compartment of the Star Cruz'R. I don't really feel like sorting through all of the contents inside. So, I end up removing the compartment and taking it along with me.

"What's that for?" he asks, as I place the compartment inside the backseat.

"Souvenir," I say behind Justin.

Justin points at the Star Cruz'R.

"You know that car?"

"Yeah" is all I give Justin. "Yeah" is, as of now, all he's entitled to. I don't explain anymore to Justin. Right now, I don't have to.

Since Justin hasn't fully regained his strength, he decides to switch seats with me. He slides over into the passenger seat, grimacing while doing so, as I take the command of the wheel.

I turn on the headlights and drive away.

🚗

AFTER what feels like an hour of driving through the cave, we finally arrive at two tunnels forking outward.

I stop the car at the fork in the dirt road.

Justin asks, "Which way?"

"Left," I say over some thought. "We go left."

DON'T @ ME

"You sure?"

"Yes."

It's fair to say Justin earns himself points by not questioning me as to how exactly I know my way around the place, of all the places, a motorized graveyard hidden underneath civilization, in the fumy darkness where the monsters dwell.

🚗

WE drive for another thirty minutes or so in tense silence before hitting a dead end at the end of the tunnel. Justin points out something strange about the wall in front of us.

"You notice how the wall looks different from the sides."

"Yeah," I say, looking closer. "It looks almost metal opposed to rock."

Justin suggests, "Try flipping on your high beams."

I switch on the high beams—or at least, I think I do—but the headlights don't change at all.

"What's this switch do?" Justin asks, pointing at a flip-knob along the dashboard.

He flips it anyway before I have a chance to figure out what it is.

All of a sudden, a bright light switches on inside the head ornament.

"That's cool yet creepy," Justin comments.

With the old and decrepit white-haired man's head displaying a stark orangish-reddish glow, beams of bright light shoot out from both the eyes and mouth. The extra light helps bring out the massive door in front of us.

"Watch the car," I say and step out.

I walk over to the metal door and try to remove the metal drop bar from the lock brackets.

Peering through the bright light, I shout out to Justin inside the car, "Give me a hand, will you?"

Justin exits and helps me with the drop bar. Once the bar is free, I slide open the door.

Daylight suddenly pours into the tunnel, temporarily blinding me.

I shield the afternoon sun with my hands.

Once my eyes adjust to the brightness, I look around an abandoned train yard covered in an overgrowth of weeds and vegetation and crumbled structures once decorated with graffiti. Now, all that remains are the faded tagging of old gang signs and twisted silhouettes of monsters. Scattered around are a variety of piles of rock and dirt with massive trenches that zigzag from the train yard.

From a distance, I spot several gutted out train cars.

I get back into the car and drive through the massive doorway.

"This is the old Cornershore Station," Justin points out, as he glances around the abandoned stretch of land. "I mean, this place is *at least* twenty miles outside of town."

Measuring my caution with Justin, I ask him how he knows about this place but soon realize after the question that I come off more suspicious of him than a person who is more so curious.

"I've heard rumors about this place," he says casually. "People used to say it was haunted. I'll admit I once went through a 'paranormal phase' where the idea of ghosts seemed way more practical than the reflection of light. Like I said," he turns to me, "a phase."

"Yeah," I say, taming my suspicion. "Guess we all go through them."

AFTER we drive away from Cornershore Station, we arrive at a locked gate at the end of a dirt road surrounding by weeds as tall as corn stalks. I grab the tire iron from the backseat and step out of the car.

After a good three to four whacks, the padlock breaks free from a rusty chain. I remove the broken padlock, as well as the chain from the chain link fence, and push the gate open.

Before getting back inside the car, I catch the head ornament in the corner of my eye and can't help but notice how it'd most likely gather unnecessary attention while driving on the main roads.

In a sudden fit of rage, I rip off the head from the hood of the car. Along the bare circular mount, electrical wires stick out like rogue hairs along the hood of the car.

Without wasting anymore time, I toss the head onto the ground. The head, as well as the light bulb inside it, goes rolling into the weeds alongside the road. I make sure to wipe my hands clean before getting back into the car.

🚗

ONCE inside the car, I turn to Justin.

I let out a sigh as if it's the end of a chapter in my life.

I ask Justin, "What now?"

"Well," he says, "first I'd like a change of clothes."

It's strange to say but I feel as if Justin has become my new partner in crime. Strangely, I don't want to take Justin back home to people who are worried about him, but I feel as if I need to ask him anyway.

So, I ask him, "You want me to take you home?"

He thinks about the answer. He *shouldn't*, but he does; in fact, he takes his time in his response.

"Not really," he says.

"Where do you wanna go?" I ask.

Somehow, Justin already knows where I'm going—or at least, whom I'm going after.

"I know where they took the others."

"What others?"

"You know, the prom kids," he says. "I overheard that Harold guy mention something about a place outside New York. A facility, I think."

"You know where in New York?"

"No," he says. "But I figure if we track down Harold, then we'll find the answers we're looking for. I want to go with you," he says, looking into my eyes, "if you don't mind. I mean, you saved my life back there. If it wasn't for you, my head would probably be—you know. So," Justin pauses, "I think helping you in whatever you need helping with is the least I can do." Before I consider his proposal, he throws in another remark: "—As long as it doesn't get me killed."

I say to him, "It could be dangerous, you know? Harold Roman is a powerful man who probably has the cops under his thumb."

"Then that's *exactly* why I wanna come with you," he says, more intensely.

"You sure?"

"Well, I think I need this just as much as you do. Yeah," he says. "I'm in."

I seal the deal with a handshake.

"I'm Squints, by the way."

"You're what?"

"Squints," I say. "That's what people call me. I never told you my name, I don't think."

"Squints, huh? I like it." He turns to me. "Justin."

"Yeah," I say. "I know. Your name's been all over the news."

"Has it, really?"

"Yeah."

"That's crazy."

"How so?"

"Well," he says, hanging his head. "I didn't think people cared about me."

I shrug.

"I care," I say to Justin.

He lifts up his head and smiles.

"Thanks," he says tearfully.

"But first," I say bluntly, "you definitely need to change clothes. No offense, but you smell like shit. Literally."

WE stop at a rundown gas station two towns away in the desert. Justin fills up the car while I run inside the convenient store and grab him a new pair of clothes, as well as hygienic supplies that he so desperately needs. When I take my items to the checkout counter, I notice the "CASH

ONLY" sign next to the register. Right then and there, I can't help but think of Bernie while looking over the sign as well as old clerk standing behind it. I think about the one day I asked Bernie why he hadn't changed anything about the car wash considering most car washes have all turned to kiosks machines, making it for a more convenient yet impersonal experience. He gave me a response like "If it's not broke, then why fix it" or something like that. I shake off the memory. The old clerk starts talking. He asks me how my day has gone so far. Where do I even begin? Even if I told him the truth, he'd think I was making up some ridiculous story to amuse him. My hesitation—or lack of answer—makes it clear for him.

I hand him money for the items.

Then, in return, he hands me change and places the items in a paper bag. He hands me the bag and says, "Sometimes, the answers are harder to put into words. Sometimes—not all the time, but sometimes—they're right under our noses."

I look down at the bag of items in my hands, smile at the kind clerk, and exit the convenient store.

On the way to the car, my mind starts to race.

I suddenly retrace a conversation Bernie and I shared. For whatever reason, I specifically remember the words he spoke to me: *"The body—male or female—is no different than a car. Every now and then, it's needs to be washed or given a tune-up."*

Then, I think about that homerun swing to RJ's jaw. The word he spoke—or better yet, screamed out— moments before I knocked his teeth from his mouth. It was the word *wait*, as if he wanted me to wait and hear what he had to say, to wait and listen before I reacted. He had killed Bernie. That, I am sure of. *But why?* I recall my first strange encounter with Bernie, his nosiness, then, several encounters later, opening up to him. During our conversation, I'd often see his hand partially hidden behind the countertop, as if his fingers were nestled on a button underneath, like a panic button or a switch.

Did I kill the wrong—

"Squints?" Justin says from the passenger side. "You okay?"

I shake away the thought.

"Yeah," I say and hand him the bag. "It's all I could find."

He pulls out a pair of mesh paints, as well as the red T-shirt with an animated car saying, *"Keep it rollin'!"*

"Fitting," he says, displaying the shirt for me.

Then, he goes through other items, like the butt cream and baby wipes.

He says, "You're a guardian angel, you know that?"

"Bathrooms are located behind the ice machine."

As Justin walks off, I stop him before he gets too far.

"Hey, Justin," I say.

He stops and turns around.

I ask Justin about the man who was talking with Harold when he was bound and if he was an older or younger man.

He says, "Older, why?"

"No particular reason," I say.

Justin turns back around and walks to the bathroom.

WHILE I'm sitting in the car waiting on Justin to change, I think about what Justin said to me not long ago, about tracking down Harold and then finding the answers we're looking for.

The answers.

I reach behind the seat and grab the glove compartment and pull it in front of my body. I search through old papers and receipts until I find an empty envelope with the word *Agency.* The first word before *Agency* is partially ripped away and I can only make out a couple of letters. I don't exactly know why, but I'm drawn to the envelope. I think maybe this is our first clue into finding Damianos, as well as the others who have been abducted—or as Justin put it, the "relevant ones."

Justin returns from the bathroom, looking new and hopefully, fresher, despite a serious infection that he might have. Which has me thinking that we may need to make another pit stop at an urgent care center along our journey.

He gets inside and sits in the passenger seat beside me.

"Better?"

"You have no idea," he says. "It took me forever trying to—"

"—Stop," I say abruptly. "That's a little too much information," I say to him, knowing exactly where he's going with the summary. I show Justin the envelope. "I think I may have an idea as to where we can start. Harold and my dad weren't just friends. They were partners."

"What? Like partner-partner?"

He taps the tips of his two index fingers together.

"No," I say before he can get any more ideas in his head. "Like business partners. You got a dirty mind, you know that?"

"I'm a guy," he says innocently.

I start up the car and shake my head.

"That's no excuse," I say and drive off.

Only a couple minutes into the drive, Justin turns to me as if he's had something on his mind for quite sometime.

"So, what are we going to do when we find Harold?" he asks me.

"*First*," I say, "we're going to find where he's hiding the missing people and *then* we're going to kill him."

"Wow," Justin says. "Just like that, huh?"

"Just like that. What do you think?"

"Sounds like a plan to me," Justin says after some thought.

As the sunset burns out behind us, Justin faces forward and gazes at the road fading into a distant twilight. After having emerged from a world of darkness, it's clear not only to Justin, but also to myself as to what awaits us on the other side of night.

And that alone is all worth the fight.

LUNA'S projected due date was the thirteenth of January, which was a Saturday.

Which meant Luna Salcedo could breathe a little bit easier knowing the *crazy* gene had possibly skipped a generation.

Ever since last June, Luna had the "big day" marked and highlighted on her calendar, had the date memorized like Jörg's nervous tick of cracking his jaw, had spoke often of the date, had considered naming the baby January, if it was a girl, and Cap—short for Capricorn—if it was a boy, had even brought up the subject of babies, particular *her* baby, in conversations with friends and family, even strangers, not to boast or brag but to remind herself of the life developing inside her and that one day, her "big day," she was going to bring new life into the world.

When the baby never arrived on the thirteenth, Luna started to freak, thinking maybe the baby wasn't ready to enter the world or there possibly something wrong with the baby or maybe its vital organs weren't fully developed or *maybe* there was a chance that her mother would find a way to haunt her from the grave.

The next Friday the thirteenth wasn't until September—another eight months away!

Then, two weeks after Luna's due date, all of her worries were put to rest. It was the last Sunday of January when she felt the life inside her trying to crawl out into the world.

The scene was like she had imagined for last few months when she started to show, except for one piece of the picture: Jörg.

He was nowhere to be found.

He was a ghost.

Horror ran through her mind and all Luna could think about on that Sunday afternoon was the worst possible scenario: Jörg was gone for good, "dipped" on her, ran off to Mexico where he'd assume his new identity under the name George Shilling.

One minute Luna was spending an afternoon at the Baby Emporium picking out onesies, pink for a girl and blue for a boy. The next minute, while placing the different onesies into the shopping cart, she felt contractions coming on. The contractions, however, were much different from before. They were shorter, tighter.

The baby was ready.

But Luna wasn't.

Neither was Jörg, so Luna thought.

As night fell, the scene was upon Luna: legs spread wide open, body sticky with sweat, every inch of her pushing while, at the same time, screaming at one of the nurses to contact Jörg once more on his cellular phone.

The nurse tried his cell—as she had been doing throughout the entire afternoon—even tried his office at work, but nothing. She left urgent messages on his voicemail.

At that moment, Jörg Schäfer had become of the most hated men in the world until he came barreling through the door.

"I'm here," he said, his labored breath helping to disguise his slurred words.

He was pale, had dark circles around his eyes. Luna, as well as everybody in the room, was aware that he was stoned out of his mind not only from his strung-out appearance, but also from the pungent smell he was giving off.

But he was there in one piece.

And it was Jörg's presence that had given Luna that final push to deliver her baby. . .

"*Girl*!" the obstetrician hollered out. "It's a baby girl!"

Jörg remained speechless.

Luna, crying.

Once the umbilical cord was cut and clamped near the navel, nurses cleaned the amniotic fluid from the baby and placed her against Luna's chest. The touch of skin-to-skin contact with her daughter filled Luna with emotion.

As Luna embraced her baby girl for the first time, all she could think about was where Jörg had been when she needed him the most.

HOURS passed.

Baby Girl Renata, now wrapped in a warm blanket, was sleeping soundlessly in Luna's arms. Jörg couldn't sleep a wink; in fact, he couldn't even sit still.

Being a diehard Cowboy's fan, he couldn't resist taking advantage of the opportunity at hand. Hoping—even praying to a merciful God—not to disturb Luna from her rest, he carefully grabbed the TV controller from the side railing, flipped on the TV mounted above, and made sure to keep his finger planted on the volume button in case the volume spiked.

Luna stirred in bed from the change in volume but remained in a rested state.

Once Jörg read the score of the big game, he nearly leaped from his seat. He grabbed the nearest pillow from the windowsill and pressed it over his mouth to muffle his excitement. It was the third quarter of Super Bowl XXX, and the Dallas Cowboys had a 20 to 7 lead over the Pittsburg Steelers.

The broadcast cut to a commercial for *Jimbo's Auto Parts*. Jörg couldn't help but turn up the volume.

On the TV, "Jumpin'" Jimbo himself was promoting his new auto parts store located a couple of miles away in the town of Monitack. Somehow, in the brief thirty-second TV spot, which had to cost at least a million dollars, Jumpin' Jimbo, who was doing exactly what his nickname suggested and jumping from one department of the store to another in a dizzying SERIES OF quick SHOTS, managed to squeeze in nearly every part of the automobile while, at the same time, going back and forth with a scraggly-looking customer who'd rather save the money by repairing his 1969 Volkswagen van himself than take it to a dealership where he'd pay an "arm and a leg." But "don't fret, Dude! Jumpin' Jimbo was here to save the day!" Jumpin' Jimbo supplied the customer with what he needed, brand new headlight, new radiator cap, new washer fluid—even had "his guy out back" handle the installation "FREE" of charge. The word *FREE* being used throughout the thirty-second TV spot. Once the Volkswagen was looking good as new, the exterior sparkling to a mirror-shine all thanks to a *FREE* car wash, the customer was on his way to explore the New Frontier. Together, they celebrated the newness of the customer's ride with a strange dance routine, which looked more like a refined shimmy, called "Da Whoop."

In the final three seconds of the TV spot, a voice over actor reading at lightning speed promoted a FREE "Monster Gulp" with a single purchase of a car part. And two purchases of car parts would get you a FREE submarine sandwich.

As the commercial ended, Jörg snapped from his trance and heard Luna stirring once more. Jörg rotated around and found Luna staring directly at him as if by him even having the audacity to turn on the television after she had given birth to their child was a mortal sin.

"Sorry," Jörg said, the color coming back to his face.

He immediately switched off the TV.

Through Luna's pounding stare, he could feel his body shrinking with embarrassment.

Trying not to wake Baby Renata, Luna asked, "Who's winning the game?"

Jörg waved his hand.

"It doesn't matter," he said and tended to Luna. "How you feeling?"

"I feel like I've just given birth," she said flatly.

A laugh slipped from Jörg's mouth. He kissed Luna on top of her forehead.

Silence formed between the two of them.

Luna asked the inevitable question: "Where were you?"

Jörg hung his head in shame.

"I'm sorry," he said. "I should've been there for you."

"That's twice you've apologized, Jörg."

"*But*, Luna, I'm here now and I'm not going anywhere."

Jörg sealed his answer with a promise.

As they embraced each other once more as a family, Jörg asked Luna if she was hungry.

"Starved" was her response.

"How about a sub?" Jörg suggested.

Luna smiled and responded, "You read my mind."

JÖRG found a sports bar called Wings and Things not too far from the hospital.

As Jörg was about to pull into the parking lot, he spotted the same place from the TV commercial—Jimbo's Auto Parts—across the street. He kept driving until he passed the auto store. Noticed it was still open. Which was a surprise because, except for sports bars or anything with the word *bar* in it, most of the businesses around here closed early on Sunday. He slowed down and peered inside. Above the front counter, he saw a TV playing.

On a whim, he pulled into the parking lot in front of Jimbo's Auto Parts. The parking lot was empty, except for a man—possible employee—wandering around inside.

For a minute, he waited in the back of the parking lot, contemplating whether or not to go inside. He thought more about the TV commercial, the *free* Monster Gulp, the *free* subs. After all, Jörg did need a new headlight. One was burned out and he was getting sick and tired of watching other drivers kiss their knuckles and punch the ceiling of their car as they mouthed the name "Popeye" for good luck every time he drove past them. Plus, since Jumpin' Jimbo himself claimed he not only sold auto parts, but also provided basic car maintenance, he thought he could use a new tire rotation.

Three birds, one stone, he thought.

With his mind made up, Jörg parked the car in front of Jimbo's. He checked the store hours on the front door. Then, checked the time on his wristwatch. The store closed in fifteen minutes. He didn't exactly know how much time it took to rotate tires, but he figured it'd take longer than fifteen minutes.

Jörg looked inside the store one last time before he decided it was best to wait till tomorrow.

As he was about to turn around, he saw the same man from earlier in the corner of his eye. Jörg directed his attention toward the man, as suspected, an employee, who was waving Jörg to enter the store.

The employee's aura was strange, Jörg noticed. He looked as if he wanted to help out Jörg with whatever he needed to make his car running "good as new."

Jörg opened the door.

"You opened?" he asked the employee.

"Come on in," the employee said gladly. "Welcome to Jimbo's."

"Yeah," Jörg said, making his way to the counter. "Hey. How's it going?"

"I can't complain. The boys are winning and I'd be ah-grinning."

"Go Cowboys," Jörg replied, the excitement drained from his voice.

He glanced up at the TV above the counter and saw that the game still on. It was halfway through the fourth and the Cowboys still had a commanding lead.

"So," the employee said, drying his hands with a rag that was too white to be found in an auto parts shop, which had a garage "out back."

"I need a new headlight for my car," Jörg said.

The employee pulled out a notepad from his breast pocket as if he was taking Jörg's food order.

"Left or right?"

Jörg paused for a moment and tried to make sense of the vague response.

"Right," he said aloud. "I mean, it's the left," Jörg suddenly clarified before the employee scribbled in his notepad. "The front left headlight."

"No problem," the employee followed before Jörg could finish the rest of his thought. "We got what you need."

"And a tire rotation," Jörg said unsurely, "if that's possible."

"Sure," the employee replied, not missing a beat.

"Is that it?"

"That should about do it," Jörg said.

"If that's it, then I'll get working on the tire rotation and by the time I'm finished, you should be back home before the end of the game."

"Sounds good."

"I just need your keys," the employee said.

"Of course," Jörg said and pulled out his car keys.

During the slow and tedious moments of the transaction, Jörg decided to pass the time by telling the employee about how nice the place was. Which wasn't all bullshit. Jörg was more than impressed by the various departments and how easily accessible they were. The automobile broken down into sections: tires, windshields, steering wheels, headlights, grills and grates, rims, mats, seats, stereo systems, and interfaces.

"Yep," the employee said, gazing around the store, "before James started to spitball names for the place, I told him he should call it 'Crapht,' but spelled with a *ph* instead of a *f*. You know, like ph-phat," he touched his belly, "*not* fat-fat."

"Not bad," Jörg said. "Catchy."

"That's what I thought," the employee said ecstatically. "But you know how it goes. Boss man has the final say-so. He's like a cat, you see—a really big cat with a big head—pissing on everything that belongs to him. But anyway. . . "

The thought came to him as soon as he handed the keys to the employee—Robbie—he said his name was; however, the name on his shirt read "Robert."

"I just remembered," Jörg said while following Robbie to his car parked outside, "I also saw in the commercial about some *free* sandwiches—"

"—Absolutely," Robbie said. "You saw that silly commercial? It was a trip, wasn't it?" He stopped in his tracks and pointed to a room, which looked like a luxurious waiting room, next to the tire department. "We got subs. We got Monster Gulps." He pointed at the TV above. "We got the big game playing. We got basically everything."

Not everything, Jörg thought to himself.

Robbie said jokingly, "All we need now is some women and we'd have ourselves a party. You know what I mean?"

"Yeah," Jörg said, his voice fading. "Sure."

Robbie waited for Jörg to expand on his response, possibly come back with a joke of his own, but when all he received in return was a cold "yeah" followed by a stingy "sure" that trailed off like a snake in the bushes, a darkness swelled over Robbie's face and everything about him was business-like.

"Well," he said, twirling Jörg's keys, "I'll get started on your car. And don't worry about the headlight. It's on the house."

"Really?"

"Just sit back, relax, enjoy the game," he said and pointed at the room next to the tire department, "and help yourself to one of our delicious Monster Gulps."

"Thanks," Jörg said, as Robbie stepped outside. He watched Robbie drive his car around the back of the store.

Impressed by the five-star customer service minus the poor humor, Jörg wandered back to the counter and watched the game from the smaller TV; however, he couldn't resist the food, the game being played on a much "bigger" screen, and he heard the slushy machine calling out his name. Not only that, he had a hungry momma waiting to bring her food.

Three birds, one stone, he remembered. *Two birds down.* One to go.

As Jörg arrived at the waiting room area next to the tire department, he came across a spread of sandwiches stacked like a pyramid on the marbled countertop, as well as a slushy machine with the decal of the scribbly, cartoonish word *MONSTER*. Jörg noticed yet another TV mounted in the upper corner of the room. Of course, the "big game" was on.

Feeling more at ease by the homey vibe, he grabbed a paper bag from a stack of paper bags that was at least two feet high and stuffed at least four six-inch subs into the bag. He picked from a variety, from turkey to roast beef, decided to give Luna a couple of options to choose from. Surprisingly, the sandwiches appeared remarkably fresh, the lettuce still crispy, tomatoes plump and juicy, meat faintly glistening from the fluorescent lights above.

To be on the safe side, he gave the meat a whiff. The smell alone caused his mouth to salivate and his stomach to rumble, as if it was a natural reaction. Jörg couldn't help but grab a ham sandwich for himself. He stopped at the condiment station and loaded up the sub with yellow mustard.

Next, Jörg paid a visit to the Monster Gulp machine. He grabbed himself a large cup nearly the size of a tub of popcorn. He took a moment to decide which flavor he was craving: Super-Duper Strawberry, Wonderful and Whacky Watermelon, Orange Shock, Electric Blueberry.

After a strenuous debate, he finally went with Electric Blueberry. Which was odd, to say the least, because he didn't care for blueberries. In fact, Jörg couldn't even remember the last time he ate blueberries. Maybe he was drawn to that one particular color, blue.

Jörg placed the Monster Gulp aside and searched for a cap, as well as a plastic straw. He went through the cabinets both above and below, but all he found were stacks of bags and extra large cups.

Eventually, after scanning the room, he found a couple of half-opened boxes stacked along the wall. Sure enough, inside the boxes were hundreds of unopened caps and straws.

THE game was over.

The Cowboys had claimed victory over the Steelers.

And Jörg, with his belly full, was beaming.

As he slurped down the last bit of his Monster Gulp and was tempted to refill his cup, he completely lost track of the time. For a moment, he almost forgot why he was sitting in a waiting room—the car!

He checked his wristwatch. Over thirty minutes had gone by, and his car still wasn't ready—*How long does it take to rotate tires?* He thought about the other times he got his tires rotated and it only took fifteen to twenty minutes. A strange feeling suddenly came over Jörg. A danger. Stranger danger. The food, all of the enticements, the friendly customer service at a particular time of night when most people wanted to go home and shelter themselves away from the outside world.

Most importantly, he thought about Luna, Renata, his baby girl. He saw himself from the outside. A man who somehow got sucked into a football game only hours after he had welcomed a new life into the world.

In a state of frenzy, Jörg grabbed his bags of sandwiches and tossed the Monster Gulp in the trash. He walked around the desolate store, calling out Robbie's name but only receiving the echo of his own voice.

By the time he made it to the garage toward the back of the store, the Monster Gulp was trying to run right through him. What made it even worse was that his car was still on the lift and Robbie was nowhere in sight.

A flash of anger came over Jörg and all he wanted to do right now was to pay the man for the job—or lack of job—and get back to the hospital where a starved Luna was waiting. The thought alone of the snarling witch Luna transformed into when she was hungry sent Jörg to a more frenzied state.

As Jörg called out to Robbie once more, Robbie appeared right behind him.

"I'm right here," he said casually. "Ain't a need to yell, man."

Startled, Jörg spun around.

"What's going on?" he asked, his tone clearly hostile.

"Sorry for the wait," he said and held up the wrench in his hand. "I couldn't find my wrench."

"Right," Jörg said, backing off. "Well, how much longer will it take?"

"The tire rotation should take no more than ten minutes."

This whole time, Jörg thought, *thirty minutes of looking for a wrench. What a bunch of bull! The man was probably off somewhere watching the game when he should've been working on my car.*

Despite the *free* food, the *free* Monster Gulp, the *free* labor, the thought alone caused Jörg's stomach to turn. The whole situation felt off, weird.

"You know, forget about it," Jörg said. "I can come back tomorrow when I have more time," he lied. "Just take my car down from there and I'll pay you for your trouble."

"Sure," Robbie said, more serious. "Just give me a couple of minutes, will you? And I'll have you back on the road."

With his bladder full, Jörg used his legs and walked in place to help ease the discomfort.

"By the way," he said, "where's your restroom?"

"We don't have one."

More anger flashed over Jörg.

"Serious?"

"Nah," Robbie said loosely. "Just messing with you." He pointed toward a hallway. "Down the hall. Second door on the right."

Jörg was so over Jimbo's Auto Parts, so over Robbie and his untimely sense of humor, ready to take empty his bladder and be done with this place. *The hell with Jumpin' Jimbo! What I'd like to do with that tire iron, you no good piece of shhh. . .*

Once Jörg entered the men's restroom, he expected to race to one of the urinals along the wall but there weren't any. For a moment, he thought he mistakenly entered the women's restroom. Jörg didn't care, though. He was about to piss his pants!

He rushed to the first stall he could find, entered, then closed the door behind him. He unloaded his bladder, as if he barely got through watching a three hour-long movie without taking any breaks.

Once he was all done and feeling much lighter, he heard a grating sound below him. He ignored the noise and reached over the seat to flush the toilet; however, as he was about to punch the handle, the noise intensified and caused him to freeze.

In a looming suspicion, he cautiously eased away from the toilet. He kneeled down and looked underneath the stall and checked the other stalls but all of them were empty—or at least, appeared to be.

The noise, he realized, which was coming from below his feet, sounded like a bunch of metal gears moving around followed by the *click-clank* cranking sound of what he could only imagine as a rollercoaster moving along a track.

Before he could rush from the stall, the floor suddenly opened up into a dark tunnel below him!

As Jörg fell into the tunnel, he violently smacked his chin on the edge of the toilet bowl. The upper part of his body bounced along the slick tile floor, as well as the sidewalls of the square-shaped tunnel. Somehow, he managed to grab hold of the floor with his right hand; however, the floor was so slick with piss and toilet water that his fingers slipped and his body plummeted into the dark hole.

Jörg screamed out in horror, but even the sound of his voice faded into darkness.

The disguised door along the floor closed, as if it was being controlled automatically.

And just like that. . .

```
HAROLD snaps his fingers together.
```

. . . Jörg was car parts.

```
Keen, glossy EYES brim with flickering waves of
fire.

EXT. CRAPHT'S AUTO PARTS - NIGHT - PRESENT DAY

A young black woman, SQUINTS, 19, stands at a safe
distance in the parking lot and with a vacant ex-
pression on her face, watches the flames devour
the entire store.
```

Squints (V.O): *Ever since I was a little girl, I always found comfort in fire. It always brought me a sense of calm yet, at the same time, a sense of delegation, as if fire was king, the ultimate one, and I was only its hallowed servant. Even on the cool, mundane spring nights whenever I'd stare at the flame of a lighter or watch inanimate objects burn, I felt inferior as soon as the heat pressed against my skin. Fire was life and death, savior and destroyer. And whenever it made its presence known, I was caught under its spell. The way it moved by unapologetically licking across everything it touched. Like a virus: spreading, infecting, consuming, corrupting.*

```
The flames SLOWLY rise to the ceiling of the
store, eating, consuming. A series of explosions
rip through the front aisle, causing the windows
to shatter. The flames spread to display shelves
of tires, turning the black smoke even blacker.
```

Eventually, the fire ran its course.

The letters HT in the showy sign CRAPHT fall from the facade of the store and crash into the fiery rumble below.

Squints hears the sounds of sirens coming from a distant highway.

> JUSTIN (O.S.)
> Time to split.

A shadowy-faced JUSTIN DEVOID, 28, wearing a hoody, and Squints, who is dressed in black as well, race to the Viper parked in the back of the lot. The two enter the sports car, Squints taking the wheel while Justin riding shotgun, and speed away before fire trucks arrive.

EXT. HIGHWAY, SOMEWHERE IN DESERT - NIGHT

The Viper ZOOMS past a gaudy billboard with the bold words:

WAKE ME TOMORROW

Submitted By
Anonymous

FADE IN:

EXT. CRAPHT'S AUTO PARTS - NIGHT

As the firefighters work on the raging fire with water hoses, ATHANOR DOWE, aka THE CLEANER, a middle-age man with shoulders as broad as a telephone pole, sporting a black cowboy hat, slips from the crowd of police officers to make a phone call away from all the commotion.

INT. MANHATTAN SUITE 101B, HIGH DISTRICT - SAME

Behind the window stands HAROLD ROMAN, early 50's, who is gazing out at the brilliant cityscape below.

The phone rings on the desk behind Harold. He answers the phone call and puts the caller on speaker.

INTERCUT - TELEPHONE CONVERSATION

> ATHANOR
> They've taken out another one.

> HAROLD
> Which one?

> ATHANOR
> The Monitack location.

> HAROLD
> Crapht.

> ATHANOR
> They're trying to send you a message. You know we can end this right here and right now, if we do it my way—

> HAROLD
> Your way is too messy, too many loose ends. Besides, the last thing I need right now is some bigheaded whistle-blower, like Cameron Dobbs, breathing down my neck. We know exactly where they're going next. Find them before they get there. Bring them to me. Can you handle that?

EXT. EXT. CRAPHT'S AUTO PARTS - CONTINUOUS

The SHERIFF approaches Athanor.

> ATHANOR
> I'm already on it.

> HAROLD (V.O.)
> And Dowe, don't do anything stupid.

Athanor hangs up the phone with Harold and nods at the sheriff.

> ATHANOR

Put out an APB on a black 2017 Car-
nelian Viper.

                    SHERIFF
On whose authority?

                    ATHANOR
The United States federal government.

INT. VIPER - NIGHT

Squints takes her eyes off the road and turns to a
quiet Justin.

                    SQUINTS
        Quiet much.

                    JUSTIN
        Just thinking, that's all.

                    SQUINTS
        About?

                    JUSTIN
        The future.

                    SQUINTS
        Future is overrated. All that mat-
        ters is the now. If we don't stop
        Roman, then there won't be any future
        left to salvage.

Justin lets out a sigh and readjusts himself.

                    JUSTIN
        What are you going to do when this is
        all over?

                    SQUINTS
            (drifting in thought)
        I guess I really haven't thought
        about it. You?

                    JUSTIN
        I dunno.
            (facing Squints)
        I'm just curious. What's driving
        you?

Squints smirks and glances down at the speedome-
ter.

                    SQUINTS
                 (sarcastically)
        A Carnelian Viper with a V-10 engine.
        That's what.

                    JUSTIN
        You know what I mean?   This.   What
        we're doing.   Why not go back to Do-
        ver and start a family?   Move on?   I
        mean, this can't all be just because
        of one guy you hardly even know.

                    SQUINTS
        Don't tell me who I know or don't
        know.

                    JUSTIN
        Sorry.   I didn't mean it like that—

                    SQUINTS
        And why are you doing this?   You
        could've just stayed in Dover.   But
        you didn't.

A tense silence swells over Squints and Justin.

                    SQUINTS
        When I was five years old, I was ter-
        rified of water.   Just the sight of
        water made me panic.   So, my mom felt
        the only way to curb my phobia was by
        treating it head-on.

INT. STOP N' SHOP CAR WASH - DAY - FLASHBACK

Squints's mom, TIARA, late 30's, drives the Star
Cruz'R into the car wash and stops the car once
the light turns RED.   Squints, 5, frantically
looks around at massive brushers alongside the
car.

                    SQUINTS
                 (frightened)
        Mom?

Tiara grabs her daughter by the hand.

                    TIARA
                 (calmly)
        Listen to me, Candace. Remember what
        I told you, about the world inside
        you?

                   SQUINTS
                (more frightened)
        Mom?

                    TIARA
        Whenever you feel sad or scared, you
        can go there.
                  (smiling)
        Free admission.

The water jets suddenly kick on, showering the car
in a gentle mist. Startled by the chaos around
her, Squints opens the passenger door and slips
out of the car.

                    TIARA
                 (reaching out)
        Candace! Wait!

BACK TO PRESENT DAY

                   SQUINTS
        I watched her fall into that trap un-
        derneath the car wash. The only rea-
        son why I wasn't in the car when she
        went under was because I freaked out.
        My jacket got caught in the door.
        After I freed myself, it was already
        too late. She had fallen in.
                  (shaking her head with disgust)
        A week later my father died in a car
        accident. Investigators said he had
        enough drugs and alcohol in his sys-
        tem to kill an elephant. Some even
        said he purposefully ran his car off
        the road because he was involved in
        my mom's disappearance.

                    JUSTIN
        What do you think really happened?

158

                    SQUINTS
I think my father found out about
Harold's dark secret. Threatened to
expose him. So, Harold went after
those closest to my father.

Justin pauses in thought. Looks at Squints with a
hard gaze.

                    JUSTIN
Did they ever find her body?

                    SQUINTS
No. Eventually, the case went cold.
A part of me went cold. I guess,
when you're that age, you'd do about
anything to forget the nightmare. So
I shut off, chose to block it out,
like it never happened, like it was
all in my head, like I never had a
mother or father. I needed to remember them. I have to remember in order to make things right.

                    JUSTIN
That was your mom back there in the
caves, wasn't it?

With tears brimming from her eyes, Squints struggles to nod her head.

                    JUSTIN
I didn't want to say anything earlier. But it makes sense now. I'm
sorry for your losses, Squints. Serious.

                    SQUINTS
                  (quietly)
          Thanks.

Squints wipes away the tears.

                    JUSTIN
                  (hesitates)
Why do you think Roman does it? I
mean, what does he get out of capturing people and doing whatever he
pleases to their bodies?

                       159

                    SQUINTS
                 (sniffling)
        Why do you think he does it?

                    JUSTIN
        Sick hobby spawned from a fucked up
        childhood. I dunno.

                    SQUINTS
        I have a theory that he only targets
        certain age groups during certain
        times. The year my mom disappeared,
        six other people, both men and women,
        all around same age, disappeared as
        well. I also think he's targeting
        those with a strong social media
        presence, like Damianos...
                 (turning to Justin)
        ...Like you.

                    JUSTIN
        I wouldn't exactly call my presence
        strong, but I'll admit I used to be
        online a lot.
                 (with air quotes)
        Used to.

                    SQUINTS
        And how's that working out for you,
        being offline?

                    JUSTIN
        Well...
                 (more seriously)
        ...I never would've met you.

        Squints glances at Justin, they share eye contact.
        Then, Squints directs her attention back toward
        the road.

                    JUSTIN
                 (awkwardly)
        Do you want me to drive?

                    SQUINTS
        No. I'm fine.

        EXT. PARADISE MOTEL - NIGHT

                      160

Waiting inside the parked Viper underneath the overhang in front of the main lobby, Squints watches Justin from her hunkered position in the driver's seat.

Biddable in manner, the old MOTEL CLERK turns his back on Justin, walks to a shelf behind the counter, and grabs a key from a wall of keys. Behind the clerk's back, Justin turns toward Squints's direction and barely able to control his enthusiasm, gives her a secretive thumbs-up below the check-in counter.

INT. ROOM 36 - NIGHT

Justin holds the door open for Squints, who creeps into the dimly lit room. As she wanders around the room, inspecting its cleanliness, Justin closes the door and switches on a table lamp.

> JUSTIN
> (nodding at the two beds)
> Least I won't have to sleep on the floor anymore.

Justin places the backpack on the bed closest to the door, as if he's already claimed his territory.

> SQUINTS
> Why'd you get two beds? You know we're tight on money.

> JUSTIN
> It's all good. The old man hooked me up, since they were out of single-bed rooms.

> SQUINTS
> (looking over the dresser)
> Whatever.

> JUSTIN
> Is this doable?

> SQUINTS
> (facing Justin)
> Doable.

More at ease, Justin grabs the remote from the nightstand and turns on the TV behind Squints. He flips through a couple of channels before he arrives at the news.

ON THE TV

Squints's face is plastered on the square box to the right of the news anchor's shoulder.

BACK TO SQUINTS

who remains in awe from a two-year old photo of her taken by her Uncle Jojo while she's painting a sea creature in her bedroom.

                    NEWS ANCHOR (O.S.)
          Still no sign of nineteen-year-old
          Candace Norwood.

                    JUSTIN
          Looks like you're now more popular
          than me.

                    SQUINTS
          Not funny.

                    JUSTIN
          Wasn't trying to be.

With the TV remote, Justin turns up the volume.

                    ANCHOR (on TV)
          The last known footage of Candace was
          taken at Stop N' Shop in Dover, Cali-
          fornia, where the remains of dozens
          of missing persons were discovered in
          a dungeon below a car wash in what
          has been dubbed by investigators as a
          bizarre Car Collection.

                    Squints
                 (overlapping)
          Can you change the channel please?

                    JUSTIN
          Sorry. Of course.

162

Justin immediately changes the channel to the show
FAMILY GUY. He places the TV remote on the nightstand, grabs the toothbrush from the side pocket
of the backpack, and brushes his teeth at the
sink.

                    JUSTIN
            (while brushing his teeth)
        I was thinking we'd go grab some bet-
        ter disguises tomorrow, now with your
        face being all over TV.

In the reflection of the mirror, Squints turns off
the TV. She proceeds to remove her shirt, then
bra. Bare-chested, she drops the shirt and bra on
the dresser.

Unaware of Squints approaching from behind, Justin
spits a mouthful of foamy toothpaste into the
sink.

                    JUSTIN
            (turning around)
        We can be like a modern day Bonnie
        and—

Inches away from Justin stands Squints, her breath
labored, her face serious, breasts exposed.

                JUSTIN (CONT'D)
            (confused)
        What you doing, Squints?

Squints leans in to kiss Justin. She plants a
soft peck on his lips; however, Justin doesn't attempt to kiss her back. Yet, he remains frozen.

                JUSTIN (CONT'D)
        Are you sure this is a good idea—

                    SQUINTS
        Shut up.

Once more, Squints kisses Justin. This time,
Justin throws his toothbrush aside and returns the
kiss.

Stumbling toward the closest bed near the sink,
both Squints and Justin passionately kiss while,

163

at the same time, remove the remaining articles of clothing from their bodies.

Once fully undressed, Squints slides both the pants and boxers from Justin's legs and flings them across the room. The boxers land on the top of the lamp, dimming the light in a strange reddish hue throughout ROOM 36.

Concealed inside the SMOKE DETECTOR on the ceiling above the door a camera privately records Squints and Justin.

INT. SURVEILLANCE ROOM - CONTINUOUS

Standing in front of a row of grainy TV monitors, the motel clerk watches Squints and Justin having sex in bed. He picks up the phone and makes a call to Harold.

> MOTEL CLERK
> Forgive me for disturbing you, sir. Normally, I wouldn't be calling you if it was important—

> HAROLD (V.O.)
> What do you have for me, Mr. Hardy?

> MOTEL CLERK
> Two kids. I've seen one of them on the news not too long ago. I think he might be one of yours.

> HAROLD (V.O.)
> Where are they now?

ON THE MONITOR

While kissing Squints's neck, Justin rolls on top of Squints and straddles her in a more dominant position.

BACK TO THE CLERK

who is anxiously biting the edge of his lip.

> MOTEL CLERK
> They're currently tied up at the moment, but they ain't going anywhere

for the night. That's for damn sure. What you want me to do?

The motel clerk turns his eyes to another MONITOR displaying a recording coming from yet another hidden camera inside the bathroom.

INT. BATHROOM, ROOM 36 - NIGHT

With her eyes closed and the top of her forehead pressed against the wall, Squints embraces the warm water against the back of her head. She lifts her head, allowing water to run down her face.

Squints turns off the shower faucet, opens the curtain, and steps out of the bathtub. She grabs a clean towel from the holder and dries off, starting with her body and then, lastly, her hair.

Once somewhat dry, Squints grabs a white Tee shirt resting on top of the toilet seat and throws it on.

As Squints is about to exit the bathroom, she notices an obvious structural flaw along the very base of the wall -- a two-inch gap separating the baseboard from the vinyl floor.

Exercising the utmost caution, she kneels down and runs fingers across the recess. More intrigued, she shifts her weight by leaning toward the wall. Part of the floor slightly dips down as if the integrity of the foundation has been compromised. Squints exits the bathroom where Justin is lying on the floor in front of the bed. The sight of Justin's peaceful state brings warmth to Squint's face. She walks over to him, slips underneath the wrinkled covers, and tries to rest without disturbing him.

Justin stirs, then lays on his back, his head turning to Squints.

                    JUSTIN
          You good?

                    SQUINTS

I'm great. I'd advise against taking
a shower, though. The floor looks
like it's about to collapse at any
moment.

                    JUSTIN
Really? Well, we'll be out of here
by morning.

Squints turns on her side until her body is
squared up against Justin. She runs her hand
across Justin's bare chest, playing with a small
patch of hair.

                    SQUINTS
I never imagined someone like you,
who acts like sex is the last thing
on his mind, having good moves in
bed.

                    JUSTIN
Well, maybe I'm <u>that good</u> at hiding
it.

                    SQUINTS
I was thinking, after this is all
over, if we're ever going to be able
to go back to our lives—

                    JUSTIN
I thought the future was overrated.

                    SQUINTS
It is, but sometimes, I think about
my future.
        (staring into Justin's eyes)
Our future.

                    JUSTIN
I guess all that matters is the now,
right?

Squints barely brings herself to nod. A calming
silence forms between the two, resulting in
Squints to rest her head along the side of
Justin's shoulder.

                    SQUINTS
                (over the silence)

Why'd you move to a small town like
Dover?

                    JUSTIN
School, remember?

                    SQUINTS
Yeah, but you could've gone anywhere.

                    JUSTIN
I guess I could. I guess I was—I
dunno...

Justin shakes away the thought. More concerned,
Squints lifts up her head from Justin's shoulder
and faces him.

                    SQUINTS
It was a girl, wasn't it? She
must've been the one—or at least what
you thought was the one.

                    JUSTIN
How come, of all the people I've ever
known, you're the only one who can
see right through me?

                    SQUINTS
                 (nonchalantly)
I didn't see you being good in bed.

Justin turns away from Squints's answer. She acknowledges a sudden change in his manner -- the
crinkle in his brow displaying a cloaked pensive-
ness.

                 SQUINTS (CONT'D)
So, what was her name?

                    JUSTIN
Grace.

                    SQUINTS
That's a lovely name. So, what was
it that Grace did that made you run
away from Seattle to Dover?

                    JUSTIN
                 (somberly)

167

I wasn't the one who was running. It was Grace. When we started to get serious, she got cold feet. One day, she tells me about a new job -- a curating job -- in New York City. At first, I thought she was just talking. Plus, she was close to her parents, who lived right outside Seattle. They were getting older, too, and I knew she'd never leave them to pursue some pipedream in New York City. But then I found out she wasn't <u>just</u> talking. My back was up against a wall. I had no other choice. So, I gave her an ultimatum.

                    SQUINTS
Which was?

                    JUSTIN
Either me or the job in New York. Clearly, she chose the job.

Squints sits upright on both of her elbows.

                    SQUINTS
Could you have gone to New York with her?

                    JUSTIN
I could, I guess. But I didn't want to be that pathetic guy who followed his girlfriend across the country.

                    SQUINTS
Justin, you <u>had</u> a choice. If you really did love her, you would've followed her wherever she went -- even in hell. Are you sure it was Grace who was scared? Or, was it you?

Teary-eyed, Justin rolls over on his side, turning his back to Squints. Ignoring his half-ass attempt at seclusion, Squints cozies up behind Justin and slips her arm around his side.

EXT. DOVER TOWN SQUARE - NIGHT - SQUINTS'S DREAM

Confused, Squints looks around a crowd of townspeople holding a vigil for the missing teen, DAMI-
ANOS PIPES, 18, wavy dark hair, soap opera-
handsome. Flickers of candlelight bring forth the
sullen, shadowy faces in the night darkness.
Shouldering through a sea of bodies, Squints makes
her way to the front of the Square. Her walk is
forced to a creep by the sight of a blonde haired
WOMAN, who is standing not too far away from Damianos's PARENTS, DAMIANOS'S MOTHER holding a framed
photograph of her son.

Intrigued by the back of the glowing mane of the
woman, Squints inches closer to her. She touches
the strangely still woman on the shoulder. Holding a candle in her palms, the woman mechanically
rotates around and faces Squints. The woman is
Squints!

Squints backpedals and as she rotates around to an
open space, the crowd is no longer standing there.
Instead, replaced by the crowd are dozens of cars,
all circled around her on a stage-like atmosphere.
The headlights are blazing, shining directly on
her like spotlights. Despite the constant revs of
engines, the cars remained without drivers; however, the only human features of the cars are the
severed heads mounted on the front grill.

Frightened, Squints searches for an escape, but
she's completely boxed in. One of the car doors
opens. A dark figure, a MAN, steps out of the
driver's seat and then, as he shuts the car door
behind him, Squints opens her eyes.

INT. ROOM 36 - DAY

Squints violently wakes up to the booming THUD of
a door closing behind her...

Startled, Squints throws out her hand across the
blanket, only to caress an empty space. The floor
CREAKS behind her. She arches her head upward and
finds a more upbeat Justin standing at the doorway
with a cup holder in his hands. In the cup
holder: two cups of coffee, two muffins, and a
bottle of orange juice.

                    JUSTIN

                    (jubilantly)
          Rise and shine.

                         SQUINTS
                    (rubbing her eyelids)
          What's this? Breakfast in bed?

                         JUSTIN
          I know how you like to put in your
          own sugar, so I just made it black.

Justin sets aside the cup holder on the dresser
and pulls out a handful of bags of sugar and mini-
cartons of cream from his pockets. He places the
sugar and cream on the dresser as well.

                         SQUINTS
          I'm that picky, huh?

With her eyes drifting toward the floor, Squints's
face melts into a vacant expression.

                         JUSTIN
          So, did you sleep well?

Squints snaps from her trance and looks up at
Justin.

                         SQUINTS
                    (hesitating)
          Yeah. I did. You?

                         JUSTIN
          Like a newborn baby.

                         SQUINTS
                    (standing to her feet)
          I'm sure you did.

Squints locates her underwear on the top of the
bed, which has been stripped of covers. She
dresses. Staggering at first, she eventually
makes her way over to Justin, who removes the cup
of coffee from the holder and places it on the
dresser.

As Squints removes the lid from the cup, Justin
holds up two muffins for Squints to pick from.

170

                         JUSTIN
            Apple or blueberry?

                         SQUINTS
                  (adding sugar into her coffee)
            Doesn't matter. You pick?

                         JUSTIN
            Apple it is.

Justin sets the apple muffin next to Squints's
coffee. Once Squints stirs the sugar and cream
into her coffee, she takes a bird-like sip. She
savors the sweetness.

                         SQUINTS
            Thanks.

                         JUSTIN
            You're very welcome.

EXT. ROOM 36 - DAY

Once dressed, Squints and Justin exit the room.
As Squints walks to the parked Viper while cautiously scanning the parking lot, Justin closes
the door to the motel room.

INT. MUSTANG - CONTINUOUS

From across the street, parked in the parking lot
of a rundown strip mall, Athanor stops combing the
thin strands of hair over the metal plate along
the side of his head and pulls his eyes from the
rear view mirror. He hones in on Squints and
Justin, who are playfully fighting over a set of
car keys.

Anthanor watches Squints burst out in laughter as
Justin tickles her side. Eventually, she gives
in, hands over the car keys, and lets Justin drive
for once.

The Viper drives away, and Athanor follows.

INT. D.J.'S FILL 'UR UP - DAY

Before Squints can open the door, Justin swoops in
at the last second and holds the door for her.

171

                    SQUINTS
Such a gentleman today, aren't you?

                    JUSTIN
                  (closely)
Well, maybe we should do what we did
last night in the motel more often.

                    SQUINTS
Don't push your luck, buddy boy.

Justin smiles off the remark. Squints walks to
the refrigerators in the back of the store while
Justin heads straight to the snack aisle.

                SQUINTS (CONT'D)
And remember, nothing with peanuts.

                    JUSTIN
      Yes, ma'am.

Squints grabs a couple of bottled waters, as well
as a grape and orange soda from the refrigerator.

Carrying a couple of dark chocolate bars in his
hand, Justin meets back up with Squints at the
front of the store where the two wait in a line in
front of the checkout counter.

                    JUSTIN
            (holding out his hand)
      I'll take those off your hands.

Squints smirks off Justin's niceness. He frees
one of her hands by wedging the two bottles of water underneath his armpit.

With Justin's right hand free, he drops his hand
by his side, grazing Squints's left hand. Without
her knowing, he slips his hand into hers. Squints
doesn't react to the gesture. Instead, she inter-
locks her fingers into his.

With only one customer left in front of them,
Squints and Justin shuffle closer to the checkout
counter.

While waiting in a comfortable silence, Squints
rotates around and looks over her shoulder where

                    172

Athanor is standing with a bag of sunflower seeds in his hand. Her eyes fall from his steely eyes and land on the gun handle protruding from his armpit.

Athanor
(nodding hello)

Ma'am.

Discreetly, Squints faces forward and removes her hand from Justin's just as the line moves forward. Both Squints and Justin place their items on the checkout counter.

JUSTIN

Twenty on Pump #7.

Justin pays for the items, as well as the gaso-line, while Squints glances over her shoulder one last time.

After the CLERK hands Justin his change, Squints and Justin make their way to the exit.

ATHANOR (O.S.)

Excuse me, ma'am.
(holding out a lighter)
Does this belong to you?

Squints pauses at the doorway, looks over the Zippo lighter with the blue dragon sticker in Athanor's hand, and with hesitation, walks toward him.

ATHANOR (CONT'D)

I believe you dropped it on the floor.

Athanor hands Squints the Zippo.

Squints
(timidly)

Thank you.

ATHANOR

Not a problem at all, ma'am.

EXT. D.J.'S FILL 'UR UP - DAY

Both Squints and Justin walk to the Viper parked next to Pump #7.

                    Justin
          You wanna drive?

Unresponsive to Justin's question, Squints remains
in a trance.

                    Justin
          Squints?

                    Squints
          No. You can drive.

                    Justin
          You sure?

Squints nods her head.

INT. VIPER - CONTINUOUS

Squints plumps herself down into the passenger
seat and places the Zippo lighter in the cup
holder. She stares at the lighter.

EXT. I-30 - NIGHT

The Viper speeds under the bridge where the Texas
state line ends and Arkansas begins.

INT. VIPER - CONTINUOUS

Behind the steering wheel, Squints glances in the
rear view mirror.

                    SQUINTS
                 (whispering)
          I sure am glad to be out of Texas.

With his eyes closed, Justin stirs from his sleep
in the passenger seat.

                    JUSTIN
                 (mumbling)
          What'd you say?

                    SQUINTS
          Nothing.

                    JUSTIN
          Just remember to stay off 30.

Squints passes a sign on the side of the road: "30 EAST." Her sweaty grip tightens over the steering wheel.

All of a sudden, the red and blue flashes of a dashboard-siren appear in the rear view mirror.

                    SQUINTS
        Shit.
                (nudging Justin's arm)
        Wake up.

Justin's eyes bolt open. Looking around in confusion, he sits upright in his seat.

                    JUSTIN
                (more aware)
        What is it?

                    SQUINTS
        Cops. What'd you want me to do?

More concerned for their safety, Justin turns his shoulder and watches the strange car closing in on the Viper.

                    JUSTIN
        Were you speeding?

                    SQUINTS (O.S.)
        No. I was going the speed limit.

With his eyes narrowed, Justin hones in on the car as it quickly approaches.

                    JUSTIN
        It doesn't look like a cop car.

                    SQUINTS
        What?

                    JUSTIN
                (facing forward)
        It's not a cop.

                    SQUINTS
        How'd you know?

Justin opens the glove compartment and grabs the
PISTOL from inside. Checks the magazine. Then,
the chamber. He snaps the magazine into the bottom of the pistol.

                    SQUINTS (CONT'D)
          What in the hell you doing?

                         JUSTIN
                    (more paranoid)
          It's not a cop—

                         SQUINTS
          —And what makes you so sure that it's
          not?

                         JUSTIN
          You really think Roman is going to
          let us anywhere near him? We knew
          this was going to happen at one point
          or another.

Squints glances in the rear view mirror. Red and
blue lights flash over her eyes. The car closes
in. Any closer, it'd ram the back of the Viper.

                    JUSTIN (CONT'D)
              (flipping off the SAFETY)
          Pull over.

Once more, Squints turns to the rear view mirror
and looks at the dark shadow behind the steering
wheel of the Mustang behind her.

                    JUSTIN (CONT'D)
          Don't worry. I got this, Squints.

After looking straight in Justin's eyes, Squints
finally pulls the car over on the side of the
road. She puts the gear in park but doesn't shut
off the car.

                         SQUINTS
              (staring in the side-view mirror)
          Where's the backup?

                         JUSTIN
          Exactly.

176

In their tense wait, Squints watches the driver
finally exit the Mustang. In the flickering
lights, she recognizes the cowboy hat, the brown
blazer, the face...

INT. D.J.'S FILL 'UR UP - DAY - FLASHBACK

Squints rotates around toward the stranger calling
out to her. Standing in the checkout line, Athanor holds out a Zippo lighter in his hand and
waits for Squints to fetch it from his grip.

INT. VIPER - NIGHT - PRESENT DAY

As Athanor cautiously approaches the side of the
Viper with his holster unbuttoned, Squints lets
out a gasp.

                    SQUINTS
          It's him.

Squints suddenly SLAMS the gear in drive.

                    JUSTIN
          Him who?

                    SQUINTS
          I can take him.

                    JUSTIN
          Wait!

Before Justin can take a shot at Athanor, Squints
SLAMS her foot against the gas pedal.

EXT. I-30 - CONTINUOUS

As the Viper skids away, Athanor withdraws the gun
from his shoulder holster and fires a couple of
rounds at the fleeing vehicle.

INT. VIPER - CONTINUOUS

Both Squints and Justin duck for cover as bullets
strike the back windshield, one bullet cutting the
rear view mirror in two.

                    JUSTIN
          Still think it's a cop?

Squints checks the rear view mirror, but she has no view for the glass is completely shattered.

> SQUINTS
> What's he doing now?

After the shooting stops, Justin shakes away the shards of glass from his hair, lifts up his head from behind the center console, and watches Athanor casually walk back to his car.

> JUSTIN
> He's getting back in the car.

EXT. I-30 - CONTINUOUS

The chase intensifies once Athanor catches back up with Squints and Justin. With Squints accelerating the Viper past eighty miles per hour, Athanor still manages to keep up with her.

Athanor BUMPS the back of the Viper's bumper, forcing Squints to readjust her grip along the steering wheel.

> SQUINTS
> Fuck! Can't you do something!

Justin rolls down the passenger's side window.

> JUSTIN
> Just keep it steady.

> SQUINTS
> I'm trying!

Squints accelerates once more, giving the Viper a little extra space from the Mustang. Justin leans his upper body out of the window and fires off a couple of rounds at the Mustang.

INT. MUSTANG - CONTINUOUS

With steering with his left hand, Athanor pulls out his gun and sticks the barrel into a bullet hole in the bottom of the windshield.

> ATHANOR
> Gotcha.

178

As Justin stops firing and leans back into the Viper, Athanor takes a shot. He only needs one shot. He's that good.

INT. VIPER - CONTINUOUS

Justin is shot in his right shoulder, forcing the pistol from his hand. As Justin hollers out in great agony, the pistol falls onto the highway and skips away.

> SQUINTS
> Are you hit?

Clutching his shoulder, Justin pulls away a palmful of blood. He looks over the blood in shock, then shows the blood to Squints.

> SQUINTS (CONT'D)
> (disappointedly)
> Damn it.

Squints turns her shoulder and watches the Mustang closing in once more.

> SQUINTS
> Buckle up!

With his left hand, Justin buckles his seat belt. Once Justin is secured in his seat, Squints SLAMS on the brakes.

EXT. I-30 - CONTINUOUS

The Mustang suddenly swerves around the Viper, forcing the Mustang to spin out. Athanor overcorrects. The Mustang ends up flipping over. Violently, the Mustang barrels off the highway, kicking up clouds of dust. Eventually, the Mustang comes to a halt upside down in a ditch.

INT. VIPER - CONTINUOUS

Justin peers out at the overturned Mustang fading off into the dark, cloudy highway behind them.

> JUSTIN
> Nice move!

179

INT. MUSTANG - CONTINUOUS

Seated upside down, Athanor smiles off Squints's
timely maneuver to shake him from her tail.

                    ATHANOR
          Bitch wants to play. Let's play.

Grimacing, Athanor pulls out a flip phone from his
pocket and dials a number.

                    FELIX (V.O.)
          Felix here.

                    ATHANOR
          Go to Plan B.

INT. VIPER - CONTINUOUS

Justin faces forward and looks over his gunshot
wound.

                    SQUINTS
          How bad is it?

Once the adrenaline wears off, the shock sets in
over Justin. His face goes pale and vacant.

                    JUSTIN
               (nursing his right arm)
          I've never been shot before.

                    SQUINTS
          You know you never struck me as the
          kind of guy who gets shot at often.

                    JUSTIN
               (jokingly)
          Not if you count Playstation.

Squints removes her flannel shirt from her body
and hands it to Justin.

                    SQUINTS
          Here. Use this to wrap around your
          arm. It should stop the bleeding.

In a last second decision, Squints takes a right
onto an off-ramp and once she reaches the end,

makes a left, then drives down a two-lane road
over 30-East and turns left into a spit of a town.

> JUSTIN
> Where you going?

> SQUINTS
> We have to get off the highway.

> JUSTIN
> I thought I told you to stay away from the
> main highways.

Squints looks at Justin with a scowl on her face.
Justin backs off and instead of arguing with
Squints, wraps the sleeves of the flannel shirt
around the wound. Tightens the shirt with a knot.

> JUSTIN
> So, who the fuck was that guy back
> there?

> SQUINTS
> I saw him back at the gas station
> when we were passing through Texas.
> I think he's been following us ever
> since.

Squints drives past a road sign: "OLD LIBERTY."
She makes a right onto AR-195.

> JUSTIN
> Fucking great. You think he's work-
> ing with Harold?

Squints doesn't respond, doesn't even move for
that matter.

> JUSTIN (CONT'D)
> Squints? What is it?

> SQUINTS
> You hear that?

Justin listens closer to the pulsating SOUNDS of a
helicopter flying above the Viper. Squints takes
her eyes off the road and peeks out the window.
Above the Viper, a helicopter is descending closer
to the road.

                    SQUINTS (CONT'D)
          Shit. I think it's him.

                        JUSTIN
          This guy doesn't stop, does he?

                       SQUINTS
          He won't stop until we're dead.

INT. HELICOPTER - CONTINUOUS

Athanor leans forward to the pilot, FELIX, 30's,
and taps him on the shoulder.

                       ATHANOR
          Get me as close as you can.

Felix returns by giving Athanor a thumbs-up.
Athanor turns to the person sitting next to him --
a bound ROSCOE DÍAZ, bloody and beaten, his mouth
wrapped in duct tape, arms tied behind his back.

                       ATHANOR
                      (grinning)
          Sit back and enjoy the show, hombre.

EXT. AR-195 - CONTINUOUS

The Viper speeds up and starts swerving from one
side of the road to another.

INT. VIPER - CONTINUOUS

With her hands loosening from the steering wheel,
Squints turns to Justin with a look of defeat on
her face.

INT. HELICOPTER - CONTINUOUS

As the helicopter descends just above the power
lines running along the side of the road, Athanor
aims the gun at the back left tire of the Viper.

                    SQUINTS (V.O.)
          If you had a chance to go back in the
          time to the moment after I found you
          below that car wash, would you have
          come with me?

INT. VIPER - CONTINUOUS

Squints glances over at Justin.

> SQUINTS (CONT'D)
> Or, would you have stayed back in Do-
> ver?

> JUSTIN
> You're asking me this now?

> SQUINTS
> Well, would you have come with me or
> not?

Justin looks into Squints's eyes and as he's about to answer Squints's question, a sudden gunshot from above RINGS out.

INT. HELICOPTER - CONTINUOUS

Athanor leans back in the passenger cabin and watches the back left tire of the Viper explode to shreds.

INT. VIPER - CONTINUOUS

Squints loses control of the car and ends up swerving off the road. The front end of the car strikes a telephone pole and ends up violently spinning out of control and onto its side.

INT. HELICOPTER - CONTINUOUS

Once more, Athanor taps Felix on the shoulder and motions downward.

> ATHANOR
> Set us down.

Felix nods his head and lands the helicopter in an open stretch of land next to the road.

EXT. AR-195 - CONTINUOUS

As the Viper starts to catch fire, Athanor steps out of the helicopter and walks toward the flaming Viper. The fire spreads to the engine and erupts in massive flames.

From a safe distance, Athanor inspects the damage.
He kneels down for a closer look, where he finds
both Squints and Justin dead inside, their bodies
burning in the fire.

Once Athanor confirms their deaths, he steps away
from the fire and spots a car slowly approaching.
He flags down the DRIVER, a middle-aged man, inside the car. The driver, in return, pulls up
next to Athanor.

                    DRIVER
          You a'ight, mister?

                    ATHANOR
          Yeah. Just fine.

Athanor pulls the gun from his holster.

                    ATHANOR (CONT'D)
          But I can't say the same about you.

Before the driver can react, Athanor shoots him
directly in the head. Then he OPENS the passenger
door to make it look like he had a passenger -- or
carjacker. He walks back to the helicopter and
drags out Roscoe from inside the cabin. He es-
corts Roscoe over to the flaming car and shoots
him in the side of the head.

Lastly, Athanor kneels down and places his gun in
Roscoe's hand. Once the scene is staged, Athanor
removes the duct tape, as well as the bounds from
Roscoe's face and wrists, and walks back to the
helicopter.

                    ATHANOR (CONT'D)
          Take me back to the wreckage.

                    FELIX
          You got it.

With the rotary blades blowing around the thick
black smoke spewing from the Viper, the helicopter
flies away into the night sky. From the cabin,
Athanor keenly watches the flames burn below.

As the fire continues to rage on and burn the Viper to a crisp, Squints's lifeless arm flops from

184

the window. Fire chews through the surface layer
of her skin -- the epidermis -- resiliently peeling away dark pigmentation, only to reveal the red
tissue underneath.

MATCH CUT:

WITH her chin and neck area caked with dried blood, Renata vacantly stared at the flames inside the fireplace.

She snapped from her hypnotized state that the fire had
left her in for the past twenty minutes and looked down at
her hands, which were spotted with shades of blood. The
notion alone of what she had recently done with her two
hands caused them to tremble, as if it was her own body's
reaction, the good that dwelled inside her informing her of
the shit she was in. Her hands still remained as evidence
for cops, detectives, investigators, anyone who would want
to analyze them and want to know what she was wearing—
or better yet, *who* she was wearing. Even though Renata
had run water over both her hands, the blood was still
there: speckles of it wedged underneath worn hangnails;
streaks of it outlined around her fingernails, as well as
tucked underneath the cuticles; red geometrical blotches
stained over parts of her skin like old ink. Her right hand
was red and swollen and incredibly sore, especially the
knuckles, which were no longer visible. Murder was the
only thought on her mind.

Flashes of red murder rose up inside her, as if the fire
had somehow tamed it, if only for a while. Renata urged to
move her eyes back to the fire and keep them there, on its
warmth and glow, to remedy the very act that she had
committed earlier that night. However, if Renata was going to make it out alive, she *had* to remember.

Hoping to bring forth anything that she might have forgotten, Renata moved her eyes back to her shaky hands:
both of them wrapped around Kira's neck like a ribbon.
The very last image that Renata remembered before
everything went gray and hazy were Kira's once-soulless
eyes and whatever entity that had a command over her finally escaping them. In that moment, Renata witnessed a

glimpse of her old friend and the life thriving inside her being turned off, as if it was being controlled by a switch.

Renata's chest tightened. She inhaled deeply and stared at the fire, hoping to drive the images away.

Another wave of panic came over her and choked any attempt she had at focusing in on anything but murder.

The once comforting warmth of the fire hit her with sudden heat flashes. The pinprick sensation of sweat poking at her skin flooded her mind with a collage of red murder.

While scrambling around the kitchen for the closest weapon, Kira grabbed a knife from the cutting board of already chopped herbs and vegetables and stabbed at Renata.

Suddenly, *Renata ducked.*

But *Kira kept attacking at Renata. Her face expressionless, eyes empty. Her tongue, different.*

Trying to rid the memory, Renata leaned forward in agony. She removed her head from her cupped hands and ran two fingers across the backside of both eyelids. The black mascara provocatively spread across the sides of her temples like Nike swooshes.

Choking and clawing, Renata wrestled Kira to the kitchen floor, wrestled the knife from Kira's grip, and while desperately pleading for Kira to stop fighting, accidentally cut her along the forearm deep enough to draw blood.

Pulling her hands from her face, Renata sat back upright and focused back on the fire.

During the struggle, the knife nicked Kira on a main artery on the side of her neck, causing the blood to squirt out.

Renata stood up from her seat and paced laps around the dark living room.

In the corner of her eye, a beam of headlights cut across the living room until the light came to rest along a picture frame of Kira and a group of coworkers who had spent the weekend at the cabin.

With caution, Renata walked to the window and saw Jevon's Beamer parked in the gravel driveway. She could breathe a little easier once she witnessed a tall and lanky, broad shouldered man stepping out of the car. She only knew of one man, who had shoulders like that, shoulders that could be easily mistaken for the shoulders of a highly trained swimmer.

Jevon locked his car with a beeper on his keychain and walked to the cabin where Renata was waiting for him as soon as he stepped onto the front porch.

Not bothering to flip on the light switch, Renata held the door open for Jevon. As soon as she closed the door behind Jevon, Jevon looked over the blood on her clothes, then the blood on her neck and face, as well as arms. He disregarded the blood and embraced Renata.

"I was worried sick about you," Jevon said over her shoulder.

Renata's eyes swelled with tears.

First, he heard the sniffles coming from below. Then, he felt a tiny vibration against his chest of what he realized was Renata crying. He held her tighter.

"Rennie," Jevon said in her ear, "you have absolutely nothing to worry about. We're going to get through this. . ."

The sound of Jevon's voice and the unusual softness in it caused her to break down even harder in his arms.

"I had no other choice, Jevon," Renata cried. "I tried to convince her to leave town, but she wouldn't listen to me. She was going to—"

Renata couldn't even speak the words.

Jevon escorted Renata back into the living room where he sat her down on a sofa across from the fireplace.

Once Renata calmed, Jevon asked Renata: "Where is she?"

Jevon leaned in closer to Renata's range of vision.

Her face was blank, the words not there.

"Rennie?" Jevon asked once more. "Where's the body?"

Renata continued to stare at the fire.

SIX MONTHS AGO

"IS anybody home, Renata?"

Renata snapped from her deep trance and pulled her eyes from a giant flame shooting up from the onion rings, which were arranged accordingly to showcase a flaming volcano on the surface of the teppan grill.

The chef began to juggle the spatula and fork, drawing awe among the guests seated around the grill. Following the trick, the chef tapped the utensils along the grill in a rhythmical fashion while, in between each beat, he spun the spatula between the prongs of the fork. He incorporated a knife, as well as a salt and pepper shaker, striking each one together, from top to bottom, from side to side, as if they were musical instruments used to season the vegetables by sound and rhythm.

Over the hypnotic *clink* of utensils, Kira called out Renata's name once more.

Renata acknowledged Kira, who was seated to the right of her.

"Yes?"

"Paul asked you a question."

To Renata's left was Paul Lauter, who, despite a few banal questions that one would receive by a teacher on the first day of preschool, had remained mostly absent throughout the night.

"I was just asking you where you're from?"

Renata, more or less, rolled her eyes toward Paul's general direction, as if she was forcing herself to look at him. She briefly acknowledged the question; however, most of her attention was focused on yet another flame igniting before her.

"Monitack originally," Renata said, as if she was speaking from the corner of her mouth. "But I was raised in Queens until I moved to Manhattan." More curious, she pointed at the flame and asked the chef, "How'd you do that?"

Paul backed away, his face red, his body shrinking in his seat.

"A little bit of oil and rum," the chef responded, a smile building behind his face. "*But* please," he said strictly to

Renata first, then to the others seated around her, "I wouldn't recommend trying it at home."

The comment drew a couple of laughs from the counter.

Besides Renata, Paul, Kira and her date Albert Nnadi, two other couples, one, the owner of the San Jose Marauders, Mory Foochs and his wife, retired fashion model and host of the TV show, *Skin Deep*, Vivian Klein, and the other, clothing designer, Claude Le Font, who were both good friends with Kira's uncle, Kin Nakamura, the owner of yaki, were seated at opposite ends of the counter.

Kira held up the glass of Naughty Empire pilsner and said loosely, "Leave it to the professionals, right?"

The chef acknowledged Kira's remark, forced a rather submissive smile onto his face, and moved onto the egg trick.

Captivated by the chef's skill in the blade and how, with any wrong move or slip-up, it could nick an artery or gauge an eyeball or, regardless, cause some serious damage if handled improperly, Renata was caught off guard by yet another question from her date.

"How about your parents?" asked Paul.

With her tone hovering along a sharp edge, she returned: "What about them?"

"What do they do for a living?"

The question immediately offended Renata; however, she tried her best not to show her resentment.

I've only known the guy for an hour and he wants to know my family history. She figured that Paul, being a data analyst for one of the most popular social media platforms on the Internet, should already know everything about her and then some. He probably even checked out Renata's meticulously "revised" profile before agreeing to go on the date, which had been all orchestrated by Kira.

Renata was tempted to return with a question of her own—in fact, the words were dangling on the edge of her tongue—"Why do you care, Paul From California?" Sorry, Silicon Valley! Renata wanted to wave a flag and say it proud and punctual, as if she was making it abundantly clear to Paul *From Silicon Valley* in her derisive tone that where an individual was "from" had absolutely no basis or bearing as to where an individual was "going" and Renata was destined to be going straight to the bar or, even better, the exit, if her date insisted on getting to the bottom of her origin story.

As the warm emotion rose inside her, the repercussions of any outburst would resonant well past the date.

She took a deep yet subtle breath, remembered to stay positive—*have fun*—and swallowed those ugly words, which were attempting to escape her head.

"*Not* they," Renata said. "Just my mother." Another guardian came to mind, the one who had looked after her for two years when she was between the ages of six and eight. "And my aunt, too," she said distantly, wondering whether or not she was revealing too much about herself to a man whom she met only one hour ago. She shortened her story and focused on her mother. "She worked two jobs, my mother, housecleaner during the day, janitor at night. Whenever I wasn't tagging along with her to work, I was probably spending most of my time with Elmo the Cat. Then, after we moved from Monitack to New York, she decided to finish up college and get a business degree. Now, she runs her own cleaning business."

"How about your father?" Paul asked. "So, what's his story?"

Renata repeated, "What's his story? Well, he has no story—at least, he was never a part of *my* story, if you know what I mean."

"Sorry," Paul stuttered, "I didn't mean—"

"—Mean what exactly," Renata said, her tone sharper. "You know what I mean."

These techy guys from Asshole Valley are so goddamn boring.

Paul looked over Renata in what she can only imagine resembling a life-size version of a sad emoji face—take that back, a sad face emoji with a tear drop.

Picking up the hostility in Renata's voice, Kira couldn't help but pull herself away from Albert and leaned in closer to Renata, as if she knew that specific tone, especially

when the subject of parents—in particularly the father figure—came up in a conversation.

With a half Elvis-like snarl of her lip, Kira nodded
across the dining room at the latest pop singer, the nineteen-year-old tween sensation, Mammilla, who, as of lately,
had recently been, as Kira rancorously put it, "literally"
everywhere: at the top of the Billboard charts; on front covers of *Vogue* and other magazines; all over TV, YouTube,
soda and makeup commercials; constantly "trending" on
Twitter; doing concerts for sellout crowds; who did *Saturday Night Live* last week.

Kira leaned in closer to Renata and pointed at the pop
singer, who was wearing her hair in an upright ponytail.
Mammilla was speaking caveman to her "hot" producers
and engineers and a PR team, dictating the conversation
while, at times, laughing so obnoxiously loud that the
guests, who were in town for a film festival, could hear her
on the other side of the restaurant—her vocabulary mostly
consisting of lots of "OMGs" or "LOLs" or "totallys" or
"fucks" and "shits" scattered in her text-heavy dialogue.

Kira whispered in Renata's ear, "I think that ponytail is
cutting off the blood to her brain."

The comment drew a snicker from Renata.

Kira said over Renata's laugh, "Care to join me in the
ladies room?"

"Hell yes," Renata whispered sourly in Kira's ear.

In return, Kira broadcasted to both Paul and Albert
that the two ladies had to "freshen up" and excused themselves from the dining area.

ON the way the ladies room, both Kira and Renata passed
the ever so famous, Instagram-friendly, twenty-foot tall
bronze statue of the ferocious-looking, mutative dragon,
ikay, which was created by Newbay native, Earl Lake.
Yaki happened to be one of the hottest locations for every
tourist who ever visited New York City, not only for its tep-
panyaki cuisine or the dazzling performances of each

remarkably talented chef who prepared each meal in front of guests, but also for the statue of ikay himself.

Standing on the edge of the tongue of yet another more skeletal, more alien dragon emerging from the other dragon's jaw, which had been stretched open in a gaping yawn as if it was about to shoot out a massive fireball, was a boy holding a flaming torch in one hand while, with his other hand, which appeared skeletal, he was bracing himself against a tooth the size of a street cone. Tourists even had to make reservations way ahead of time—three to four months was the average wait. Some came to yaki to dine while others came for their own personal gratification to snap a selfie of themselves standing in front of the boy, the Great and Powerful ikay, who had, over the years, taken on an open-world lure with comics, movies, and video games, bursting open the door for imaginative minds to decipher each detail of its intricate design.

Having visited the restaurant twice, once with her mother when she was a girl and another with a once-respected boyfriend whom she ended up dumping after she walked in on him making love to his laptop, Renata couldn't help but stop and admire ikay and its mystical, yet theme park-like vibe. Even though she now felt as if the statue was, more or less, an elaborate candle, the sight of it brought back a wave of nostalgia.

As Kira unknowingly proceeded ahead of Renata, walked past the kitchens, and headed toward the restrooms, she bumped into Kin, who nearly spilled a cup of green tea all over his seven thousand dollar blue ombre plaid two-piece suit.

Renata turned to the commotion to the far right of her.

Kin recoiled with exaggerated surprise and removed the white clout goggles, which were once made popular by Kurt Cobain, from his face.

"Kira, my dear," he said, his voice high and gay. "I wasn't expecting you till later this evening."

Renata overhead Kira: "Albert mentioned something about heading over to NoMo afterwards for drinks."

Hesitant to meet Kira's uncle whom Kira had talked so much about—all in the highest honor—Renata walked over and joined Kira and her jovial uncle.

"Kin," Kira said with her arms held outward as if she was showcasing Renata to her uncle, "this is Renata Salcedo. She works with me at CC."

"Is that so?" Kin said, stepping closer to Renata. He folded his sunglasses in his breast pocket and held out a limp hand for Renata. For a moment, she didn't know whether to shake it, as in what most humans do, or kiss the top of it, as if it belonged to royalty. "It's always a pleasure to meet Kira's friends," he said.

Renata bowed slightly as she shook Kin's hand.

"How do you do, Ms. Salcedo?"

"I'm good," Renata said, glancing around at the Japanese decor. "You know, this is a nice place you got here. I can remember the last time I was here like—"

"Why thank you, sweetie," Kin interrupted right before Renata had a chance to share a story about her last visit to yaki—which was actually quite an interesting story about her boyfriend's sleeve getting caught on fire while trying to interfere with the chef's trick. "I would love to chat with you, but apparently, the legendary, Gary Worthington, is in the building and I'm dying to hear what he's been up to."

"Why does that name sound familiar?" Renata asked Kira.

"*The* Gary Worthington," she said. "Artist turned survivor turned *New York Times* #1 Best-Seller. After his bestselling novel, *Unfollowed*, was turned into a major blockbuster, he launched his career in what was known as one of the most epic comebacks of all time."

"I think I remember," Renata said, thinking. "He was a victim of The Snipper, right?"

"Ah-*yeah*," Kira said. "The man had his tongue literally cut off and lived to tell his story."

"So poetic yet so heroic," Kin said to himself, as he drifted off for a moment, as if the thought alone of Gary's touching story always forced himself into a state of deep thought. He pulled his attention back to Kira. "Anyway, gotta jam." He kissed his niece on the cheek, said his see-ya-laters to her, and once more, shook Renata's hand on his way to the main dining room. "Nice meeting you, Ms. Sal-cedo."

"Nice meeting you, Mr. Nakamura," she said after Kin had already thrown on his shades and sashayed away. Overwhelmed by her uncle's energy, she turned to Kira. "Your uncle sounds like a busy man."

"I don't see how he does it," Kira returned. "Rubbing shoulders with celebrities everyday, running into movie stars like it's no different than catching up with old friends. Me," she said, closer, "I get terrified every time I come here because I know I'm going to see someone famous."

"You know, I was wondering why you looked so ravishing tonight," Renata teased. "Expecting to run into Casa Blacka?"

"You know I don't dig that fool's music?"

"*But* you dig him."

Kira paused.

"Only his body," he said over the gap of silence.

Then, Kira flippantly laughed off her secret crush on the up and coming R&B singer known as Casa Blacka and continued toward to the ladies room.

Renata followed.

WHILE wiping away the smudge of mauve lipstick off her two front teeth with the corner of a paper towel, Renata couldn't help but listen in on Kira in the stall behind her. Just when Renata thought Kira would stop, she kept going and going.

Kira flushed the toilet—finally—slid open the powder-coated glass door, and exited the stall. She looked down and made sure her skirt was "straight," and then moved her eyes to Renata's reflection before her. Renata didn't realize it, but she was staring at Kira.

In return, Kira arched her shoulders upright and said, "What?"

"Nothing," Renata said, turning her attention back to her own reflection.

Kira joined Renata at the white marble vanity.

"I swear beer makes me piss like a racehorse," Kira stated the obvious, as she held her hand next the sensor underneath to the faucet.

"Kira Nakamura," Renata said, her tone drawn out, as if the use of such language in such a fancy place was considered inappropriate.

"What?"

"I can tell," Renata said back and grabbed a paper towel from an arrangement of expensive oils and lotions and handed it to Kira.

"Nosy much," Kira said, grinning.

Renata fell silent not from Kira's remark, but from something else, something that had been on her mind ever since she left the dining area.

"So, what do you think of Paul so far?" Kira asked.

Renata found herself rolling her eyes. Her lack of answer was more than the answer itself.

"Forget I asked," Kira said, tossing the crumbled up paper tower in the trashcan.

Renata followed with a series of questions: "So, what about you and Albert? You think he has potential?"

"Potential for what?"

"Boyfriend."

"Girl, please," Kira said sassily. "It's coming up on two weeks. You know I am incapable of holding a productive relationship longer than three weeks." She paused as she pulled out the tube of lipstick from her purse. "Abiola is a sweet guy and all, but sweet only goes so far."

"If I recall correctly, didn't I hear him mention something about you two going to Barbados for the weekend?"

Kira shrugged.

"Yeah, but I dunno."

"Barbados, Kira," Renata said louder.

"Yeah, so what?"

"Are you serious? I'd kill someone to go to Barbados."

Kira let out a mousy noise from her mouth.

"I'm jealous," Renata said over Kira's sudden quietness. "Me, I wish I could travel around the world one day, explore exotic locations, but Je. . . "

Renata stopped halfway through his name.

"But?"

All of a sudden, her skin flushed. She struggled to look Kira in the eyes. For a moment, she thought her cover was blown.

Renata retracted her thoughts.

"Too busy, I guess," she muttered.

Quietly, Renata directed her attention back to the mirror.

Kira furrowed her brow from Renata's strange behavior and reapplied a layer of scarlet red lipstick. During the smooth stroke, she shot short glances at Renata in the mirror. Then, she moved onto her hair, primped hastily yet strategically, as if she was searching for not a new look but the right look. Once more, she caught Renata in the corner of her eye. Kira stopped primping, stopped making adjustments.

Thoughtfully, Kira faced Renata, who was smoothing out a wrinkle along the top of her silk pale blue halter top.

Renata turned to Kira's reflection, then Kira herself.

She waited in limbo for a reaction from Kira.

"Can I ask you something personal, Renata?" Kira asked heavily.

Renata furrowed her brow.

"Sure," she said hesitantly. "Okay."

Kira asked bluntly, "What happened to him?"

"What happened to *who*?"

"Your father," Kira said. "Was that really true what you said to Paul?"

Renata didn't immediately respond. Yet, she let the question marinate for a moment.

Kira dipped her head downward.

"You know," she said, looking up at Renata, "I lost my father when I was just a young girl."

Kira's words rippled through Renata, drawing her full attention.

"I'm sorry to hear," she said.

"Don't be," Kira said abruptly, as if she already knew Renata's response before it even left her mouth. "It was ages ago."

Another silence fell between them, a deeper silence, as if Kira had given the floor to Renata.

Unsure whether or not to share with Kira, Renata brought herself back to the gray days when she'd accidentally walk in on her mother embracing an old letter written by a man who was shrouded by conflicting stories.

"He left when I was born," Renata finally said, her tone way more subdued, "at least, that's what everybody said, but, I dunno. My mother was—and still is— convinced that he never abandoned us or 'ran away,' which was what everybody was telling her. She was so convinced that something awful had happened to him that she even hired a private investigator to help track him down, but, after years of investigation, nothing panned out. Sometimes," Renata hung her head in similar fashion to Kira and then raised it, "I dunno," she said, looking directly into Kira's eyes, "I think maybe he's still out there, perhaps he has another family, a daughter maybe. I sometimes think about what that conversation would be like if I ever ran into him one day. All those times I needed him when he wasn't there for me. The times I needed the guidance. The times when I felt all alone or cast aside, as if I was the 'thing' that often got talked about whenever I wasn't in the same room, the mistake. Mostly, I think about the times I cursed that man without even knowing him. He was only one man, and yet he was a million different people in my mind. *But*," she paused, her eyes watery, "at least I had Elmo, though. God didn't take him away."

"Must've been some cat," Kira said jokingly. Then, leaned in and followed: "I have good ears. They're only good for one thing."

Renata looked downward at the sink and forced out a tight, unraveling laugh, which helped loosened up the tension that the night had brought her. In that globe of silence, Kira's focus wasn't drawn to the laugh but to the laugher. She soberly studied Renata, who had the profile of a falcon. With her steady eyes, Kira traced the shape of her face and the last bits of laugher trailing out and bringing about a glow in her face that had been dimmed all night by the dullness of Paul's abysmal conversational skills.

"Listen, Renata," Kira said patiently, as she took one step closer to Renata, "I know these past couple of weeks have been tough at Carla and Corvine—I mean, I think everybody at the agency is freaked out about the new launch and you certainly shouldn't be the one to feel the brunt of everybody's frustration. I have this cabin—well, it's not my cabin. My mother looked after the cabin after my father died. Then, when she got sick, she handed it down to me. It's become sort of like this family heirloom. Whenever you feel like it, Renata, the cabin is yours."

Renata tilted her head in confusion.

"What are you saying?"

"I'm saying, whenever you're feeling like you want to *murder* somebody and you're dying to go somewhere for the weekend, even week, or whatever, just let me know and the keys to the cabin are yours."

Renata mulled over Kira's offer.

"Whenever I'm feeling frustrated with work," Kira said, "I go to the cabin for a weekend and then, when I come back, it's as if all that negativity washes away."

Renata hesitated.

"I don't know what to say," she said.

Kira's face formed into a part smile, part frown.

"Just say 'thank you.'"

"Of course," Renata leaned in and hugged Kira, "Thank you."

She couldn't help but turn her gaze toward the mirror behind Kira's shoulder.

PRESENT DAY

WITH her head down, Renata stood in front of the bathroom mirror.

She could barely bring herself to look at herself in the mirror.

With her trembling hand, she turned on the faucet.

She leaned forward and splashed her face with cool water.

Finally, she moved her eyes up at the mirror and in horror, watched the wet, red blood run down her face like a crimson mask.

The sound of two hard *knocks* on the bathroom door pulled Renata's attention away from herself and the horror.

Standing in a loud, humming silence, she listened closely for another knock but instead heard a voice.

"*Rennie*," Jevon said from behind the door, "you good?"

Renata didn't respond. She didn't know how to respond to the question.

"Rennie?"

The doorknob twisted in a clockwise direction.

"Yes, Jevon," she snapped over the running water. "Good."

As she turned off the water, her eyes caught the needle mark on her forearm and the infection starting to spread around it. She poked at the swollen red dot on her arm and recoiled in pain.

She was pulled away from the strange marking by the sound of Jevon's back sliding against the other side of the door. A shadow was plumped underneath that narrow slit of the doorway. Next, she heard the sound of metal jiggling together. In all probability, it was Jevon readjusting the metal band of his wristwatch. But, in that moment, the sound of metal, whether it be a *jingle* or a *clink* or *clank* or the sharp *shing*-sound that a blade made whenever removed from a sheath, triggered a lost memory, like one from a dream or bad nightmare, one that shared the characterstics of reality. She lifted up a worn Tee shirt of the pale face of a silicon creature from the hit manga series, *BLAME!* The shirt was old, the lost remnants cast from Kira's tweens. Renata specifically recalled her mentioning something about keeping the clothes at the cabin for, more or less, sentimental value. But it wasn't the Tee shirt that Renata was most worried about. It was that stab wound underneath the shirt—or *lack* of stab wound. She touched her belly, then ran her hand across her belly, but couldn't find a single mark on her skin, not one!

Renata ignored the infection, ignored the actual thought of being stabbed, and took a seat on the edge of the toilet.

From the other side of the door, Jevon asked Renata, "Did I ever tell you that I, too, lost someone close to me?"

Jevon didn't expect any answer in return and that was exactly what he got, a wall of silence and the subtle movements of a slender shadow moving below him.

"His name was Richard," Jevon said with his back pressed against the bathroom door. "Filthy Rich was what people who knew him well called him because he was born with a silver spoon in his mouth, basically had everything any person could ask for handed down to him. He preferred to go by Ricky better than Filthy Rich; in fact, he hated that name. One night, I met Ricky at a bar, which sat in the shadows of Dunmire Stadium, called The Bucket. He was doing a show at a local theatre outside Tucker's Ridge. He created marionettes and put on these 'grandiose' plays all by himself. I swear he was something else. For years, he had been putting together this entire world of characters, all marionettes, all with a specific trait and background, until one day he finally reached a point in his life where he no longer wanted to look at what he was creating as a mere hobby. So he went on the road, conducted different shows with the marionettes. Ricky didn't make a lot of money, didn't draw much of an audience either, but I believe he was happy at what he was doing. That night, we exchanged phone numbers. I met up with him in Hamshaw, a small town outside Nashville. The more I got to know Ricky, the more I realized Ricky was hiding something from me—*a darkness*. He was the type of person who didn't want people thinking he had money or had come from money. I figured he was embarrassed by the notion of having a much bigger bank account than an average nine-to-fiver who made enough money in a workday than Ricky brought home from a show. He was quite an interesting individual, Ricky was. *But* he had demons. And Ricky battled those demons with drugs and alcohol. I didn't realize—at least, not until much later—he was in pain. He was suffering." Renata could hear the pain in his voice, then a sigh. "The man probably lived eight lives before I even met him. Burning through enough money to build an island. By the time I intervened and got him the help he deserved, it was already too late. The damage he had done to his body was irreparable. His liver was shot. He needed a new one. Doctors were astonished he was still alive. But, being the rich kid he was, he figured he'd just buy himself a new one. He assumed he'd be a high priority. *Nope.* He had to get in line like everybody else."

Silence built behind the door.

Renata was tempted to speak, even open her mouth.

Jevon cleared his throat.

Spoke.

"I think the last few months after he cleaned up—before everything turned to shit—were probably some of the best moments of my life. I started to understand more about Ricky and why he went down the road he did. You see, he never told his parents about his personal life. He told me that they'd disown him if they ever found out about him. Which meant they would cut him off financially, emotionally—"

His words got to Renata. Words that were often spoken to her as a child being raised by a devote Catholic who held the word of God above everything else.

With both hands, she tightly covered her mouth in order to smother the sobbing.

"—But this sort of 'fearful' mindset wasn't only created by his parents alone. It was society, religion. It was everything and everyone who pointed at Ricky and said, 'No. *You're not allowed to be that way. You have to be like us. You have to be normal.'* I haven't loathed such a word as I did after I met Ricky. He hid from society because society was told to shun people like Ricky. Society was forced to look at Ricky differently because he was different from everybody else. When he should've been looking at who he was as a good thing—perhaps his greatest quality—Ricky only saw it as a bad thing. 'Evil,' some would even say. Me, having lived in the metropolitans for most of my life, I didn't have it nearly as rough as Ricky. The bullying. The hazing. *The rejection.* There were a few who messed with me when I was younger. But mostly just name-calling. Which I could handle. So, even up until the very end, Ricky continued to live a lie. I saw his parents at the hospital. Whenever I would visit, I'd have to wait until his parents left before I could see him. There was this one time when I showed up in his room. I thought his parents had gone; but surprise, surprise they were downstairs grabbing a bite to eat in the cafeteria. When they saw me in the room with their son, I think they knew who I was to Ricky. I could see the disappointment filling their eyes, *the tragedy.* His parents knew all along about their son and yet, they spent years rejecting the idea like a body trying to naturally rid a virus. If there was one thing they couldn't take away from their son, it was his bond with me. The connection. Together, we ruled the world, showed it how it could be. We created memories, memories that will stay with me till the day I die. . . At the end, when Ricky was all doped up, he wasn't making any sense whatsoever. In a way, he didn't have to say anything at all to me. He didn't have to make sense. Our connection had already been forged by the roads we took in life. Two roads that lead us together. And one that showed us a glimpse of life without *fear* or judgment."

A memory flashed inside Jevon's mind: the moment he first met Ricky at the bar, his head slowly turning toward Jevon while he continued to laugh at a joke he cracked with the bartender. The image of a sickly Ricky lying in the hospital bed crept back in. But it was that other image, the one image with Ricky sitting at the bar and laughing, that painted over Ricky's final moments.

"It's the bond," Jevon said, "that connection, the one that will unite us rather than divide us, that Carla and Corvine is trying to take away from us. Imagine a world without connection, Renata. A cold and dark world constantly plugged in, manipulated by powers beyond our control and those whose greatest profit comes from driving a stake in the heart of civilization. We need that 'connection' in order to survive as a species, otherwise, all will be lost in the darkness."

The bathroom door *finally* cracked open, startling Jevon.

A sword of bright light shone over the right side of his body.

"Renata?"

"Hey," she said flatly.

Standing to his feet, Jevon replied, "Hey."

The two stood in the doorway and stared at each other.

Jevon finally broke through the silence.

"Listen, Rennie—"

"—Forget it," she interrupted. "Let's get this over with, shall we?"

"Of course."

JEVON walked with Renata to her navy blue Ford Taurus, which was located at the side of the cabin.

When they arrived at back of the car, Renata stepped aside and without uttering a single word, maintained a clear understanding as to who was going to open the trunk.

Jevon sighed, snatched the car keys from Renata's hand, and inserted the key into the lock.

Before he opened the trunk, he turned to Renata.

"I'm aware you might've been close to her, Renata," he said. "Possibly even considered her as a friend outside of work. But, Renata, you must understand that she wasn't that person back there; in fact, she wasn't a person at all. *They* got to her, you see. By then, it was all over. Once *they* get to you, *they* own you—your thoughts, your body, even your soul. So, you can forget about everything that you know—or once knew. Once they have you, there's no escaping. And that's what makes what we're doing so important."

"I know," Renata uttered.

Her look was wounded, her words and thoughts tender.

Jevon sighed once more, as if he was sending subtle, unspoken messages to Renata that he was upset with her behavior.

Without any hesitation, he unlocked the trunk.

The trunk *squeaked* open.

THREE DAYS AGO

RENATA grabbed as many bags of groceries as she could fit in two hands from the trunk of her Taurus and closed the door with the bottom of her chin.

While carrying the bags to the front porch of the townhouse, her butt beeped. She placed the groceries on the porch and pulled the phone from her back pocket.

She read the name on the screen of the phone: Kira.

After the third beep-beep, she decided to answer the call.

"Hey, Gurl," Renata said ecstatically.

"Why hello, Renata," Kira replied.

"What's going on?"

"Nothing," she said. "I was just calling to see how the trip went?"

Renata didn't expect to hear the question so soon in the conversation, but the last thing she wanted to do was continue to lie to Kira.

She embraced a deep breath.

The only word that came to mind: "*Exhausting.*"

"Really," Kira said, her voice curling with suspicion. "Well, did you at least have a good time?"

"I did actually," Renata said, her voice slightly higher, "but you wouldn't believe the traffic home. Talk about a nightmare."

"That bad, huh?"

"You wouldn't believe."

"I was also going to ask you about the water—"

"—Don't worry," Renata said. "I turned it off just like you asked."

"Just checking because the last time we went up there I totally forgot to cut off the water and you know how that went—"

"—Kira," Renata said shortly. "It's all good."

"Yes," Kira said, more quietly. "Of course it is. I just wish I could've joined you this time around, but the other day I swear I felt as if someone was hammering a nail into my forehead. I haven't felt like shit in years. For a while, I had a nice non-sick streak going on."

"Well, that only means you're human, Kira."

Suspense cut between the break in the conversation.

Renata could sense the *other* question manifesting over the airy silence.

"So, was it just you? Or did you go with anybody?"

Renata leaned against the railing of the porch.

Be honest, she thought to herself.

More casually, she asked, "Remember that one guy, Paul Lauter?"

A noisy silence filled the other end of the phone.

"The name doesn't ring a bell," Kira said finally.

"The guy whom I went on a date with, remember?" Renata said. "We went on a double date with you and Al?"

"Oh yeah," Kira said. "Paul the Sta-Sta-Sta-Stall."

"Yes. Paul the. . . yeah."

"What a total scumbag," Kira said angrily, as her voice trailed off into a dead silence. "Wait a second!" Kira chirped before Renata had any chance of redeeming herself. "You didn't take him to the cabin, did you? Renata—"

"—Yeah," Renata said flatly. "Eww. No. Remember Paul's friend? We ran into him later that night off North

205

Morrison?" Still no response from Kira on the other end. Renata thought of the one thing—or *things*—that would jar her memory. "We had kamikazes?" No response. "The website developer?" Again, dead silence. "You said you liked his jaw."

"Yes," Kira said abruptly. "Ah! What's his name? Trevor?"

"*Trent*," both Renata and Kira said simultaneously.

"Yeah," Renata said over Kira. "That's the one."

"Wasn't he a lot older than you?"

"Forty-three."

"Forty-three?" Kira suddenly repeated, her voice louder and laced with confusion. "He's forty-three?"

"Yeah," Renata said. "So. Why you tripping?"

"He's twenty years older than you."

"Yes," Renata said. "I'm aware of his age. Thanks for stating the obvious."

"I'm just saying—"

"—Well, I'm just saying he doesn't at all act or 'look' like he's forty-three, if you know what I mean." Renata waited for a response from Kira but all she received was more silence. "But," Renata said over the silence, "there weren't even sparks there. You know, all thunder, no lightning."

Finally, Kira put together the clues that Renata had been seeding throughout the conversation.

"You see," she said, her voice sharper, "now, I feel bad."

"Bad? Why?"

Renata caught the glimpse of the front door in the corner of her eye.

"If I knew that you were going to the cabin on some romantic getaway with Trent the forty-three Stud, then I would've at least straightened up the place—"

"—No," she said, her voice facing as she stepped toward the front door. "It's not like that. . ."

More intrigued, Renata looked closer at the front door, as well as the damage around the doorframe. The door was cracked open. The doorknob was loose and hanging from the door like a baby tooth ready to be pulled. The area next to the faceplate looked partially caved in by what might have been from a crowbar.

"This is the part where you give me details—"

"—Listen, Kira, can I call you back?"

"Call me back? Gurl, I want to know what happened between you and what's-his-name—"

"—Kira, I'll call you back."

Renata hung up before Kira could lash out.

Cautiously, she opened the wobbly door and stepped inside the townhouse.

"Hello?"

Nobody answered.

Renata grabbed the closest weapon that she could find, which happened to be a small metal pole from a lamp that had been destroyed on the floor. Everything was either destroyed or overturned: lamps, coffee table, furniture. In her bedroom her underwear, shirts, and socks had been removed from the drawers and scattered around the floor. The outfits in her closet had been removed as well and scattered everywhere. Even in the kitchen the food from the pantry, as well as the refrigerator had been emptied onto the floors. Even the walls were covered in various colors of liquid and foods. The inside of the apartment appeared as if a hurricane had blown through each room, throwing and scattering things in the most destructive manner. But nothing was stolen, though.

Which was the first of many red flags.

RENATA arranged an emergency meeting with Jevon at the abandoned Eastwake Theatre outside Middletown, New Jersey.

She arrived extra early, which had given her more time to think about who or *what* had torn through her townhouse.

After about twenty minutes of waiting around, Jevon was still a no-show; and even though she was expecting Jevon to arrive rather late since the meeting was close to rush hour, she was still a hot mess. She spent the whole time pacing back and forth around the lobby area, which was overgrown with weeds and all sorts of plant vegetation. Surprisingly, the place had power; and every now and then, the lights would flicker along the sunburst lighting, sending Renata into a higher state of alarm.

Renata resorted to biting her nails—which was an old habit that she kicked a year after she graduated from high school. Once she heard the door *squeak* open and witnessed a sword of light cutting through the lobby, she removed her fingers from her mouth and stepped forward for a closer look.

At first, a shadow appeared on the slanted rectangular the sunlit doorway was casting on the floor, then, secondly, a figure emerged from around the corner.

Eventually, after calling out twice to the dark stranger, a worried Jevon appeared before her.

With her brow furrowed in concentration, she stormed straight to Jevon.

Before Renata could unburden herself, Jevon asked her, "Did you remove the battery from your phone?"

"Yes," she said annoyingly. "I removed the battery. I did exactly what you told me to do."

"Good," he said, "because they can track us through the phones."

"I know," Renata returned. "You don't have to talk to me like I'm some goddamn child—"

"—How about your tail? Were you followed?"

"No," she said and swiftly corrected, "I mean, I was followed. Someone was following me. I mean, not here."

"Are you sure—"

"—Yes," Renata snapped. "I'm sure. Were you followed?"

"No."

"Then, we wouldn't be having this meeting if we were followed. Now would we, Jevon?"

Patiently, Jevon held out his hands and tried to calm Renata.

"What's going on?" he asked, holding back his frustration.

"They know about me."

"It could've been anybody, Rennie," Jevon suggested. "Some kid. A neighbor? Have you made any enemies with anyone in the past few days?"

"Gee," Renata thought aloud. "Let me think." Then snapped at Jevon, "Perhaps Carla and Corvine—"

"—What makes you so sure they know about you? You've covered all your tracks. As far as I'm concerned, you haven't raised any red flags. Hypothetically speaking, if they did know about you—which I highly doubt it—I don't think we would be having this conversation. You're still here, aren't you?"

"What the hell is that supposed to mean?"

Trying to keep the civility, Jevon held out his hands.

"Sorry," he uttered. "I shouldn't have said that."

Turned off by Jevon's poor attempt at reassuring her—which, to Renata, felt quite the contrary—Renata gave Jevon the cold shoulder, as if the lack of Jevon's presence would make her think more clearly.

"I dunno," she said quietly to herself. "Who in the hell breaks into a house and doesn't steal anything?" Renata turned around and faced Jevon before he had a chance to answer her question, "I'll tell you who? Some asshole from Carla and Corvine who's trying to send me a message. That's who."

"And what message is that?"

"What do you think, Jevon?" Renata shook her head in disgust. "You know, I thought you were a lot smarter than that—"

"—Well," he said, the frustration rising his voice, "I'd say if they're trying to scare you, then I think they've done a pretty good job at it, don't you think?" He backed off for a moment. Then, stepped closer to Renata and touched her on the shoulder. "Listen to me, Renata," he said, his voice tender. "We both knew that something like this was eventually going to happen and it's better that it happened sooner than later."

"Later?" Renata shrugged off Jevon's hand from her shoulder. "Exactly how much longer do you expect me to stay on this story?"

He ignored the question: "Even if you are right, Renata, then it clearly demonstrates that we've tapped into something that they don't want tapping into. We have come way too far to give up now. And you certainly can't keep. . . " Jevon searched for the right words, ". . . *running off* every chance you get."

Renata reacted to the words. Her face filled with hot rage.

"Running off? Correct me if I'm wrong but it was you who said I needed to find some kind of normalcy in my life. *Cool off*, if I remember correctly. Those were the words you used. No. I'm sorry. *Get away—*"

"—I need you present right now," Jevon said.

The comment prompted Renata to clench her jaw together, as if she was restraining the words in her mouth.

Patiently, Jevon said, "After all of this is over, you can do whatever you want with your life, start a family, travel like you've been talking about, whatever. Just remember, Renata: it's our resiliency that has gotten us where we are today—"

"—And where are we exactly, Jevon?"

"Close."

"Close?" Renata snapped. "I know I'm not in any position to tell you how to run your magazine, but it's time to publish the story. You saw what they did with MindChant and how they're deliberately targeting the vulnerabilities of those who are most vulnerable, tracking people's every keystroke and using subliminal messages in their ads to suck them into whatever product they're promoting. It's no different than a disease, Jevon. And if we don't stop the spread now, then it's going to be too late." Renata paused and gathered herself. She couldn't make herself more clear: "I've brought you more than enough 'sufficient' evidence to expose Roman and Elmahdy."

"You have, Renata, and I'm grateful for all you've done—"

"—So, I say let the people see the facts for what they are and let them decide what to do with Roman and Elmahdy. If we don't have the people's back on this story, you and I know both know that it's the end of us. Like you said, we're talking about people powerful enough to erase us from existence. If they can make Rubin's death look like a suicide, then who knows what they can do to us?"

"The man was unstable," Jevon argued. "You saw his background."

"I did and it was all fabricated, Jevon," Renata said. "Smoke and mirrors."

"Well, maybe you should've dug deeper, Renata."

Renata picked up the hostility in Jevon's voice.

"My own 'vetted' resource," she said, more convincingly, "a man who has no grudges with Carla and Corvine, who has absolutely no reason to talk to me, who arranges a meeting in the middle of nowhere in fear for his own safety, who was paid hush money to keep his damn mouth shut, winds up dead twenty-four hours after he spills his guts to me. *Not* a coincidence." Determined, she stepped closer to Jevon and said clearly, "They haven't erased us just yet. But it's only a matter of time now. Just look at what happened in Dover. All fingers pointed at Harold Roman, yet literally every network runs some heartfelt story about how he lost his second wife to cancer two years after his marriage with Elmahdy was annulled in order to regain sympathy for him and change the public's perception and, just like that, he gets off scot-free, as if he had absolutely no involvement in what was going on with Bernie Shore or Rankin Jericho. How does that even happen? When the hell did 'playing dumb' exempt a man from the very inkling of being charged with murder?"

"And that's why we need to present the strongest case forward, otherwise the story isn't going to stick," Jevon urged. "We still have gaping holes in the story, such as the person responsible for setting these fires or the fact someone out there clearly knows what Roman is up to. And," Jevon emphasized, "what about this doctor character? We still have absolutely no information about him, who he is, or what experiments they're running at this secret facility you speak of. We may have Chione Elmahdy, all of her ties to Roman's crimes, the outrageous donations and contributions to police departments all around the country, but Renata, it's *not* enough. We have to convince the public that 'literally' everything they've been told is a complete fabrication of the truth."

"Why does it matter how much we have," Renata argued. "We have enough to plant doubts in their minds. Most importantly, enough to warrant an investigation!"

"By whom exactly? Corrupted officials? Bought-politicians?" Jevon's cheeks clouded with red heat released from his voice. "What we cannot do at this point is jeopardize the story by presenting it to those who have already been turned!"

"What does it matter? We have a story!"

"It's matters!" Jevon shouted. "We need every single person who's involved, including every single individual who has received so much as a penny from Harold Roman. We haven't even scratched the surface—"

"—That could take God knows how much longer—weeks, months, possibly even years."

Jevon closed his eyes for a moment and took a breath.

"We're talking about bringing down a company that's turned into a monster, a monster that grows stronger while we sleep, a monster that thrives off attention, a monster with an endless appetite feeding off our weaknesses and using them to manipulate us. In order to destroy this monster, we have to do the job that nobody else will do. . . Renata, we have to tell its story not the way it wants to be told but the way it doesn't. And if we waver now, then all the progress we've made will be for nothing. Our work won't even be an afterthought. I know it sucks, but it's the job."

Jevon stared at Renata and gave her an opportunity to respond. That pissed-off look he once wore on his face like pride melted into an expression of utter disappointment.

The deep sting of defeat suddenly poked at Renata.

She felt speechless, destroyed.

"What do you think you signed up for, Rennie?" asked Jevon.

Holding back the tears, Renata uttered, "I dunno."

SEVEN DAYS AGO

"HEY, *Junior*, you want anything from Café Cloud?" one of the drones from Marketing called out to Renata.

Renata didn't even have to turn around. She could recognize LeBron's voice and the arrogance that emitted from his aura like noxious fumes. Even though the word *junior* was officially part of Renata's new title—after all, it beat names like *newbie* or "noob" or new blood or anything with the word *new* or remotely close to the word *new* in it or even worse, *hey, you*—she never got used to being called Junior.

Biting the words in her mouth, Renata pulled herself from the printer and rotated around where LeBron, the conceited, slack-jawed bastard he was, waited by the doorway for an answer.

"No thank you," she said, remaining professional. "I'm good. . . "

She gave LeBron a professional smile and finished the conversation with a professional acknowledgment by stating LeBron's name back to him. She didn't put any emphasizes on either his name or his title. However, she let it be known to LeBron that he had rightfully earned his name the moment it was given to him. Renata couldn't say the same about his title.

"Suit yourself," LeBron said, his voice and face changing. He appeared as if he was invisibly waving off Renata not with a hand but, more or less, with a slight dip in his facial expression, as well as the rolling of his eyes. Somehow, he took Renata's answer more so as a retaliative response rather than a simple rejection to his kind proposal to the universal link, which was, of course, food.

As LeBron went away, Renata felt a sudden buzz swarming around her. She could feel it in the recycled air—that electricity—while she continued to print out a list of competitive trends, as well as noteworthy news items, that she had found during an intense yet highly productive surf through what she had grown accustomed to calling the "Underworld," including social media and social networking services and other popular platforms, such as the addictive MindChant, which had recently gone "public," as well as the two swiping apps that MindChant, Inc. currently owned, *Men Only* and its counterpart, *Women Only*.

She ignored the strange sensation and watched each page fall into the tray of the printer. While falling into a trance of the mundaneness of watching paper fall out of the printer—which was no different than one watching paint dry—Renata came across one page in particular, which piqued her interest. She removed the page from the stack of papers and skimmed it over.

The trend consisted of articles written about other competitors like Zinc Way and Foley and Sons, other marketing companies that targeted a majority of their audiences through online advertising with certain SROs like "AdRight," by using various emojis, particularly "food emojis," such as fruits, vegetables, or meat, as innuendos to depict parts of the human anatomy based on their size or shape.

Even though Renata had an idea as to why people—particularly the younger demographic, according to the data, younger males—commonly used an eggplant emoji to describe one of the most "trendy" organs of the male body, she was still confused as to why people, of all the phallic-shaped foods out there, chose a fruit that often bore the shape of a stumped big toe.

Renata removed the pages from the tray, placed them on top of the scanner in a neat stack, and slid the other page into the stack.

The buzz was back—that electricity.

In a state of frenzy, she looked around the office, through each glass corridor and office where a team of incredibly insightful strategists—whose job description specifically required a knack for telling a story, in other words, a "master storyteller"—was pitching fresh ideas for new projects and advertisements to directors while, in other transparent conference rooms, graphic designers were sketching potential slogans along glass boards, as well as shuffling through a variety of mock-posters displaying multifaceted marketing packages.

One particular slogan stood out the most: the words *Be the Better You* written in bold font on a poster. Other adjectives like "new," "revamped," or other catchy words, were being pitched and often replacing the word *better*.

Renata immediately noticed the head turns, the widened-eyes, and the change in facial expressions or lack of expressions: each strategist, each project manager or director, each assistant or accountant, all directing their attention to a brooding entourage moving like a quiet storm from the elevators to the main offices.

Deeply intrigued—partly mesmerized—Renata dropped what she was doing and peered closer at the entourage. She figured they were "big wigs," "investors," "potential clients perhaps," worse "lawyers"—it wasn't at all uncommon to come across gangs of lawyers gliding throughout the building every now and then like elusive undead armies— even "competitors from competing Ad Agencies." Each expression on each member's face, similar to the ones on each employee scattered around the office, appeared in unison; however, they were darkly grim, war-like in nature, as if the individual at the very center of the wall-like entourage had produced such a contagious vibe.

Renata stepped from the printers and exited the nook where she was working and caught a glimpse of the elusive one rounding the corner along an intersection of hallways, the one in the middle, the boss *wo*-man who had been aggrandized by myths and legends—even as Renata kept a mental snapshot of Chione Elmahdy in her mind, the black and white striped v-neck, those plump shoulder pads tucked underneath a sharp, black blazer that she was sporting like an athlete of the highest caliber strutting into the back of a coliseum, game face on, ready to vanquish the worthiest of opponents, as well as a vacant Michael Myers-type mask which, rumored, had covered her "other face," such lore was being murmured throughout the office, such as the reasons as to why she wore the mask, which was "to cover her disfigurement caused by the overuse of cosmetics that she was marketing, as well as countless botched facial reconstructive surgeries from when she was one of the most sought after fashion models who was later cast aside by the industry when she was a teenager."

Other rumors buzzed throughout a hornet's nest of chatter: Chione Elmahdy was said to "wear that same outfit every single day, not the same way Albert Einstein did, but because the outfit was somehow 'a part' of her," or "Her nickname, *The Redactor*, which she had earned because she was known to figuratively redact anybody who got in her way" or "She sleeps in a hyperbaric oxygen chamber at night" or "She only eats canned tuna fish" and "there's something about the mercury in tuna that her body needs to survive" or "All of her toes were amputated when she was only five years old in order to compete at the highest level of ballet for dictators around the world" or "She has the ability to see in the dark" or "She was once close friends with Saddam Hussein" or "She and Andy Warhol 'supposedly' had a child together when she was eighteen and this child was raised by a family somewhere in Oslo where it was developing the cure to the world's energy problem under several pseudonyms" or "She was able to seize all bodily functions of an individual with the single *snap* of her fingers; however, these unique powers weren't given to her or passed down to her from birth, but rather mastered after spending twelve years tucked far away in the Himalayan Mountains with quasi-Tibetan monks training her how to master the perfect *snap* of her fingers."

Renata even heard a rumor in the midst of the commotion—which she knew wasn't a rumor at all but, more or less, an accurate statement which was closest to the truth—that Chione "murdered Carla and Corvine in cold blood in order to take over the sibling's once failing company."

After the entourage breezed by, Renata found an opportunity to strike.

She left her nook and tracked down the marketing assistant, Selma, who was about to join a meeting with the rest of the marketing team. She handed her report to Selma and insisted on going on a food run.

Selma immediately waved off Renata. "No sweat," she said. "We'll just do it on Munch Run." Renata wasn't aware of Munch Run. Selma explained, "It's a new app."

"I can have the food here quicker," Renata argued.

Someone, Renata thought it was one of the strategists, was complaining how hungry he was. Once more, Renata insisted—nearly begged—to pick up food.

LeBron chimed in: "I thought you were 'good.'"

"*I am good*," she responded swiftly. "But I don't mind picking up the food for everybody; in fact, it would be my pleasure. And not only that, I'll have it here much quicker than Food Run—"

"—Munch Run," someone seated across the conference table corrected.

Selma presented the team with Renata's report, which was the final sell. The team came to an agreement to let Renata go on a food run. They handed her a list of orders. Once Renata acquired the list, she was out of there.

RENATA zoomed through a couple of hallways before she reached the entourage.

She slowed down her pace and eventually, after a couple of swift maneuvers, caught up with the entourage. Without drawing any attention to herself, she crept behind the entourage and blended in as soon as they reached the security desk in front of Chione's office.

The security guard let the entourage through the lobby without even questioning Renata's presence; in fact, she wasn't even sure the security guard had spotted her because her head was kept down and her eyes to the floor the whole time.

Once through the lobby, she followed the entourage to two oak doors—which she assumed led to Chione's office. The closer they approached the doors, the more nervous she became. Her heart pounded in a drum-like resonance throughout her chest. Her palms and other areas of her body, sweaty. She couldn't even believe she had gotten this close to the so-called Redactor; in fact, she couldn't even hold a thought in her head and it was as if she was having some outer body experience and watching herself from the outside.

Chione's secretary acknowledged the entourage and swiftly stood to her feet and opened the doors for everyone.

As the entourage poured into the office, Renata realized she had to make yet another move. With little-to-no options, Renata made a snap decision; and just as the secretary moved her eyes toward one of the members of the entourage, Renata darted behind the vase of a large areca palm plant in the corner of the room.

Renata ducked, her body balled up as tight and tiny as she would allow it.

The door *finally* closed.

Curious, Renata poked her head from the areca palm. The secretary was nowhere in sight. The entourage, gone.

With her heart pounding harder against her chest, Renata tiptoed to the doors.

She eavesdropped over the conversation from within the office. The conversation sounded as if the secretary was taking a possible lunch order. She thought she heard a woman talking about "California rolls." Possibly the secretary. The conversation came to a halt. Over the gap of silence, she heard another woman's voice. The voice was much deeper and pronounced, imperial.

Over the thrumming of her heartbeat, she heard the words "*check on*" a "*Dr. Essen*" and "*update on.*" From there, Renata filled in the blanks. "Go check on Dr. Essen and provide me with the latest update on. . . ?" The last word trailed off and left Renata scrambling through her mind, trying to piece together the remaining word—*or words*—of the sentence.

Renata mistook the sound of footsteps for the sound of her heartbeat. The beating suddenly got louder and louder and she suddenly realized it was footsteps and they were heading directly at her! At the very last second, Renata ducked behind the secretary's desk. From behind the desk, she watched a member from the entourage walking away. Keeping close to the desk, Renata stood upright.

As the door started to close, Renata caught yet another glimpse of Chione as the other members of the entourage began to take their seats around the medieval-sized table.

Renata specifically honed in on the tall woman in the sharp black blazer who was standing at the end of the table—whom Renata assumed was, in fact, the one and only Chione from not only the outfit she was wearing, but also the manners that she exhibited. With her back turned and her head slightly arched upright to a cathedral-like rose window below the high ceiling, she whispered something to the secretary. Her mode was dour and domineering. The secretary submissively nodded her head in return; however, the gesture looked more like a subserviently bow than an act of acknowledgement. Just a couple of inches before the door *finally* swung close, Chione turned her shoulder, her head dipped downward, revealing her unmasked face. Renata's mouth cracked open like a lazy yawn, her insides left gasping from the sight of Chione's face. She froze, as if she had been caught in the eye of Medusa's gaze.

In her statue-like state, Renata heard more footsteps, sharper. The sound reminded her of a horse, only without the *clop*. She soon realized it was a *clip-clip* sound of silhouettes, more importantly, the secretary's silhouettes.

As the door swung open, Renata looked around in a state of utter frenzy. With her mind swirling, she found a trashcan next to the secretary's desk. Then a cup holder inside, as well as two coffee cups.

The secretary called out from behind, "Excuse me!"

Renata snatched the cup holder and coffee cups from the trashcan. Her body erected upright like a freshly watered plant. As she secured the last second coffee cup into the holder, she used way too much vim and vigor in her grip—she possibly had the adrenaline to thank for the sudden burst of energy. The cup caved in but didn't completely crush. Cold coffee spilled from the sides of the white and brown cup and dribbled all over her hand.

Ignoring the coffee, Renata faced the secretary.

"Excuse me," she parroted, trying to rid the surprise from her face.

"You're not allowed up here," the secretary snapped. "Who are you? What department are you from?"

"I truly apologize," Renata said, pretending to be a dumb intern. "I believe I may be lost. I'm looking for marketing. As you can see, I'm running a little late and my boss will kill me if I don't have his coffee on time."

With her painted brows furrowed in several different kinds of emotion, the secretary looked over Renata, the "dumb intern."

"Wrong floor," she said, pointing downward. "It's the floor below."

"Got it," Renata said, more casually. "Thank you."

The secretary looked over Renata once more, her face less busy.

"You're quite welcome."

Renata hurried away.

❦

SOMEHOW, after taking a shortcut downstairs, Renata managed to beat the man in the black suit to the main entrance.

Renata maintained a steady lead over the strange man, lawyer, Chione's assistant, errand boy—whoever; however, he could've been a lawyer from the way he was dressed or the fact that lawyers were always going in and out of Carla and Corvine. Renata was leaning more toward an assistant. Her assumption was mostly based on the man's presence, his look, mainly how she had seen him many times in the building, carrying coffee, bags, purses, or boxes—or what Renata expected to be deliveries—all done in a hasty manner.

Once she reached the parking garage, she jetted to her car and took cover behind the steering wheel.

While Renata was waiting on the assistant, an image of Chione's face flashed through her mind. She could see her vivid face as if it was right in front of her: all the scars along the sides of her face, the chemical burns around her dark eyes, the gaping hole in the side of her cheek, exposing the teeth inside her mouth.

Eventually, the assistant entered the parking lot.

Renata refocused.

From the inside of her car, Renata kept her eyes on him as he walked directly to his car, which was parked at the other side of the parking garage. Once he got inside his car and drove off, she waited for him to do a half lap around the level and eventually pass her car before starting up the ignition.

As he proceeded down the ramp to the next floor, Renata followed.

RENATA was a car behind him at the front gate, which could've worked to her advantage; however, it all depended on the driver in front of her. Once the attendant inside the booth collected the assistant's ticket and waved him through, he exited the parking garage.

All Renata could hold onto was that he took a right out of the parking garage. And that was it. The driver in front did exactly what she dreaded: he was a talker. And he wouldn't shut the hell up! In order to keep the traffic moving, she honked her horn. The loudmouth in front of her turned around and threw up his arm in a typical privileged "how-dare-you" attitude.

Renata honked yet again.

The driver finished his transaction with the attendant and sped off. Once Renata pulled up to the booth, she handed the attendant her ticket. The attendant, realizing the rush Renata was in, opened the gate for her.

Renata sped off.

EVENTUALLY, after making a last-second guess to make a left on Galvin Avenue, which would take her through the Lincoln Tunnel, instead of staying on West 41st Street, Renata caught up with the assistant's car.

Enormously relieved from the sight of the car, Renata made sure to keep her distance. They stayed on 495 until they crossed over into New Jersey. She ended up following the assistant for about forty minutes to what looked like a business park right outside Caldwell. Renata counted at least four separate buildings; however, each one connected to one another by long enclosed walkways.

As she approached the park, she searched for a sign outside but couldn't find one. Except for a number on the top corner of the buildings, the buildings didn't give much away. A gate with barbwire surrounded the buildings—Renata immediately thought the buildings might've been government, even military, from the cold vibe she was getting. The assistant pulled up to a booth in front of a front gate where a security guard with a gun came out to greet him. He showed the security guard some type of badge. The guard opened the gate and waved him through.

Renata hung back and weighed her options. She clearly couldn't drive up to the main gates and drive right in, considering a possible "badge" was a requirement for entry. She had to look for another way in. She resorted back to her old days, those young and rebellious days where a term like consequences was about as irrelevant as showing a picture of a helping hand to a man suspensefully dangling from the ledge of a high-rise with only three sweaty fingers preventing him from plummeting to his ultimate death.

After the decision was made, Renata moved swiftly. She parked her car at a safe distance and waited until the security guard went back to his cozy hole before she made her next move. Once the guard was distracted by the smartphone in his hand, Renata sprinted toward a chain link fence which surrounded the entire complex and scaled it as quickly as her body would let her.

The climb was easy—maybe too easy—however, when Renata arrived at the top, she was forced into a caution mode.

Using an old jacket to cover up the sharp spikes, she carefully stepped over the barbwire; and on her way down, the jacket snagged on the spikes. She ended up having to tear away the jacket, which had left behind a small square of jacket between two clusters of spikes. The piece wasn't big enough to raise red flags—at least from where the guard's booth was located; however, she didn't have any time to scale back up the fence and fetch the rest of her jacket for there were cameras mounted everywhere around the building.

She *had* to move.

And move, she did.

RENATA prayed to whatever merciful god out there that the person working in the surveillance room was either on a break or not paying an iota of attention toward the monitors or simply too lazy or slow to witness a twenty-three year old woman darting through a well-manicured lawn and seeking cover behind one of the many evergreen shrubs along the side of the building. Really, all Renata could do was pray for the best and expect the very worse.

As Renata waited to make her next move, she wrinkled her nose and smelled a strange stench lingering in the air. With her head down, she peeked around the shrub and spotted two men, possible employees, one a heavyset man with a heavy beard, and the other a slender man with a rather premature beard. Both men appeared to be on a smoke break. The heavyset one, chiefing on a vapor pen, while the other man, puffing away on what the #Truth kids called an old fashioned cigarette. She immediately took interest in the door and how it wasn't at all guarded like the other main entries in the front of the building. She was more interested in the lock, as well as the door handle, and how it was like a typical door that probably locked from the outside.

Hey, she thought. *Maybe it's my lucky day.*

Maybe it was the *people working in the surveillance room.*

Renata doubted it.

But she still prayed.

She fished around her pocket, pulled out an old receipt form earlier that day, and folded it tightly. She looked down at the piece of paper in her hand and wondered what in the hell she was thinking—really! She knew that she was about to do something incredibly stupid, but she thought to herself: *What other choice do I have?* She had a hard time believing how exactly she got herself in this particular situation—What a situation it was!

She waited until the two men finished smoking—and vaping—and made her move.

The two men opened the door and stepped inside.

Renata sprinted toward the door and wedged the piece of paper into the lock inches away before it closed. She waited a few seconds outside, listening closely to the sound of the two men's voices fading farther and farther away.

In her anxious wait, she couldn't help but look up.

What do you know?

Another camera, this one aimed directly at Renata.

Shit.

Once the two voices faded, Renata gave the door a tug.

What do you know?

Relieved, Renata opened the door and stepped inside the cool building. She immediately noticed the hospital-like staleness. She carefully closed the door behind her; and once her eyes adjusted to the change in light, she spotted those same two men rounding the corner at the end of a hallway.

"What is this place?" she whispered to herself.

Only one way to find out.

Again, with her head down, she moved quickly down the hallway. Once she made it to the end, she had two different routes, the hallway to the left leading to a sketchy set of double doors, which looked like they required a special key, while the other, the hallway to the right, stretching as far as her eyes could see.

Dumbfounded as to which direction to take, Renata's deliberation caused her to draw her eyes upward.

What do you know?

Of course, she found herself standing directly in the crosshairs of yet another surveillance camera. She put aside her thoughts and prayers and said the hell with it and took a right.

She proceeded down the hallway and passed a sign that read: "Zone C." She steadied her walk and made herself look less obvious while, at the same time, trying to make sense as to what organization uses "zones" to identify a level.

Even though the Zone C fellows had vanished, Renata managed to track their scent to "Lab 4." Inside the narrow room were glass vials and test tubes scattered about worktables. On one side of the wall were many rows of animal cages, each one occupied by a furry creature. The "meows" was what gave them away.

"Cats?" Renata mouthed to herself.

She guessed—more or less, assumed—that the cats were used the same way rats were used, which was for testing, but her guess was as good as the next. She could hear the two men talking inside over a harsh symphony of cat meows; however, she couldn't quite tell what they were talking about. Hugging the side of the wall and trying to block out the cats, Renata leaned in closer to the doorway for a closer listen. Suspended on top of a fluorescent table were various prototypes of strange headgear, from helmets to toboggan-like hats with cables hanging downward like octopus tentacles, all smaller in size, smaller than a baby's head, clearly not intended for humans. She was suddenly hit by her own *duh!* Glancing around at the cat cages inside the room and the headgear, which, clearly, matched the size of a cat's head, Renata was left in a deeper state of confusion.

The two men suddenly came back into frame, their appearance different.

Renata ducked back behind the wall before she could be spotted. She noticed the two men were no longer dressed in casual clothes. Yet, they were both wearing white lab coats.

One of the men, the slender one, removed a lifeless cat from one of the cages. The cat appeared sedated by the way the man was carefully handling it.

He gently placed the cat on a metal table while the other man, the heavyset man, was snapping a couple of plugs into the very back of a small cat-size helmet at his workstation, which was covered in various electronic gear.

The two men continued to argue while prepping the cat for "collection."

The heavyset man: *"There's absolutely no question in my mind that Bethany murdered Jon."*

The slender man: *"What!?! You're completely insane, dude! You're telling me that the sneaky witch Fiona didn't play a role in Jon's untimely demise?"*

The heavyset man: *"Hey! She might have. But all evidence points directly at Bethany. You know, if turns out, Bethany is the murderer, a part of me will be somewhat glad, especially after the way she treated Mark. Talk about a heartless bitch."*

The slender man: *"What's your deal with Bethany, dude? You're not one of those Bethany haters, are you?"*

The heavyset man: *"No!"*

"Bethany?" Renata said to herself, leaning back behind the doorway. "Who the hell is Bethany?"

After a heated argument ensued, Renata soon realized the two men were talking about fictional characters on an HBO show and not real-life murderers.

The headgear was placed over the cat's head. Once it was secured, the two men turned their attention toward a computer. All she could see were wavy lines of what looked like maybe vitals on the monitor; however, Renata wasn't entirely sure as to what the lines were indicating—*brainwaves*, if that was such a thing?

As Renata leaned in even closer, she saw more people in other rooms conjoining the laboratory. The room was smaller and appeared to be an operating room. Inside were doctors wearing gloves and masks and protective gear. Re-nata couldn't see exactly who *or* what was lying on top of the operation table for a pale blue curtain, which covered nearly the entire length of the table, was obstructing her view. Whatever it was, it was quite a large thing that cast a large, round, and most importantly, *still* silhouette behind the curtain. One of the nurses removed a gas mask from the thing's face while the other one handed the doctor a sharp instrument—possibly a scalpel—and readjusted the surgical light above the. . . subject? The change in lighting dissolved the silhouette, making it harder to see what was going on behind the curtain. Renata wasn't sure as to what the doctor had called the strange, sleeping thing, but she swore the word "subject" was used on several occasions—or was it *specimen?*

Leaning dangerously close into the corner of the slender man's range of vision, Renata saw the massive paw of what looked like a Siberian tiger.

RENATA continued her search toward the end of the hall-way where she nearly got spotted by a bundled-up team of casually dressed, multitasking dudes who were—more or less—gliding along like phantoms. If it wasn't for their pin-sharp focus on the electronic tablets in their hands, which, from second glance, appeared to be controlling their every movement, then she would've been spotted for sure. The way each one of these puppet-like dudes quickly tapped and scrolled through the greasy screens of each tablet with their *clicking* centipede-leg moving fingers appeared un-natural, machine-like. With no other alternative, she was forced to seek cover in an ominous-looking staircase.

As sudden terror started to take hold, Renata inched closer to the opening between the two flights of stairs and peeked over the railing along the landing.

There, in the deep swell of darkness, she witnessed flights of stairs traveling down at least twelve more sto-ries—*at least*. Her heart beat faster, chest tightened. Her whole body trembled. The notion alone of being inside some kind of underground facility caused Renata's head to spin. Her breathing gradually increased. Words like *trapped* and *lost* came screeching at her, intensifying the terror.

She ignored the head noise and focused on the story— *It's all about the story!*

After she gained control over her breathing, Renata ended up walking down a flight of stairs. She stopped at the floor below, which was called "Zone D." She couldn't help but wonder what came after "D." She walked to the floor below: "Zone E." She continued to travel down the stairs, spiraling her way into darkness. She reached "Zone Z." Renata thought she reached the end of these "zones," but after she leaned over the railing and peered down into the darkness, she soon realized that she wasn't even close to the bottom—there had to be *at least* ten more stories below her! She had gotten this far, so why not go a little farther.

Poised for the truth, she made her way down to the bottom of the facility.

Outside the stairwell door, a red sign read: "WARNING NO SMOKING."

When she cracked open the door and carefully stepped into a stale hallway as if the floor was covered in glass, she looked to her right, then her left. The floor appeared the exact same as the floor she had recently come from. She duly noted the elevator to the far left, which would possibly come to good use if she was to get spotted—which was strange to Renata, just thinking about it, since she hadn't been spotted once while sneaking around a facility that was littered with surveillance cameras.

About twenty paces from the stairwell door was another warning sign outside a closed door: "DO NOT DISTURB THE SLEEPERS."

Renata pulled away from the sign.

"Sleepers?"

Above the door, a red TV studio-like "recording" light was glowing.

Renata's eyes were drawn to the red light and the way it was begging to her.

She walked to the red light and right before entering the room, she came back to the sign.

Sleepers?

Carefully, she pulled on the door handle, immediately feeling resistance. She managed to barely crack open the door but not far enough to sneak inside.

Renata tried once more, this time using more muscle.

With a stronger pull, she opened the door and when she closed it behind her, the room created a suction effect, causing the door to slam shut. She thought the sound would draw attention; but like before with her presence, it went unnoticed.

More poised, she scanned the dimly lit room, which stretched into darkness. She immediately felt cold by the gunmetal gray walls, the lack of lighting, the atmosphere itself unnerving.

Most of the source of lighting came from a station—a control room of some kind—behind a pair of glass panes. A man was operating a control panel, testing levels, and whatnot. Renata witnessed those same wavy lines on a monitor in the center of the control panel. She honed in on a label directly above a row of surveillance monitors that read "The Cloud Room."

All of a sudden, a scratchy voice came on through a speaker, telling the man, the "operator," to "give us the room."

Us?

The operator gathered his things, his tablet, as well as an empty cup of coffee from his workstation, and stepped out of the control room.

Before the operator glanced up from his electronic tablet, Renata immediately took cover in the dark shadows in the corner of the room.

Once the operator left, Renata crept toward the control room. She took cover behind a wall while two strange men were talking inside another, darker room just outside the control room. She peeked over the side of the wall. What she thought was going to be a simple peek-and-duck turned out to be crippling stare. Renata's jaw fell into a gawking expression.

Before her very eyes were hundreds of bodies—the "sleepers," all positioned in midair with the front of their bodies facing upward, while their arms, their legs, as well as their torsos were being held by wires suspended above them and to Renata—at least, at first thought—the bodies appeared as if they were floating in the air. Each body was separated by a length of five feet on all sides, including the top as well as the bottom. Each column consisted of twelve bodies. Above hung an intricate pulley system, which allowed a nurse to access the body. The suspension of the bodies, Renata could only suspect, was to prevent bedsores.

Each body had what Renata believed to be a feeding tube hooked up to their abdomens like a power cord. The creamy beige-colored liquid—or *food*, Renata suspected—inside a clear thirty-gallon communal bag hanging next to the pulley system appeared as if it was being automatically controlled by a suspended device next to each body. What really caught Renata's attention were the hats with wires on their heads and how each one looked similar—if not, identical—to the strange hat that one cat from earlier was wearing.

Renata ducked back behind the wall, tried to make sense of what she had just witnessed; however, she couldn't make any sense of it. She peeked around the corner once more, followed all the wires past the feeding bag, past the pulley system, past to the dark rafters along the ceiling, until she reached a soft pinkish light radiating in the center of the room.

Renata was pulled away by a disturbance coming from one of the bodies.

Every now and then, a quiet alarm would sound, causing the upper torso of a body to automatically elevate either upward or dip downward in a seesaw motion, depending on a blood pressure regulator.

A blonde-haired nurse entered the room from another door to check on one of the sleeper's—or patient's—body. She also checked the device next to the body, punched a couple of buttons on the control pad. Then stroked the hair of a young male, telling him that he was having a "nightmare."

Once the young man's blood pressure returned to normal, his body was automatically lowered to a straight sleeping position.

The nurse left room, bringing the two men's voices back into the foreground. Renata heard a man talking vaguely about "applicable candidates"—she specifically heard the word, *quota*, several times throughout a heated conversation. She tracked down the voice to the assistant, who was talking to a rough-faced man, who appeared to be the head doctor based on a gold lab coat he was wearing—she figured the color of coats had something to do with certain rank.

"You just make sure to tell your boss that there is no turning back from this," the doctor said, handing the assistant a metal briefcase with the word **FRAGILE** written in bold red lettering on the side. *"Once she puts it on. . . she will have access to an entire generation. I hope she's ready."*

The assistant responded with a tone of defiance, *"My boss? She's your boss too—"*

"—Just be a good boy and relay the message for me. Is that so hard to ask, Merlot? If Chione has a problem, then she doesn't have to send over her errand boy. She knows where to find me—"

"—What about the couple?"

"What couple?"

"You know, the troublemakers. He's created a buzz around the office. As far as the other one, it's only a matter a time before she does something stupid."

"And why does this concern me?"

"Well, what are you going to do with him?"

"I think Roman has plans for him. Frankly, it's none of my business. Neither is it any of yours."

"Whatever you say. We all know who the real doctor around here is."

The air between the two grew tense. Neither one had anything else to say.

After a long pause, the assistant threw his head up in a resentful nod and said, *"See you around. . . Doc."*

The doctor waved off the assistant.

Renata's skin was drenched with a layer of sweat. Her stomach was churning by the idea that she was possibly this so-called "troublemaker" who the two were speaking of. As for whom the "him" might be, only one "him" came to mind and she had absolutely no clue as to what Roman—more than likely, Harold Roman—was going to do to "him."

As Renata slowly sunk back in her squatted position behind the wall, the doctor turned toward Renata's direction but never made any eye contact with her.

Keeping her gaze on the doctor, Renata caught a glimpse of his face and the old scars from premature acne speckled along the sides of his face like dimples on a golf ball.

The assistant left the room. Then, eventually, after a brief scan of all the bodies suspended throughout the entire room, the doctor was next to leave.

Once the room was finally clear, Renata walked over to the nearest body that was suspended in the air. She stood over the young light skinned man, whom Renata figured to be in his late teens to early twenties. What stood out the most was the contraption on his head. This particular hat, unlike the one that cat was wearing, appeared translucent and covered with even more cables. She cracked open one of his eyelids. His eye was neither fixed nor dilated. Which was a good sign. She checked the other eye and, like the one before, it was rapidly moving. Which clearly indicated activity in the brain.

Out of desperation, she tried to wake the young man; however, he was stuck in some kind of deep, *deep* sleep—REM sleep?

Renata drew her eyes away from the young man and noticed the other young men and women all around, all suspended, all asleep, all plugged up to. . .

A massive glass tank in the middle of all the bodies.

She followed the wires above, which were all connected to the top of the cylindrical glass tank, which was filled with a pink liquidy substance.

All Renata could make out was the shape inside—that's all. Even though the creature was roughly the size of a human, its shape, as well as tentacle-like arms, suggested animal, possibly in the phylum category, mollusks which included octopuses and snails. That, she knew.

She shuffled around the other bodies and as she proceeded toward the tank, a beam of yellow light cut through the darkness to the left of her.

The same nurse casually entered. Good thing for Renata the entire level was dark—except for the artificial light inside the control room, which was on the far side of these sleepers, the only source of decent light was coming from the giant nightlight that was the glass tank—otherwise, Renata would've been immediately spotted. But, no, like before, it was as if she was a ghost. Strangely enough, she managed to remain undetected.

A few rows away, one of the bodies was slightly dipping downward.

By the time the nurse tended to the sleeper, Renata joined the shadows.

PRESENT DAY

INSIDE the trunk, her body was wrapped like a burrito inside a gray comforter spotted with continent-shaped stains of dark blood. Jevon wasted no time in peeling back the upper part of the comforter, revealing Kira's pallid face. The lower part of the corpse's face was caked with blood. Her hazel eyes were still wide open, still staring *straight* at Renata, as if, even after death, Kira's spirit somehow knew exactly what her so-called "friend" had done to her.

Jevon attempted to close Kira's eyelids, as they do in the Hollywood movies, but the eyelids sprung back open like a doll's eyes. He placed the comforter back over Kira's face.

Next to Jevon, Renata suddenly started to backpedal from the trunk.

Baffled by the movement, Jevon rotated around and faced Renata, whose face was riddled with horror.

"*Renata*," Jevon said softly, "it's going to be okay." He held out both hands, as if he was using them to help calm down Renata. "Renata. . ."

Renata continued to backpedal, her head shaking back and forth.

"No, no, no," she cried. "I killed her. . ."

"Renata," Jevon pleaded, as he stepped away from the trunk, "you must understand you had no other choice. If I could swap positions with you right now, believe me, I would in a heartbeat. But—"

"—I don't think you would," Renata said grimly.

Before her eyes, Kira was removing the comforter from her body and climbing out of the back of the trunk. She shouldered directly past Jevon. As soon as Renata witnessed Jevon's reaction—or lack of reaction—the horror intensified.

Renata cried, "You—you can't see her, can you?"

Jevon turned to the open trunk.

"Of course, Renata," he said, pointing at the stained comforter inside. "I see her." Once more, he faced Renata. "Renata," Jevon said, his voice more fatherly, "we're going to get through this, okay?"

Renata backpedaled, and Jevon closed in right behind Kira.

"She's right in front of you!" Renata shouted out.

Jevon returned, "Who's right in front of me?"

Apparently, Kira hadn't bled out entirely. When Kira started to speak, it reopened the wound on her neck, causing the blood to pour out.

"Is this how you treat all your friends, Renata," she said vacantly. "I thought you were my friend—"

"—I was," Renata corrected, "I am!"

"Renata," Jevon said over Kira's voice, "you're acting strange. What's going on with you?"

Kira continued to walk toward Renata while Renata continued to backpedal. Her heel tripped over a rock stuck in the ground and caused her to fall backwards. Jevon caught up with Renata, his body passing straight through Kira's body. Kira stayed with Jevon, her motions nearly mimicking his.

As Jevon leaned over to help up Renata, so did Kira. However, Kira wasn't trying to help Renata at all. Kira's face merged with Jevon's.

As the world started to spin before Renata, one body with two faces appeared in front of her. She didn't know which one to trust; in fact, she didn't even know whether or not either one was real. The blurry faces morphed in and out of one another, Jevon's worried-looking face, then Kira's blank dead face, until the face before her was only one face, Kira's more masculine face. Renata's eyes rolled in the back of her head and her body did what only came natural.

SECONDS passed.

Renata charged through the blackness.

Her eyes bolted open.

As she sat upright along the gravel driveway, she noticed that Jevon and Kira were gone. The trunk door was still open.

Renata called out to Jevon but didn't receive any response. The firelight inside the cabin was no longer flickering. Renata remembered that the fire was still burning when she and Jevon went outside. Which made her wonder exactly how much time had passed. It felt like seconds, but perhaps it was hours.

In the corner of her eye, she found another light, a soft pinkish light pulsating deep within the woods. She decided to check it out.

ONCE Renata stepped foot into the dark woods, the environment started to change all around her. The farther she walked into the woods, the more the ground below her started to harden and turn more unnatural. She saw less trees and foliage. Similar bodies to the ones she saw at the unmarked facility—the "sleepers" in the "Cloud"—appeared as if they were part of the woods. She came across one with his head partially sticking out of the ground. Another one a part of a tree trunk. Renata arrived at a control panel, which was covered in tall weeds and dirt. She followed the same pinkish light until she eventually arrived in that same place where the sleepers were suspended in the air, the Cloud Room. All of the sleepers were gone; however, the glass tank still remained. She made her way to the tank where a gray-skinned, emaciated man with a wispy white beard floated inside. He had to be somewhere around seven feet tall in height, eight when fully straight and erect. He was rail-thin, zombie-like, cheeks hollowed, eyes sunken deep inside the sockets of his skull, skeleton exposed, including ribcage; his skin was worn extra-extra loose, hipbone and elbows showing the most flab, mainly excess skin which appeared as if it was an old suit that didn't fit anymore and was ready to be donated away.

As he lifelessly floated inside the pink liquid inside the tank, Renata pressed her hand against the surface of the glass.

The strange man's white eyes bolted open, startling Renata.

As he stirred with life, he floated down to Renata's eye level. Carefully, she studied the strange man's face, looked well past his dead milky eyes, past the airy white beard, and traced the contours of his skeletal face with her finger.

THREE WEEKS AGO

STILL slightly hungover from last night's romantic entanglement, Renata ran into the couch and nearly tripped over the coffee table in the center of the living room. The noise caused the warm body underneath the bed sheets to stir in bed and readjust sleeping positions.

Renata froze in her tracks, as if she was playing red light-green light and she was given a glaring red light. With her eyes still bloodshot from the lack of sleep, she looked over her shoulder, waiting for her to rise, to *hear* her voice, to *see* her smile. She saw none of that. Instead, that awful symphony resumed. She tried to block out the snoring by putting her mind to work. Last night, she shared a story about her father. She also told Renata the history of this cabin. Renata specifically recalled her walking to the triple dresser and standing in front of it while she told the story, and it was as if she was defensive. Renata picked it up in her body gestures, the way her tone changed, the way she stood, and how she appeared as if she was guarding the dresser.

Careful not to make anymore noise, Renata opened the top drawer.

Inside were overturned picture frames of Kira's mother and father, as well as Kira when she was a young girl: photographs of Kira doing girl-stuff around the cabin like hanging upside down on a tree branch or flying a kite or painting her father's face with her mother's makeup.

Renata opened the next drawer and came across both Japanese and American newspapers of Kira's father, who was a famous basketball player in both Japan and America, where he played four years in the NBA before he retired due to a knee injury, which had followed him throughout his professional career.

After combing through the basketball memorabilia, Renata moved to the next drawer, the third and last drawer. She found a newspaper article on Kira's father. His wife had reported him missing after he disappeared while having drinks with former teammates at a bar. According to the newspaper, the former NBA player was missing for over forty-eight hours. The people he was with that night had the same story: "*One minute, they were hanging out at the bar, catching up while having drinks. He excused himself and went to use the restroom. He never came back.*" The investigators never suspected any foul play. Eventually, the case went cold.

Renata heard the *rustling* of bed sheets behind her. She threw the article back where she found it and closed the drawer.

"Hey, Fire Crotch," Kira said childishly, her bare body leaning over the edge of the bed. "Come back to bed, will you?"

A wide smile stretched across Kira's face.

Still wrapped in her thoughts about Kira's father and his disappearance many years ago, Renata rotated around and saw half of Kira's body poking through the opening of the bedroom doorway.

From the bed, Kira begged, "I need your body heat. I'm fucking *freezing*."

PRESENT DAY

KIRA'S father placed his sticklike hand exactly where Renata had placed hers.

Both of their hands touched through the glass, the frail hand of Kira's father looking like an exaggerated Halloween ornament that was three times the size as Renata's hand. Renata stared into his ghostly eyes, the once dark irises appearing as if they were penciled-in, then erased. She knew what she had to do. She didn't know why, *but she knew*. She searched the area for a blunt object. After combing the room, Renata ended up ripping off a metal handle about the size of a softball bat from the side of the control panel. She ended up using the handle to beat away at the tank. Only after a couple of strikes in, the glass barely even cracked. During each swing, she could feel the impact of metal hitting solid glass vibrating through her entire body and causing her bones to ache. She tried once more, gave everything she had, and ended up chipping away at the glass. Several pebble-sized chunks of glass fell to the ground. Renata's bones hurt like no pain she had ever felt before. Her hands were sore and throbbing as if the blood was trying to rip through her skin. Renata picked up the handle, gripped it tightly, and once more, reared back for a swing.

A voice from the darkness: "*I wouldn't do that if I were you.*"

She abruptly paused right as she was about to unleash her unfettered wrath.

A dark, hellish-faced figure stepped forward into the pinkish glow.

"*You're going to severely* regret doing that. . . "

Renata lowered the handle by her side.

Chione appeared before her. She was dressed in the same clothes she always wore: a dark blazer customized by the notorious fashion designer Toufik 2.0 worn over a black and white striped long sleeve v-neck shirt that was so skin-tight that it looked painted on her skin; signature bootcut pants in modern stretch to match her blazer; black stilettos that appeared to add at least six inches to her height; a gold Rolex given to her by the syndicate commonly referred to as "The Network," the wristwatch matching gold looped earrings. The only attire missing from her sleek wardrobe was *that* mask.

"Why's that?" Renata finally asked after studying Chione.

In a nonchalant manner, Chione nodded at Kira's father.

"If that thing gets out, then everyone you have ever loved will be gone. The world that you know—or at least you thought you knew—gone."

"That thing has a name," Renata snapped. "His name is Reo Nakamura."

Chione's face slackened, the scars making her frown look wavy and warped.

"Why are you doing this?" Renata asked.

"And why exactly do people of power do what they do?" Promptly, Chione answered her own question before Renata could ponder her own: "More power, of course. *More* control. You come from a 'unique' generation—a 'guinea pig generation'—one raised by televisions, phones, devices with one purpose only, which is to distract you from reality." She stepped forward, revealing more scars on her shadowy face. She turned to the tank and touched the glass with her index finger. "The brain is no different than a computer. Once you *hack* it, the possibilities are endless." Her attention was drawn back to the tank and for a moment, she witnessed Kira inside the tank, *not* her father. She appeared to be in a similar state as her father: gray, cloudy skin, skinny, white hair, whiter eyes, could easily pass as the walking dead. "Everything you do," Chione said to Renata, "every choice you make, every thought that enters your head is controlled by us. You are a generation incapable of any individual thought. You *read* the same books. You *watch* the same movies. *Listen* to the same songs. You all *speak* the same. Even *act* the same. Most importantly, you all *think* the same."

"How's this for thinking the same?" Renata said furiously, as she held up the metal handle.

Without the slightest hesitation, she swung at the glass tank.

As soon as the handle collided with the tank, the glass exploded and all that pink slimy fluid came gushing outward.

Renata was hit by incredible force surging directly at her, causing her to fall and bang her head against the floor. The tank eventually emptied. All that pink slimy stuff pooled around Renata's soaked body.

Dazed, she looked around and tried to find her bearings. By the time she finally came to and wiped away the pink sludge from her eyes and face, it was already on top of her body. The weight alone of it pressed against her chest caused her breathing to shorten. She tried to push whatever it was from her body but she felt paralyzed.

With her senses more heightened, she looked closer. It was nearly half the size of her; however, it had no distinguishable shape. The only shape that came to my mind was the look of a heart with the valves and arteries still intact and hanging outward. The texture of its skin pressed against hers was fuzzy and moss-like, gray-brownish in color. The organs inside it buzzed in spastic-jarring beats, as if each one was working in harmony. Somewhere, underneath that tangled mess of wiry bristles before her, Renata witnessed—or at least, thought she witnessed—dozens of beady black eyes protruding outward like Braille.

Eight phallic-shaped tentacles suddenly stretched from its shelled underbelly, one of which slithered up her neck, as well as chin. The slimy tentacle sensually combed over Renata's lips and mouth. She kept her jaw clenched so tight that she thought she might've broken a tooth.

Other tentacles slithered upward, two of which plugged the two holes in her nose that were her nostrils.

Unable to breathe, Renata held on as long as she could until she couldn't hold on any longer.

Fighting for a breath, she gasped.

As soon as Renata embraced the air, the tentacle entered her mouth and slithered down her throat.

Renata resisted, at first. But after her breath was cut short, her vision turned gray and she started to drift. The last images Renata witnessed before she fell into the blackness were of Chione's "other" self, an alter ego. As her throat started to swell, images started to change in shape and character. In those last few moments before the inevitable blackout, she couldn't help but wonder if she was falling directly through the ground, as if her body and soul were somehow melting into that pink sludge pooled around her. The blazer slipped from Chione's shoulders. The gold looped earrings straightened and projected upward like antennas along the side of her head. The black stripes along the v-neck shirt peeled outward, revealing a set of spider-like legs underneath. The legs were incredibly long, too, and stretched well past her *human* legs. Chione grew taller and taller, more domineering. And that was the very last image Renata carried before a black world washed over her.

TWO DAYS AGO

RENATA woke up sweating bullets on Jevon's couch.

She was hit by a fishy stench in the air. She tracked down the putrid smell to Jevon's tortoiseshell, Freddy, and the what-smelled-like-week-old tuna fish it was eating from its *Hello Kitty* bowl on top of the dresser.

Rubbing the crust wedged between the corners of her eyes, Renata sat upright and peeked through the blinds where, outside, the sun was shining just above the treeline. The time on the nightstand read a quarter past six. Renata contemplated shutting her eyes and trying to grab a couple more hours of sleep—perhaps venture back into the recent nightmare—but she heard someone who was larger than a cat moving around in the kitchen.

Wearing a XXL Grape Rush T-shirt that Jevon loaned her to sleep in for the night, she was slow to stand from the couch. Since the bottom of the shirt extended well past her thighs, she didn't even bother slipping into any pants. Renata dragged herself around the room, first checking her cell phone, which she turned off last night. She had "1" missed call and "1" voicemail. She checked the number of the missed call and immediately recognized Kira's phone number. Renata realized that she completely forgot to call Kira back after she arrived at Jevon's. With everything that had been going on lately, coming home to a vandalized townhouse, the sketchy people following her, those "sleepers," Renata decided to give herself a pass and listen to the voicemail. In the message, she heard muffled voices talking—if it was Kira, she wasn't making any sense. The closer she listened, the more she realized that Kira had more than likely "butt dialed" her number by accident. Halfway through the message, Renata heard Kira screaming out loud. Then, other muffled voices came in and out of focus. Renata specifically heard one particular voice while Kira begged for the man to stop. She heard a rustling sound. Then, a man's voice: "What the fuck is this shit?" It was clear, as if the whole time they had been talking over an obstructed speaker. The obstruction sounded as if it had been removed—possibly from Kira's pocket. She heard Kira's voice: "I swear, I didn't know I had it on me," she said. The "it" that she was referring to was possibly her phone. The last words she heard before the phone crunched into a sharp silence were *you sneaky bitch*.

Left in a state of horror, Renata listened to the message once more, trying to make sense of what they were talking about before one of their voices—clearly, a man's voice—started talking into the phone.

After the message ended, she listened to it again.

Then, again.

All that she could take away from the message was that something had happened to Kira.

And it didn't sound good.

WITH the sound of Kira's voice etched in her mind, Renata dragged herself from the living room and made her way into a cramped kitchen where Jevon was frying a white egg for himself. She passed the guest bedroom. Stopped. Turned back around. Inside the room were Jevon's ailing mother, Aurora, and Aurora's aide, Ezra. A lift was attached to the ceiling, which was used to transport Aurora in and out of her hospital bed. Next to the bed were a wheelchair, a tray, as well as a shelf of medical supplies.

Renata stopped at the edge of the doorway and took a closer look inside.

While Ezra was stuffing a couple of pillows underneath Aurora's side to prevent Aurora from getting bedsores, she stopped what she was doing and shot Renata an unfriendly glance. Renata's silent nod of hello was accompanied by a soft wave of her hand. Ezra acknowledged her gesture with a slight dip of her head, which wasn't exactly in the ballpark of Renata's nod but, more or less, a motion indicating that she was aware of Renata's presence.

Renata, who was now aware of the "situation" Jevon always chose to deflect whenever it was brought up in a conversation, proceeded into the kitchen.

Jevon was turning the egg.

Renata acknowledged a pot of oatmeal bubbling on the stovetop. Next to the pot were containers of fresh strawberries and blueberries and other fruits laid out on the countertop. Renata felt compelled to grab herself a handful of blueberries; but, after realizing all of the strings Jevon had to pull in order for her to stay here, she remained polite.

The coffee was already made—which brought great comfort to Renata. An avocado had been gutted, the stone removed, and the oily edible flesh was laid out on a paper plate in six decorative slices. The wheat bread was in the toaster. She wasn't at all hungry—at least not hungry enough to enjoy a decent meal—but she knew she had to eat. The way the day was destined to go, Renata knew that she needed her strength.

"Sorry if I woke you," he said, sensing Renata's presence. "Surely, I thought you'd sleep in."

"Well," Renata said and while yawning, "I'm up now." Then, from the corner of her mouth, "All thanks to you."

Renata tried to rid the thought of Kira from her mind, Kira possibly hurt or in danger, but she couldn't shake the violent images.

Jevon grinned and said over his shoulder, "Looks like someone woke up on the wrong side of the couch."

"Don't start with me," Renata responded, more grumpily. "So," Renata said sheepishly as she turned toward Aurora's bedroom, "are you sure I'm not getting in the way—"

Jevon waved off Renata before she finished her question. "I'm not going to tell you again, Renata. It's no big deal; in fact, I'm pretty sure my mother enjoys the company."

Renata leaned in closer, as the two slices of toast popped from the toaster.

"Can she talk?" whispered Renata.

"Not yet," Jevon said, surprisingly casual. "But she has a therapist who sees her twice a week. I think she's making progress."

"That's good."

Jevon removed the hot white egg from the pan. He placed the egg, the slices of avocado, and toast on a paper plate in an orderly fashion, and carried it to the table where he placed it next to a glass of orange juice.

"Here," Jevon said and pointed at the plate of food. "Eat some breakfast."

"Thanks," Renata said and sat down.

"You're very welcome," Jevon replied and walked back to the stove. Before he could reach the stove, he was drawn to a news report on TV. He pointed at the TV perched on the end of the countertop, as if he was redirecting a frustration that he had been holding onto all morning—the fallout from his own "Serenity Now" moment. "You see this bullshit? I swear, it's becoming an epidemic and nobody seems to give a rat's fuck about it—"

His rant was put to a sudden halt as soon as he saw Ezra entering the kitchen. He immediately apologized for his language. Business-like, Ezra ignored Jevon's usage of words to describe the "homeless problem" in the city and fixed a bowl of oatmeal for Aurora.

"Thank you, Ezra," Jevon said, as Ezra placed the bowl of oatmeal, as well as the berries on a tray and carried it to Aurora's bedroom.

Jevon walked back to the table, his attention focused on both the TV and Renata. "You know, perhaps that should be our next story—expose these corrupted doctors who are getting their patients hooked on snake's milk."

"Snake's milk?"

"Have you been living under a rock for the past year?"

From the redness in Jevon's face, it was apparent that he wanted to take back the words as soon as they left his mouth.

Turned off by Jevon's comment, Renata responded with a harsh tone laced in her voice, "*Really?*"

"Sorry," he said regretfully. "That was out of line. It just. . ."

Renata felt compelled to argue with Jevon, to tell him about this "rock" that was she had been living under for the past year and it was called "Carla and Corvine;" however, for one, it was too early to fight; and two, she had nowhere else to stay.

"It just pisses me off," Jevon said, as Renata redirected her attention toward the news reporter who was standing outside Tent Square, a Mecca for the homeless, in Lower Manhattan. "Seeing all of these god. . ." he trailed off, as if he was still mindful of Ezra's presence, ". . . damn drug companies profit off people, as if they've been reduced to nothing more than dollar signs, pawns exploited by politicians, sound bites, 'hot takes' for headlines, expendable—'x'd out, huh?" Jevon pointed at Renata with a partial grin on his face, as if the groundwork of this so-called "new story" was already in development inside his head. "It's not a complicated issue. The doctors over-prescribe drugs to patients, get patients addicted, then the insurance companies cut them off, forcing patients on the streets to buy harder, cheaper drugs, like snake's milk. I mean, we're talking about a drug that can destroy a person's life. The damage is irreparable. If you want proof, all you have to do is walk down North Morrison Street. *They're* everywhere."

"What makes 'snake's milk' so different than crack or heroin or any of these other drugs on the streets?" asked Renata.

"What makes it so different?" he repeated. "Nobody knows where in the hell it came from."

"But surely somebody knows," Renata stuttered. "Nobody?"

"Nobody knows," Jevon said.

"Have researchers run tests?"

Jevon bobbed his head.

"Tried."

"And?"

"They don't know," he said.

"They don't know?"

"Crazy, huh?"

"Yeah," Renata mumbled. "Crazy."

The news cut to a commercial break.

Renata couldn't help but draw her attention toward the commercial.

"*Sometimes athlete's foot can leave you on itchy ground.*" In the TV commercial, a soccer player kicked off his cleats and started scratching his feet moments before the game-winning penalty shot. "*Help fight the itch by asking your health care provider about Damianix. Damianix treats those suffering from athlete's foot. Damianix should not be used. . .*" Renata drifted in a trance from the soothing sound of the voice-over actor's voice, "*. . . Call your doctor about fever. This may be a sign of a life-threatening reaction. Side effects may include. . .*"

Heated by the latest news report, Jevon turned off the TV.

The silence in the kitchen forced Renata inward where violent images of Kira filled her mind.

As Jevon was about to walk to the stove, he noticed Renata's paranoid state. Clearly, food was the last thing on her mind. She was looking around the kitchen, as if she was being watched from a window or a closet.

Jevon reassured her, "You're safe here."

Renata faced Jevon and forced a smile on her face.

WHILE Jevon was washing the dishes, Renata turned on the shower faucet inside the hallway bathroom and snuck into Jevon's bedroom. Thinking about the best place where he would put it, she snooped around his room. She checked the most obvious place first, which was the nightstand. She had no luck. Next, she looked under the bed and checked under the mattress and pillows. She moved her search to the closet where she found a suspicious-looking box on the top shelf. What she thought might've been it was only a box of cigars with a note attached inside from Barron, who was the senior editor at *X'D*. Lastly,

Renata checked the dresser and went through each drawer, including his sock and underwear drawer. Not a damn thing. As Renata pulled her eyes from the dresser, she found a picture frame of a young man on the top of the dresser. She looked over the photo of the man inside and thought about whether or not Jevon had any brothers or cousins. If Jevon did, he never mentioned it to her. She picked up the frame, held it closer to her face, and took a closer look at the young man. She shielded the top of his face with her hand, searching for Jevon's mouth or jaw. Then, did the same with the bottom of his face and searched for Jevon's eyes or nose. She couldn't find any features on his face that resembled Jevon, except for maybe his brow; however, he could've been related to him outside of blood. Renata flipped over the picture frame and opened the back. A key fell out onto Renata's hand. Key found. *Check.* Now all she had to do was find where he was hiding it.

As soon as Renata closed the picture frame and placed it back on the dresser, Jevon was standing at the doorway.

"I thought you were taking a shower," he said, leaning against the doorway.

"I was," Renata stuttered, "I mean, I am. I'm waiting for the water to warm." She immediately changed the subject and nodded at the photo of the young man, who clearly wasn't Jevon. She asked, "Who's the guy?"

"He's nobody," Jevon said flatly.

"Nobody? He has to be somebody; otherwise, what is he doing in your bedroom?"

"Don't you have somewhere to be soon?" Jevon asked, the boss in him coming out in his voice.

"Yeah, *Dad*," Renata said sarcastically.

"I don't mean to—"

"—I know," she said swiftly "I shouldn't have been snooping around."

Jevon turned around and pointed toward the bathroom, which was filling with thick steam.

"Think the water is warm," he said.

"Right," Renata said flippantly. "Thanks."

"Listen. . . Renata. . . " Jevon said through the unexpected tension before Renata could make any sort of move toward the shower, "I'm going to step out for a minute while you take your shower."

"Where you going?" she asked.

"I just have to pick up a few things at the Lion's Den," Jevon said. "I should be back before you head to work." He pulled out a cell phone from his pocket. "Got you a new phone." He stepped into the room and handed the phone to Renata. "I programmed my number in there, like the other one."

"So, this one has a tracking device on it as well?"

"Renata," Jevon sighed, "you know, I can't take any chances, right?"

Renata sighed as well, as if she was mocking Jevon.

"Right."

"Trust me," Jevon said, trying to relief the tension in the air, "I can't tell you how much I miss my old phone. I'm now realizing how much it spoiled me. But it's the sacrifice we have to make, right?"

"What are you going to do with the other phone?"

"I already destroyed it."

"You know I could've done that," Renata said, letting out more emotion than she intended to let out. She retracted the anger before it took hold. "I mean," she said, trying to tone back the anger, "you know, I destroy them every time you get me a new one."

"I know you do," Jevon replied sharply with a strange look on his face. "*But* I thought you were taking a shower. So, I did it for you. So, you're welcome."

"Okay, well," she held up the phone, "thanks anyway."

Jevon left the room.

"I'll be back soon," he said, walking away.

ONCE Jevon drove away, Renata basically had the whole place to herself. Considering Aurora's aide, Ezra, spent most of the morning taking care of Aurora's in the bedroom opposite Jevon's office, Renata decided to skip a shower and went straight to Jevon's office.

Mounted on the walls in sturdy black frames were the front covers of nearly every issue of *X'D*. There was very little space on the walls for other issues—and those, which couldn't fit on the wall, Jevon had tucked away in a far corner of the closet where they were collecting dust. Renata wandered through the office, looking over each magazine cover as if she was touring an art gallery. She wound up at the poster-sized cover of the once-cultural icon turned shamed actor, Vincent Brentano, who was ousted from Hollywood after he was accused of raping a nineteen-year-old actress, Marina Coyle. Whenever Jevon needed to rally the troops at the Lion's Den, he often talked about the importance of this particular issue, not because it happened to be the very first issue ever published, but because it helped launch an external investigation that ended up clearing Vincent Brentano's name many years later. Despite being acquitted, Brentano's reputation was ruined, reduced to false tabloids and parody TV cameos, and left many people with doubts about whether or not he committed the crime. Brentano was unable to find decent acting jobs—hence the cameos—whereas the young, up and coming actress, Marina Coyle, was featured in two summer blockbusters during the time of the accusations. One of the blockbusters happened to set a box office record for the highest grossed movie in opening weekend; however, two years later, Coyle got involved in drugs and alcohol; her career fizzled out like a popped balloon; and by the time Coyle's twenty-third birthday arrived, she was doing low budget amateur porn and barely scraping by. As for Vincent Brentano, who, by then, had turned into a blacklisted actor, he ended up doing Indie films for about four years until he hung up his acting hat. Sixteen years after Brentano's career tanked itself into a coma, Jevon approached him about making a comeback. After some convincing, Brentano sat down for an "Exclusive Interview" that appeared in the first issue of the controversial magazine, *X'D*. Throughout all of these years, Brentano maintained his innocence and denied the charges filed against him. After the magazine was released, just a few months later Vincent Brentano's career took off again, landing him lead roles in three Oscar-nominated movies—he even received a nod in the Best Supporting Actor category for his tour-de-force performance as a struggling hit man turned drug addict in the film, *Home Free*.

With the key in hand, Renata stepped closer to the first issue of *XD* hanging on the wall. In a way, the poster was begging for attention, as if it had a huge sign on the front that said, "Pull here."

And Renata did exactly that. She pulled back the poster and on the wall behind the poster was a lockbox. She opened the box with the key. It worked. Inside were stacks of cash—at least six-figures inside—and a Glock 19.

She grabbed the pistol from the lockbox, left the cash. She closed the lockbox, placed the poster back in its rightful position on the wall, and midway toward the door, she paused. For a moment, she contemplated turning around and taking the cash, just enough to get by until the story she was working on ran itself into a dead end. In that moment, she felt free. If only for a moment.

RENATA spent the whole subway ride thinking about the voicemail on her phone.

Once she arrived at her stop, she sat frozen in her seat. Her workbag, which held Jevon's Glock 19, was gripped tightly in her lap. Other passengers walked past her. A voice on the intercom pulled her from a trance. She came back to reality; and as soon as the doors started to close, she darted off the train. She caught her arm in the two doors but ended up yanking it out just as the train took off.

She walked up the stairs leading to the street. The whole time, she felt as if she was being followed. She looked over her shoulder to see if anyone was following her. When she turned back around, she was hit by the sudden force of another pedestrian. Both Renata's shoulder and the pedestrian's shoulder collided in harmony, forcing them to drop their belongings. Renata couldn't be sorry enough for the accidental bump. The pedestrian, who wasn't displaying the least amount of emotion—and if she was, Renata couldn't see it for her face was hiding behind a dark hoody—kneeled down and with her gloved hand, picked up a Zippo lighter that she had dropped on the sidewalk, while Renata grabbed her workbag, as well as the data research papers that had flown from it. Renata couldn't help but notice the Zippo in the pedestrian's hand and the blue cartoon-like dragon sticker, which was partially peeled away on the side of the lighter.

As the strange pedestrian scurried away as if she had just committed a crime or something, Renata felt a sudden pain in her forearm. She looked down, examined her arm, and saw a tiny red dot just below her elbow. She couldn't help but wonder if she was stabbed by a sharp object on the pedestrian's hoody—perhaps a sharp zipper?

Renata stood to her feet and was struck by a sudden dizzy spell. She stopped walking for a moment, grabbed her forehead, and tried to catch her balance while distracted phone addicts shouldered past her in a hasty, rude rat-race manner, texting, MindChanting, Twerkstreaming, or whatever was more important than paying any attention to their surroundings.

Eventually, after the crowds thinned out on the sidewalk, Renata managed to find her bearings. The dizzy spell eased a bit, enough for Renata to make it work without falling over; however, she could still feel it lingering.

THE first clue that something wasn't quite right with Renata all began when she was forced into small talk with Arnold, the friendly security guard who worked on the first floor of the Carla and Corvine building. As she did every morning while passing through the lobby, she went through a series of responses, right on command, as if she was sending quick emails using words from a stockpile of expressions. A thought popped in Arnold's head. Everything about Arnold appeared as if it popped, his eyes, mouth, index finger that erected upward in cartoon fashion. Before Renata could ease her way to the elevators, Arnold pulled out a folded up piece of paper from his pocket.

"What's this?" Renata asked but already had an idea of what it was.

Arnold walked over to Renata. He handed the piece of paper to Renata. She looked down and was slow—in fact, scared—to grab the paper from not Arnold's hand but something else's hand. The color of his skin was sandy brown. The texture, rough and partly covered in scales, like the wrinkly skin along the neck of a hundred year old tortoise. Renata recoiled from the sight of the strange hand.

In a state of shock, she drew her wide eyes up at Arnold, whose facial expression changed slightly.

"It's a recipe for the pineapple upside down cake," he said.

Once more, Renata glanced down. Arnold's hand changed and appeared like any normal hand of a sixty-year-old man.

Arnold extended his head downward toward Renata's falling eyes.

"Remember you asked about it the other day?"

"Yes," Renata said suddenly. "Right. Of course."

She grabbed the piece of paper from Arnold's hand.

"And just remember to butter the inside of the pan before you pour in the batter, otherwise—"

"I know," Renata interrupted, "the cake will stick. Got it."

Arnold smiled and waved goodbye to Renata.

"I don't need to tell you."

"Thanks, Arnold," Renata said, turning toward the elevators.

"You're welcome, Renata. Enjoy your day."

Arnold placed his thumbs around his belt along his hips and watched Renata walk away.

RENATA was printing off the latest trends, in particular one trend which happened to be certain types of dances from one of the most popular video games in the market, *Camp Kill,* which was a long awaited sequel to game developers Finger Warrior's debut smash hit, BΔSEHEΔD, an online video game which offered players an opportunity to play a campaign or a free-to-play *Battle Royale.* All the sales data suggested that players weren't actually buying the game. Instead, they were playing the free *Battle Royale.* However, Finger Warriors made most of the revenue from the in-game loot. Each day, new skins and emotes were available to purchase with game loot—or BΔSEHEΔD coins. Also, the more points you earned the more loot. It was like playing a slot machine. Similar to BΔSEHEΔD, *Camp Kill* was a free online game where players spent money on various loot inside the game. According to recent studies that Renata had found while scouring the Underworld, *Camp Kill* was one of the leading causes of a spike in divorces between the ages of 25 and 50. The popular game also reached children ages 12 through 18 and was said to play a pivotal factor in a sudden surge in high school dropouts. Kids were basically making a living off subscriptions or "views" from their own YouTube channels.

After Renata handed off the latest "dance" trends to LeBron, she walked back to the printer where she left her coffee. She saw that the coffee was gone, only a brown ring where her coffee cup once sat on top of the scanner. She thought that maybe one of the interns tossed the coffee. She looked around, first to the right and then the left toward the other offices. As Renata rotated around, she saw Kira standing only a couple of feet from her. The sight of Kira startled her.

"Kira? Hey."

"Hey," Kira said expressionlessly.

"What are you doing?"

"I'm working," she said, her face still blank and emotionless. "What does it look like I'm doing?"

"Sorry." She hesitated. "I didn't mean it like that."

"What did you mean?"

Even though some kind of anger or frustration would come out from such a comment, Kira said it robotically, as if she was somehow heavily medicated.

"I mean," Renata stuttered, "you know, the message."

"What message?"

"You left a message on my voicemail last night. Don't you remember?"

"No."

"Quit yanking my chain," Renata said loosely, tapping Kira on the shoulder. "You know what I mean?"

Kira looked down at her shoulder, her face still blank.

"Yanking your chain?" Kira repeated. "What chain?"

"You know," Renata said, using laughter to lessen the innocent remark, "it's an *expression*." Trying to hide her concern with a smile, she looked over Kira for any injuries or marks on her body. "You honestly don't remember? That's strange. Maybe someone got a hold of your phone."

"Maybe."

Over the one-way conversation, Renata finally asked the inevitable question, "Are you ok—"

"—Now that I think about it," Kira said before Renata could finish asking the question, "it might've been my cousin."

"I didn't know you had a cousin."

"Dovydas Mazeika," Kira said. "David, for short. He's not my actual cousin. Kin adopted David from Lithuania when he was just a baby. You know how kids can be when they get a hold of a phone."

"Sure," Renata said, more relieved as the conversation started to loosen up a bit. "So, how old is Dovydas—David?"

"He's fourteen. He's actually in town performing at Merkin Hall. The show starts tonight at eight-thirty."

"Merkin Hall? Really?"

"He's sort of a boy wonder, the next prodigy—so they say."

"Sounds like it," Renata said, then asked: "Curious, what instrument?"

"The cello."

LeBron called out Renata's name from outside the printer room. Renata turned toward LeBron and acknowledged his interest in the recent report she had given to him.

"*Listen, Kira. . .*" Renata said, as she turned back around to face Kira.

She had only taken her eyes off Kira for no more than three seconds. Baffled by Kira's disappearance, she looked around the office but couldn't find her anywhere.

WITH the recent conversation with Kira on her mind, Renata excused herself from the meeting with the marketing team and located the nearest computer inside an unoccupied office where she googled the schedule for Merkin Concert Hall. She read through all of the names in the ensemble. She came across the name *Dovydas Mazeika* among the musicians performing tonight at "eight-thirty."

Still not entirely convinced, she decided to type in Dovydas Mazeika's name in the search browser.

While scrolling through a gallery of images—some of which shared no relation to Dovydas Mazeika—Renata scrolled past one particular image that immediately caught her eye: a photo of Kira's uncle, Kin, posing with young Dovydas in front of yaki. Kin's arm was wrapped around Dovydas's shoulder, not at all in any kind of fatherly or guardian-like way but more so like a fan wanting to take a photo with someone whom he admired. They were both smiling and throwing up the two-finger peace sign for the camera. She could tell the photo was taken during the late afternoon due to the setting of the sun and a glare on the sides of both their faces; however, one detail grabbed Renata: the cameraman—or cameramen. In the reflection of the glass doors outside the restaurant, a forty-something year old, blonde haired man, who looked as if he could've passed for Dovydas's father—real one, that is—was holding the camera. Next to him stood a dirty blonde haired woman of the similar age who could've passed as Dovydas's mother. She, too, had a camera in her hand.

Renata read the date the photo was posted on Kin's Instagram page. It was taken last year.

Out of curiosity, she clicked on a link that sent her to Kin's Instagram page. She scrolled through hundreds and hundreds of his personal photographs, most of them taken with other well-known celebrities at his restaurant, fashion designers, authors, movie stars, sharks, artists, musicians, Broadway actors, none of Dovydas, except for the one he posted roughly "one year ago."

Renata pulled her eyes from the computer screen. More confused, she looked around the office, only to find Kira, of all people, standing at the front of a conference room at the other end of the office. She was staring at Renata. As soon as Renata's eyes crossed Kira's, Kira turned away and proceeded with her meeting.

Defeated, she dropped her head in thought, wondering as to why Kira, a person whom she once considered as a good friend—even "one time," much more than a friend—would make up lies about her uncle. In her defeated state, she noticed that strange red dot on her forearm and the red cloudy skin around it, as if a large zit was forming underneath it. She gently ran her finger across the red spot on her arm. The area was incredibly tender to touch and felt the same way a day-old bruise would feel. The hot flash of pain on her arm radiated through her body, causing her to flush with sickness. She was hit by yet another one of those dizzy spells. The insides of her mouth started to moisten, as if it was preparing itself for what was soon going to come. Her stomach lurched forward. A bubble of nausea hit her once, then, in an attempt to fight back the urge to vomit, hit her yet again.

With her face all pale and sweaty, Renata rushed to the bathroom where she sought out the last stall. She quickly shut the door behind her and right when she was about to explode, she fell toward the toilet. The vomit splashed on the side of the rim and bowl. Some even hit the floor. Whenever she felt as if she was about to stop and stand up, Renata was forced back to the toilet where she continued to vomit. She ended up dry heaving until she had nothing left in her stomach. For a moment, her eyes rolled in the back of her head. Her surroundings turned gray. The world, spinning. All of that straining caused Renata to temporarily blackout.

After she pushed through consciousness, she found herself pressed up against the side of the wall. The side of her head was throbbing from where she possibly hit her head during the blackout.

Feeling less dizzy, she wiped her mouth cleaned, flushed the toilet, and while grabbing the forming knot on her forehead, stepped out of the stall. The life was drained from her face and body.

Renata ambled toward the vanity where she inspected the red mark on her head. The knot was raised. Which was a good sign. She continued to primp her hair and re-adjust her clothing. Renata blew her nose into a paper towel and when she pulled the towel away from her face, a Rorschach test of phlegm was revealed inside. She tossed the damp towel in the trash, leaned over the sink, and used her hand as a cup to take a few bird-like sips of water from the faucet. She pulled her face from the sink below and looked into the mirror before her.

Standing motionlessly in the open stall behind her was Chione.

Renata's heart skipped a bit from the sight of Chione's grim presence. In that moment, Renata was no longer exhausted or sick. Instead, she was fully aware—woke. Poised, she kept her keen eyes on Chione, who, in return, stretched open her mouth in a yawning gape, revealing *not* the normal tongue of a human but a set of dark legs that were curled up like two tightly clenched fists. Hairy spider-like legs slowly uncurled and stretched out the sides of her mouth.

Frightened by Chione, Renata suddenly rotated around, only to find an empty space inside the stall. Renata ran through a series of thoughts, all of which were guided by the idea of hallucinations. Clearly, she didn't feel like herself. And her only rush to judgment was that she had eaten something tainted.

She pushed aside the thoughts and crept toward the stall. Halfway toward the stall, she heard strange noises coming from inside the stall. A *winding* noise followed by a strange *clicking* noise. As she stood at the edge of the stall, contemplating whether or not to further investigate the noise, the bathroom door opened, giving way to a glaring white light.

Sensitive to the bright light, Renata was hit by yet another dizzy spell!

She blinked and squinted, hoping to see more clearly through the light. Her eyes felt no different than they did when staring at the sun. An alien-like figure manifested from the light and its body became fuller as it approached. The bathroom door shut, dampening the brightness in the bathroom doorway. Renata blinked and focused until those red blotches in the corners of her eyes were gone from view. She witnessed a petite woman entering the bathroom. She thought it might have been Kathleen from Human Resources; however, she didn't give off a vibe that she was any kind of threat.

DEEPLY disturbed by her current condition, Renata left the Carla and Corvine building without telling anyone where she was going.

As she stepped onto the sidewalk outside, she felt the same sense that she was being followed. Renata couldn't explain how or why, but she could, more or less, sense it in her bones. She decided to hail a taxi.

The taxi pulled up beside her. She hopped into the taxi, placed her workbag on the seat, and told the taxi driver to take her to "Madison Square Park."

As the taxi driver drove away, Renata texted Jevon on her flip phone.

Meet me at Madison Square Park ASAP.

Only a few seconds later, her phone rang. She looked down at the number on her phone. Jevon was calling her. She didn't answer the phone. Instead, she texted him back.

Can't talk.

Jevon responded: **K.**

The return text threw Renata for a loop. Ever since she had known Jevon—which was going on for a year now and certainly long enough to understand his usage in words and stock responses—Renata had never read *or* even heard, for that matter, her boss answer with such an abbreviated response.

As Renata put aside her cell phone, she couldn't help but notice the turn that the taxi driver had missed; in fact, the taxi driver was driving in the opposite direction of Madison Avenue. Dread crept into Renata's thoughts—*stranger danger!* Renata realized he was taking her to Lincoln Tunnel. She looked at the taxi driver in the rear view mirror. In that narrow strip of mirror, the driver didn't appear at all to be the same scruffy-looking Middle Eastern man who picked her up; in fact, he didn't appear to be a man at all. His skin was smooth and glossy like hard candy. Along the sides of his protruding insect-like mouth were two fuzzy-looking palps that one would normally find on an arthropod. Two antennas hung from his navy blue Yankees ball cap and stretched down the sides of his face. His eyes appeared yellowish, almost translucent in nature.

Renata remembered the gun in her bag.

As she took her eyes off the taxi driver for a moment to grab the Glock from her bag, the taxi driver changed appearance. He looked just like he did when he picked up Renata. *But* Renata wasn't fooled.

"You're going the wrong direction," Renata said to the taxi driver.

While occasionally glancing at Renata through the rear view mirror, the taxi driver said casually to Renata, "She just wants to talk with you, that's all."

"Please stop the car."

"I'm afraid I can't do—"

Before the taxi driver could finish his sentence, Renata already had the barrel of the gun pressed firmly against the side of his hairy neck.

"Stop the fucking car," she demanded.

The taxi was slow to stop, but eventually, he eased off the side of the road as other cars came screaming by.

With her eyes not leaving the taxi driver, Renata blindly reached for the door handle. She found it. Tugged on it. The door was locked.

"Open the door. *Now!*"

The taxi driver unlocked the doors from his end.

Renata opened the door.

The traffic ambience was clearer; however, Renata made sure to keep the gun pointed at the taxi driver.

With the gun drawn, Renata grabbed her bag and carefully stepped out of the taxi.

Before Renata stepped onto the sidewalk, the taxi driver said from inside the taxi, "There's nowhere to run, Renata. We have eyes everywhere."

Renata digested the comment, didn't put too much stock in it, then took off.

PERIODICALLY looking over her shoulder, Renata walked briskly through Koreatown. Somehow, the taxi driver's words had stayed with her throughout her walk. Her paranoia was heightened. She checked her six o'clock once more and spotted a sketchy-looking man closing in on her. She had no other choice than try to lose him. She ended up seeking cover inside a restaurant called Noodle Shop, which was located under the second floor of a sleazy video store that sold amateur oriental sex tapes and DVDs. Renata looked as if she was wearing a huge red hat and a Tee shirt with a "Kick Me" sign on the back of it. The guests inside—mostly Korean—moved their eyes from the steaming bowls of noodles and stared at Renata with blank expressions.

Trying to act as normal as she could, Renata proceeded toward the very back of the restaurant, occasionally nodding *hello* to the other guests who were sitting inside the booths that lined both sides of the restaurant.

Renata glanced down at one of the guests' bowls on the table covered in a red and white checked plastic tablecloth. Inside the bowl were cellophane noodles—or "glass noodles," which were known for their translucent grayish color. At first glance, she thought the noodles were moving around inside the bowl. But, after a second glance, the noodles appeared like noodles. She passed another table, saw yet another bowl with noodles. This time, she watched the noodles moving inside the bowl like live worms. Another guest slurped up the worms inside his mouth, the ends of the worms squirming around on the corners of his chin. Her stomach lurched heavily. Her skin perspired with layers of sweat. That dizzying sensation was back. Her world started to spin. Passing each guest, watching each wiggle of the worm, listening to each and every *slurp* and exaggerated *gulp*, Renata quickened her pace. She stormed into the kitchen where mean-faced cooks hollered at her in a foreign language. The words were slowed down. Even after she charged toward the back door with cooks dumbly shouting out behind her, the world itself felt as if it had slowed down. She knew the only way to combat this slowing effect was to do what only came natural: run. And that, she did.

Before she could find the exit, her foot slipped, causing her to stumble into a shelf of pots and pans.

Infuriated by Renata's presence, one of the cooks suddenly came at her with a bird's beak knife. Renata brandished her gun, but the cook stabbed Renata right in the gut before she could open fire.

Clutching her stomach in great agony, Renata managed to shoulder her way outside. With the cook right on her tail, she grabbed a stack of cardboard boxes and pushed them against the back of the exit door. The boxes avalanched onto the ground, preventing the cook from exiting. Through the narrow crack of the door, the cook reached out to grab Renata by the hair, his hand like a pincer snapping back and forth.

Renata managed to escape. *But the gun*—the gun was gone!

She must've dropped it during the attack.

With her eyes honing in on a red STOP sign on the corner of the street ahead of her, Renata ran through the alleyway behind Noodle Shop. She pulled out her cell phone, gripping it tightly in case she needed to call Jevon. Only a few strides in her daring escape, the "slowing" dramatically worsened. She was sprinting in slow motion.

All of a sudden, her legs grew stiff and heavy. Even the pavement below her started to thicken, as if it was made of quicksand. Each stride became harder for Renata. Each motion, each movement, more rigid. Right then and there, Renata found herself sinking into the soft pavement. Her feet were first to go under, then her shins, knees next.

Once the pavement reached her waist, she held out her hand, flagging out the pedestrian crossing the alleyway. The man ignored her.

Another one came by.

With every fiber of her being, Renata called out for help but received no response.

More came walking by.

All ignored.

The pavement was now up to her chest, crushing each word she could muster. Nobody—not one—was paying any attention to Renata.

Each pedestrian, each phone addict, were too distracted by their phones held in their hands below; their heads were frozen in downward positions, the glow of the phones casting a pale light over each one of their faces.

The cell phone slipped from her sweaty hand and came crashing down on the hard pavement.

She continued to sink farther into the ground below until she was eventually swallowed whole.

PRESENT DAY

FRANTICALLY swinging out her arms, Renata searched through the blackness until she found a glimmer of light. She swam toward the light, but the light kept pulling away from her. She reached and reached and reached, the edges of her fingers clawing at the light. Out of desperation, she surged forward and managed to wrap her hands around the light. She embraced the light, as if it was her own.

Gasping for air, her eyes bolted open.

The cold, damp washcloth, which once rested on her forehead, slid down the side of her face.

Jevon, who was sitting at Renata's feet on the couch, grabbed a glass of water next to the bloody blouse on the coffee table, and rushed to her side. She finally settled and in that moment of peace, she was struck by a coughing spell.

Mindful not to spill any water, Jevon handed her the glass of water. With his help, he nursed the water into Renata's mouth.

"I got it," she said, taking hold of the glass on her own. "Thanks."

"You scared me for a moment," said Jevon, as he felt Renata's forehead with the backside of his hand.

The cough finally subsided, which presented yet another issue: her arm. She tried to scratch at the infection on her forearm. Jevon grabbed Renata's wrist during mid-scratch and specifically told Renata to stop scratching.

"It itches," Renata said and looked around and found herself back in the living room of the cabin. The fire in the fireplace was still burning. The mood was less tense. She directed her attention back to Jevon, who told her, "I think maybe your arm is infected. You remember how you got it?"

Renata thought back as far as the last few moments, in particular, Kira rising from the dead.

Jevon stood from the couch.

"I'll look for some Neosporin," he said.

Renata asked Jevon, "What happened?"

Jevon walked back to the couch and stood over Renata.

"You had a panic attack," he said, grabbing the glass from Renata's hand. "If I didn't catch you before you passed out, you probably would've been more worse for wear."

"My hero," she said with a trace of sarcasm and sat upright against the arm of the couch.

"You know, Rennie, this is now twice I've come to your rescue. I tell you," Jevon said undoubtedly, "it's not getting easier."

"Thanks again," she said, more quietly. "I just... I don't know what in the hell's going on with me. I feel like I'm losing, you know?"

"You're in shock, Rennie," Jevon said, sitting back down on the couch. "After everything you've just been through, who wouldn't be?"

Renata looked twice at Jevon. The second time, she witnessed the softness in his face. She smiled, but, eventually, after Jevon spoke her name in a darker manner, her face melted into a look of deep concern. He had something on his chest, she realized, something *heavy*, something that he was hiding from her.

As soon as he was about to clear the air, two headlights flashed over the living room walls. Jevon stood, first, then Renata, who followed close behind to the living room window. A car was parked at the end of the driveway, its headlights still blazing. They both stood at opposite sides of the window.

More concerned, Renata asked, "What's really going on, Jevon?"

With a shameful look on his face, Jevon turned to Renata.

"I'm sorry," he said. "It's part of the deal."

"*Deal?*" Renata parroted. "What deal?"

"The other day, after I found you unconscious in that alleyway, they came to my place," Jevon said. "I thought it might have been Mom's physical therapist. I went to answer the door and there they were."

"Where was I?" asked Renata.

"You were resting in my bedroom when they arrived." Jevon shook his head in utter disgust, as if the disgust was directed toward himself. "I didn't even have a chance to react. They were already on top of me. I had no other choice. I cut a deal with them." Jevon stepped closer to Renata. "You must understand, Renata. If I didn't do exactly what they told me to do, they were going to destroy everything—*everything*—including the ones closest to me."

Jevon looked into Renata's eyes and held his eyes on her.

"What did you do?" asked Renata.

"They gave me no other choice," he said shortly. "They bought me."

"Bought you? This isn't about money, Jevon. It never was—"

"—Not money. *My* life." He turned to Renata. "*Your* life. Face it, Renata. They own us now. They've been following us ever since we started tightening up our investigation into Carla and Corvine. We swung for the fences. Came close. *Really close.* But, in the end, we struck out—"

"—We can still expose them for *what* they are. We have the evidence linking them to *multiple* crimes, enough to put them away for good."

That awful look was back on Jevon's face, and he wore it as if it was a mask that weighed twice the weight of his head.

"Jevon," Renata seethed, "we still have the evidence, don't we?"

Jevon raised his head and peered into Renata's eyes as if, for a moment, he'd actually cause her bodily harm in order to protect her.

"Did you not just hear me, Renata?" Jevon asked, his voice louder. "They'll kill us! End of story!"

"So, that's it, huh? We're giving up that easily? The story's over and we're just going to sit back and watch while they fuck the human race into extinction?"

The headlights flashed twice, as if they were blinking at them.

"We can't stay here," Jevon said, as he acknowledged the signal in the corner of his eye. "We have to leave."

Renata didn't budge an inch.

"Come on. Time to leave."

"And go where?"

With clarity, Jevon said, "*Home.*"

RENATA left the car keys inside the cup holder of the center console, just as Jevon was told, and got into Jevon's car. Jevon started the ignition and as soon as Renata closed the passenger door behind her, he made sure to lock the doors—even secretly flipped on the child's safety lock without Renata paying any mind. She was too busy checking the contents of the glove compartment. After a quick survey, she saw that, except for several owner's manuals and receipts, it was nearly empty. In a cautious glance, Jevon acknowledged Renata's strange behavior.

With one eye on the driveway and the other one on Renata, he drove toward the mysterious car.

"So who the hell is this guy?" Renata asked, as they approached the car idling at the end of the driveway.

Jevon blew out a heavy sigh, as if the thought alone of "this guy" caused him great stress.

EXT. ALLEYWAY, DOWNTOWN DALLAS - NIGHT

Athanor steps out of the stolen police cruiser, grabs the can of gasoline from the trunk with his gloved hand, and douses the police cruiser -- inside and out -- with gasoline.

                    JEVON (V.O.)
        His name is Athanor Dowe.

Athanor leaves himself a sloppy trail of gasoline
along the pavement and strikes a match on the side
of the building. He drops a flaming match onto
the ground, igniting the trail of gasoline.

Jevon took his eyes off the gravel road for a moment and
turned to Renata, who appeared curious to know more
about this "Athanor" character.

INT. ALLEYWAY, DOWNTOWN DALLAS - SAME

Appearing only as a tall, strikingly handsome silhouette, Athanor struts from the massive fire raging only feet behind him.

> JEVON (V.O.)
> I've only heard stories about him.
> Ghost stories. People say he was
> born on the run from the cartel.

SERIES OF SHOTS - ATHANOR'S ORIGINS

-- EXT. SAFEHOUSE - NIGHT -- In the midst of heavy
gunfire, ATHANOR'S MOTHER plucks Baby Athanor from
the makeshift crib, places him inside a cardboard
box, and with ninja-like movements, pokes holes in
top of box with a blade. With a gun gripped in
one hand and a box curled by her side like a football in the other, Athanor's Mother escapes
through a bedroom window as bullets plug the
walls.

"People? What people?"

"I dunno, *people*," Jevon said. "They say he spent most of
his childhood in and out of juvenile hall."

-- INT. CANTERBURY ELEMENTARY - DAY -- Boy Athanor
rolls up his book report on "To Kill A Mocking-
bird," his knuckles tight and white, the paper
making leathery sounds. He hits a BULLY in the
back of his head, stuffs the end of the report
down the bully's throat and smothers him to death.

-- INT. PRINCIPAL'S OFFICE, CANTERBURY ELEMENTARY
- DAY -- POLICE OFFICERS remove Boy Athanor from
the office in handcuffs.

-- INT. JUVY COURT - DAY -- The JUDGE barks and wags her finger at Boy Athanor. Then, she SLAMS down the gavel.

> JEVON (V.O.)
> By the time he turned eighteen, he enlisted in the Marines.

-- EXT. VILLAGE, IRAQ - DAY -- Young Athanor breaks into a small hut, murdering armed members of the al-Qaeda organization.

> JEVON (V.O.)
> When he came back to America, he joined the Force.

-- INT. POLICE ACADEMY GRADUATION - DAY -- On the stage in front of a crowd of friends and family members, Athanor shakes the hand of the SUPERIN-TENDENT.

> JEVON (V.O.)
> He used his skills he picked up over-seas to hunt down bad guys.

-- INT. CRACK HOUSE - DAY -- Detective Dowe breaks down the door and fires at an armed DRUG DEALER, who draws an Uzi. Detective Dowe kills the drug dealer and uncovers a stockpile of cocaine and il-legal weapons. His PARTNERS congratulate him.

Jevon drove closer to the mysterious car parked at the end of the driveway. A shadowy face appeared behind the glare of the headlights.

-- INT. DOWNTOWN - NIGHT -- Athanor chases an armed suspect into a shady building.

> JEVON (V.O.)
> One night, Athanor's life was almost cut short.

-- INT. PARKING GARAGE - NIGHT -- With a shotgun in his hands, a CRIMINAL creeps up behind Athanor and shoots him in side of head, blowing off part of Athanor's skull.

Jevon slowly drove past the car, revealing the side of Athanor's face in the driver's seat. He dragged from a lit cigarette, which cast an orange glow over his stern, shadowy mien.

-- INT. OPERATION ROOM, HOSPITAL - NIGHT -- A surgeon installs a metal plate in the side of Athanor's bloody head.

> JEVON (V.O.)
> Rumor has it that the gun blast destroyed part of his brain, the part that felt emotion.

"*They* say a lot of things, don't they? So, does he work for Chione?"

"He works for no one."

-- INT. HELICOPTER - NIGHT -- Athanor mercilessly rains down gunfire on a Viper speeding down the highway, the flashes of gunfire flickering over his face like a strobe light inside a dance club.

BACK TO SCENE

"He doesn't exist in the real world," Jevon said, as he looked at Athanor's car in the rear view mirror. Athanor flicked the cherry from the end of the cigarette. The tiny flaming ball of ash settled in the gravel below. "He's a ghost," he said to Renata. "He only exists to carry out the dirty work so that people like you and me can stay clean."

"Me? Clean?" Renata laughed hysterically. "Jevon, I just *killed* an innocent person. Some 'cleaner' isn't going to take that away."

"He will."

"But I can't, Jevon. I can't take that away."

"Well, Renata," Jevon said, as he pulled out on the main road. "You're going to have to try."

"How?"

"You can start by acknowledging what happened." He took his eyes off the road and glanced at Renata. "You can't block it out. You wouldn't be human, if you could.

First off, Renata, you have to *accept* what you did, then *move on* with your life. Understood?"

"It's *not* that easy."

"Nobody ever said it was."

ONE DAY AGO

THE pothole in the road jarred Renata to consciousness.

The sounds all around her intensified: the siren blaring outside the ambulance and then two people talking, one of them a paramedic and the other, Jevon, who was holding Renata's hand.

Wringing wet with sweat, Renata pulled the side of her flushed face from the gurney and straightened her focus upward at the light above.

A paramedic's face entered her field of vision. She was reading a thermometer.

"A hundred and three," she said to herself.

"It's lowering," another more familiar voice said.

As soon as Jevon's face entered Renata's view, she tried to sit upright but the paramedic held her down. Renata looked around the inside of the ambulance with a sense of great urgency.

"What happened?" asked Renata. The fear was evident in her voice. "Where are you taking me?"

"Easy now, Renata. I told you," Jevon said clearly. "We're taking you to the hospital. You're not well."

"I'm fine," she said with a swallow and once more, tried to sit upright. More aggressively, the paramedic held Renata to the gurney. "Just take me back to the cabin. I want to go back to the cabin."

Perplexed, Jevon said, "What cabin, Renata?"

Renata wasn't quick to respond.

"Kira's cabin?"

Renata closed her eyes to block out that "sinking" feeling. The pink darkness behind her eyelids drew an image in her mind: Jevon's frail mother standing behind the crack in the doorway, half of her cryptic face visible, the other half lost in the shadows. Somehow, Renata felt as if she was still back in the bed, still sinking through the mattress, still tangled in heavy bed sheets, still unable to free herself from the horrors that plagued her.

"Renata," Jevon said, pulling Renata from her feverish daze, "I'm not going to just sit back and watch you suffer like this. It's unacceptable, you hear? You need to see a doctor—"

"—You didn't see what I saw," Renata cried out, her hands shaking as if she was trying to hold the words in her hands. "His face changed, Jevon. And if you would just listen to me for once, I'm trying to tell you that this wasn't some kind of expression. His face *wasn't* his face. And. . . and. . . and as for Chione," Renata stammered breathlessly, "you should've seen her. She's *not* human either!"

"Renata," Jevon said, his tone softer, "you're not making any sense."

"Relax, Ms. Salcedo," the paramedic reassured Renata. "Everything is going to be fine."

Renata completely withdrew from the paramedic, as well as Jevon.

The inside of the ambulance became smaller and smaller, so small that it was starting to get crowded.

Renata honed in on a small compartment to the left of her, only inches away from where the paramedic was sitting. She didn't exactly know why, but she was compelled to open the compartment. As she reached for the latch, the paramedic grabbed Renata's wrist and guided her arm back to the gurney. The compartment trembled—which caused Renata to shift to the edge of the gurney. The trembling stopped; then, as Renata attempted to open the compartment once more while the paramedic's attention was concentrated on the *beeping* alarm of a blood pressure monitor, the trembling continued, this time more violently. She recoiled and once the trembling stopped, tried to open the compartment again.

"Ms. Salcedo," the paramedic said, as she grabbed Renata's wrist tighter this time, "you *have* to relax."

In a brisk movement, Renata opened the compartment of bagged syringes. A couple of syringes fell out onto the floor.

"Ms. Salcedo!"

The other paramedic driving the ambulance turned to his partner.

"*Bee*," he said sharply, "*control the patient.*"

"What is it, Renata?" Jevon asked, as the ambulance slowed down through a busy intersection.

The paramedic eased back Jevon with her hand.

"Ms. Salcedo," the paramedic said while checking Renata's eyes with a flashlight, "if you don't relax, I'm going to have to restrain you. Do you understand me. . . "

Still withdrawn from Jevon and the paramedic, Renata moved her eyes to the contents of the compartment. Her eyes flicked. She witnessed something moving underneath a couple of bags and oxygen masks in the back of the compartment.

Renata heard two voices whispering to one another: "*Has your friend been taking any drugs?*"

As she kept her hands by her side, as the paramedic demanded, other syringes and medical supplies stirred without Renata even touching them.

From behind the compartment, at least four tentacles stretched outward, slithering along the drawers and cabinetry and around the paramedic's legs and moving up the sides of the gurney.

As the tentacles reached Renata's legs, her body trembled violently.

With a serpentine slither, one tentacle moved up her thigh.

Frantically trying to move to the farthest end of the gurney, Renata attempted to brush off the tentacles; however, another one slithered underneath the gurney, making its way up her shirt. She swatted at it while, at the same time, Jevon and the paramedic were grabbing at her, her head, her arms, and demanding that she lay back down on the gurney, as if, in her mind, they were completely unaware—in fact, oblivious—as to what she was witnessing.

The paramedic tried to slip Renata's wrist through a restraint, but Renata resisted.

As soon as it was clear to Renata that she had nowhere else to escape, except for one option, which she didn't have time to ponder over since the tentacles were now wrapping around her body, she suddenly bolted forward through the tentacles and the arms, using the gurney to propel herself to the doors. She kicked open the back door and threw herself from the ambulance!

Jevon reached out to grab her arm—or any part of her body for that matter—but half of her body was already out of the ambulance. Right before she hit the pavement, she curled her legs inward, tucked her shoulder into her chest—like she saw one time in a movie—took the brunt of the fall directly on her shoulder, then rolled several rotations over the street.

Just ahead, the paramedic slammed on the brakes.

With horns blaring, cars swerved around the ambulance and nearly crashed into them. Once it was safe, Jevon stepped outside and ran to Renata as other cars screeched by. An awful dread immediately washed over him as soon as he spotted Renata in the middle of the road.

Zigzagging his way through traffic, he rushed toward Renata, who appeared injured from the way her body was lying in a fetal position. Once she saw Jevon running toward her, she stumbled to her feet and drunkenly ran away. She made it to the sidewalk without getting struck by any cars. She ran a couple of blocks, as if she was powered by adrenaline. She came across a dim alleyway, which—at first—looked like a good place to lose him. She was hesitant to cut through. That awful feeling of sinking was creeping up inside her, not entirely but dully like a bad thought. She took only one step into the alleyway before she froze. The dark pavement rippled, causing Renata to immediately back away. She decided that it was best to keep running and hoping that she could lose him on foot. A couple of blocks down, after dodging a couple of pedestrians shopping for fruit at a local stand outside a food market, Renata glanced over her shoulder and saw that Jevon was too far behind to catch up to her. *But still*, he wasn't giving up.

As Renata rounded the corner of a bagel shop, she found herself staring directly at Central Park. Without a doubt in her mind, she knew that she could *definitely lose* him inside the park. She darted through heavy traffic, juking out several cars and taxicabs. She leaped over a brick wall and entered the park through the south end. She ran past joggers, strollers, and sightseers, rested once against a tree to catch her breath, and then took off running as if Jevon was still on her tail.

Racing around both children and parents as if they were obstacles, she ended up cutting through a playground and finally, after both of her legs were about to buckle from exhaustion, taking cover behind the steepest side of Umpire Rock—or "*Rat Rock*," a name which the popular outcrop had acquired after it was once known for not only being a hangout for those who walked upright, but also those who walked on all fours.

While sucking down gulps of air, she bent over and rested against her knees to help ease the sting in her throat.

Eventually, she caught her breath and was ready to run again; however, right as she was about to take off, her eye caught a strangeness in the bedrock below. One rock in particular appeared to be out of place, as if it had absolutely no business being there, like, somehow, the rock was trying to blend in with the other rocks but failed miserably. *But why couldn't other people see it?* She tapped on the flat rock with the tip of her sole as if she was checking for life and received a hollow *thud* in return. She carefully kneeled down and with her knuckles, knocked on the soft rock; and it was as if she was knocking on a door that was shaped like a rock. She dug around the dirt, searching for a door handle but only finding a glacial striation-like gouge on the right side of the rock. She stuck two fingers into the crack and tugged upward until she heard a *click*! The rock suddenly sprung open like a door. She made sure nobody was watching. Then, she swung the rock open and stepped inside a sewer-like shaft that led to a dark space below.

AFTER climbing down a ladder, Renata finally reached the bottom of the shaft.

Surrounded by darkness, Renata's eyes adjusted. She found an orangish light coming from the end of the corridor. Cautiously, she walked to the light.

ONCE Renata reached the end of the corridor, she found herself in a boiler room. Various sized pipes were running along the walls and hard concrete. From a distance, she heard the monstrous *screeches*, the *howls*, the *roars*, raw mayhem getting louder and louder. Following the guttural sounds were noises of metal bars beating against pipes, the *clinking* and *clanking*, as well as a piercing, cringe worthy *ring* of what sounded like sharp talons scrapping against rusted metal. Renata ducked behind a pile of waterlogged boxes and fell witness to giant warped shadows stretching like carnival mirror reflections along the beat of firelight cast along the massive walls: shadows running on two legs, as well as all four legs, shadows jumping, shadows dancing, shadows fighting, shadows morphing from humans to eight-armed creatures.

Terrified as to what was storming her way, Renata curled herself into a ball. She prayed to God—*any* God— to protect her from whatever evil was headed her way. Under the breath of her muffled voice, Renata spoke of forgiveness and made vows to make atonement for all of the wrongdoings in her life.

At that moment in time, she was a pious woman.

A woman who was ready to make a change.

RENATA went undetected as the inhuman vandals raged on. She forced herself to sleep. And that night, she

dreamt of blackness. And in that blackness, various unrec-
ognizable shapes appeared like distant apparitions.

She was jolted from sleep by an image of fangs coming
forth in the dark.

More aware, more refreshed by the long sleep, Renata
scanned the massive boiler room. She couldn't tell whether
it was day or night. All she knew was that in such a place
neither time existed. She finally found the courage to
stand. She exited the boiler room and made her way to a
locker room, which looked the same way any locker room
would look if suddenly abandoned due to a natural disaster
over dozens of presidential campaigns ago. Old, dusty,
faded clothes were randomly scattered everywhere. She
picked up one shirt in particular that had long slits in the
side, as if a wild animal had gotten a hold of it. Some were
covered in strange resin; others, a sticky phlegm-like goo.

She walked down yet another corridor, this one nar-
rower than the one before, until she reached an "EXIT"
door.

Carefully, she opened the door. The afternoon sunlight
temporarily blinded her. Once her eyes adjusted to the
change in light, Renata realized that she was standing underneath a railroad bridge on Randalls and Wards Island.
She stepped outside and closed the door behind her. She
looked up and clarified that it was, in fact, Hell Gate
Bridge. But *how in the hell did I get all the way out here?*

During her trip back into Manhattan, she spent the rest
of the afternoon trying to figure out how she wound up on
Randalls and Wards Island.

But she had no answers to her queries.

SIX HOURS AGO

KIRA was preparing her to-go meal, a sort of throw-it-
altogether type of Japanese roman noodle soup that she no-
toriously branded "Hangover Food," when the buzzard
sounded. She stopped chopping the shallots on the cutting
board and walked to the door where she answered the call.

"Hello," she said into the intercom.

"Kira," Renata said from the other end, "it's me, Renata. I need to see you."

Kira paused, thought for a moment, and then opened the downstairs door for Renata.

"Come on up," she said and paced around the kitchen while Renata made her way upstairs. She finished the glass of Chardonnay and as she was about to pour herself another glass, Renata was already at her door.

Kira opened the door for Renata. She immediately noticed Renata's posture, her strung-out state, and how she was struggling to stand upright in the hallway. Kira stepped aside and waved Renata inside her apartment.

"What happened?" Kira asked Renata, as Renata awkwardly stood next to a bookshelf.

"I think I'm losing my mind," she said, looking away from Kira.

Kira asked, "What do you mean?"

"I'm seeing things," Renata said, holding back tears.

"What *things?*" asked Kira.

Renata shrugged.

"I don't know," she drawled, the emotion showing through her cracked voice.

Kira wrapped her arm around Renata's shoulder and escorted her to the living room where they both sat down next to each other on the beige leather couch.

Renata could no longer hold back her tears.

"Do you want something to drink?" Kira asked, as she leaned forward to look into Renata's eyes. "I can make you some tea, if you like," she said, studying Renata. "For me, a cup of hot tea always makes me feel better—"

"—Do you have anything stronger?" Renata asked, as she wiped away tears and phlegm with the backside of her hand.

"All I have is wine," Kira suggested.

"Wine is fine."

Kira went back into the kitchen; and once she found herself away from Renata's view, she embraced a deep breath behind the refrigerator. She poured two glasses of wine. In secret, she chugged the glass of wine in only a couple of gulps and then poured herself another glass of wine. She brought the two glasses back to the living room. She handed Renata the glass.

Renata sipped from the wine.

"Thanks," Renata said depressingly. Before Kira had a chance to offer a polite response, Renata said abruptly as if she had an important issue to discuss with Kira, "What was up with you the other day?"

Kira's thin eyebrows curled into a question mark.

"What you mean?"

"You acted like you hardly even knew me, Kira," Renata said more clearly. "Like we weren't friends anymore." Once more, she brushed away the tears. "I needed a friend, someone whom I could trust, and you weren't there for me."

"I'm here now, aren't I?" Kira responded and touched Renata high enough on the thigh to warrant Renata's attention.

They both shared eye contact.

"I'm sorry for whatever's going on with you," Kira said. "If there's anything I can do for you, then. . . " her eyes trailed downward on Renata's thigh and then flicked back up at Renata's eyes, ". . . I'm yours."

As soon as Kira made a move up Renata's thigh, Renata grabbed Kira's hand and tried to stir it away from her belt buckle.

In return, Kira aggressively leaned in to kiss Renata. At the last second, Renata turned her head away. Kira kissed Renata on the cheek.

Renata made it obvious by her gentle recoil that she wasn't at all interested in Kira's affection.

"I can't," Renata said, backing off.

"Just relax," Kira said and leaned in once more. She grabbed Renata's wrist and pushed it aside. Her grip was disturbingly tight and when Renata pushed her hand away yet again, she felt a strong resistance from Kira.

"Stop, Kira," Renata said, as Kira attempted to kiss Renata. "Kira," she said, trying to push off Kira, "I said, 'Stop!'"

Kira ignored Renata's demands and pinned down her shoulders. She ripped through Renata's blouse. Renata managed to kick off Kira from the couch. She made a flee toward the door, but Kira grabbed Renata and pinned her down to the floor. She was kissing, licking, and rubbing herself against Renata, as if she was driven by a primordial lust that went beyond any desire.

With a gaping yawn, Kira opened up her mouth to bite Renata. Her tongue, which was as long as a limb, stretched out from Kira's mouth as if it was unrolling like a red carpet and then licked at the side of Renata's face, leaving behind a gummy trail of saliva along her cheek. The tongue slithered around the bottom of Renata's chin, ran down her cleavage, and proceeded toward her abdomen.

Totally aware of Kira's actions, Renata quickly snatched the tongue before it could penetrate her and used it like a leash to yank Kira off her body.

The fight ensued into the kitchen where Kira tackled Renata into the table.

Renata looked around at anything she could grab, a plate, a vase, a floral picture framed on the wall, and tossed it all at Kira. Like a boxer, Kira ducked and dodged each projectile. She shielded herself from the picture frame; however, the corner of it caught her on the top of her forehead, drawing a string of blood to run down her face.

Panting heavily, Renata pushed the words out from her mouth as if each one was carrying her last breath: "*What's gotten into you, Kira?*"

Kira never responded, couldn't. To Renata, the woman circling her appeared as if she had regressed to her most primordial self and had the look of something inhuman, something pre-human. Her fingers were flexed outward, nails drawn and ready to scratch or rake, her pupils swollen black; and that tongue hanging from her mouth like a loose necktie acted as if it was her most underrated weapon.

The fight intensified farther in the cramped kitchen where sharper projectiles were used for defense, as well as offense. With her back against the refrigerator, Kira whipped her tongue around Renata's neck. Renata had no other choice than to remove her hands from Kira and remove the tongue, which was now choking her to death. She blindly felt for a weapon along the countertop. She fingered for the knife. Slid it closer with her index and middle finger. Once she grabbed the knife, she brought the knife forward and severed Kira's tongue with a clean and swift stroke.

Bloody and bruised and now tongueless, Kira elbowed Renata directly in the nose. The blow temporarily dazed Renata, which gave Kira an opening to wrestle the knife from Renata's hand. She turned the blade on Renata; however, Renata overpowered Kira and redirected the tip of the knife at Kira's throat.

With the blade only inches from Kira's throat, Renata begged Kira to stop.

Kira wildly swung at Renata.

Struggling to watch, Renata had no other choice than to make one final thrust forward with the blade.

She stabbed Kira in the throat and cut through a major artery, causing Kira to bleed out on the kitchen floor.

In a state of shock, Renata looked downward at her palms and they were both drenched with blood.

PRESENT DAY

"HOME sweet home," Jevon said, as he pulled his car in front of his brownstone.

After being caught in a daze of staring at the passing city lights, Renata lifted the side of her face from the headrest and turned to Jevon, who was removing the seat belt from his body. She looked him over with suspicion.

"What?" he said once he noticed Renata staring at him.

"Nothing," she said. "Just tired. That's all."

Jevon responded to Renata with a half-smile and exited the car. He walked to the passenger side of the car and opened the door for Renata. Gentlemanly, Jevon helped Renata from the seat and walked her into the brownstone. He flipped on a lamp in the foyer.

During the slow and tired amble into the living room, Renata passed Aurora's bedroom, which was dark and empty.

"Where's Aurora?" asked Renata.

"I ended up putting her in a home," he said and immediately followed before Renata could question him as to why he put his mother in one of "those" places in which he often spoke about with such rancor, "*but* only for the time being. With everything going on right now, I couldn't put her at risk. Eventually, things will settle down, though. That's the beauty of time."

Jevon disappeared in the darkness as he grabbed two pillows and a folded up blanket from the hallway closet.

Renata stood at the edge of the dark living room and asked Jevon over a tense silence, "Are you saying we're safe here, Jevon?"

"Of course, we are," he said and returned to the living room where he placed the pillows and blanket on top of the couch. Without turning on another light—which Renata didn't think too much about—Jevon walked up to Renata and reassured her, "You don't need a gun to feel safe."

"About that—"

"—It's done," Jevon interrupted, as if he wasn't in any mood to talk about the Glock 19 that she stole from his office. "You're safe here. Trust me."

"Trust is hard to come by these days," she said coldly, as she leaned against the doorway.

"After everything we've been through, you still don't trust me?"

Renata defensively folded her arms across her chest and shifted her weight to one side of her body.

"It's not that I don't trust you," Renata said and hesitated. "It's that—"

"—You don't trust yourself," Jevon finished for her.

Renata nodded her head *yes*.

Jevon stepped closer to Renata. His moonlit eyes trailed away for a moment. Then came back to Renata's eyes.

"You have shown me—" he said thoughtfully, "—proven to me actually, that you are capable of bringing down Chione based on the sacrifices you have made not only for me, but also for those whose voice has been stifled by powers greater than you or me. And now you're in a *unique* position where you can do anything you set your mind to." He touched her on the shoulder in a fatherly way. "*You* have the power, *Renata*. One day, when the time is right, you will use that power to tell your story to the world. And those who don't look like you or speak like you or act like you or even *think* like you, they will cheer for you and parade you into the new world."

Renata had an idea of what Jevon was telling her, but she didn't know exactly where he was going with the "point."

Before Jevon could even arrive at the "point," he touched the side of Renata's chin. "It's been a long day," he said softly. "Get some rest."

Jevon walked into his bedroom, closed the door behind him, and flipped on a lamp inside.

Renata made a bed on the couch and rested for a while.

As soon as she closed her eyes, she heard the *click* of a lamp switch—which she assumed was Jevon switching off his lamp. Renata didn't bother to open her eyes. Yet she remained comfortable on the couch, thinking about what Jevon had said to her moments ago. Only a few seconds into deep thought, her eyes flicked open. Unaware of the dark figure sitting in the recliner chair next to her, Renata walked into the kitchen and paced around. Another dark figure was sitting at the kitchen table; however, she was so deep in thought that she completely ignored her surroundings.

Immediately, Jevon's words—those particular *words*—leaped at her.

She marched back into the living room and as she was about to open Jevon's bedroom door, Renata caught a disfigured-faced figure sitting in the recliner. The blood ran from her face, leaving it pale and ghostly. She swallowed a gulp of air down her parched throat.

Before Renata could make sense as to who was sitting in the recliner, a lamp switched on beside the recliner. Part of Chione's scarred face was revealed in the shaded light. In her lap, she was petting a creature—in fact, the same telepath that Renata had witnessed floating inside that large cylindrical glass tank filled with a pinkish substance. The creature's hissy breath made robust purring sounds whenever Chione stroked the back of its scaly skin. Several tentacles slithered outward from its shell, caressing Chione's belly the same way a cat would knead through soft fabric.

"*You,*" Renata said, her voice trembling, "what did you do with Jevon?"

Chione grabbed the remote from the end table and turned on the TV.

The bold graphic of a BREAKING NEWS REPORT scrolled past the screen. The news anchor appeared shortly after, reading from the teleprompter. In the report, forty-seven year old, Jevon D'Agostino, the creator of the controversial magazine, *X'D*, was found dead in a hotel room at The Villages in NoMo. A video appeared on TV, one which was taken "EARLIER" that night. In the footage, coroners were carrying out a body inside a black bag from a sleazy hotel room. News crews and reporters were stationed around the crime scene. Stringers were trying to get the best angle for the shot while reporters were interviewing witnesses and other hotel guests. For the latest report, the news anchor sent it over to Jessica Varner, who was "live" at Jevon's residence.

There, on the TV, was "LIVE" footage of a brownstone, which looked identical to Jevon's, roped off with caution tape. The police, as well as detectives, were gathered outside the brownstone.

Overwrought with emotion, Renata turned to the front door. She didn't see any cops outside or anybody for that matter. She turned back to the TV. Saw that "LIVE" feed.

Confusion swept beneath her.

How can it be?

She tried to scrape the bottom of her thoughts but came up empty.

More confused, Renata focused on what the reporter was saying.

"Investigators are searching D'Agostino's residence, hoping to find more answers into his death," the reporter said, as activity increased behind her.

"It's been on TV all night long," Chione said over the report.

Renata rushed to Jevon's bedroom, checked inside, and saw an empty bed.

As a warm rage built up inside her, Renata turned to Chione, who was sitting comfortably in the recliner.

"What did you do?" she asked Chione.

"Well," Chione started, as she continued to pet the strange creature in her lap, "if you want to know the truth—I mean—if it makes you feel better, Dowe said he put up quite a fight."

The words coming from the recent report caught Renata's attention.

"Police currently have the twenty-eight year old from Seattle, Justin Devoid, in custody. Just recently, Mr. Devoid was reported missing in the town of Dover where he was currently attending community college. As of now, police are currently going through all of Mr. Devoid's social media pages and searching for any possible motives. According to D'Agostino's phone records, D'Agostino met Mr. Devoid through an online dating app called 'Men Only.' The two arranged a meeting at The Villages where several eyewitnesses claimed they saw the two entering the hotel room together. However, police believe that Mr. Devoid did not act alone. Candace Norwood, a nineteen- year-old from Dover, California, who, like Justin Devoid, was also recently reported missing, is wanted for questioning in the death of Jevon D'Agostino."

"Turn it off," Renata demanded, the rage simmering inside her.

The sound of the reporter's voice was like knives stabbing at Renata.

"I said, 'Turn it off!'"

Chione turned off the TV.

"It's bullshit," Renata seethed, shaking her head in utter disgust. "The whole story, it's all fabricated. *Why?*"

"Why do you think, Renata?" asked Chione.

Renata stopped and did exactly what Chione had asked. She thought. She thought about the dead body in her trunk, *not Kira's body*, but Jevon's dead body—*take that back. As a matter of fact, there was nobody in the trunk of my car;* then, she thought about the person whom she was talking to the whole time inside Kira's cabin, *not Jevon, but Chione.*

"This whole time. . . " Renata seethed. The tears streamed down the corners of her face, and they burned like acid. "Why pretend to be him? Why lie to me?"

"Not *all* lies, dear," Chione said. "Push past the emotion that blinds you, Renata. You're a smart woman. You already know the answer to those questions."

Renata had another vision, a sharp and stingy one that knocked the wind out of her.

All of these fabricated images—hallucinations—Renata realized, all stemmed from the infection on her arm.

"The woman back there," Renata said, out of breath, "the one who bumped into me on the street—or should I say, who 'deliberately' bumped into me—what the fuck did she put inside me?"

"It's starting to make sense, isn't it?" Chione asked with disdain. "Pieces to form a greater puzzle. I'm sure you can imagine that it wasn't easy for me pinning your boss's murder on those two lovebirds. Somewhere, buried underneath the pile of bodies, the foolish girl in me admires Candace Norwood for what she did after she uncovered her mystery, how, unlike most people, she decided to act not on impulse but, justifiably so, on the fundamental truth of self-righteousness. Most importantly, I admire how Candace Norwood traveled across an entire country to rescue the one person whom she loved—or thought she loved—when, turns out, love, her true love, her 'perfect match,' was right beside her the whole time. *However*, as a result of Candace Norwood's careless actions and the. . . unwanted attention she and Justin were drawing to our operation, *the public* will now see the two not as 'vigilantes' but deviants. When you're madly in love—or, in Candace Norwood's case, one who didn't know she was in love—you'll do about anything to hold onto it, that *feeling*," Chione's eyes honed in on Renata's. She held them there like blades. "Even if it means ruining another person's life."

"What the fuck did she put inside me?" asked Renata, as she carefully took a step away from Chione.

Without drawing any attention, she glanced around the living room. In a second glance, she spotted a pair of scissors on the edge of a table next to the TV.

She backpedaled toward the scissors and stood directly behind them.

Villainously, Chione said to Renata, "I've pulled back your eyelids and given you a glimpse into the other side of midnight, into a dark world gnawing away at the very fringes of your own reality."

Renata's eyes flicked toward the creature squirming in Chione's lap. Chione shushed and calmed the creature by repeatedly petting it.

"Is little Genie Beanie making you uncomfortable?"

"Genie. . . ?"

"Genie Beanie can be whoever you want him to be," Chione said childishly. Her voice was higher in pitch as if she was communicating to the creature through baby talk. She leaned in closer and rubbed the bottom of her chin along its scaly skin. Her voice changed. "Isn't that right, Dr. Love?"

The creature appeared different in Chione's lap; in fact, it didn't look like any creature at all. Renata looked twice and saw Chione holding a newborn baby in her arms, not the same grotesque creature with tentacles.

With her index finger, Chione tickled the baby's stomach, causing him to let out an explosive cackle.

"How's my little Lovie Dovie? You're a good Lovie Dovie, aren't you?"

Chione tilted forward and started blowing farts along
the baby's stomach; and when she pulled her head away,
Renata witnessed a tabby in her arms. She petted the
sides of the cat's neck; and in return, the cat purred softly.

"Aren't you, my Love Muffin—"

"—Stop it!"

Chione paused and looked at Renata as if her comment
was criminal.

"Stop what?"

"*She still doesn't know*," a manly voice said from the dark
kitchen.

Renata turned toward the kitchen, saw the dark figure
sitting at the table; and then, as soon as she found an opportunity to act while Chione was distracted by the voice,
she reached behind her back and secretly grabbed the pair
of scissors from the table.

With her arm tucked against her waist, she curled her
hand into her wrist and shielded as much as the scissors as
she possibly could without getting caught in the act.
Chione glanced at Renata, who, in return, kept a hard gaze
on Chione, as well as her eyes, making sure neither one of
them moved in the general direction of her right hand.
They didn't.

"Know what?" Renata said over the stretch of silence.

"She knows enough," Chione said to the voice inside the
kitchen.

Without Chione looking, Renata slipped the scissors in
her back pocket and covered the grip with her shirt. She
walked into the kitchen and switched on the light. There,
at the kitchen table, sat an older man with his back facing
Renata. He was eating from a bowl of *Apple Jacks*. Next to
the bowl, the box of *Apple Jacks* was overturned on its side,
empty. Renata walked to the side of the table for a closer
look. In a slight head turn, Harold acknowledged Renata.

"What are you not telling me?" asked Renata. A gap of
silence brought about a sharp rage inside her. She barked,
"Answer me—"

"—Don't you see, Ms. Salcedo?" he said, holding his head down toward the bowl of Apple Jacks. He scooped up a spoonful of cereal and stuffed the spoon into his mouth. A trail of milk dribbled down the corner of his mouth. With his thumb, Harold wiped away the milk from his face and said after chewing the rest of the crunching cereal, "You remain a vital piece of the puzzle and without your sacrifice, everything else fails—all the dominoes do not fall in the correct order, if you know what I mean."

"No," Renata snapped. "I don't know what you mean."

Harold finished chewing, swallowed.

Clearing his throat, he said, "After MindChant was launched last year, Carla and Corvine was given access to the phones and tablets of every single person in the world who downloaded their app, which enabled us to know your likes, your dislikes. Nothing new, right?" he asked Renata but didn't expect for her to answer. "However, we wanted to go *further*, to push the boundaries, to go beyond the limits, to venture uncharted waters, to go where no man has ever gone in order to create something truly special. Believe it or not, Ms. Salcedo," Harold said, "it was the people like your father who paved the way for the next generation—*your* generation—people who sacrificed themselves for the greater good, people who, essentially, gave us a way in." Harold tapped on the side of his temple with his finger. He drifted off in reflection. Not once did he ever turn toward Renata, to look at her or even acknowledge her. Yet, it was as if he was talking to himself. "The people of your generation don't have the slightest clue as to how *easy* they have it, how much generations before them sacrificed in order for your generation to have the privileges that were once considered unobtainable. You have no clue, Renata, that in an instant," Harold faced Renata, his murky eyes sharpening, "we can take it all away from you. Gone." He snaps his fingers together. "Just like that."

Unable to think properly, Renata felt paralyzed by Harold's words, especially about what he had said about her father.

"For the sake of curiosity," Harold leaned in, "tell me. Where exactly do *you* think *you* are right now?"

She glanced around the kitchen, glanced at Chione, as well as that mindfuck of a thing in her lap, then glanced back at Harold.

"We're at *Jevon's place*," she said but her tone suggested that she making an educated guess to an answer on *Jeopardy*, as if she was better off saying, "What is Jevon's place?"

"Correct," Harold said. "We are at Jevon's place, *but* where are you?"

Renata's heart started to beat faster. Her palms were sticky with sweat. Skin clammy. She tried to calm down that tribal drum of a heart in her chest by taking a deep breath. A sudden flash of heat swelled over her body. The "sinking feeling" was back, pulling from below, enticing Renata to not fight it but embrace it. She blocked out that creeping sensation and focused on Harold, his face, his body, his *words*.

"I guess there's only way to find out," she said, her voice fragile.

Renata's face went vacant, dead-like.

Without any hesitation, she pulled out the scissors from her back pocket and stabbed Harold directly in his temple.

His eyes swelled open in surprise. His face, slack—but only for a moment.

The hair on the backside of Renata's neck suddenly shot like quills on a porcupine. She felt the handle of the scissors softening inside her palm. The scissors melted between her fingers. Warm steel oozed from her balled fist, dripped down the side of her wrist, and artfully veined across her forearm. As gently as possible she pulled back her right hand from Harold's head. Opened her palm. Her entire hand was covered in black and silver goo.

Harold appeared unfazed by her unsuccessful attempt at killing him; in fact, he appeared more frustrated as he wiped the goo from the side of his face. Harold glanced down at his clothing attire and found smudges of goo stained on his sweater.

Pissed off, Harold cried out, "Goddamn it, Gene! Couldn't you have turned the scissors into goddamn corn- flakes or something less messy?"

As Harold turned his shoulder, he witnessed a blurry, cryptic figure stretched out and covering the entire length of the wide doorway. Renata couldn't help but notice the horror on Harold's face, as if he was staring at the very in- carnation of horror. She heard a sharp *clicking* sound com- ing from over her shoulder. Before she could turn to wit- ness the great monster looming beyond her, she felt a rough nub, which was about the size of an elbow, prodding against the back of her neck.

From behind, she heard Chione's voice: *"I'm disappointed in you, Renata."*

Renata was hesitant to turn around. When she finally did, she was left frozen in shock. Spread out directly be- hind her in the most grandiose, insectile posture wasn't Chione, rather another more archaic version of Chione with her eight legs stretched outward, one of which was pressed like the barrel of a gun against the backside of Renata's neck, while the others covered the entire length of the doorway. Her eyes were pitch black, demonic. At the base of her abdomen her belly was protruding outward as well, similar to the womb of a woman who was eight months pregnant, however, the bulge was shaped like the thorax of a spider. Renata had a good idea of what the tiny hole, which used to be her belly button, was designed to do. Gusts of wind came at her in waves. She never questioned where the wind was coming from since they were indoors; however, Renata figured that Chione's metamorphosis had something to do with a change in atmosphere. The living room behind Chione was no longer visible, as well. Yet, all that remained was a void as black as space.

The *screech* of a chair skidding along the hardwood floor startled Renata.

"I'll be waiting in the car," Harold said shortly, as he hurried outside.

With her eyes, Renata followed Harold to the street outside. She peered out the window and witnessed Kira sitting collectively in the driver's seat of a modified black Beamer with Trent's severed head stilled in the most shocking expression glowing on the front grill like a three-pronged headlight.

She thought about running far from Chione, running anywhere but right here, from this nightmare. Even when the thought turned to action and she attempted to move both her legs, Renata felt more paralyzed than before, as if the only part of her body that was working properly was her mouth, and even that part felt as if it was failing.

"All I have to do is wake up, right?" she suggested, her chest getting tighter with each breath. "I'll just climb up a tall building. Jump off a ledge somewhere. The fall will wake me up. . . "

"I wouldn't be so sure."

Chione's voice doubled, as if she was speaking through an electric box fan.

"Then, I'll just buy a gun and blow my brains out—"

"—I'm afraid it's not that *easy*, Renata," Chione said statically. "You're either *with us* or you're *against us*. I'm afraid, dear, you've made your choice."

Numbness crept into Renata's right hand, starting with her fingertips first and then coursing through her hand like a prickly wave.

"Please," Renata begged, "I choose to live. . . "

"Oh," Chione said grimly, as her black eyes lit up diabolically, "you *will* live. Where you're going, you are going to *thrivvve*."

"I just wanna go home," Renata cried, as shadows crept up her fingers. "Just please take me home—"

"—As you wish."

Panicked, Renata held up her right hand to her face, and all that remained of her hand was a shadow of a hand.

The shadowing effect continued throughout Renata's entire body, ridding all physical nature as well as being, until nothing remained of her but only a blacked out version of herself.

THREE YEARS LATER

TWENTY-six year old librarian, Emma Newtral—"Em," as she was often called by her peers throughout the Main Library in the small town of Maynard, Ohio—had spent the first week of November gathering enough courage to take the ultimate way out, her final destination, not "deleted" but, in a sense, "escaped," as in, once pushed, she would transport herself to another place that bore neither memory nor regret. The place where no one returned alive.

The months prior to Emma Newtral's predicament, she found ways to get by, as if "getting by" had become her own theme, a tagline used to promote her sad movie. Everyday, she found ways to escape the mundaneness which her life had become through the power of a story, either fictional and non, whether it be from taking in small excerpts like gulps from a book while placing it back on the shelf or helping track down a book for a Reader or chatting up a storm with other garrulous Readers who looked nothing like her but shared common interests about various characters, their flaws, or the decisions a particular character made, as well as offering renditions or long-winded accounts and analysis or "breakdowns" of the author's private thoughts or even, apart from reading, tracking down the notorious "Book Thief" who had been evading Emma for the past two years. She'd school those who were less schooled during political debates and basic ground coverings of classical literature from Jane Austen's *Pride and Prejudice* to John Steinbeck's *Of Mice and Men*. If there was one thing she knew a computer could—and *never* would—convey, it was the experience, a positive or negative one, a human being received after reading a book, good or bad.

However, after the reading stopped, when visual chaos deteriorated from the page, when transition from wits to wane left translation smoldering in a cold toke, when Emma Newtral closed whatever book she had escaped to, life viciously returned to an upright position. Her brain stopped. Initially, the adventure stopped. Yet, a new one began the day Emma met a man—a "boy," was what she skeptically told her mother on the phone—who went by Phil, whose name was easy to remember because it rhymed with Bill. Phil was three years younger than Emma but, despite his normie status, acted twice his age. After a month of dating, happy hour drinks and awkward dinners, walks in the park and late night movies, their relationship grew into titles: "Boyfriend" and "Girlfriend." Emma didn't pin it to one particular moment, but if she had to guess where their relationship felt as if it could've been an unbreakable alliance, she'd say the moment she decided to buy Phil a toothbrush when she was out grocery shopping, since he had spent the night over at her place several times and went to bed with stinky breath. It was the *little* moments like those which kept piling up until, one day, the thought of marriage and even the imagery of it surfaced inside her head; in fact, it was more plausible than anything she had ever known. Phil Watts could be *the man* who'd take her hand in marriage, Emma once thought. She even thought about kids, two of them, a boy and a girl.

Then, one day, Emma decided to bring up a conversation about having kids when they walked past a young woman with a baby bump. Not once during the six months of seeing each other did Emma and Phil ever talk about kids; in fact, the subject seemed as if it was sacrilegious and avoided at all costs. Unlike trying to pinpoint a moment when the relationship solidified, Emma knew exactly when the bond that she had strengthened with Phil started to disintegrate: the "Kid" talk. *Why*, she thought over sleepless nights, *why did I have to open up my big mouth?* The conversation scared Phil so much that he sabotaged their relationship. He'd list off excuses from left field not to see her. He'd speak out of turn and talk ugly to her—nasty, unmanly. He'd often push her away when she went so far as to bat an eyelash at him. He'd tell her that he had a "headache" or was "too tired" to offer any affection. Eventually, after two weeks of Phil's unruly behavior, Phil decided to end it with Emma. Broke up with her through a best-selling text. Even told her to "keep the darn tooth-brush."

A month after the breakup, while Emma was sitting on a patio outside a coffee spot where she and Phil used to hang out and trying to soak up a crisp autumn day, Emma witnessed other couples around her—"cute" couples, "hot" couples, "perfect" and "imperfect" couples—all enjoying the afternoon sun and acting as if the world around them didn't exist. She once had that with Phil. Someone whom she could grow old with. Someone who would accompany her on trips around the world—they often shared dreams and aspirations, places to travel, experiencing new foods to eat, new faces to see, new people to meet, new cultures to embrace. She let it slip right through her fingertips. At that particular moment in her life, a black hole blotted out the sun, as if it was suspended above her all this time. The sky went gray. The mood darkened. Faces changed. November hadn't felt colder. After a week of planning her escape, thinking of different ways to do so, from jumping out in front of a car, to taking dangerous routes to work, to overindulging, Emma went with her last option, a less-brave or daring one. She was going to hit the "escape button" once and for all. Without any thrill or glory. Without any grand exit or her symbolic middle finger to the world. And a piece of her laughed off the humiliation. Some "boy," whom Emma Watts had once referred to, had driven her to this state, some "boy" had ripped out her heart from her chest Temple of Doom-style, tossed it on the ground while it was still beating, and then crushed it with his foot like a soda can, some "boy" was going to be her masked executioner and the last face she'd see in her mind before she fell down that rabbit hole. The thing—because there was always a "thing"—Emma wasn't even in love with Phil. But maybe that was the whole point.

That night, Emma picked up a bottle of Tylenol PM from the drug store. Unlike the moment she was brought into the world, she wanted to go out like a quiet riot, not punching or kicking, not screaming or crying out for the warm bosom of her mother, but rather ride a current and let the liquid remedy sweep her away into the great abyss and drift into a final sleep, her eternal sleep, her greatest escape.

She dumped the entire bottle into her palm up, held the pills in her hand like popcorn and stuffed as many as she could fit into her mouth.

Soon, she thought, she'd hit that escape button. Watch it open up like a cellar door and reveal on the top right corner of the keyboard, a flight of stairs drifting off into a dark world, one that shared neither memory nor regret.

As soon as she washed back the mouthful of pills with a sip of water, she received a message via TV spot, as if it was her own "SOS" reflecting back at her.

Earlier that day, Emma came across the same advertisement twice, one, a ten-second video clip on the right side column of a ".org" website on ingesting "toxic chemicals" and another, an enticing click bait window displaying the same actress from the video clip standing proudly on a white beach promoting a recently FDA approved drug on the market. She ignored the video clip while scrolling through the page of harmful household chemicals on her laptop. She "x'd" out the window attached with a link redirecting her to the drug's website while entering some shady health forum on rat poison on her phone.

In the advertisement, *a young woman who looked identical to Renata but was not Renata was sitting in a slouched, turtle-like posture by a garden window while scrolling through old photographs of a young woman who looked identical to Kira but was not Kira on her phone. The two women, both in the bedroom and on the phone, could've passed as siblings. Similar to the way one viewed the sibling of a celebrity or somebody famous. He or she looked identical to the celebrity or famous person; however, a facial feature, a nose, a jawline, the brow—even the shape of his or her face—felt as if it was somehow out of place, whether it be too small or large or misshapen. The mood of the bedroom was heavy and damp. Outside, it was pouring rain.* In the background the song "Mad World" by Michael Andrews and Gary Jules was softly playing. *As the rain dribbled down the garden window, so did the tears along the young woman's face.*

The next scene cut to *the same young woman sitting on the couch in the living room. She was flipping through the channels on TV. Each channel highlighted her grief, either it be from a commercial on the latest perfume—the super model, who was promoting the perfume, looked identical to the woman on her phone—or live coverage of the Oscars—the dolled up actress, who was strutting the red carpet while, at the same time, posing for photographers, like the commercial before, looked identical to the woman on her phone or an episode from the hit television series— the driven detective, who was escorting a criminal, her White Whale, into the back of a squad car, like the previous channels, looked identical to the woman on her phone.*

The next few scenes followed *the young woman through her daily routine: eating dinner alone, watching a movie alone, sleeping alone, eating breakfast alone, working alone, browsing through the aisles of a bookstore alone.*

At the bookstore, a young handsome man made eye contact with the young woman, made a one-sided conversation with the young woman, made his five-star attempt to lighten up the tense mood with an innocent joke but the young woman could barely bring herself to crack a smile. The young man asked her if she'd like to join him for a cup of coffee, but she shook her head. Said she had things to do.

One-by-one, the sleeping pills slowly spilled from Emma's mouth.

Her eyes were glued to the flat screen.

Back to the advertisement where *the young woman was looking over several brochures: exotic places like India, Belize, Madagascar, the Bay of Kotor in Montenegro, Gozo, Malta, Greece, Nepal, French Polynesia, Chile, Fiji, Cook Islands, Burma, Australia, Ireland, Scotland.*

The next scene showed *the young woman sitting at the kitchen table watching YouTube "travel" videos on her laptop.*

In the next scene, *the young woman was riding a carousel in the park. While riding the back of the stationary horse, she visualized the moment where everything went wrong, where her life turned to one of great solitude and depression, the moment when the other young woman, whose photos were on her phone, decided to walk out that door where the light outside was bright enough to blind her.*

Emma emptied out her mouth completely until her mouth was ridded of pills, leaned forward, and turned up the volume on the TV.

As the young woman exited a coffee shop, a city bus with the bold purple sign drove past her.

The young woman came across a similar sign on the billboard when she was driving home. The first part of the word, **Renata***, caught the corner of her eye. Lastly, the young woman fully acknowledged the poster on the wall inside the exam room. Curious, the young woman looked over the poster*

Renatafill™

When the doctor entered the exam room, the young woman pointed at the poster and asked the doctor about the latest FDA approved drug on the market

Renatafill™

The next scene showed *the young woman and her doctor talking about the new drug in the doctor's office. The young woman nodded carefully as she listened to the advice that her doctor was giving her.*

The following scenes showed *the young woman restarting her life on*

Renatafill™

Smiling from ear to ear, the young woman strolled through an airport with her carry-on luggage; she handed a ticket to the stewardess, laughing while doing so; the young woman, still smiling, boarded the airplane. The young woman arrived at the Bay of Kotor—or "Boka."

Gleefully walking through the town of Perast, the young woman sampled the local cuisine; she met a waiter whom she shared a wonderful conversation with. Later that night, the young woman went out for drinks with the waiter. The two traveled farther inland where they both rode horseback on Shagya Arabians.

Emma stood up from couch, walked to the flat screen TV mounted on the living room wall, and listened closely to the advertisement.

Back to the advertisement: *While the young woman was having a loving dinner at a fancy restaurant, the same young woman from the photo on her phone walked past her table. The young woman didn't even recognize her. Ignoring the other young woman whom she had deleted from ther phone, the young woman continued to drink, eat, and laugh with her new boy-friend.*

In the next scene, *the young woman was in the kitchen preparing a cup of coffee when, all of a sudden, her new tortoiseshell cat jumped up on the countertop, startling the young woman yet, at the same time, causing her to laugh away her frustration. With a smile on her face, she embraced the cat.*

"Look beyond the skin with. . . "

Renatafill™

As the young woman walked on a white beach glistening like diamonds in rays of sunlight stretching over the horizon, Emma carefully placed her hand onto the television screen. With the advertisement drawing to an end, the glare of light bloomed over the screen and caused Emma to squint. The glare was so strong and brilliant that it coursed through Emma's warm hand, her once pink skin now outlined with a red glow. The glare continued to brighten until Emma's hand thinned and whitened and eventually, faded into the white light.

YOU *may not know it—maybe you do—but you've seen it all before, on television, on your phone, in* the Movies, *or even read about it in that book you read every night in your bed:* the Similarity.

Don't think of this Similarity *as merely a coincidence; but, instead, think of it as a smokescreen for those with great power and influence—more or less, a deliberately checked* (wink-wink) *avenue swayed by the blood of those whose voice still remains voiceless despite their efforts to be heard and then made profitable by stylized renditions of themselves. For centuries, they've been manipulating us, telling us how to act or how to speak, and most importantly, how to think for ourselves. Even as I write this manifesto, they're attempting to shut me up, to silence me, to end me.*

(The pop-pop-pop-pop of gunfire RINGS out throughout The Maw. Bullets scream over May's head)

Ever since I was a little girl, I've always been captivated by bears: American black bears, brown bears—or you may know it as the grizzly bear—Polar bears, pandas—who in the hell doesn't like a panda?—and, of course, the Pizzly bear, which is a hybrid of a grizzly and polar bear—and yes, believe it or not, such a thing exists.

(Smoking out of control, the canister of a smoke grenade spins below her feet)

When we're young, we're taught that bears are cute and cuddly, stuffed animals to embrace whenever we feel upset or afraid, vessels for education, mentors, characters in nursery rhymes or fables, and most importantly, friends, whether it be good, best, or 'special.' For instance, take Smokey's more proactive brother, Brutus the Bear: a noble figure one could look up to, to admire, to rally behind, and most importantly, to cherish, for he was handed down the role as the protector of the forest and his universal message which had been passed down for generations, albeit elementary, carries a weight that touches all of mankind from the far seas to the highest mountaintops. But, let's be honest, you should've been wondering—if you're not, then maybe it's best that you turn back now while you still can—'Realistically, how the fuck can a bear speak?'

(An armed mercenary whispers into his radio on his shoulder, "Target acquired," from behind the re-gurgitator-coaster)

What they never told us is that, in Reality, *where facts matter, where actions have consequences, where folklore and fairy tales are nonexistent, Brutus—the real one, that is—comes from a species that would tear your face off with claws the size of pocket-knives and rip your body to shreds and then devour you before you even have a chance to call out for help because a word like 'help' would be the last thought on your mind when Brutus starts to pick through your vital organs as if they were a basket of rotten tomatoes.*

Not so cute and cuddly anymore, huh?

(The brutish mercenary approaches May's body, which
is lying lifelessly on the floor)

*I'm not going to take you as a fool, but what you're doing is
straight up foolish. You may know what they're doing to you—
maybe you don't. Maybe you're like everybody else who goes along
with the 'crowd,' lacking the ability to question the motives behind
their masquerades.*

Is it all for a 'like' or perhaps even a follower?

*I hope you're better than that—man, I hope you are. If you're
not, if you are unable to 'delete,' if you feel as if you've reached the
point where your voice is the only one that matters, I'm here to tell
you that you don't matter—not to them, at least. But don't get
mad. They celebrate you when you're mad. Mad is better.*

Mad is king, and the throne is up for grabs.

I'm here to tell you that you do matter.

You're not expendable.

(The cloud of smoke consumes the mercenary, obscur-
ing parts of his shadowy face)

*In order to get where you need to be, you must understand that
they're in the process of high jacking everything you hold sacred.
They're exploiting you. Your memories.* Moments. *Your friends
and family. Your loved ones. They want your ass plugged in,
clicking, posting, sharing—make sure to hashtag it! If you don't,
you won't be liked. You will be shunned from society. Even better, pigeonholed. Mocked. Belittled. Your voice, squelched. And
it would be as if you never did have a voice or even worse, never
existed. You don't take me as a fish, but your actions are pretty
fishy. And they don't own you—not yet, that is.*

(Brushing away the smoke, the mercenary kneels down
and picks up a permanent marker off the floor)

But you ask: Who are they?

Don't worry.

Think of me as your tour guide.

I'll show you where everything went to shit.

(The barrel of a Glock 19 slowly emerges from the smoke)

And then, maybe, I'll answer the question you're dying to ask.

(A thumb pulls back on the hammer of the pistol, ready to fire)

✉

ERICKA heard that Bufferman99's latest review on the spin recently posted on the video-sharing website, ↑Load (Upload)—or "Arrow Up," as the kids called it.

And millions of people were commenting below the video.

Ericka scrolled through the hundreds of new videos on ↑Load until she finally came across that one particular video. She clicked on the *play* button:

> "Sup, my lil' Bummies! It's ya favorite spin critic here, the one and only Bufferman comin' straight to you from the Bufferboard! Today, I'm gonna fill you in on a lil' sumthin, sumthin called *Wake Me Tomorrow*, the latest spin from the dreamineers behind Spin-to-Play. Now, if you're unfamiliar with Spin-to-Play or you've been like livin' under a fuckin' rock or was recently thawed out after being cryogenically frozen for the past two years, Spin-to-Play is a relatively new interactive attraction at Fantasy World where spinners—aka your 'story developers'—hook your ass up to this weird ass thingamajig called a schwab, which, from what I've been told, absorbs what's inside your brain. I'm talkin' about thoughts, desires, memories, and then, depending on whatever mood you're in during the 'extraction process,' your assigned spinner will then take all them thoughts and images and sequence them all together in what we humans once called a 'movie.' Yes. Those. Remember those? I mean, 'What are those?' Haha! But trust me, lil' Bummies. I didn't understand how it worked at first, but if you're ever in the Lagoon Park area, then I suggest you stop by Fantasy World and give it a shot. Me, personally, I haven't tried it myself. I ain't in the business of having some mysterious modified life form digging around upstairs. But, like I've said, it ain't for anybody. But—and I'm talkin' a big BUT—from

what I've seen with my eyeballs, it's boss. My lil' cousin took a spin last summer and he compared it to experiencing a dozen of movies all wrapped into one. What are those?!? So, caught up? All right. Let's talk about *Wake Me Tomorrow*.

Randomly chosen from the National Lottery, *Wake Me Tomorrow*, which was anonymously submitted to Spin-to-Play, is the first of 'five' spins to appear on Spin-Place last week. Fantasy World's new streaming service, Hotcakes, is set to unveil the next four spins later this month—and for reals, if *Wake Me Tomorrow* is a sign of the next spins to come from the National Lottery, then, holy guacamole! We are in for one helluva ride! But first, just a side note: from what I've heard in an exclusive interview with Spin-to-Play's designer, Sidney Kovacs, Spinner, Laurel Green, who's been straight-up killing it as of lately for her outstanding work in the hit streaming series, *Street Tones*, was brought on at the last minute for final respins—or in other words, 're-shoots,' for those of you who've been *Fragile Rock*-ing it for the past two years. You've also probably recognized Laurel from last year's controversial spin, *The Wetlands,* which made it to número dos on Spin Geek's 'Top Ten Spins of 2028.' With *Wake Me Tomorrow*, Laurel Green didn't just bring her A-game. Hands down, she 'factually' owns the muthafuckin' competition!

Now, before I begin, I wanna warn you that this is a SPOILER review. So, if you haven't seen *Wake Me Tomorrow*, then what is you doing here? Please save us all the trollin'. Leave now while you still can; otherwise, don't say I didn't warn you, lil' Bummie.

Wake Me Tomorrow stars the beautiful Grace Holiday, a twenty-seven year old former artist who works as a curator for an art gallery in New York City. The spin starts off with Grace waking up to a shocking news report on TV about a strange murder-suicide on a highway in Arkansas. Four people dead. Two of them cla-zapped! The other two found inside a car that had caught fire. If it wasn't for the people involved, especially the two people inside the burnt car, the story may have *never* made it to the national news—two people are 'factually' being clapped as I speak right now (I mean, don't clap the messenger, just look at the data, folks); but you have to remember, *Wake Me Tomorrow* takes place in the year 2019, so, for those of you who don't remember what the times were like ten years ago, this spin is a good reminder of how 'easy' we had it. Anywhodunit, according to investigators, an ex-convict named Oscar Hernandez high jacked a car on the highway, cla-zapped the driver, and then, out of road rage, went after a couple who were passing through Arkansas. But, the catch! It wasn't just any ordinary couple cruisin' along the highway like Alice and Alice. They were 'May Warren' and 'Desiree Newton,' two vigilantes who had recently been all over the news for their involvement in multiple arsons throughout the country where each business destroyed in the fire was owned by a powerful warlock named Harold Roman, aka 'The Assembler,' who—fun fact—happens to be one of the largest shareholders for Fantasy World. What? What is Harold Roman doing in this spin? I'll get to that in a minute. For now, what does May Warren or Desiree Newton have to do with Grace's story? Well, for one, apparently, Desiree Newton and Grace Holiday used to be a 'thing,' well, not really a thing. They hooked up like one time back in the day. But, clearly, Desiree was completely out of Grace's league. And two. . . well, we'll get to that later.

So, with the recent news about Desiree's death on her mind, Grace goes about her day. We follow Grace's story while she's preparing an exhibition for an artist named Jpeg—Jpeg, being one of these 'trash artists' who embraces the whole 'revenge culture' mainstream, as my Pawpaw would say, 'poppycock.' However, in Jpeg's words, it's a 'revenge against the norm.' Which I dig. But nothing about Jpeg is normal. Jpeg was featured in an eMag called *Normal*, which exploits people who have been ousted from society. In Jpeg's case, his looks. In years past, Jpeg would've been compared to the Elephant man for his deformed, freakish features—Can you actually believe they used to call them 'Freak Shows' back in the day? I'm serious. Just doodle it. But Jpeg did what most people had a hard time doing. Jpeg embraced his looks—and his art. He was one of the 'hottest' artists in town. And why is Jpeg so important to the spin? Me, personally, I believe Laurel decided to add Jpeg's artwork throughout the spin for more symbolic reasons— if you've seen *The Wetlands*, you know that Laurel is a stickler for symbolism. Most importantly, I believe the spin *does* present a message, as subtle as it may be, and that's to exploit our obsessions with perfection and how we, humans, view ourselves to the public. Regardless of how we look or what someone might find is ugly, another might find as beautiful.

Aesthetically, *Wake Me Tomorrow* is both ugly at times while, other times, beautiful. The two stark contrasts are deliberate throughout the story as we follow Grace through her success with Jpeg, who, in return, ends up opening the door for other 'trash artists' like him.

Eventually, Grace reaches a point in her life where she wants to settle down. While spending a weekend with a close friend at a horse race event upstate, Grace stumbles upon a romance writer named Charles Patterson who writes under the pen name Evan Darling. Grace is attracted to Charley. After a couple of mishaps, the two go on a date. One date leads to another and the next thing Grace knows, she's crazy in love with Charley. A year passes. Grace and Charley end up getting married. We follow her through the next couple of years. She's living the perfect life. She has a great job. Successful parents. She goes on vacations to Fantasy every year. She is living the dream. However, as Grace's story progresses, her mental state strangely starts to deteriorate. She ends up having a child with Charley. A girl named Isabel. Although it's clear that Grace is not content with her life after her pregnancy, her focus is directed inward at herself. Bizarre things start happening whenever Grace finds herself looking into the mirror. She sees distortions of herself, her face as well as her body.

If you've ever seen one of Laurel Green's spins, you should know that she's not into explaining anything—I mean, *anything*. She'll put in enough details for viewers to be able to think for themselves. And, at times, you can miss them if you blink.

DETAILS YOU MISSED: For example, the mirrors and the mirrors reflections commonly used whenever Grace is a part of the scene. There's even one scene in particular—major SPOILER ALERT!!!—where you see a reflection of someone else inside the mirror while Grace is having dinner with Charley's friends. This is a sign of things to come. For the hearing impaired, hint hint!

Once Grace gives up her career as a curator and devotes her life to being a mother, her appearance starts to slowly change—at least, through her point of view. Other DETAILS like, at the beginning, with Grace *bumping* into the young woman on the street in New York City or Grace witnessing a strange man at the art gallery during Jpeg's exhibition: these are all subtle clues for the glaring questions to come in the latter part of the story. Laurel makes sure to plant these answers earlier in the story, then distracts you with other stuff in the middle of the story—particularly, the complicated husband and wife issues between her and Charley.

Toward the end of Act 2 of the spin, *Wake Me Tomorrow* becomes an entirely different story. Act 1 is what I hear most of these wannabe spin critics out there call a 'slow burn.' This is me in my best spin critic impersonation. Yeah, that's right, my fellow human being, it's a slow burn. I'd say 'man,' but I don't want to offend the ladies out there. Nobody gives a shit about these 'pandering fools!' Am I right, lil' Bummie?

Wannabe spin critic douches aside, I'd say I was more drawn to the parallels of the two characters and their stark differences. In a way, Grace is everything that May wanted to be. Grace was in a stable relationship, whereas May, who wasn't truly in love with Desiree, not physically, that is, however, more so the idea of who Desiree could be: a partner and lover. Once Grace starts to realize who she *really* is, her life does a complete one-eighty. She starts having hallucinations of seeing herself as someone else. She starts waking up in strange places, not knowing how in the hell she got there or what she did the night before. She doesn't know whether she's losing her mind or what.

Now, for those with light stomachs, you may want to step out of the room right now because I have to—I mean, I must—bring up the famous eye scene that people are talking about. Laurel Green went straight Cronenberg on us! The master of body horror himself! Having lived through the TV era and having seen a lot of movies and TV shows in my time, I've never seen anything like the infamous 'eye scene.' I mean, we have all seen transformations in film, from man to werewolf, man to monster—we've even seen something in the same vein as Raimi's classic, *Army of Darkness*—but I have never seen a woman 'factually' transformed into another woman. And the way it was done was masterful. I 'factually' vomited a bit in my mouth as soon as I saw that eyeball poking out of Grace's shoulder while she was brushing her hair in front of the bathroom mirror. I knew that something was about to happen but I didn't know exactly what and then, when it *did* happen and Grace starts peeling off her fucking skin, I was like 'Get out here, bitch? What the hell did I just see?' Did that white bitch just rip off her skin, only to find a black bitch hiding underneath? And not just any black bitch. That's da fuckin' Bonnie wannabe bitch, May Fuckin' Warren! I've probably watched the scene at least ten times. But every time I got to pop a Dramamine in order *not* to lose my shit, if you know what I mean. So, you're probably wondering—because I was factually wondering it myself—*How in the hell are my eyes seeing May Warren when she 'supposedly' went out in a blaze?* SPOLIER ALERT!!! Turns out May Warren DID die. BUT not in real life! WHAAAAAT!!!

The whole time throughout the spin, May Warren has been inside her own spin—think of it as a spin within a spin—WHAAAAAT!!! And, after she finally emerges from

Grace's body, she ends up going after the last person involved in her parents' deaths. WHAAAAAT!!! Origin
story! So, let's back up a sec. As May Warren slowly
starts to take over Grace, she uses Grace's body as one,
for cover, and two, to not draw any attention to herself.
Talk about going full-on *Moonlight* on her ass! Wearing
Grace's body as disguise, May Warren goes after the
people who were involved in her parents' death, starting
with The Assembler—the one scene where Grace cuts off
The Assembler's head and delivers it to Chione Elmahdy's office with a bomb stuffed inside has that over-the-
top *Total Recall* vibe (STFU! I mean, the similarities are
uncanny. But it works! Talk about sending a message!
Clearly, whoever anonymously submitted the spin had
seen the movie a few times, enough for it to bury deep
within his or her subconscious). Then, after the snip-snip,
she goes after every single person in charge of Fantasy
World, including the elusive Mirrorman from *Mirrorworld*,
that lil' little dude, Dab, then Kira the Rappin' Jap, who
are all a part of a syndicate called The Web.

Finally, at the end of *Wake Me Tomorrow*, when May
Warren pays a visit to Fantasy World, we find her entering through a secret 'Employees Only' door inside
Dreamland. Turns out the strange man who Grace saw
at the art gallery was Curtis Scarborough, a well-known
whistleblower who was not only trying to undercover the
killer(s) of the genius behind *Normal*, Tony Peseta, who
was under investigation for insurance fraud before he
was found dead inside a nightclub, but also May's source
into breaking into Spin-to-Play. Scarborough knew a guy
who knew a guy who was one of the technicians at Fantasy World. Once inside, May tracks down the last person involved in her parents' death. The man behind the
curtain. The wizard of Oz—if you will. At the end of the
corridor awaits the one and only Sidney Kovacs, the
creator of Spin-to-Play! I know what you're thinking: *How
in the hell was this spin released on Hotcakes?* Most importantly, *how in the hell did this 'anonymous' person
NOT get sued for slander or copyright infringement?* The
answer to all of the above: *Controversy*, my lil' Bummies.
Obviously, whoever 'Anonymous' is, they were certainly
having fun by accusing the people behind Fantasy World
for killing his or her parents. I mean, why not? Having
theme parks across the entire world, Fantasy World is
one of the must lucrative businesses in the world. So,
why not portray them as a supervillain? '*Mad is king*,' as
May puts it so boldly. As far as getting involved in the
creative process, companies have been doing it for years.
The whole point is to release a product that will create

controversy. And you know as well as I do that controversy, like sex, sells. Fantasy World took a huge risk in
releasing a product—or in this case, a spin—that painted
them in a rather negative light. Talk about not giving a
fudge! Does it really matter, though? No. Hell nah! The
payoff worked! Besides, Fantasy World already owns our
asses anyway. They could 'factually' hand out a shit bar
covered in a red ribbon and you'd still buy it. You'd even
say that it tasted pretty good. But if you rewind the
clocks, filmmakers and spinners alike have been creating
alternate realities and timelines for years. Just browse
through Hotcakes or SpinPlace. I'm sure you'll find at
least a dozen or more fantasy spins where the story is
about some homie time traveling all the way back to
World War II or even disguising himself as a member of
the Third Reich and clappin' Hitler's sorry ass or instead
of landin' on the moon, landin' on Mars and startin' up an
ALL-female colony or livin' in a nation where one particular person became president instead of another and
showin' what life would've been like. Alternate realities
were made popular during the time of *Wake Me Tomorrow* and now, it's starting to make a comeback.

But REAL TALK: Controversy is the 'new' sex.

So, after May cla-zaps Sidney Kovacs, you'd think the
story would be over, right? With May finally avenging her
parents? Wrong! Apparently, before Sidney Kovacs was
greeted by the Grim Fuckin' Reaper—yes, there's factually a Grim Reaper character in the story, although he
ain't what you think he'd look like—he hit a panic button
next to his chair, which, in return, activated an elite group
of mercenaries. May is outnumbered. She seeks cover
inside The Maw.

ENDING EXPLAIN: The reason why May decided to
call Curtis Scarborough when she was trapped inside The
Maw was that she had no other way of telling her story to
the public. Scarborough had connections to the police—
the good ones, that is. The ones who weren't paid off by
Harold Roman. May knew that if she didn't tell her story
to the public, then Kovacs and his men would erase her
from the earth. So, she grabbed a marker and wrote
down her manifesto on every inch of her body. That way
it would never be lost. After a violent shootout, May
barely survived. She ended up turning herself into the
cops. I know a lot of you wanted May to escape, but I believe Laurel Green chose this particular ending because
she was sending a 'subtle' message about the idea of revenge and once a person goes down the road of revenge, it's no different than living life in a jail cell. You're
stuck. You no longer have your freedom. At the end of

the day, you still have to live with the same person looking back at you in the mirror. And that's a wrap. For
now, keep spinnin'. And if you haven't done so already,
make sure to subscribe to my channel on ↑Load. What
you waitin' for? Bufferman over and out!"

Ericka suddenly received a *dig* on her MessageBox!

She closed Bufferman's latest review on *Wake Me Tomorrow* and clicked on the message with an "arrival" notice on
the bottom screen of her laptop.

Still astonished by the quickness of the deliver, she
walked to the front door and heard a remote control-like
buzz fizzling out. She knew that sound. For the past couple of years, she had grown accustomed to hearing that particular sound outside her door. She opened the door and to
her exhausted surprise found a BB drone flying away into
the gray sky. On the porch was a package from YourCart.

Right on schedule, as always.

Ericka grabbed that trademark royal blue package from
the front steps of her townhouse and carried it inside. She
used a knife from the kitchen to cut open the box. Ericka
could feel the anticipation building up inside her as soon as
she dug through the bubblewrap. First, she pulled out a
lithograph of an advertisement for the "new and approved"
Spinner Jack 2000 by the brand Phun Co "The 'Ph' Fun
Company," as well as the new spinner "kit," which allowed
anyone to make their own spin from their own home, and
then submit their spin directly onto Fantasy World's website.

Uninterested, she placed aside the lithograph.

The child-like Christmas morning filled up Ericka, if
only for a moment. She carelessly tossed sheets of bubblewrap aside on the countertop, first revealing the **FW** logo,
then the name *May Warren*, written on the green box
inside.

She pulled out the box from inside the cardboard box
and held it before her. There it was neatly tucked behind
the cellophane wrap: an action figure of herself. However,
the closer Ericka looked at the action figure, she realized it

wasn't herself—not entirely. The action figure looked nothing like Ericka.

First, they screw up my spin, Ericka thought. *Now, this! They can't even get my face right!*

She examined the action figure closer. The nose was all wrong, she immediately pointed out. Her nose was much wider, her lips fuller, whereas the nose, as well as the lips on the action figure were thinner, less full. The nose and lips of a white woman. Even May's skin was lighter in tone, not dark, as if, oddly enough, she was supposed to be a more "enhanced" version of herself, a TV-friendly, photogenic version that corrected her "nappy" look.

As the excitement melted away as quickly as it first came to her, Ericka threw the action figure in the trash and stormed to her bedroom where she spent the next hour cleaning the bathroom.

LATER that afternoon, Ericka canceled her delivery order and decided that she was going to be the one to pick up her food. Ericka didn't know why, of all days, that this day would be the day to change. For the past few months, Ericka had become sick and tired of having machines wait on her hand and foot and watching drones and bots standing on her doorstep, dropping off whatever then pulling a Houdini on her. She could vaguely remember a time when her teenage-mind thought it'd possibly be a cool, not-so farfetched idea—even so, an idea that would benefit all of mankind—of having robots be a part of daily life, as in interacting with them, even dragging one of them along with her as if it was an obedient pet. She never thought in a million years that being twenty-nine—such a "ready" age where she was going to be at the cusp of her prime, a soon-to-be queen—would feel so goddamn old. Yet, she felt worse than a peasant. Ericka felt expendable, as if, at any moment, she could be replaced by someone who looked similar to her. And the thought alone made her grumpy, that old-kind of grumpy where resisting against the "status quo" was more than likely to become a mantra, where nostalgia was masked by short tempers, long tirades, and out-of-pocket excuses, and all she wanted was to get back to a simpler time where emotions were earned, *not* bought or posted.

After a brief debate, she'd convince herself that she needed to get out of the house for some "fresh air" since she had been cooped in all morning.

As Ericka was about to step outside to grab herself dinner before her graveyard shift started at the local Food Circle, she backtracked, walked to the trashcan, and fished out the action figure underneath an empty bag of potato chips.

She brushed off the crumbs from the greasy action figure and placed it on the kitchen countertop.

Convincing herself that it wasn't going to be as bad as she originally thought, Ericka stepped out of the townhouse with an artificial sense of optimism.

She only made it a couple of steps from the front porch before her neighbor, Symphony, poked out her head from the front door of the townhouse next to her and called out to Ericka.

Annoyed by the sound of Symphony's voice, Ericka turned to her neighbor as if she was carrying out an unpleasant choir that caused way more grief than it did relief.

"Hello, Symphony," Ericka said and witnessed her neighbor tiptoeing around the hedges as if she was dodging obstacles.

"I don't mean to bother you, Ericka, but I heard a strange noise coming from her place a couple of hours ago, which had me deeply concerned. You know how I am, with living alone over there and all. We have to look after each other, especially with all of these break-ins these past couple of days. I'm sure you heard all about them."

You live alone too, Ericka wanted to say but held back her tongue.

"No," Ericka said instead. "Not really. Probably just a drone," she said, trying to avoid the soon-to-be conversation with Symphony. She soon realized that her first response could've come off as an invitation for Symphony to further explain these string of so-called "break-ins."

"A drone?" She watched Symphony's face change from concerned to confused. "You mean like those—"

"—Yes," Ericka said shortly. "Those. Welcome to the future, Symphony."

"Right." Symphony laughed off Ericka's dark sense of humor. "I certainly wish my Lawrence was alive today to see what this world has turned into. You know, Ericka, he worked for a movie production company in Los Angeles. Lawrence used to work on science fiction movies—"

"—Listen, Symphony," Ericka said, pointing at her car parked in the parking pad, "I don't have time to talk right now. I have to be somewhere."

"Right," Symphony said, her mood more deflated. "I forgot how busy you are. We'll talk later."

"Sure," she said, walking to her car.

Ericka was waiting for Symphony to say something else in order to keep the conversation alive—she always did.

But strangely, she heard nothing.

Not a peep.

BEFORE Ericka picked up her Thai food, she drove about twenty minutes out of her way to Waynesville Beach. She always liked to drive. There was a brief two-to-three year period during the sweeping transition to driverless cars where she wouldn't even contemplate whether or not she'd drive. After all the glitches were finally resolved, she liked driving again. Once she arrived at the beach, she stood along the edge of the shore where the sand was hard and smooth enough to evenly walk on and watched the rolling waves crashing at her feet. Ericka embraced the serenity of the sounds and smells of the ocean, the comforts it offered, as if they were rights, *not* privileges, to those who had the willpower to journey to the place from where they came. From a distance, a dark ominous-looking storm was brewing over the Atlantic. Ericka knew what was coming; yet, she didn't care. The ocean was resilient like that.

✉

THE madness all started when she passed the *third* sign on the way to pick up her Thai food. Except for early screenings two weeks ago, *Wake Me Tomorrow* had only been released to the public for a week. Yet, it had become an overnight sensation. Even though the lenticular billboard with green undertones was rather impressive—the way Grace's face slowly changed to May's depending on the angle she looked at it (each time Ericka first witnessing Grace's white face on the billboard ahead of her, and then, while driving past the massive sign, suddenly witnessing May's black face)—Ericka swore to herself that, if she saw another one, she'd kill herself.

✉

THE images were back.

Those words *Wake Me Tomorrow* "brought to you by the 'new and approved' Spinner Jack 2000!"

Ericka didn't want to look. But a part of her felt as if she had to look.

As she grabbed her food from the Everyday Thai dispenser, she turned to the image. She looked twice at the green *Wake Me Tomorrow* T-shirt that the young kid was wearing. Too not far away in the waiting area another kid, who was waiting to be seated with her parents, was playing with an eight-legged Chione action figure in one hand and a Desiree action figure in the other. Making verbal explosions and sound effects with her mouth, the kid was creating her own imaginative fight inside her head with the two action figures.

If they only knew, Ericka thought.

I wonder *how they would react.*

As soon as Ericka stepped outside the Thai restaurant, an e-bus drove past the busy intersection. On the side of the e-bus was that same sign, the two faces staring at her, ever-changing. Before she could even react, she saw yet another massive sign on the side of a building. She was tempted to scream. She even went so far as to take in a deep breath, as if she was about to give her best roar.

Frustrated, Ericka marched to her car with that scream held tight in her chest. She couldn't help but overhear these two other kids, older, tech-school age, remnants of the Window Generation—or what she often referred to as the "Whatever Generation"—arguing about the latest spin, *Wake Me Tomorrow*.

One of them was arguing that the spin was so authentic that it was based off a real life story. "According to Low-down, the spin was 'factually' based off the life and times of—"

The other one cut off his friend before he could finish and retorted by talking about what color of mood he was currently feeling—the color being red, "crimson red," to be exact. The comment sparked a debate on who was the better spinner in the "green" category: Either Kelly Green or Laurel Green. Another kid, who was lagging behind, joined in on the debate, "Don't forget Acid Green? His last spin was next level—"

"Or, what about Paris Green?" the other kid chimed in. "He went straight up *Matrix* in that spin, *Infinity Hack*. Know what I mean, Red—"

"—That's Crimson Red to you, bot. Not like your ass would know anything about jacking in. All you do is watch 'em."

"You spun one time and you're acting all boss. . . "

Like the scream she had bottled-up inside her, Ericka was tempted to unburden herself, confront the Window Kids, these so-called "fans," these "haters," and ornery "in-stigators," grab them by the shoulders and shake them until they turned purple and let them all know what really went down in *Wake Me Tomorrow*. She wanted to scream it loud to the world that it's her story, *not* Laurel Green's. That it was she, Ericka Barnes, who made the spin *Wake Me To-morrow* and that opportunist, Laurel Green, was the one who made it more commercialized by dumbing down the plot in order to make a quick buck.

Doubt crept in.

Then fear.

Ericka thought about the repercussions, as well as the "fine print" she signed before submitting the spin.

Even when she tried to close her eyes and rid the horrible nightmare that she was currently trapped in, that more "popular" version of her story was lingering in the darkness, as if, somehow, her memories of the past events had started to alter.

They'd never believe her anyway, though. That, she knew.

After all, she looked nothing like May Warren. And what they did to Justin, the whole gender swap, caused Ericka to clench her teeth as if she was smothering the rage before it could escape and bring about physical and mental harm to anyone who crossed her path.

As the impulse came and went, Ericka proceeded toward her car. In the corner of her eye, she saw one of those new pop-up bookstores.

Neatly displayed behind the front window were all sorts of *Wake Me Tomorrow* merchandise: comic books, hats, coffee mugs, puzzles, and board games.

Curious, she walked over to the window.

Again, in annoyance, *she looks nothing like me*, Ericka thought.

Next to the display case, she noticed a rack of Spinner Jack 2000s. Each one of the schwabs inside the tightly concealed packages appeared as if they were in a "sleep mode."

Across the street was an ice cream parlor. On the front window of the parlor, she saw a similar WMT-themed poster advertising a brand-"spanking" new flavor called Bloody Revenge, which was inspired by *Wake Me Tomorrow*. Bloody Revenge was two scoops of chocolate ice cream topped with hot strawberry sauce and bullet-shaped pieces of butterscotch inside a vanilla cone. Ericka recognized a couple of TwoWay kids with their new whips hanging outside the parlor licking Bloody Revenge ice cream cones.

The rage suddenly melted from her insides.

A cold emptiness washed over her. She experienced the same emptiness during her spin. To her, it felt no different than losing a close parent to Alzheimer's or a loved one who didn't recognize her anymore. In a way, Ericka felt as if she was losing herself to a world that she no longer recognized. The emptiness faded from the idea of what her story had become and brought forth an anger that made her skin hot. A new anger.

With her jaw tightly clenched, Ericka turned toward the general direction of where her car was parked and just as she was about to storm away, a bearded man with glasses bumped into her. The blood suddenly raced through her veins. She lurched forward and for a moment, imagined herself dropping a satchel of artwork onto the sidewalk. In that moment, she was in New York, surrounding by throngs of New Yorkers and tourists alike. Ericka had seen this particular moment before, like déjà vu, yet it wasn't déjà vu because there was no satchel on the sidewalk.

Immediately, Ericka felt something sticky and cold pressed against her stomach. She looked down and witnessed a circular blotch of red liquid all over her shirt. Her first reaction: *Blood.* She had been stabbed by a blade. Then, she witnessed the vanilla cone inside the man's hand.

"So—so—sorry," he stuttered.

Ericka swallowed her words as the google-eyed man tried to wipe away the warm strawberry sauce with a napkin.

"Forget it," Ericka said.

The man continued to wipe away the sauce.

"I said 'Forget it!'"

Finally, he backed off.

Ericka stormed away.

NOT too far away was a clothing store called Refinery.

With both her hands and arms sticky with strawberry sauce, Ericka debated whether or not to wash up inside the industrial-looking store. She didn't want to track the sauce into her car. She could feel it crawling over her skin, as if it was an entity spreading over her body. She had no other choice. Mainly, she wanted to get away from all of the chaos outside. She entered the store and was immediately greeted by a wall of manufactured freshness—that kind of new shoe smell. The sight of clothes hanging on clothing racks brought back a sense of nostalgia. Stores like these didn't exist anymore; in fact, considering most of the consumers' shopping was done through the Internet and convenient smartphone apps, a majority of retail stores had either been bought out by super companies like YourCart, which focused on e-commerce, or declared bankruptcy.

Ericka located the bathroom in the back of the store. Three employees, who looked as if they were about to pounce on Ericka to ward off the tedious grip of boredom, hovered around Ericka and prodded her with questions, which received short, unequivocal answers. She dismissed each one of the hungry-eyed, slack-jawed employees and eventually made it to the bathroom without being torn to pieces. Once Ericka stepped inside the bathroom, the thought of relieving herself came to her; however, she still had doubts about using the toilet inside the stall. After debating whether or not to use the toilet, she decided it was best to hold it.

When Ericka returned from the bathroom free of strawberry sauce, she came across a nice-looking red blouse on a clothing rack. The red blouse rid any negative thought she had of Refinery, the thought of *them*, as well as the strange tremble in the mirror when she was washing the sauce from her skin. She held up the blouse to her chest, envisioning herself inside it. While she was "here," she might as well try it on. *Why not?* Normally, in order to stay out of the public' eye, like most of the population, she bought her clothes online. But Ericka constantly reminded herself that she was, in fact, "here," walking among her own kind—or at least, what she thought was her own kind.

Ericka took the blouse to a dressing room. She passed yet another funhouse-like mirror, which distorted her body to the point where certain areas were disproportionate. She ignored the mirror and proceeded toward the last stall. Once she stepped inside, she didn't hesitate. She removed her shirt and tried on the blouse. She stepped outside the stall and walked to the mirrors where she modeled the red blouse. Ericka experimented with various mirrors, each one displaying a different size and shape of her body. After looking through one particular mirror, she was sold. The red blouse was going to be hers—*mine*, she claimed.

As Ericka was about to head back to the stall, the floor suddenly shook! She threw out her hands, trying to balance herself. The very first thought that came to mind was *earthquake*. But how? This area never received earthquakes; in fact, it wasn't even near a fault line. The shaking eventually stopped. Then, it appeared as if the walls were moving. She looked toward the floor. Then, the walls. Yes, she knew, the room was moving as if it was on a turntable. Ericka tried to make sense as to what was happening. She immediately eliminated earthquake. Now, all she could think about was *them*. They found her.

With the walls moving all around her, Ericka raced toward the exit.

The doorway filled with yet another wall in its place. Even the mirrors had vanished behind another wall.

Once the room finally came to a stop, Ericka heard a *clicking* sound coming from the same stall where she changed clothes.

With caution, she walked back to the stall and opened the door. As soon as she stepped inside the stall, the back wall slid open, revealing a dark, misty, narrow hallway before her. With nowhere else to go, Ericka walked through the secret door. Once she stepped into the hallway, the wall closed behind her.

Despite all of the disruption, Ericka didn't feel at all frightened.

On the contrary, she felt calm.

Maybe too calm.

☷

ONCE she reached the end of the hallway, the calmness shattered and rough waves of panic rushed through her body, causing her airways to tighten.

Before Ericka hung these massive pink curtains, which stretched into a ceiling that faded into darkness.

Carefully, she searched for an opening in the curtains but couldn't find one at first reach. She started to push and pull and punch through the heavy curtains until she eventually found herself lost in a pinkish mass of soft velvet. The smooth texture of the curtains became pricklier and changed in weight.

Out of curiosity, she ran her hand across a loose, over-lapping fold in the curtain. To Ericka, the feel of the curtain felt almost like. . . skin. Such a ridiculous notion came and went. She blindly pushed her way to the other side and managed to peel back a narrow slit in the pink curtain, revealing a circular room with dark burgundy carpet. Strangely, it was the busy-carpet below that both of her strained eyes first saw, the veiny pattern which reminded her of the blood vessels and connective tissue inside the hypodermis. Then, secondly, each and every member of The Web scattered throughout the studio-like room. Except for Chione, who was standing as if she was a host, the members of The Web were sitting patiently as if they were waiting on Ericka's arrival.

Chione Elmahdy was there without her mask, Ericka first noticed. She was wearing a black and white striped shirt under a black blazer.

Dab, the little person whom she remembered from ten years ago, was coming and going with a silver tray of hot tea and finger foods, such as pigs in a blanket and lettuce wraps filled with a smelly minced meat, through a pinned-up opening in the curtain which acted like a doorway.

Harold Roman was there, as well. He was seated in a slouched position in a bulky wheelchair. He was wearing an oxygen mask on his face; however, Ericka never saw the oxygen tank. Despite Harold's incredibly frail appearance, he had a monk-like tranquility about him.

Kira was present too. Dressed in all black. Her dark hair worn tight in a ponytail. Her head was rested against her arm in a bored teenager manner. She was hanging out in a round pink booth in the very back of the room. Ericka couldn't tell whether Kira was actually bored or *drunk*—the four empty glasses of beer on the table hinted at a greater issue.

Seated across from Kira was R.C. Crimp, an employee at Fantasy World who Ericka used—or better yet, "manipulated" through the power of female persuasion into having her spin produced without raising any eyebrows. Both his shoulders were slouched. He was wearing a look of defeat on his face, as if he had recently been called to the principal's office and was waiting for his punishment to be handed out. R.C. was cut from the same cloth of people who meant nothing to Ericka, not because he once meant something to her, but because he, like all of the others, acted as if he had already figured her out and despite any progress she made, she'd always be that girl he once "hooked up" with, that "Shy Girl," or that "Useless Thing," or as others who crossed the same circles, "Rabid Dog," or the once "Disobedient Student," or that bitch who was "Too Good To Talk To Anyone," or like her gym coach once said, a "Waste of Flesh." Ericka didn't have to prove anything to anybody, including some kid whose last name rhymed with the word *pimp*.

Another person, one whom she had never seen before, was there as well. His entire head was covered in a mask that looked as if it was a mirror. He was wearing a raggedy brown trench coat over glittery chain mail.

Last but not least, Ericka's spinner Laurel Green was sitting in another booth with two other spinners. She didn't know who they were, but she could tell from their celebrity-type aura that they were, in fact, "spinners."

"Welcome," Chione was first to speak, as she ushered Ericka farther into the pink room. "I'm aware you may be feeling like *Alice in Wonderland* by now. . . "

Ericka witnessed a flicker of light in the corner of her eye. She turned to the mirror-faced person—whom she assumed was a man based off his broad shoulders and tall frame, as well as the way he was dressed—and noticed the display of a brown confused emoji face behind the surface of the mirror as if he was wearing the emoji like a New Age e-mask.

". . . But rest assured," Chione said, grabbing Ericka's attention, "you are exactly where you need to be."

"I—I need to be?" Ericka's voice cracked. "And where exactly am I?"

Chione paused.

A tense silence filled the room.

"*Home*," a dark voice said from behind the opening in the curtain.

A dark-skinned woman stepped into the pink room.

The expression of Ericka's face fell. Her jaw slackened. She drawled, "Mom?"

"Hello, Candace," Tiara said, as she entered the room. She was dressed in a white nightgown. Whenever Ericka thought of her mom outside those frozen images she had of her while being trapped inside the car wash, she always visualized her in that white nightgown. She'd be wearing it at the most vulnerable moments of her life: childhood. She could see her mother gliding into her bedroom at night as if she was the descendent of an angel. She'd be wearing that same nightgown when she tucked her into bed and sent her away to the place where dreams were made. She'd be wearing that same nightgown when she sat comfortably by her bedside and checked her temperature with the backside of her hand pressed softly against her forehead or other areas of her face as if she was locating sickness and was prompt to eliminate it. She'd be wearing that same nightgown when she reassured her that the day beyond the other side of night would be brighter than the day before. She'd be wearing that same nightgown when she read her a bedtime story with grace and fluidity, and the sounds of her mother's voice and the words coming from her mouth were miniature artists painting sumptuous portraits, climatic scenes, and rich landscapes inside the vastness of her mind.

Ericka examined each detail of her mother's face. Then, her eyes fell toward the white nightgown and after a second glance, it looked faded. The white cotton, dull and gray, as if the nightgown had carried its color from the hazy memory itself.

The reflection in the mirror changed. Another brown emoji appeared on the glass screen, this time a brown-faced emoji with a tear drop.

"What?" Ericka uttered. "What are you doing here—"

"—Your mother is here to support you, Ms. Norwood," Chione cut in. "Or, do you prefer to go by the name Squints?"

"My name is Ericka," Ericka said, more convincingly. "Ericka Barnes."

"Yes," Chione responded. "We know. For years, you've been hiding under that name. But you and I both know who you really are."

As Chione approached Ericka, Ericka took a step back.

"I am Ericka Barnes," she said, her breath labored.

"Yes," Chione said arrogantly. "And so were thousands of other people. But Ericka Barnes—the real one that is— is dead." Chione tilted her head like a dog did at the first sight of confusion. "Did you think by using that poor girl's name you would carry on her legacy?" She didn't respond to the question—couldn't—for she was too confounded by the sight of her mother standing feet away from a bitch who was badgering her. "You didn't know. You went along with the crowd like they all do. Despite your efforts to bring us down, we *collectively*," Chione looked around the room, "believe the credit should be rightfully given to where it is due. After all, if it weren't for your spin and all the attention it received, then—more than likely—Spin-to-

Play would've eventually died out like any other trend. It was inevitable. *However*, any trend that could last beyond its life cycle—that is called a gift—"

"—Just tell her already," Kira said from the back of the room. Her voice was slurred and bitter in tone.

Chione glared at Kira through the corner of her eye.

After the heated stare down, Chione faced Ericka.

"And that brings me to exactly *why* you are here, Squints."

"I don't go by that name anymore," Ericka seethed.

Another emoji appeared on the screen: a red-faced bad tempered emoji.

"Enough with goddamn emojis, Mirrorhead!"

Chione turned to the strange man with a mirrored-face and pointed at Ericka, as if she was using Ericka's sudden outburst as an example to a past argument.

"And this is exactly why we didn't vote you to be the spokesperson for Spin-to-Play. No offense, Mirage, but the American people would never trust a person who speaks in emojis."

Harold removed the oxygen mask from his face.

"Like that surrogate, Sidney Kovacs, is any better," he coughed while talking, as if the words alone itched his throat. "The man's a goddamn flake."

Harold violently coughed. He was forced to put his mask back on.

"Enough Harold," Chione said sharply, as Dab rolled a recliner chair into the center of the room. "As I was saying, Ms. Norwood, we are extremely excited to say that we are officially in the May Warren business. With that said, we want to capitalize on *Wake Me Tomorrow*'s success and expand its universe." She showcased the chair before her. "Please," she said calmly, "have a seat."

Ericka didn't sit. She didn't even budge for that matter, which forced a sigh from Chione.

"Let me ask you, Ms. Norwood: *Why?*"

Ericka snapped, "Why what?"

"*Why* change your identity? *Why* use one of the Fantasy World's employees to blackmail your way into our theme

327

park? *Why* sign a user agreement and legally authorize us to alter your spin as we see fit to our platform?"

Ericka thought carefully about her answer.

"I don't know the answers to your questions," she said finally. "All I know is that it's not complicated. It *never* was. Maybe I wanted to relive what happened to me ten years ago, when a part of me felt alive. Maybe I just wanted to experience that feeling again. For so long, I thought that feeling was gone. For good. That I'd never get it back. But let's to be honest. Life sucks. Only so often does something come along that makes life *less* suck. I had that with Justin, if only for a while. So what's wrong with holding onto that? Or. . . " she said before Chione or the other members of The Web could respond, ". . . maybe I was simply bored. Maybe I was tired of living life in the shadows. Maybe I just wanted to recourse the direction of my past, to *change* my memories. Be somebody else—at least for one day. So, I guess I figured if I couldn't bring you down in the real world, then why not bring you down inside my head. Why not destroy the people who killed Justin? Because, in a way, even though Justin is not dead, what you lying monsters did to him—what you did to us— *we* might as well be."

"You and I both know, Ms. Norwood," Chione said, as she stepped closer to Ericka, "we couldn't just sit back and do nothing while you and Justin were off on your self-righteous road trip. Collectively, we did what we had to do in order to stay afloat; and if that required you to carry out a job for us, then so be it." She glanced over at Harold. "Isn't that right, Harold?"

Once more, Harold removed his oxygen mask.

He had a strange puckered look on his face, as if he was trying to laugh but was aware of the repercussions.

"Other individuals," Harold said weakly, "spinners who have been elementarily reduced to nothing more than a *color* in order to cater to the needs of a public that has become incredibly hypersensitive and prone to conflict, will undeservedly earn recognition for the work you have done. *Your* successes, Candace Norwood, will be only *their* suc-

cesses and nobody—I mean, not a single soul from Monitack to Modesto—will celebrate you. Let alone, remember
you. You, my dear," Harold said grimly, as another coughing spell came on, "you will go to your grave knowing that
everything you've ever accomplished in life was all for nothing. . . ."

"Yeah," Kira said obnoxiously, as she blew out a fart
from her lips. "You're one to talk, *Night Rider*!"

The room fell to silence over Kira's outburst.

Somewhere, in the back of the room, someone was holding in a laugh.

Through another doorway in the pink curtains, Dab reentered the room with a dropper on a tray. Before the two
curtains closed, Ericka was able to get a closer look into
another smaller, storage-like room behind the pink curtains. Inside were wooden shelves of hundreds of glass jars
filled with a pink liquid. Floating inside each jar were
snake worms.

Dab placed the tray on the stand next to Harold's
wheelchair and grabbed the dropper.

"Ahh," Dab said, opening his mouth wide as if he was
mimicking a common gesture made by a doctor.

Harold followed suit and opened his mouth while Dab
squeezed a drop onto the back of his tongue.

"One more," Harold begged, smacking his gums.

"What did I tell you about taking too much of that
stuff?" Chione said wifely.

"Hush, Spider Lady," Harold groaned.

During the quarrel between Chione and Harold, Ericka
drifted in thought. A memory came to her, one that had
been buried deep for so many years, as if it was there all
along and certain words or smells or even particular images
had caused it to surface. Right then and there, while
Chione was snapping at Harold for overusing snake's milk,
Ericka remembered her words, Mom's words: *open it.* The
two words that had traveled years to find her. Two innocent words that were attached to so much pain and misery.
The words came at Ericka like a warm blade, forcing her to
jump to a moment in her life where innocence was held

sacred. And in that moment in time, Ericka was a young girl desperately trying to open a car door before her mother, who was locked inside, fell into the trap underneath the car wash. *Open it*, she said, only many years later after the fall. *Open it*. Not the car door. But another door, one decades-deep inside her head. Ericka first thought it was some Bizarro world type of bullshit where expressions or gestures were the complete opposite. Hello being goodbye. What's up was what's down. Hang in there champ was give it up, loser. Keep your head up, keep your down. Open it, close it. But with doubts emerged the truth.

Disappointed in her silence, Ericka turned toward her mother. She witnessed a bead of sweat rolling down the side of her forehead. Her eyes trailed downward to her mother's warped reflection in Dab's tray. She was neither Mom nor Tiara; in fact, she wasn't at all human—well, not entirely. Yet, this supposed woman in her mother's white nightgown appeared to be a Fantasy World employee holding what she thought to be a larger "schwab" in his arms. He was holding the schwab no different than a person would hold a pet. Her eyes flicked toward her mother; and in a brief survey, she searched for a seam or zipper along her mother's skin, any opening. She couldn't find anything out of the ordinary—at least, not on the surface. The thought alone of not being able to distinguish *what* was real or who exactly was wearing who as a disguise caused her brain to cramp.

As soon as the imposter acknowledged Ericka with a half-smile that trembled into a dimple, Ericka pulled her eyes away from the grotesque reflection and directed her eyes toward the woman pretending to be "Mom." In a glimpse, Ericka caught what looked like a tentacle slithering back up into the white nightgown.

"Please disregard, Mr. Roman," Chione said to Ericka. "As you can see, he's not well."

Ericka was slow to follow.

"Ms. Norwood?"

Left in a wobbly daze, Ericka tracked down Chione's voice.

"Yeah," she said vaguely.

"I'm sure all of this is overwhelming right now," Chione said and once more, pointed at the chair. "I assure you everything will make sense soon enough."

"It all makes perfect sense," Ericka said with more clarity. "You want to exploit me, as you do with the others. That's the whole concept, right? To squeeze every drop of blood from me until you bleed me dry. Then, after you're done with me, toss me in the trash."

"Not exploit, Ms. Norwood," she said confidently. "Showcase." She pointed at the two spinners sitting next to Laurel Green. "And that brings me to the next chapter in your epic saga. Now, it gives me great pleasure to introduce you to the Queen of Cool, Champagne Pink, and the one-of-a-kind, Mystic Maroon, the next two spinners who have agreed to collaborate in a sequel to *Wake Me Tomorrow*." Chione nodded at the two spinners. Then pointed at Ericka. "Ladies and gentleman, I'd like you to meet the real life May Warren."

In return, Champagne Pink and Mystic Maroon reverently bowed their heads down at Ericka. Then, raised their glasses in a toast.

"Look forward to spinning your story," Mystic Maroon said to Ericka.

Once more, Chione pointed at the chair in the center of the room as if she was no longer asking but demanding for Ericka to have a seat.

Dab reentered the room with a white box in his hands. He placed the box on top of the tray next to Harold and gently removed a smaller version of the same creature that she witnessed posing as "Mom." The creature was roughly the size of a Bluetooth and had been modified with a two-button style interface along the back of its hardened shell.

As if he was handling a bomb ready to go off at the slightest disturbance, Dab handed the creature to Chione.

She wasn't as careful as Dab handling the creature. She snatched the schwab from his palms, held it up in better light, and momentarily admired it. Two tentacles released from underneath the curved shell and dangled below it, one of which would be inserted directly into Ericka's ear while the other tentacle into her left or right nostril—whichever one she preferred.

"Believe it or not, Ms. Norwood, it was people like you and that Rat Bastard, Cameron Dobbs—who's now lying six feet under—who forced us to conduct our business much differently. After awhile, capturing people was starting to become riskier. From doctor offices to photo booths to any confined space, we *factually* had to redo the entire fabric of this country. But now," Chione said, as she looked over the tiny schwab in her hand, "we found a new way to get inside consumers' heads. With help from the most talented scientists we could buy, we managed to genetically modify Gene and his telekinetic powers in order to create a more marketable product for the average consumer. Look at it as a shrunken down, bite-size version of an *ancient being* from an *ancient world* parallel to our own inside the palm of your hand. And with our new and approved schwab interface, we haven't even scratched the surface on the possibilities—"

"—Looks all the same to me," Ericka seethed.

"You know how it works," Chione said, ignoring Ericka's comment. "You might feel a slight pinch while I link up mini-Gene here to your brain. However, there's absolutely nothing to worry about. I assure you lil' Genie-Poo is perfectly safe. Like our motto: 'Straight from your dome directly to any electronic device inside your home.' In other words, as Kira coined it, from head to home."

Kira rolled her eyes from the remark and continued to look as if she was the least interested in what was going down.

With her patience running thin, Chione pointed at the recliner chair. "Please don't make me force you," she said, as she teased the two long spider legs starting to peel outward from behind the two black stripes of her shirt.

Ericka looked over the schwab in Chione's hand and the two angel hair-sized tentacles hanging below like electrical cables.

With deflation, Ericka asked, "I don't have a choice, do I?"

"Nope," Chione said sinisterly.

With no other choice, she sat down in the recliner and as Chione was about to insert the schwab into her ear, a booming voice suddenly called out, "*Freeze!*"

Everybody in the room was startled, especially Ericka, who, despite her lack of appreciation for cops, surprisingly welcomed the sound of that infamous word and the stony-faced detective behind it. Ericka thought she had seen the familiar-looking detective once or twice before; however, she couldn't quite pin the exact moment in time. He was aiming a highly pressure-sensitive boom stick directly at Chione. One blast of the sound wave could temporarily cause paralysis.

"Drop the schwab, ma'am," the detective said to Chione.

"This must be some kind of misunderstanding, young man—"

"—*Detective*," he emphasized.

"Do you know who I am? I could crush you like a fly."

The detective charged the boom stick, which was ready to fire.

"Being someone in your position," he said, grinning, "you have to appreciate the irony right now."

Armed with stun clubs and loop cuffs, a swarm of police officers poured into the room.

"Not too smart, are you *Detective?*"

"I'm not gonna ask you again," the detective said, readjusting the boom stick in his hands.

Eventually, Chione placed the schwab on the tray and held up her hands in surrender. All eight of them.

"Sir," one officer said from the corner of the room, "you might wanna take a look at this. . . "

With his eyes never leaving Chione, the detective called over a police officer to take his place. The officer swiftly grabbed the boom stick from the detective's hands and traded places with him.

"If she moves, *crush* her."

"Yes, sir."

The detective checked on the other police officer, who was holding back the curtain. He nodded at the snake worms inside the jars on the shelves.

"Is that what I think they are?"

"Jackpot," the detective said in awe. Excited about the big bust, the detective stepped back into the room and grabbed the boom stick from the police officer's hands. "Officer Brace, these people are all under arrest for the illegal possession of toxioplexus," he nodded at Ericka, "except for her."

As soon as Ericka locked eyes with the detective, she knew exactly where she had seen him before. The face around his eyes was all but foreign to her. But his eyes, she knew his eyes.

"*Kush?*"

Her tongue slipped.

With the thought of being arrested as well—her arrest being more severe than the others—Ericka tried to take back the words as soon as they left her mouth.

"They used to call me that in a past life," he said smoothly. "It's Hush now."

The police officers subdued the other people in the room with cool cuffs, including Harold Roman, and then escorted each one from the room. Ericka looked around the room and saw Chione nowhere to be found.

Maybe they had already taken her outside, she thought to herself.

She redirected her attention back to Detective "Hush."

Who was looking back at her with that very same look on his face.

One of remembrance.

☲

DETECTIVE Hush walked Ericka outside where it was still daylight.

Shielding her eyes from the bright light, Ericka scanned the underpass of the bridge and heard drones and hover cars humming overhead. The sight and sounds of day stirred her insides. A flash of panic suddenly came over her.

With her heart racing, she asked the detective, "How long have I been gone?"

"Two days," he said. "Good thing you have a neighbor who cares about you; otherwise, we never would've found you."

"How'd you find me?"

The detective displayed a holophone along the band on his wrist. The hologram displayed their exact position on a GPS graphic.

"Tracked you through your phone."

Ericka pulled out a flip phone from her pocket.

"Damn!" the detective said in surprise. "Still rocking the flip-flip!"

"The whole point of having this was *not* to be tracked," Ericka said, loosening up from Hush's excited nature.

"I don't know where you heard that," he said, the excitement trailing from his voice. "Ever since Robert's Law was passed two years ago, all phones, including that ancient piece of shit in your hand, are required to be tracked."

"But how'd I get all the way out here?"

"With your two legs."

Ericka rolled her eyes from the dud of a comment and looked up at the bridge above her.

"I was shopping," she drawled. "Then, the next thing, I know—well, I don't know what happened."

"Funny how time plays tricks on the mind these days," he said. "One minute, it's day. The next, night. Strange times, huh?"

"You got that right," she said, facing the detective. "So, your name's Hush."

"And your name's Ericka."

Ericka's stomach tightened. Her palms grew sweaty.

"Yeah," she said, unsure.

"Don't worry," the detective said with a smirk. "I've got bigger fish to fry. I know you didn't do all those things you were accused of doing ten years ago."

An officer interrupted the detective, who immediately turned business-like.

"We seem to be missing one," he informed Hush.

"Yeah," the detective said, already knowing who was missing. "She's quite a sneaky one. Put an APB on her," he said casually. "We'll find her."

"Yes, sir."

The officer went away.

"Calling the shots now, huh?" She cracked a smile, which was worn tight on her face. "Former criminal who was once on the opposite side of the law, now the man who locks up bad guys."

"Criminals make the best cops, don't they?"

In a state of euphoria, she watched the officers escort the rest of the Web, including Mirage, who was wearing a brown smiley face emoji, into the back of the police van. With e-jacks, other officers were pulling out pallets of snake worms, which were contained inside jars and shrink wrapped to pallets, and loading them into the back of un-marked trucks.

"It's strange," she trailed off.

"What's strange?"

"Bumping into you like this," she said, "after all these years."

"Not really," Hush said. "It's a small world."

As Hush joined the rest of his team, Ericka couldn't help but stand back and mull over Hush's comment.

Never had the world seemed so big as it did right now.

THE following day after the bust in New Centre, millions of Americans watched Ericka Barnes in an exclusive tell-all interview from their television sets, smartphones, laptops, e-tablets, and holophones.

They watched Ericka go on a "live" broadcast and tell the truth about her encounter with the creators behind Fantasy World's most popular attraction called Spin-to-Play, where, under the timely edits of his or her designated story developer or "spinner," guests were allowed to cognitively live out his or her desired fantasy in movie-style formats later viewable through Fantasy World's streaming service, Hotcakes.

They watched Ericka talk about how these creators, out of financial gain, attempted to coerce her into making the sequel to *Wake Me Tomorrow* by any force necessary.

They watched Ericka breach her contract by revealing herself as the "real life May Warren!"

They watched Ericka reject *Wake Me Tomorrow*'s success. But the main focus of the interview wasn't directed toward herself or why she submitted the spin in the first place or even stating the message behind the "uncut" spin whether it be satirical or cautionary. Her focus was solely directed at the people *watching* her.

They watched Ericka go on a twelve-minute tirade about America and its everlasting hunger for violence and savagery and how not the idea but the word *justice* had turned into a marketer's wet dream, a symbol used for mainstream, a talking point in a politician's script, a cartoon disguised by cheap gimmicks and clip-on neckties, a stuffed animal filled with sewage waste, a toy laced with poison, a trite punch line, a dumb snippet on a cereal box, a dirty joke.

They watched Ericka call out *all* Americans in their inability to "unplug."

They watched Ericka Barnes stare down the very people who interviewed her and question the strategic tactics used throughout their broadcasts in order to corral more viewers. Their agenda was as clear to her as it had ever been: No longer was it a race to the bottom of the brain stem. It was a fucking marathon without a finish line.

And millions of Americans watched, but did they listen?

"THEY'RE going to eat you alive."

Ericka woke up to the sound of her manager's voice escaping from the darkness. She rid the screeching rats from her dreams by stretching her body. Looser, she rolled out of bed and nearly tripped over the aluminum baseball bat perched against the headboard. First, Ericka checked the window closest to her bed. Once she opened the blinds, the sun greeted her and never had she felt so welcomed by the light. For years, she found nothing but anguish in the daylight. For years, she imagined exactly what it felt like to be a vampire. To resist the sun's warm bite by sleeping through the majority of the day and to work through the night as an overnight stocker at Food Circle, a job that didn't pay enough to live comfortably. A job that never offered any reassurance for an inevitable future where a "robot" replacing a human was a bill away from being passed into law. A job that created more setbacks than advantages. A job where planning a weekend trip to Fantasy World meant starving for three months.

Despite Ericka's finical insecurity, for years she earned an unexplainable ease in the natural cover of night, as well as the unbroken promises it constantly provided. A part of Ericka enjoyed not having to interact with the public. A part of Ericka questioned where such joy had originated and scorned such answers. That pain was gone, though, as if the release of her great burden, one which she had been carrying around for ten years, had expelled the pain from her body.

In spite of yesterday's contentious interview, she told herself it was going to be not a good day but a "great day."

She walked up to the locked bedroom door and removed a barricade of books and weights, as well as a chair wedged against the back of the door.

Once the door was clear of debris, she headed straight to the kitchen. Craving a strong cup of coffee, Ericka grabbed the bag of coffee grounds from the pantry's shelf. She opened the bag. Of course, it was empty. But Ericka took it as a sign, to get out more, to join the very crowd that she had liberated. She didn't need to make her own coffee when she could go buy herself a cup of coffee in the public, where people walked together in harmony, where they talked face-to-face to one another, where they thrived at a continually learned skill. She would pay a visit to one of these people—take that back—an artist who was skilled in crafting coffee.

MORE optimistic about the new day, Ericka grabbed her Zippo lighter, as well as her lucky coins, thirty-three cents, from the warped clay bowl that she made when she was a child, and placed the belongings in her pocket. She rode her jet scooter to the nearest coffee shop, Cup of Joy, which was located only two miles from her townhouse.

As soon as Ericka stepped inside the coffee shop, she immediately received exaggerated head turns and stares that lasted long enough to be considered rude.

Above the lounge area, a sixty-inch hologram was re-playing yesterday's interview. Ericka witnessed her face on the hologram. She swallowed the cartoon-like gulp down her throat.

Undeterred, she proceeded to the front counter and constantly reminded herself that today wasn't going to be a great day but an extraordinary day.

Ericka didn't even make it halfway toward the front counter before they came at her. First, a man in his late sixties walked straight up to her and spit directly in her face. She didn't even have a chance to wipe off the spit from her cheek before another man groped her breast and sharply hissed the word *bitch* to her while he was leaving the coffee shop. Left in a loss of words, Ericka followed the two men toward the exit. She didn't even make it halfway toward the exit before yet another person—a woman a couple of years younger than her—shoved Ericka from be-hind and then snapped a selfie with a holophone as she stripped the very shoes Ericka was wearing from her feet. The woman placed the shoes in her purse.

"Thanks, bitch," she said, flashed the peace symbol, grabbed her to-go cup of coffee from the counter, and exited the coffee shop.

Another person even younger than the one before—who looked as if she had no business being in a coffee shop—came at Ericka and tried to rip off her shirt.

This time, she wasn't going to sit back and let these people walk all over her.

Clawing at Ericka, the girl ended up scratching the side of her face while she tore off part of the collar of her shirt.

Once humiliated, now left in a state of rage, she grabbed the girl's wrist and ended up body slamming her into a rack of coffee mugs! The crash caused shattered mugs to scatter across the lounge area. She wasn't sure whether or not she killed the girl. But the girl wasn't moving. Immediately forced into a "fight" or "flight" survival mode, Ericka surveyed her surroundings. Sipping from their coffee as if it was fueling their anger, others stood from their seats and approached Ericka.

One of them said Ericka was going to "severely" pay for what she said about him on national TV and that she wasn't going to take his spin away from her. She saw a look in his eye, which was no longer human.

As the people started to circle Ericka, she found a hole and seized the opportunity before it was too late. She ran from the coffee shop. People exited as well. Some of them followed Ericka. Others pointed at other people on the street, yelling out, "There she is! There's the backstabber!"

Ericka's pace quickened. She looked over her shoulder and a crowd of a dozen or so people had tripled in a matter of seconds.

Other people were racing toward their hover cars and grabbing weapons from inside.

Some grabbed any weapon they could find either inside their cars, hover cars, or trucks (knives, tire irons, clubs, baseball bats, loaded fanny packs), or even attached to the street itself (bricks, broken glass, road signs.)

The more extreme ones, who had been psyching themselves up all week to unleash their bottled up violence, were armed to the teeth with outlawed firearms, including shotguns, pistols, snipers, and even rare assault rifles.

Jacked up from the thrill of the chase, one man took a shot at her but missed by inches.

As soon as Ericka heard the gunfire as well as the ricochet of a bullet next to her ear, she took off running.

Armed with a variety of weapons, all intended to cause physical harm to the body, the mob chased after Ericka.

After shortcutting through several alleyways and at times, circling back to the same alleyway she originally cut through before, Ericka came across what looked like the remains of a body in the middle of the street. Cautiously, she approached the bloody mess. The arms and even a leg had been ripped from the torso. Ericka looked closer at the corpse's face. The expression on her face dropped in horror. It was R.C.—at least, what was left of R.C. They had "factually" torn him apart. Ericka heard the mob on the other side of the street. She took off down the alleyway and with nowhere else to run, sought cover inside a warehouse stocked with hundreds and thousands of boxes. Ericka came across one particular box on the shelf. Curious, she cracked open the box and found the eyes of a doll staring back at her. Her eyes, Ericka realized, as she tore open the box completely and pulled out the package from inside. She studied the doll's mutated face. Except for the same eyes, the face wasn't hers, but rather farthest from hers. All of the features, including the nose, lips, chin, cheekbones, eyebrows, appeared transparently disproportionate to the shape of her head. For example, the doll's nose was roughly the size of a pear, whereas her lips were shriveled like dried raisins. She had seen the face before; however, at that moment in time, with commotion growing outside, she couldn't pinpoint the origins of the face.

The name on the pink package read: "*Ericka Barnes*" in the next chapter of the epic saga. . .

Underneath the tagline read the title of the sequel to *Wake Me Tomorrow*.

NO REST FOR THE WICKED

Ericka wandered around the warehouse and randomly opened other boxes on the shelves: dolls, cereal boxes, action figures, puzzles, and board games, all new merchandise for *No Rest For the Wicked*.

The commotion was louder, closer.

Ericka followed the sound to a tall powdery window where the dim silhouette of a mob waiting. She could see their hands—which looked more like paws—and the sides, as well as the fronts of their faces—which looked furrier or scalier than faces of humans—pressed against the glossy glass, as if they were trying to peer inside. Ericka knew that, if they found her, they'd kill her and "eat her alive," as her manager put it so bluntly after the interview. She had no other choice than to run. So, she did exactly that, she ran. She exited through a back door behind the warehouse and continued to run until her body would no longer let her.

With the mob still fresh on her tail, Ericka round yet another alley and took cover in a dumpster. She closed the dumpster lid behind her. As the mob roared, growled, and hissed directly outside the dumpster, she cowered herself into a ball and tried to remain as still as possible.

Eventually, the animal-like sounds trailed off down the alleyway.

Ericka pulled out the Zippo lighter from her pocket and struck the flint inside. She slowly moved the tiny flame around the dumpster. Piled all around her was old, discarded *Wake Me Tomorrow* merchandise. She came across the same May Warren action figure, which partially charred, part of its face melted. Searching for a weapon to defend herself, she dug through the trash until she cut her finger on a shard of glass. She pulled out the broken mirror wedged underneath the vinyl casing of a *Wake Me Tomorrow* soundtrack.

With the Zippo held close to her face, she looked into the mirror and couldn't help but recognize the stark differences of her face. Her nose was much different, deformed. Her lips, much thinner. The only person who suddenly came to mind was Jpeg. The sight of the artist's face caused her insides to wrench. She didn't know exactly why she was wearing the deformed face of a man who only existed in her spin. But, as she poked and prodded at the various hail-sized tumors covering her entire face, she realized it was, in fact, her face, *not* Jpeg's. Ericka could only look at the face for only a few seconds before the hate of what they had done to her started to corrode her very heart.

More aware of not who, but *what* she was up against, Ericka carefully pocketed the shard and closed the Zippo.

In the coming days, Ericka knew that staying close to the darkness would be her only chance at survival. And, maybe one day, when the violence finally came to an end, she would see the light again.